SCAVENGER HUNT

ROBERT

PANTHEON BOOKS / NEW YORK

SCAVENGER

HUNT

FERRIGNO

Pantheon Books and colophon are registered trademarks of Random House, Inc.

Library of Congress Cataloging-in-Publication Data
Ferrigno, Robert.
  Scavenger hunt / Robert Ferrigno.
    p. cm.
    ISBN 0-375-42173-4
  1. Hollywood (Los Angeles. Calif.)—Fiction. 2. Motion picture industry—Fiction. 3. Journalists—Fiction. I. Title.

  PS3556.E7259 S33 2003   813′.54—dc21   2002025840

www.pantheonbooks.com

Printed in the United States of America
First Edition

9 8 7 6 5 4 3 2 1

In memory of Jack Olsen
God better not have any skeletons in his closet

Acknowledgments

My appreciation to my editor, Sonny Mehta, for his clarity and insight, to Mary Evans, my agent, for her sharp wit and encouragement, to Kim Duddy of the King County Crime Scene Investigations Unit, for her forbearance and good humor in response to my many questions, and to James Crumley, a most excellent Halloween companion. I am also endebted to M. Lee Goff's *A Fly for the Prosecution,* for its wealth of information about forensic entomology.

SCAVENGER HUNT

Prologue

"How did *you* get in here?"

Sugar stood in the doorway between the anteroom and her office, hands in the pockets of his blue suit jacket. "Gee, April, that doesn't sound too friendly."

"I was expecting you to call me with an update—you picked a funny time to come by in person." April McCoy picked up the cigarette smoldering in the clamshell ashtray on her white desk and took a short tentative drag, then stubbed it out. The clamshell was filled with broken butts, their filters ringed with red. "Did everything go all right? I haven't heard anything on the radio."

Sugar surveyed the office. "I always wondered what this place looked like. It's nice."

April watched him from behind her desk, eyes narrowed, resting her bulk on her forearms—three hundred pounds if she was an ounce, but well groomed, powdered, and manicured, every frosted hair in place, her dress black and billowy. Nice to see a big girl with her vanity intact, particularly in L.A., where the women thought they had to be built like linguini. "Heather did what she was supposed to?"

"A real trouper," Sugar assured her. "Just like you said."

April relaxed slightly. "Heather's young, but she has a good head on her shoulders, that's what's important. A lot of the young ones . . ." She dabbed at her lipstick with a fat pinkie. "I don't need to bother you with my troubles."

"Taking care of troubles—that's my job *and* my pleasure." Sugar

• 3

ambled inside. He was a hefty boy too, not in April's weight class, but a big and tall shopper, proud of his bulk, pleased with everything about himself, not in some loud and flashy way—he hated that—but he knew who he was. Too many people had to work at liking themselves, overspending, overselling, overmedicating. But Sugar—he had seen it all, and he measured up just fine.

It was almost midnight, the dingy office building deserted except for her office on the eighth floor. Sugar had taken the stairs, feeling his heart pounding as he took the steps two and three at a time, kicking up dust. Most of the lights in the hallway on the eighth floor had burned out. Sugar had moved quietly through the puddles of darkness on the balls of his feet, past the Asian food importer and the prosthetic limb supply company and the immigration attorney who had a lucrative sideline in slip-and-fall cases. The eighth floor smelled of sack lunches left unrefrigerated too long.

April lit up another cigarette, her many rings flashing. She blew smoke at him. "How *did* you get in here, anyway?"

Sugar shrugged.

Ashes tumbled onto the white surface of the desk, and April backhanded them, left a dirty smear.

Sugar stopped in front of her bookcase. There wasn't a book in it, but plenty of photos: April with that black kid who was the white guy's sidekick on a TV show that got canceled last year, April with that girl singer who was supposed to be the next Britney Spears but wasn't. Lots of photos of April with shiny young men and women who he was probably supposed to recognize but didn't. One of those fancy AM-FM radios was on the top shelf, tuned to a New Age music station, which was a waste of technology if you asked him.

"Were you able to take her home afterward?" asked April. "I know I'm just being an old mother hen—"

"You're not old. Not by a long shot."

April absently touched her hair. "So did you give her a ride home?"

"Not exactly."

"Not *exactly*? What does that mean?" April's voice croaked when she was nervous, which was not really a good quality for a talent agent or business manager or whatever it was she thought she did for a living. It seemed to Sugar that when you negotiated for your supper, it was important to hold something back.

"Not exactly means there were complications, but I took care of them." Sugar's own voice was warm and buttery, as soothing as prescription cough syrup. Good times and bad, his voice maintained its resonant timbre. A few years back he had broken his right leg in an auto accident on the 405, lacerated his scalp too, a flap of hair hanging over his ear. He didn't remember much about the car crash itself, but he still could see the look on the firefighter's face as he used the jaws of life on the crumpled Ford, the young fellow shaking as he worked to cut him free, disconcerted by Sugar's easy manner, his bad knock-knock jokes and mock apologies for all the blood.

"Heather is a fine little actress." April took another drag on her cigarette and stubbed it out. Judging from the ashtray, she never smoked them down past halfway—she probably thought that it was the last half that would kill her. "Heather—she knows what she wants, and she knows what it takes to get it. Knows how to keep her mouth shut too." April's eyes were hard behind the smoke. "A special girl."

"Fresh off the griddle, that's what I asked for."

April lit another cigarette. "And that's what I gave you. You remember that. One hand washes the other, Sugar."

"Rub-a-dub-dub." Sugar smiled, then walked to one of the large windows overlooking the street and placed his hands under the two handles.

"Don't bother trying. That thing's been stuck since Noah took his boat ride."

Sugar lifted, putting his back into it. The window creaked, then slid all the way up, and he felt the breeze cool against his sweaty forehead, heard the hum of the freeway in the distance.

"Well, that's a first," said April.

Sugar looked out at the night. The surrounding buildings were dark, the street deserted. "It was getting hard to breathe in here."

"Don't you start on me." April tapped out her cigarette after just a couple drags, then bent forward, coughing into her fist. "You remember what I said about one hand washing the other," she warned. "Heather has a lot of talent, but we both know what that's worth without the right connections. A good word whispered in the proper ear . . ."

"I hear you. If you don't mind me asking, what's your slice? Fifteen percent?"

April had lovely dimples. "Thirty-five."

Sugar whistled.

April nodded toward the file cabinet. "Ironclad too. You'd be surprised at how many try to beat me out of my commission. It's enough to shake my faith in humanity."

"You have to trust people. Otherwise, what's the point of living?" Sugar dimmed the lights, then tuned the radio to an oldies station, caught Aretha Franklin in the middle of "Chain of Fools." He walked to the desk and held his hands out. "May I have this dance?"

April stared at him.

Sugar beckoned. "Come on, beautiful, don't leave me out here all alone."

"Are you serious?" April laughed, embarrassed. "You *are*."

"Nothing wrong with a little celebration. You and me, we're just little people, but look what we did tonight." Sugar smiled at her and saw her doubts melt. It *was* a good smile, full of strong, white teeth and humor. "We made it happen, girl. We shook things up good. One way or the other, Heather is going to be famous."

April hesitated.

Sugar folded his hands in prayer.

April got slowly to her feet, moved around from behind the desk. She looked toward the doorway, as though afraid they were going to get caught, then saw him looking and blushed. "It's—it's been a while since I've been asked to dance."

"No accounting for taste, is there?" Sugar put one hand on her hip, the two of them swaying to the music, a little awkward at first, at least until she relaxed and let him lead, Sugar slipping his arm halfway around her waist, dancing closer now.

April giggled as he swept her across the carpet, amazed at his strength and poise, his deft moves. "You make me feel light as a feather."

Sugar held her tight, effortlessly lifting her off her feet as they glided around the room. She was a big girl, but she felt small in his arms, and the sensation was like an electric current traveling between them, warm and intimate as a stolen kiss. "'Chain, chain, chain,'" he crooned, "'chain of fools.'"

April rested her head against his shoulder, inhaling his aftershave. "Aqua Velva," she murmured. "It's been a long time since I smelled that."

"I'm just an old-fashioned guy." Sugar nuzzled her hair as he danced her round and round the room, and she gave in to him too, letting him whirl her faster and faster until he lost his footing and the two of them stumbled toward the open window. He pulled her back just in time, her knee already on the low sill, caught her as she started to scream. "That was a close call," he said, holding her tighter, his pulse pounding in his ears.

April disengaged herself, out of breath, shaking. She tried to close the window, leaning on the handles, tugging away without budging it. "S-sorry, Sugar," she gasped, her face flushed. "I'm so clumsy—"

"It wasn't your fault. I'm the one with the two left feet." Sugar put his arms around her again. She tried to push him away, but he had the dancing fever now. "Let's just finish out the song. Come on, beautiful, just this one song, and I'll let you go."

April stared into his eyes, searching for something, not sure what she was looking for. She finally nodded, giving in, but her body was stiffer now, her neck moist, and the moment of grace between them was lost.

Sugar moved to the music, trying to keep pace with Aretha's soulful lament of helpless love. The song was almost over. "'Chain, chain, chain . . .'", he started.

"Did you remember to tell Heather not to contact me?" said April, trying to bring things back to business.

Sugar didn't answer.

"Did you tell her?" April kept looking around as he danced her across the room in widening arcs, her hair flying like party streamers as he spun her off her feet again. "Sugar—" she gulped, eyes wild. "Sugar, I'm getting dizzy."

"Shhhhhhhhh," he said, whirling faster now, a frantic pirouette. "Sugar, *please!*"

Sugar pivoted on his hip and effortlessly tossed April headfirst through the open window. Nothing but net. An eight-story drop was hardly enough time to get out a good scream, but April gave it her best shot. He stood in the window, looked at her lying face-down on the sidewalk, one arm outstretched, reaching for the gutter, her rings gleaming in the streetlight. Rings on her fingers, bells on her toes. "Tell Heather, yourself."

The wind caught April's billowy black dress and hiked it up, exposing her pale thighs. If Sugar were a gentleman, he would have rushed right down there, tugged her hemline down, and maintained her modesty, but he stayed where he was, not moving until he saw headlights turn the corner at the end of the block. He stepped back into the room, pulled on a pair of surgical gloves, and went through the file cabinet. Heather Grimm's contract was at the very front of the G folder. Such high hopes, it was kind of touching.

Sugar took one last look around. April had probably been coming into this office for years now, coming in every morning, working the phone all day behind that cheap white desk, dreaming of hooking the big one, sitting there year after year. You'd think that after all that time a part of her would remain, some kind of lingering aura. But Sugar couldn't feel her presence, not at all. April had left the building. He was almost at the door when he turned around, went to the bookcase, and turned the radio back to the New Age station, wiping the knob clean. He could still hear her music playing as he walked down the hall, like an echo that April had left behind. It was something to think about on the drive home.

Chapter 1

"God, I *hate* blondes," said Tamra Monelli. "What's the big whoop about pink nipples anyway?"

"What's a blonde?" said Jimmy, standing with his arms around the Monelli twins, Tonya and Tamra, as Rollo checked the viewfinder of the camera, making sure the HOLLYWOOD sign was perfectly positioned behind them.

Tonya giggled and pinched Jimmy's bare ass.

"Last week we lost a part in a slasher film," complained Tamra. "Three callbacks, and at the last minute the director decides that the high-school shower scene is a blondes-only zone, because, and I quote, 'Blood contrasts better against white skin, and besides, blondes look more innocent. That's why everyone wants to fuck them.' Innocent?" She cupped her breasts, her nipples dark as anthracite. "Do *these* look guilty to you, Jimmy?"

"Smile." Jimmy Gage showed his teeth to the camera, dropping his hands to discreetly hold down his erection as the twins pressed against him, warm and naked and perfect. Jane was going to flip when she found out about this.

Rollo hit the auto-timer and rushed back, making sure they were all in the frame. The rickety HOLLYWOOD sign was behind them, paint peeling, covered in graffiti, the letters dangerously canted from the last earthquake. California Stonehenge. The timer clicked, the flash blazed, and a Polaroid slid out. Item number six on the scavenger hunt list of seven: *nude group photo at a recognizable L.A.*

landmark. "I still don't like this place, Jimmy." He glanced around at the debris that littered the ground, winced at an air-conditioner half-buried from the impact. "All kind of bad shit happens here."

"Bad shit happens everywhere." Jimmy checked the backdrop of dark sandstone bluffs above them; the HOLLYWOOD sign was built near the top of a ridge, higher hills looming overhead. Dropping bowling balls off freeway overpasses was passé among young wanna-bees. Today's future lifer took pride in hauling heavy objects up onto the bluffs and dropping them on the sight-seers below. A couple of months ago a tourist had been flattened by an empty fifty-gallon propane tank.

Rollo scooted over to where the camera was perched on a broken Styrofoam cooler, a nervous, twenty-year-old filmmaker with thick round glasses and a Trotsky goatee, wearing only a pair of two-tone bowling shoes.

The Monelli twins stretched and preened in the warm night air, smooth and sleek as weimaraner puppies.

Rollo watched the twins, fanning himself with the Polaroid to speed the development. "Do you think I look okay, Jimmy? Physically, I mean."

"You're a credit to the human genome." Jimmy slipped on black pants and steel-tipped welder's boots, a powder-blue ruffled tuxedo shirt completing the ensemble. He was tall and lanky, somewhere in his mid-thirties, with dark tangled hair and an open smile. If you didn't know better, you'd think he was just another laid-back hip-ster—until you noticed his eyes, saw the edge there. A reporter for *SLAP* magazine, Jimmy was a troublemaker by trade and inclination, with fast hands and too much curiosity for his own good. Fight or flight, it made no difference anymore.

"Do I *really* look okay?" Rollo examined the Polaroid, then stepped into a pair of tie-dyed shorts, almost falling over as he hopped on one skinny leg. He reached for his Hawaiian silky, an original aloha shirt from the 1920s, museum quality, worth more than the VW van he drove. "I mean, if you were a woman, would you find me sexually attractive?"

"Sexually? So we're past 'physically' now?"

"Yeah, it was sort of like a rolling stop. So *would* you? If you were a woman?"

"I'm not really in touch with my feminine side."

Rollo glanced at the twins cavorting among the broken TVs and shattered microwave ovens. "I think I should start working out or something. Maybe get some B-twelve shots. Or human growth hormone. They say you can get cancer from that stuff, but it takes a long time. Five or ten years at least."

"At least."

Rollo glanced up at the bluffs. "We should get out of here."

The four of them had spent the last few hours driving around Los Angeles trying to fill the scavenger hunt list that Napitano had passed out at his party. Antonin "Nino" Napitano was the autocratic publisher of *SLAP* magazine, a smash-mouth monthly with a no-corrections, no-apologies editorial policy. *Vanity Fair* had perfected the art of the Hollywood air-kiss, fawning yet dignified, but *SLAP*'s kisses drew blood, its eviscerating profiles and critiques sending the rich and famous scuttling for their spin doctors and libel attorneys.

Invitations to Napitano's lavish parties were sought after by bit actors and screenwriters with a P.O. box instead of an office, potential rock stars, and models-of-the-moment. Scavenger hunt winners had their faces splashed across the "Shock of the New" section of *SLAP*'s next issue, a guarantee that their phone numbers would be on speed-dials all over the city. For a month, anyway. Jimmy didn't need the ink—he was Napitano's favorite, the only writer who stood up to him—but Rollo and the Monelli twins could use all the help they could get.

Rollo tugged at his goatee as he stared at Tamra posing inside the giant letter O, back arched, her belly bronze in the moonlight. "Too bad Jane's not here, Jimmy. I'd like to scope out the goods." He saw Jimmy's expression and took a step back. "Jimmy's girlfriend was supposed to come to the party," he explained to the twins, "but she stiffed him when she heard I was on the guest list. She's some hotshot detective with the Laguna PD; real pretty too, but she doesn't like me."

"Jane got a call from the assistant DA. One of her cases is going south. *That's* why she had to back out of the party."

"I'm *glad* she didn't come," flirted Tamra. "Out of sight, out of mind, that's my motto."

"Why doesn't Jane like me?" asked Rollo.

"She says that every time you come by, she feels that she should count the silverware afterward." Jimmy grinned. "I convinced her to cut you some slack, but bringing the palm tree to her dinner party—that finished it."

"You know what that tree was worth?" sputtered Rollo. "Dwarf sago palms are *protected,* man. I could have sold it to a collector for a thousand bucks."

"He dug it up from a botanical garden," Jimmy told the twins. "He arrived at Jane's door with this palm tree in a shopping cart. All these lawyers and cops standing around drinking martinis, and here's Rollo pushing the cart into the living room, wheels squeaking, dirt falling all over the carpet." He shook his head. "I told you to bring *flowers.*"

"The greenhouse was locked," explained Rollo.

"You told us you were a director." Tonya looked at her sister.

"I am," said Rollo.

"He is," said Jimmy.

Jimmy and Rollo were the only people in L.A. who were convinced. His oddball documentaries devoid of commercial potential, Rollo financed his films with assorted scams and hustles: counterfeiting Disneyland tickets, peddling hot electronic gear, hacking into databases to improve credit histories. He was a gawky high-school dropout with an IQ over 140 and barely enough common sense to keep himself out of jail, and though he slept with a night-light on, he had risked his life for Jimmy and never mentioned it afterward. They were friends.

Rollo bent down and tossed Tonya her panties, the black silk rippling through the air like a fleeing octopus. "We should go. The last item on the list is the hardest."

"Where we going to find an Oscar?" said Tamra.

"A *real* Oscar," said Tonya, spinning her panties around one finger. "No best-costume or best-song crap."

"Major-category gold," finished Tamra. "That's what the rules said."

Jimmy reached into his pocket and answered his phone.

"How goes the hunt, dear boy?" cooed Napitano. "Did you get the rubbing?"

Jimmy could hear music at Nino's end, and the tinkle of glassware. "Yeah, we got it."

"Splendid. Some of the other players had difficulties with that one. Legal difficulties." Napitano clucked his disapproval. "Most of the teams saw 'A tombstone rubbing from a silent film star' and headed directly to Forest Lawn, even though it's after hours. Arrests have been made, Jimmy, it's quite tragic." He hummed softly. "I was wondering, though, how the police knew that there was going to be a mass scaling of the gates."

"I have no idea."

"Bravo. 'Admit nothing'—if that's not on your family crest, it should be." Napitano was chewing something. "Which star's tombstone did you visit?"

"Rex the wonder dog. The pet cemetery in Encino is unguarded." Napitano's laugh was a blubbery wheeze as Jimmy broke the connection. "Get dressed. We're being watched."

Rollo craned his neck toward the bluffs.

"Don't look," said Jimmy. "Just move."

The Monelli twins shimmied into their matching black dresses.

Rollo squinted. "I don't see—" A portable TV crashed onto the ground about ten feet away, exploded in a spray of glass. He screamed, grabbed at his ankle.

War whoops sounded overhead.

"Head toward the van," Jimmy said quietly. A cinder block thudded into the weeds right beside him. "*Don't* run." He watched Rollo race toward the van, arms folded over his head, the Monelli twins right behind him, wobbling on their high heels. Jimmy smiled and ambled up the path, hands in his pockets, waiting for a grand piano to land on his head.

Rollo didn't even wait for Jimmy to close the door to the VW van before peeling off. No one spoke for a long time. They were almost at the I-5 freeway before Tamra finally broke the silence. "So whose Oscar are we going to borrow?"

Rollo veered into the carpool lane. "It's a surprise."

"So is a cerebral hemorrhage," said Jimmy, suspicious now. "Who are we going to see?"

Rollo cleared his throat. "Garrett Walsh."

"Mother*fucker*," said Jimmy.

"I knew you weren't going to like it," said Rollo, accelerating.

"Who's Garrett Walsh?" said Tonya.

"He made that kinky movie from a long time ago. *Firebug*," said Tamra.

"*Firebug* won two Academy Awards," said Rollo, easing through late evening traffic. "It was his *first* movie, a cheapo thriller full of twists and reversals, with lousy distribution and no stars, but Mr. Walsh walked away with two Oscars, best director and best screenplay. Even Tarantino didn't pull off a double play his first time out." A silver Lexus cut him off, and Rollo leaned on the horn. "And it *wasn't* that long ago. Nine years, big deal."

"He murdered a teenage girl," said Jimmy. "Walsh was only released from prison a few months ago."

"Heather Grimm," said Tamra.

"Who?" said Rollo.

"The girl he killed," said Tamra. "Her name was Heather Grimm."

"Seven years for murder—he should have gotten seventy," said Jimmy.

"I remember now, we were in junior high when it happened," Tonya chirped to her twin. "There was a picture of her in *Entertainment Weekly*. She looked like a cheerleader."

"Blonde, of course," the twins said in unison, clasping pinkies.

"Where else are we going to get an Academy Award, Jimmy?" said

Rollo. "It's not like there's a black market in them." He considered it. "At least not for the major ones."

"You *sure* you know where we're going?" Jimmy asked a half-hour later.

Rollo squinted through the cracked, dusty windshield. The VW's lights barely illuminated the winding, two-lane road as the van lurched its way up Orange Hill, second gear slipping. There was a restaurant on the peak, and houses strung along the ridges of the Anaheim foothills, million-dollar crackerboxes with views of the ocean ten miles away. On a good day at least.

Jimmy stuck his head out the window to get a better look. The air pollution cut off the stars, and it was the myriad glittering lights below that looked like the Milky Way, the rakish, cocked neon halo atop the A in the ANGELS STADIUM sign shining brighter than Polaris. It was as though the world had flipped over, and they were not moving higher but *lower,* into the darkness.

"I ran into Mr. Walsh at the Strand's midnight movie a few weeks ago," Rollo said to the twins. "He was getting—"

"What is this 'Mr. Walsh' crap?" said Jimmy.

"I was the only one who recognized him," continued Rollo. "He didn't want company, but I followed him to his car afterward anyway. It wouldn't start, which I thought was a good omen, because it was three A.M. and he didn't have money for a tow truck."

"Walsh should have called O.J. and asked him for a lift," said Jimmy. "Killers helping killers—it sounds like a bumper sticker."

"How could he *not* have any money?" said Tamra. "*Firebug* did over seventy million domestic. That's a cost-return ratio of almost fifty to one. He's got to be sitting on a pile."

Jimmy turned around and stared at her.

"What?" said Tamra. "I majored in business at community college."

"Mr. Walsh was pretty nervous that night," said Rollo. "Pretty drunk too. He kept asking me to run red lights and dodge through alleys. I think he was scared we were being followed. Fans can be pretty aggressive." The van lurched, and he fed it more gas, then suddenly veered off the main road and onto a barely visible gravel path, the wheels spitting up stones. "Mr. Walsh told me to stay on the paved road, then had me drop him off in front of this big house. He said it was his place, but I watched him in my rearview as I pulled away and saw him pretending to unlock the gate." Rollo grinned. "He's a tricky guy. I guess you have to be when you're famous." The van hit a pothole, and Rollo's chin banged against the steering wheel, but he was so pleased with himself that he didn't seem to notice. "So I started back down the hill, then cut my lights, parked on the shoulder, and waited. Sure enough, ten minutes later I see Mr. Walsh walking up this path. I tagged along on foot. He had to stop a couple of times to throw up, and I thought once he heard me, but now I know where he lives. Smart, huh?"

Jimmy looked out the side window. They hadn't passed a house since the turnoff—no lights, no mailboxes, no safety rails.

Rollo gasped as the van skidded toward the edge, fighting to regain control. The road narrowed still further, not even gravel now, just dead grass and hardpack.

Tamra caressed Rollo's neck. "Is Walsh working on a new project?"

"How's my makeup?" Tonya asked her sister. "Heather Grimm. The photo of her in *Entertainment Weekly*—her hair was in a French braid. Walsh must like that."

"Yeah, he was so turned on by her hairstyle that he raped her, then stove her head in with one of his two Oscars," said Jimmy. "That's a sincere compliment."

"I don't get your point," said Tonya.

"Mr. Walsh paid his debt, Jimmy," said Rollo.

"No, he didn't."

"Yeah, well . . ." said Rollo. "Anyway, now he's just trying to get his life back together."

The VW crested the hill. Jimmy could see a large house above the ridge, and a trailer nearby, dimly lit, a beat-up Honda parked beside it. The road abruptly ended, and as Rollo hit the brakes, the van skidded to a stop. The engine idled roughly, and the headlights illuminated the landscaped slope, lit the arrangement of boulders behind a large pool of water that had white lilies floating on the surface. At the center of the pool, balanced precariously on some rocks, a man stood with his back to them, jeans hanging loosely around his hips, barefoot and bare-chested, caught in the headlights' glare as he pissed merrily into the koi pond.

Tamra giggled.

The man turned his head toward them, blinking, as he casually shook his penis, a cigarette jutting from his mouth, sunglasses pushed back on his forehead. The black water seemed to be boiling, fish churning around his toes, their gold scales flashing in the light.

"Oh yeah," said Jimmy, "he's putting his life back together. He's almost got the puzzle complete now."

Chapter 2

Walsh plucked the cigarette from his mouth and flicked it into the koi pond as Jimmy and Rollo approached. The sizzle was loud in the stillness. He started toward them, slipped on the rocks, and went into the dirty water up to his knees, staggering closer now, bringing the stink of booze and dirty water with him.

Jimmy held his ground, but Rollo took a step back. The twins were still in the van, working on their hair and makeup, preparing for their big entrance.

Seven years in prison, and Walsh still had the same insolent mouth and sleepy eyes, the same Wayfarers perched high on his head, and three days of stubble. The bags under his eyes were bigger now, his face puffier and more dissipated, but it was still the same bad-boy mug that *Newsweek* had put on the cover twice, once when he won the Oscars and again when he was convicted of murder. The tattoo on his right shoulder was a jailhouse-issue devil with a pitchfork, the tattoo as sloppy as his sunburned torso, a shim of gut drooping over the waistband of his jeans. He looked a lot better than Heather Grimm did.

"Mr. Walsh—it's me, Rollo. Remember?"

"Yeah, I remember you," growled Walsh, slouching, his thumbs hooked into the back pockets of his jeans. His eyes shifted from one to the other like he was trying to decide something. He settled on Jimmy. "The tough guy here looks familiar too."

"Hope you don't mind us dropping by," said Rollo. "We're playing a game."

"You already played me, kid," Walsh said to Rollo, still keeping watch on Jimmy. "You fooled me good with all that yakkety-yak about movies, and you being a fellow filmmaker. Well, I have only myself to blame."

"I'm not sure I understand, Mr. Walsh."

"Shut up, Rollo," said Jimmy, who *did* understand.

"Yeah, shut up, Rollo," Walsh said evenly. "You did your job, you don't have to pretend anymore." He smiled at Jimmy, his teeth uneven and nicotine-stained. "I know what you're here to do, tough guy, but don't worry, I'm not going to make you sweat for your paycheck. I just want a few minutes to make my peace."

Jimmy saw Walsh doing something with his right hand behind his back.

Walsh bowed his head. "Now I lay me down to sleep," he said, inching closer, "I pray the Lord, my soul to—" He whipped the linoleum knife out from behind his back, the curved blade catching the moonlight as he swept it low, going for Jimmy's belly. "Making spaghetti," that's what the disemboweling stroke was called in prison, intestines spilling out in a red sauce of blood.

Jimmy had been waiting for the Chef-Boyardee move ever since he saw Walsh slip his hands in his back pockets. He pivoted to his left, barely avoiding the blade, then punched Walsh in the face, caught him just under the nose, and knocked him backward. The knife spun off into the night. A linoleum knife was a smart choice for an ex-con. Anything with more than a four-and-a-half-inch blade was considered a deadly weapon, but a linoleum knife, equally deadly in the right hands, was just a tool.

"*Thanks*, Jimmy," said Rollo, rushing over toward where Walsh lay sprawled on the ground, groaning. "That's really mature."

Jimmy smiled as he rubbed the throbbing knuckles of his right hand. Moonlight shimmered on a small gold ring through Walsh's right nipple.

"Mr. Walsh is sure to help us now," Rollo muttered. "What do you care if we win the scavenger hunt?" He sat Walsh up, then picked the Wayfarers off the ground and tenderly fitted them back into place on his forehead. "You're always settling scores that aren't any of your business, Jimmy. Mr. Walsh did his time. Why is it *your* job to decide what he had coming?"

Jimmy watched the blood trickle from Walsh's nose. "It's not my job," he confided to Walsh. "It's more of a hobby."

"You hit—you hit like a girl," Walsh said to Jimmy.

"Stand up. I'll try to do better this time," Jimmy said softly.

Walsh stayed where he was, thinking. "Rollo called you Jimmy."

"That's my name."

"*You're* Jimmy Gage?" Walsh squinted at him in the dim light. "Rollo told me about you. The magazine writer . . ." He spit blood. "You're not here to kill me."

"I *tried* to tell you." Rollo looked around. "*Is* there somebody trying to kill you?"

Walsh looked at Jimmy. "You cold-cocked me just for the *fun* of it?" He dabbed at his nose with his fingertips, winced, then wiped the blood on his jeans. He stood up, still wobbly. "I've gotten bad reviews before, but this is the first time I got punched out by a critic." He grinned at Jimmy, but there was no humor in it. "I owe you one, tough guy."

"Get in line, asshole," said Jimmy.

Rollo sidled away from Walsh. "Are we in any danger being here with you?"

"Good for you, kid, no sense being a hero." Walsh rubbed his stubble. "I didn't think anybody knew where I lived, so anyone dropping by . . ." He spotted the Monelli twins slinking toward him from the van. "Then again," he said, raking his long hair back, "I could be persuaded to throw out the welcome mat."

"I'm Tamra."

"Tonya."

The sisters giggled as Walsh kissed their hands, his lips lingering. "I learned how to kiss a beautiful woman's hand when I was at

Cannes," he said, eyes glittering. "There was plenty of hands to kiss in the old days. I won the Palm d'Or, but I guess you know that."

Tamra stared at Walsh's dirty fingernails and unwashed jeans, but Tonya didn't seem to notice.

Jimmy listened for the sound of a car engine or the crunch of gravel, wondering who Walsh was expecting, but heard only the distant hum of traffic. From anywhere in Orange County, at any time of day or night, the sound of wheels on pavement was steady.

"We're on a scavenger hunt," said Rollo.

Walsh scratched his belly, checking out the twins. "You girls collecting geniuses?"

"We need an Oscar," said Jimmy.

"*Everybody* needs an Oscar, tough guy. Me, I got two of them." Walsh smiled at the twins. "The best things always come in pairs."

"We just want to borrow one of them," said Rollo. "We'll bring it back right after the party."

Walsh put his fingers to his nose, closed off one nostril, and blew a spray of blood onto the ground. "Why would I do that?" He cleared the other nostril the same way.

"Why don't we talk about it inside?" Tonya took Walsh's arm and walked him toward the Spanish-style mansion towering above them through the trees. "Rollo said you're working on a new project. Do you have a studio commitment yet, or are you riding bareback?"

"I didn't say anything about a project," protested Rollo.

"He doesn't necessarily need studio participation," Tamra said, turning to Walsh. "You could self-finance the seed money. Even if your house is a tear-down, the lot alone has to be worth at least eight or nine million—"

"Probably *twelve* with the unobstructed view," said Tonya. "Prices have skyrocketed since you . . . went away, Garrett, so even if you're carrying a couple of mortgages, you should be able to collateralize." She rolled her eyes upward, while Walsh stared at her. "Three million, easy. You roll that into a performance bond, then leverage the bond into a ten-million-dollar feature budget, coproduce it with a European consortium—"

"Asian market has more liquidity right now," said Tamra, tapping her front teeth with a forefinger. "So you lay off a coproduction deal with one of the Hong Kong outfits, and now you're bumped up to twenty, maybe twenty-five million, and then . . ."

Tonya squeezed Walsh's arm. "*Then* you start thinking of casting."

"It's not my house," Walsh said.

"The Asians are saturated with blondes," counseled Tamra, "so you should be thinking of female leads with pigmentation."

"Actresses willing to defer their salary in exchange for profit participation," said Tonya.

"It's not my fucking house!" Walsh pointed at the rusting trailer perched on concrete blocks. "*That's* where I'm camped out. The bastards who own the property are sailing around the world for the next year. They're letting me stay here because they're such patrons of the arts. My two biggest fans, that what they said. Not big enough to let me stay in the house, oh no, they got that locked up tight and secure, with their own electronic gate off the main road, but they just *love*—"

"What about all the money from *Firebug*?" Tamra said indignantly. "You couldn't have spent all that. You didn't have time."

"I had plenty of time," said Walsh. "Took about three months, but then I only retained two percent of the *Firebug* net profits. I had to sell the rest to get the money to finish the movie. I didn't care. When you want something, you do whatever you have to."

The twins looked at Walsh, then the trailer, then flipped out their cell phones in tandem.

Walsh watched them stroll back toward the van, chattering into their phones. "Easy come, easy go, story of my life," he said to Jimmy. "No big deal. I've got free room and board, fresh air, and an ocean view"—he gobbed a wad of spit toward the koi pond—"and all I have to do is take care of the goddamned fish."

"You looked like you were taking care of them when we drove up," said Jimmy.

Walsh grinned at Jimmy. He pulled a crumpled pack of cigarettes from his pocket, tapped one out, and Zippoed it with a practiced flourish, snapping the lighter shut with a distinctive snick.

"I'd really like to borrow one of your Oscars, Mr. Walsh," hurried Rollo.

Walsh watched the twins get back into the van, smoke trickling from his nostrils. "Women used to find me charming."

"Tonya and Tamra—they're high maintenance," said Rollo.

"They're *all* high maintenance, kid," said Walsh.

"Let's take off, Rollo," said Jimmy. "The philosopher king here is a train wreck."

"Nice to be a winner, isn't it, tough guy?" said Walsh. "Nice to have all the answers and not care who knows it. You never slip, never stumble. Well, enjoy it while it lasts." He peered at Jimmy, and there was no anger in him anymore, just a vast weariness. "The moment you stepped out of the van, shoulders thrown back, cocky smile—I didn't know your name, but I knew that look. Scared me too. There's not much difference between a winner and killer, not as much as you'd think."

"I just need to borrow one of your Oscars for a few hours," said Rollo.

"I can't wait to see what you sound like when it all turns to shit," Walsh said to Jimmy. "And trust me, sooner or later it *always* turns to shit."

"Are you going to loan us the Oscar or not?" said Jimmy. "It's late, and I'm bored."

"Try living with morons for seven years—you'll find out what boredom is," said Walsh, the cigarette bobbing. "Seven years, and I never once met one of those criminal masterminds you see in the movies." He opened wide the door to the trailer. "Come on in. I could use a little intelligent conversation."

"No, thanks."

Walsh blew a stream of smoke past Jimmy's face. "You think you're better than me?"

"I think a liver fluke is better than you."

Walsh smiled.

"Let's go inside," Rollo said to Jimmy. "Come on, what's it going to hurt?"

The trailer was cramped and cluttered, the sink strewn with empty cans of Dinty Moore beef stew and mandarin oranges, the couch sagging, the open windows streaked with grime. It stank of cigarettes and stale beer. *"Mi casa es su casa,"* Walsh said with a flourish. In the glare of the overhead light, he looked even more dissipated, his eyes bloodshot and watery. He slipped behind a paisley-print sheet strung across the rear of the trailer and walked out a few moments later, pumping the Academy Award over his head.

Eight or nine years ago, Jimmy had watched Walsh make the exact same move, standing in the spotlight at the Dorothy Chandler Pavilion, already drunk, looking lost and impossibly young as he waved his second Academy Award to the crowd. Jimmy remembered turning up the sound on the television as Walsh launched into a rambling acceptance speech, thanking no one, acknowledging no one but himself. Walsh was no longer the golden boy, but his eyes were still lit by the same arrogance as that night at the Academy Awards so long ago. The same fear too, the awful clarity of knowing that the ground under his feet was already shifting. Jimmy had felt sorry for Walsh then— and even after everything that Walsh had done, he felt sorry for him now.

Walsh hesitated, then handed Rollo the Oscar. "Best director."

"Whoa," said Rollo, cradling it in both hands. "The Holy Fucking Grail."

Jimmy stared at the Oscar and thought of Heather Grimm, wondering if this was the seven-pound statue Walsh had used to crush her skull with. He didn't feel sorry for Walsh anymore.

"Rollo can borrow the Oscar for your scavenger hunt," Walsh said to Jimmy. "I just want you to stay and keep me company until he brings it back. I'm offering you a gift, a page-one scoop: a new screenplay I'm working on, my best one yet. The story of a man on top of the world, a man who makes a mistake and falls right through the earth. It's the oldest story there is, but it's got some new angles. Some twists."

"You should be talking to a studio, not me," said Jimmy.

Walsh shook his head. "I'm colder than an Eskimo's pecker. That's why I need you. I want you to write an article about me, about what I'm working on. I even have a title for you: 'The Most Dangerous Screenplay in Hollywood.'"

"Give me a copy, and I'll take it home and read it," said Jimmy.

"No can do," said Walsh. "There's only one copy, and it's not finished yet anyway. Not quite." He rubbed his jaw, and it sounded like sandpaper. His eyes were locked on Jimmy. "It's a good script. So good it may even get me killed." He waited for an answer, then finally stubbed out his cigarette on the white Formica table, the surface glazed with burn marks. "I'm surprised you're not jumping at the opportunity. What's the matter, tough guy? You afraid to be alone with me?"

"I'm not a fifteen-year-old girl. What do I have to be scared about?"

Walsh jerked like he had been slapped, the pain genuine. "You're certain I was guilty?"

"You *pled* guilty."

Walsh stared at Jimmy with those sad, sleepy eyes. "Maybe I was wrong."

Chapter 3

"Cocktail?" Walsh held up two prescription bottles and gave them a shake.

"Pass."

"Your loss." Walsh shook out a couple of Percocets, added a Vicodin, and tossed them into his mouth, washing them down with a swallow of screwtop brandy. He faced Jimmy across the card table and defiantly drew out a long pungent belch. A dented, manual typewriter rested on the card table, an old Underwood, heavy enough to bring down a charging rhino. Stacked beside the typewriter was a manuscript, yellow Post-it Notes sticking out from between the pages. An accordion-style file folder lay open on the floor, next to a wastebasket filled with balled-up paper and empty pint bottles.

They had moved into the rear of the trailer after Rollo drove away with the twins, Walsh pulling aside the paisley-print sheet as though he were ushering Jimmy into Valhalla. While the main room was shabby and strewn with clothes and debris, this back area was neat and clean, furnished with only the card table, two chairs, and the typewriter. One wall was lined with books. Walsh's remaining Oscar looked lonely all by itself on the top shelf. A narrow piece of foam served for a bed, the white cotton sheet taut, the pillow shaped and flattened. The room was probably the exact size and configuration of the cell Walsh had spent the last seven years in.

"You ever been in love?" Walsh held the a bottle of brandy like a scepter. "The *real* thing, not just slamming the meat around."

Jimmy straddled the other chair, elbows resting on the wooden back. "You said you wanted to tell me about your new screenplay. Let's get to it."

"If you've never been in love, you're never going to understand the screenplay. I'd just be wasting my time." Walsh leaned back in his chair until the two front legs came off the floor, precariously balanced, but he was unconcerned. From the knees down his jeans were a darker blue where he had slipped in the koi pond, but he didn't seem to care about that either. "So *have* you or haven't you?"

"Yeah," said Jimmy, feeling like he had surrendered something, "I've been in love."

"Lucky us, huh?" Walsh brought the chair back down, picked up the sheaf of paper, and waved it in Jimmy's face. Every page had corrections written on it. "It's called *Fall Guy*." He tossed it back onto the desk. "That's all I told the studios when I shopped it around a few weeks ago. The title and my track record should have been enough. Selling the sizzle—that was all it should have taken to get an offer. Instead, all I got was thanks but no thanks, fuck you very much."

Jimmy could see Walsh's gold nipple ring tremble with every raspy breath he took.

Walsh whipped his thumb across the bottle. The cap flew off, and he batted it away with the other hand; it was one of those showy, jailhouse bits of business perfected by men with nothing but time. Jimmy had seen cons roll a cigarette with two fingers, seen them dance a quarter across their knuckles, move it back and forth across the bones. It didn't impress him. Walsh took a swallow of no-name brandy. "I once paid a thousand dollars for a bottle of cognac—"

"Did you kill the girl?"

Walsh scratched at the red devil on his shoulder—it was an ugly tattoo, the pitchfork crooked, the horns on its head uneven. "I wish I knew."

Jimmy watched Walsh pop open a prescription bottle. He wanted to believe that Walsh was lying to him, stringing him along, but the man's confusion and frustration were real.

Walsh tossed a couple more Percocets down his throat and chased them with another belt of brandy. "Best news since getting sprung was finding all the new legal dope out there. Just tell the doctor you hurt your back mowing the crabgrass, they write you a scrip."

"Let me read the screenplay. Then you can pass out in peace."

"Tough guy—yeah, I can spot them a mile away." Walsh waved the manuscript. "Well, *I'm* a certified fucking genius. *I'm* in the history books. What about you?"

Jimmy glanced at his watch.

"It's a good half-hour drive to Napitano's from here, so relax." Walsh took another pull on the bottle. "That little prick has quite a place: three or four acres it looked like, swimming pools, fountains, tennis courts, statues everywhere." He belched again. "I tried to crash Napitano's party last month. Spent ten minutes arguing with one of the security guards. Punk had never even heard of *Firebug.* Two fucking Oscars—I might as well be Shelley Winters for all the good they're doing me."

Jimmy laughed, and Walsh laughed too, shaking his head, and Jimmy almost liked him.

"How many times did you see *Firebug?*" asked Walsh. "Come on, 'fess up."

"Four times."

Walsh grinned, and it wasn't the phony leer he had turned on the twins. This one was honest, almost shy. "It *was* a good movie, wasn't it?" He banged the bottle down. "All those film school brats flocking to Sundance—I used to feel intimidated. While they were getting hands on with Coppola and Redford, I was cleaning sinks and buffing floors. I worked graveyard as a janitor when I wrote *Firebug,* did you know that?"

Jimmy nodded.

"That's how I met Harold Fong, the software geek who put up the money for *Firebug.* He was always pulling all-nighters at DataSurge, and I'd stop by on my breaks, and we'd shoot the shit about movies. It didn't matter that he owned the company and I took out the trash, we *both* loved the Coen brothers. Him and me used to do bits from *The*

Big Lebowski and *Fargo* that went on for ten minutes. Harold fucked me on the profit participation for *Firebug,* but he backed me when no one else would. Now I can't even get past his secretary's secretary." His eyes were red-rimmed. "You ever been in love?"

"You already asked me that."

"Right." Walsh blinked, clutched the screenplay. "You can't read *Fall Guy,* not yet anyway. I name names, the *real* names too, nothing changed to protect the innocent—or the guilty." He looked up. "I'll *tell* you the story, though. We'll make it a pitch meeting, and you can smile and pretend you understand, just like a real studio exec." He pushed his hair back, and there was something about that long sullen face, something that peeked through the abuse and squandered talent, that touched Jimmy. Walsh stood up, the chair falling over behind him.

"The opening shot is of our hero in prison, staring at a letter," said Walsh, pacing, sketching the scene with his hands. "He hasn't opened it. He's almost afraid to open it. He just lies there on the lower bunk, tracing the feminine handwriting of the address with the tip of his finger. It's night, the cell lit only by the dim security light overhead. We can hear his cellie snoring, and the usual noises in the background, men crying in their sleep, somebody grunting out pushups, but our guy is in a world of his own. He's waited all day for this moment. He takes a tentative sniff of the envelope and closes his eyes, savoring the memory. Then, very slowly, very carefully, he slides his pinkie under the envelope flap, and we hear the sound of paper tearing on the soundtrack. Fadeout." Walsh glanced at Jimmy, trying to gauge his reaction.

Jimmy looked back at him. Walsh had his complete attention.

"Flashback to our hero before he was in prison—a young filmmaker, so fucking hot, the sidewalk smokes under his feet. Studio executives are calling him, putting the calls in *themselves,* and the women—the pussy comes out of the woodwork when you're famous. You could be Quasimodo, and they'd still want to fuck you, and it *definitely* goes to our hero's head, but he keeps working harder than ever, burning the candle at both ends, taking a blowtorch to it, scared that he's going to wake up one morning and be back pulling Kotex out of clogged toilets. His second film is much more ambitious—instead of a million-dollar budget, it's slated at seventy million, and he's got real actors to work with this time, and a real crew, and gofers bringing him espresso.

"Then one day, right out of the blue, he meets *her*. The girl. Every good story has to have a girl, and here she is, smart and funny and so beautiful, the kind of girl he's jacked off to his whole life. Only one problem—she's married. She's signed a till-death-do-us-part contract with a powerful man, a dangerous man. But our hero doesn't care, he's used to getting what he wants, and what he wants is *her*. And because this is a Hollywood story, the girl feels the same way about him. Love, Jimmy, the real thing, ocean deep and mountain high, the kind you risk your first-class life for, the kind you have to grab for when you see it, because it may never come again. That kind of love."

Walsh sat down, their knees almost touching. "If this was a real pitch meeting, Jimmy, you'd ask me on what page do they fuck, and I'd say, without even looking at my notes, I'd say page fourteen, and you'd like that, because the audience doesn't like to wait more than fourteen minutes to see the hero and the girl fuck. You've got to feed the beast, Jimmy, and fuck they do, our hero and the good wife— that's what he calls her, their private joke. They scorch the sheets, our hero and the good wife, they tear each other apart and put themselves back together again, and what they have is so sweet, it's worth every lie, every excuse, every broken promise." He squeezed Jimmy's leg. "It's worth the *risk*. And it is a risk. For her. For him."

Jimmy was hooked.

"Our hero has made enemies on the ride to the top. Boy wonders are easy targets, and our hero, he's left himself open. He's a little afraid of the husband, if truth be told, but that only makes the loving sweeter, and besides, our hero is clever—his scripts are intricate, devious thrillers, full of twists and reversals. He's a man who knows how to get away with *anything*. Our hero gets off on the danger, but the wife, the good wife, is more . . . practical. She backs off a little bit. Not much. It's not over, she assures him, she just needs a little room, a little space, because she's having a hard time faking it at home, and she's worried that the husband is going to wise up—and maybe, just maybe, she needs a break from the boy wonder."

They were so close that Jimmy could count the broken blood vessels in the whites of Walsh's eyes.

"The little break turns into a week, and then another," said Walsh, his face shiny with sweat, "and our hero is dying inside. He leaves messages on her machine, their private call-me code, two short beeps and one long, but she doesn't respond, and he's getting mad now, angry at her for leaving him hanging, angry at himself for missing her. One afternoon he's sitting on the back porch of his beach house, working on the shooting script. This second movie, *Hammerlock,* is weeks behind schedule, and the suits are getting jumpy, and though he would never admit it, he is too. All those stolen afternoons with the wife have come with a price, and there's rumbling in the trades, anonymous, of course, that our hero is a one-hit wonder.

"So this particular day, he's sitting out in the hot sun, when who should appear but a beautiful girl in a pink bikini. Her name is Heather, a gorgeous blonde who has stepped on a piece of broken glass and cut her foot. Blood on the sand. Can you see it? Our hero is a creature of images, and the sight of the lovely Heather with blood dripping off the sole of her foot—you should have been there, tough guy. *You* should have been there instead of me.

"The director invites her in to clean up while he gets bandages. It's not a bad cut, but it hurts, and the pain in her face arouses him more than it should. The blonde has no idea who he is. She's young, nineteen she tells him, a college girl majoring in nothing in particular. She sees his two Oscars on the mantelpiece and asks him where he bought them, and she's serious. She lies back on the floor, her foot in his lap while he cleans the wound, blowing on her toes when he applies the antiseptic, and her eyes go right through him. She goes back to the beach for her blanket and towel and coconut suntan oil, and when she comes back, our hero has a couple lines of coke waiting, and one thing leads to another, and he's aware of the good wife, knows that he's cheating on her, but she's cheating on him with her husband, and then the college girl shrugs off her bikini, and that's all, Jimmy, that is *all*."

Jimmy saw Walsh fight off the shakes, but he made no move to help him.

"Our hero and Heather spend the afternoon fucking and doing coke and fucking some more. He's making up for lost time now, and he's switched to smoking heroin, the better to take the edge off, my dear, the better to push away the image of the good wife." Walsh balled his hands so tightly, his knuckles were white. "No smack for the girl though. She was curious, but he wouldn't give her any, not even a taste. He was a stone junkie, but he knew enough not to let her get started. He didn't want that on his conscience." He looked at Jimmy. "That counts for something, doesn't it?"

Jimmy nodded.

"Well sir, they fuck all afternoon, and into the evening, and the last thing our hero remembers is nodding off with his face against her soft skin. When he wakes up—when he wakes, he's on his feet, sleepwalking, and this big policeman is holding on to him, saying, *What have you done, buddy?* Our hero can barely hear the cop, his attention focused on the blonde lying at his feet with her head caved in, that soft skin ruined, and one of his Oscars is beside her, slick with blood. The policeman keeps repeating, *What have you done, buddy?* and our hero . . . he doesn't know what to say.

"The trial doesn't take long. It's not that kind of movie. The hero's team of five-hundred-dollar-an-hour attorneys suggest that he paint Heather Grimm as a coke whore, a desperate Lolita eager to fuck her way into the movies who attacked him when he put her off. Instead, our hero takes the DA's plea bargain. He's an arrogant bastard, but he remembers what Heather's face used to look like, he remembers her laugh."

"He knows that any jury in their right mind is going to hand him a life-without-parole ticket," said Jimmy. "He knows with the plea bargain and good behavior he can walk in seven. What about the good wife? What does she do?"

Walsh looked away. "Our hero never hears from her. She doesn't call him, he doesn't call her. What's he going to say? 'Sorry, I missed you so bad I fucked a stranger, than beat her skull in because she wasn't you.' No, our hero keeps quiet. Talking isn't going to help, it's only going to drag her into the mess, and our hero would do anything to avoid hurting her." He cleared his throat. "Did I mention that he loves her?"

Jimmy watched him.

"The prison sequences go fast, because the audience has already seen all the prison movies they want to see. Now we replay that opening scene, where about a month before he's due to hit the street, our hero gets a letter—a letter from *her.*" Walsh closed his eyes for a moment, savoring the memory. "All that time without any contact . . ." His voice trailed off, and it took him a while to find it. "He lies on his bunk for an hour, staring at the envelope, enjoying the curves and valleys of her handwriting. The things that run through his head. He actually thinks she's going to say she has divorced her husband, that she'll be waiting outside the gate, her hair smelling like fresh-cut flowers.

"That's not what the letter says, though. I bet you figured that out. The wife wrote to tell him that she just found out that her husband knew about them. He had known almost from the beginning. He had known and never let on, never said a word to her. He kept quiet for the whole seven years our hero was inside. When our hero's name came up in conversation at a party, the husband never reacted. He kept the secret."

"Just like our hero."

Walsh glared at Jimmy. "Our hero kept quiet to protect *her.* Maybe the husband kept quiet to protect *himself.*"

Jimmy turned that one over for a while. "You think he set you up?"

SCAVENGER HUNT • 33

"I don't know. I don't remember killing Heather, but there was plenty of evidence. All I'm saying is that if the husband knew about the affair, maybe he did something about it. I know I would."

Jimmy had heard crazier stories. Once or twice anyway. "How did the wife find out?"

Walsh looked at him, the sunglasses on his forehead like a second pair of dead eyes. "She . . . heard us."

"What does that mean?"

"She *heard* us. You deaf?" Walsh was angry again, shifting emotional gears more often than a Grand Prix racer. "She takes pills sometimes to help her sleep, but a few months ago she woke up, and her husband wasn't beside her, which is no big deal, because he often works all night. So she gets up to get some water, and she hears . . . voices downstairs, and she's curious. She goes down and listens at the door where he works, and the voices are fainter now, so faint that if it wasn't *her* voice coming from inside the room, she wouldn't have recognized it. There's my voice too and now she's got her ear pressed against the door, listening. The two of us are inside that room, the sound of us making love, so clear that she actually remembers the afternoon that we said those things. I'm a talker, Jimmy, I got things to say when we're going at it, and so does she. Her husband has a tape of that afternoon—he probably has a tape of all the *other* afternoons, all the other evenings and mornings. Tell me that's not sick. This was the first time she had caught him listening to the tapes. Maybe it's a special occasion, or maybe the fact that I'm going to get out soon has made him want to take another listen, to remind himself what I did to him. That's the first two acts, Jimmy. What do you think so far?"

"Good pitch, but it's a big stretch from knowing your wife is fooling around to orchestrating a homicide. That's why there are more divorce lawyers than hitmen."

"This guy knew for months that his wife was cheating on him, and he never said a thing," said Walsh. "The man who could pull that off, kissing her on her way to an exercise class, knowing she's really going to see me, but letting her go, sleeping beside her night after night, and never giving it away—a man who could do that, he could do *anything*."

"What does the wife think? Is she still living with him? If she is, that has to tell you something."

"It tells me she doesn't know what to think. She still loves me, that's all she knows for sure. Those seven years that I spent thinking of her, she was thinking about me too."

"What's her name?"

"Not yet." Walsh patted the manuscript. "I got it all down here: names, places, dates. I just don't have the third act finished yet, the part where the hero nails the husband and wins the girl back." He thumped the table, then tried to stand, but his legs were rubbery. "I'm going to need proof," he puffed. "*Then* you'll see it. I'll give you an exclusive."

"You can't even find your balance. How are you going to find out what really happened at the beach house all that time ago?"

Walsh nudged the bulging file folder beside the table with his big toe. "My legal team hired a private detective to investigate Heather Grimm. The plea bargain short-circuited things, but I got their raw notes here. Some interesting possibilities too." He glanced out the window, shivering now, hearing voices in the wind, screams in the trees. "The husband's not done with me."

"You're overselling it, Walsh."

Walsh's smile caved in, his confidence as fake as the rest of him. "I made phone calls. The studios don't know what the screenplay is about, but I told them it was based on a true story. The husband—he has to have heard what I'm working on. I need you to tell my story, Jimmy. He wouldn't have the balls to do anything to me then."

Jimmy shook his head.

"This scavenger hunt of yours—I played that game when I was a kid. Knocking on doors, asking for treasure and trash, and it's all the same. Well, open your eyes, tough guy, you stumbled on to something big here." Walsh clawed at Jimmy's arm. "Put me on the cover of *SLAP*, play it up big."

Jimmy shook him off. "I've been hustled by the best, Walsh, and this ancient mariner routine of yours is stale. Hire a press agent if you want publicity." He saw Walsh shudder, and Jimmy eased up on him. "Look, finish the script, and I'll read it."

"I don't have time. All those years in the joint, I can tell when shit's coming down. You need to write about me *now*."

Jimmy's phone beeped. He listened to Rollo shouting that they had won, that they were going to be famous, *all* of them. He heard the twins crowding around the phone, laughing, and the sound of glasses clinking.

"You're killing me." Walsh stared out the window, his face slack. "You're killing me, and you don't even know it."

Chapter 4

Sugar grabbed the phone on the second ring and dropped the receiver, still watching the seagulls floating overhead, looking for lunch.

"It's me."

"Been a long time," murmured Sugar, glancing around. Nothing and no one who didn't belong there. He adjusted his Dodgers cap, pulled it low over his eyes. "You're not calling me from home, are you? Not from the house or the office, remember?"

"I remember."

Sugar went back to watching the seagulls, squinting into the sunlight as the largest one swooped low, its beak sharp and cruel against the sky. Most folks liked birds, thought they were cute, and Sugar had to admit they did look graceful on the wing. But they were predators, every one of them, built to rip and tear, to gulp down life and not think twice about it. People who fed seagulls—it was an insult to Mother Nature.

"Sugar?"

"I'm here." Sugar smiled as the big gray gull came up with a fish, flapping across the water, the scales of the fish rainbowing in the sunlight as it wriggled in the gull's beak.

"I—I was expecting more surprise on your part."

"He's out. Sooner or later you're going to call. Why should I be surprised when you finally do?"

"What are we going to do about him?"

Sugar turned away from the seagulls, staring now at the three girls lying face-down on fluffy white beach towels, munching at small bags of French fries. They had their tops off. He didn't know what the big thing about tan lines was; they were sexy, if you asked him, innocent somehow. The thong bikinis that the girls were wearing—Sugar still hadn't decided about that.

"Sugar?"

Sugar sat in an aluminum chaise longue, wearing baggy blue swim trunks, his bulky torso slathered in oil. The girl in the polka-dot bikini was rolling over. Sugar watched her try to cover her breasts with an arm as she reached for her top. She wasn't completely successful, and he saw a flash of white skin, soft white skin that had never felt the sun. Still, he appreciated her efforts to maintain a semblance of modesty—so many of the young ones were whores. Pardon his language, but there was just no other word for it.

"We have to do *something*."

"I don't have to do anything." Sugar moved the phone to his other ear. "I see a sleeping dog, I let him lie there."

"I don't think that's wise."

"You don't, huh?" One of the gulls floated over the three girls and their French fries, squawking—if they weren't careful, they were going to have an unwanted visitor. Girls should know better, particularly the pretty ones. They were just asking for trouble. Sugar reached into the cooler beside his chaise longue, pulled out a bottle of organic apple juice, and took a long drink. He smacked his lips into the receiver. "Well, you know your business, I know mine."

"I want you to take a more proactive approach."

One of the other girls shifted on her beach towel, and Sugar watched the taut rise of her hip, the sweetness of her shadow. If he had had his binoculars, he could have counted the sweat beads on her inner thighs. He pinched his own belly, got a handful of fat, then smoothed his warm oiled skin. Not bad. "Proactive—that's a word you don't hear in conversation very often, and every time you do, it's an asswipe who's using it."

Chapter 5

"God damn it, Rollo, you should have told me," said Jimmy.

"B.K. is cool," said Rollo. "Relax, man. Get yourself a colonic."

Jimmy glared at him, then went back to watching the sun-baked road, heat shimmering off the blacktop. He was driving this time, not trusting Rollo's old VW van to make the steep grade up to Walsh's trailer, the black Saab whipping around the curves spewing gravel as Jimmy blinked back sweat. Walsh was going to go nuts when someone he didn't know showed up. Jimmy just hoped they got there before Rollo's new buddy.

The afternoon was hot and dry and overcast, the twelfth straight day of a thermal inversion. A shroud of pollution hovered over the L.A. basin, getting progressively thicker and more carcinogenic. Jimmy's throat was raw, and he had a headache that all the aspirin in the world didn't help. He wasn't alone. The violent-crime index had gone up seventeen percent since the smog alert had been declared, and the continuing power crisis made the use of air-conditioners problematic. Yesterday two women driving nearly identical minivans had gotten into an argument over a parking space outside a grocery store, an argument that ended with one woman beating in the other's windshield with a metal baseball bat. The bat was handy, since she was taking her daughter's T-ball team to practice. As the Channel Five news anchor intoned smugly last night, "Southern Californians now have to choose between life, liberty, or the pursuit of happiness." Jimmy had wanted to shoot the set.

It had been a month since the scavenger hunt. Rollo and the twins' triumphant arrival at the party bearing Walsh's directing Oscar had been the highlight of the evening. Rollo had called Jimmy, giddy, said Napitano was feeding the twins beluga caviar from his open mouth like a mother bird with her chicks. Jimmy had thanked him for the charming image. Walsh had clutched Jimmy's arm when Rollo's van pulled up an hour later, still pleading for Jimmy to tell his story, finally surrendering, promising to have the script finished in a month. "*Then* maybe you'll believe me."

Jimmy didn't argue; he left Walsh to stew in that broken-backed trailer, hearing him pounding away on the swapmeet typewriter, just beating away on it. Jimmy didn't feel sorry for him, not exactly; but Jimmy wished he hadn't hit him.

Walsh had stuck his head out the window as Jimmy and Rollo got into the van. "Come back in a month, and I'll barbecue some steaks. You bring the steaks—New York cut, two inches thick minimum— and a bag of mesquite charcoal and a few cases of cold Heineken. A couple of Marie Callender Dutch apple pies would be nice too, and a gallon of French vanilla. Don't forget the charcoal lighter. *I'll* supply the match," Walsh said, dissolving into drunken cackles, banging his head on the window.

"I don't know why you're complaining about B.K. coming to the barbecue," said Rollo, waving an unlabeled DVD in Jimmy's face. "Mr. Walsh hasn't seen this in seven years. You think he's going to be *upset* when I hand it to him?"

Jimmy adjusted the air vents, the hot wind blowing across him. He hadn't said anything to Rollo about what Walsh had told him in the trailer; he had promised Walsh to keep quiet about the good wife and the letter she had written to him in prison. "Silence is golden, tough guy—and *safe*. I can trust you, can't I?" Jimmy had broken at least nine of the Ten Commandments, but he kept his word. He accelerated, sending Rollo's unopened cardboard boxes sliding across the backseat—a twenty-seven-inch JVC monitor and a Sony DVD player. No receipt, of course.

"You should be proud of me," said Rollo, not letting it go. "B.K. is a film archivist at Trans-World Entertainment, a fucking *gnome,* man. He's not interested in hardware or Italian suits or any of the usual beads and mirrors I trade in. Just pulling Walsh's rough cut of *Hammerlock* from the vaults was a risk for him—the dude could go to jail for making me this copy. The only way he was willing to do it was if I introduced him to the man himself." He pushed back his floppy hair. "Besides, I had B.K bring the pie and ice cream."

Jimmy accelerated.

Rollo tightened his seatbelt as the Saab went into a skid, veering toward the sheer drop-off. He fired up a joint, took a couple hits, and started to pass it over. Then the car hit a deep pothole, and he thought better of it. "Me and Mr. Walsh—I think we connected in just the little time we spent together. I'm a filmmaker too. You see the look he gave me when I came back from the party with my camera? He knew. I got about five minutes of great footage of him and the trailer before you dragged me away. I could tell he appreciated my camera work too. No tripod, no steady cam, the real thing, guerrilla tactics, just like he used on *Firebug.* I'm hoping maybe he and I could collaborate on a project." He nudged the grocery bag between his knees. "That's why I brought something more than sirloin to the barbecue."

"You brought some of your movies too?"

"Just six of them," said Rollo. "Hey, don't give me that look. We got enough beer here for an all-night festival of Rollo's greatest hits."

Jimmy smiled. For all he knew, Rollo would be up on stage accepting an Oscar someday, squinting into the spotlight as he thanked the little people. In L.A. anything was possible. Even Walsh's innocence.

After the scavenger hunt Jimmy had run a Nexus search on Walsh's arrest and trial, hoping to find something that would either bolster or deflate the idea of a setup. The legal documents alone ran to more than four hundred single-spaced pages; Jimmy had been too busy to do more than read the highlights. There was solid forensic evidence against Walsh: His skin was under Heather Grimm's nails, his semen was in her vagina, and her blood was spattered on his purple silk pajama bottoms. No wonder Walsh had pled guilty even though he had no memory of committing the crime. The silk pajamas alone would have been enough to get a conviction in the hands of the right prosecutor. What was missing from the reports was an in-depth portrait of Heather Grimm, something over and beyond "an innocent girl, with a talent for trigonometry and Spanish club bake sales," in the memorable words of some clown from the *Times*. Nothing in her bio suggested she had the icy calculation needed to take part in setting up Walsh.

That's what it came down to. If Walsh had been framed, Heather Grimm had to have been in on it, which meant that the husband would have originally planned on Walsh getting hit with a statutory rape charge. That would have been enough to stop production of *Hammerlock* and stop Walsh's career. It wouldn't do much for the great love affair either. So what had happened? Either Walsh had really killed her, or the husband's plan had escalated. Jimmy intended to ask Walsh exactly what had happened once he invited Heather Grimm into the beach house, what she had said, how she had behaved, her tone of voice, her familiarity with drugs, and the eagerness with which she took part.

"I brought Mr. Walsh a copy of the new *SLAP* too," Rollo said proudly. "That scavenger hunt pictorial is already paying off. Next week I'm being interviewed on this public access channel, and the Seven-Eleven where I get breakfast put our page up next to the cash register."

"Oh, joy."

"I *was* a little surprised they used the HOLLYWOOD sign Polaroid," bubbled Rollo. "Full frontal nudity is cool with me, but I didn't think *SLAP* did that. I bet *now* Jane wishes she had come along." He saw Jimmy's expression. "Maybe not."

The Saab crested the hill, and Jimmy saw a red Ford Escort parked beside the trailer.

"That's B.K.'s car," said Rollo. "Party time!"

Jimmy pulled in beside the Escort, turned off the engine, and stepped out into the racket of crickets sawing away, a mating song more desperate than melodic. He lugged the three cases of beer toward the trailer, while Rollo followed behind, carrying the steaks and charcoal. Jimmy stopped so suddenly that Rollo bumped him.

"Hey, watch it," said Rollo.

Jimmy nodded at apple pies strewn on the ground, a half-gallon of vanilla ice cream melting beside them. He could hear the sound of someone sobbing nearby.

"M-maybe we should come back later," said Rollo.

Jimmy followed the sound of crying and found a balding, middle-aged man slumped against a stunted lemon tree, holding his head in his hands. He was overdressed in chocolate-brown corduroy pants and a button-down shirt, his thinning hair limp and moist around the crown of his head. Jimmy thought at first that the poor guy had had a sunstroke.

"B.K., dude, what's wrong?" said Rollo.

B.K. covered his face with his hands.

Jimmy wasn't interested in B.K. anymore—his attention was drawn now to the koi pond. A gigantic beach ball floated in the water, a bloated two-tone beach ball, red on one side, blue on the other. As Jimmy approached, a cloud of blackflies lifted up from the pond, drifting overhead like a cartoon thought-balloon of dark intentions, and then the breeze shifted, blowing the stink toward him, and Jimmy covered his mouth and nose, his eyes burning. It was Walsh—or what was left of him.

"Fuck," said Rollo, right behind Jimmy now.

Walsh floated face-down in the dirty water, unrecognizable, hands and feet chewed away. He wore jeans and no shirt, just like the night they had first met, his swollen torso lobster red from the sun, blistered, the flesh of his back split open. The devil tattoo on his shoulder was so stretched and distended, it looked like a map of terra incognita. Fat foot-long koi swam lazily around the body as the blackflies settled back down.

Jimmy stared at the body, feeling light-headed, his skin clammy in the heat, the crickets sawing away, the rhythm broken by B.K.'s sobs. "Did you tell anyone else where Walsh was staying?" he asked Rollo.

"What does that mean?"

"Did you?"

"No, man—I only gave B.K. directions this morning." Rollo was breathing heavily, but the smell didn't seem to bother him. "Mr. Walsh, I was keeping him for myself. To be honest, I was half sorry I told *you*."

Jimmy sidled toward the body, swatting at the bugs, until he reached the rock border of the koi pond. He had been in apartments that smelled worse—crackheads who bought a pound of raw hamburger, left it on the counter while they fired up a rock, and a month later it was still there. The fish had long since finished with the soft parts—Walsh's face was eaten away to the ears, and the koi were grazing now on his fingers and toes, the tips of the finger bones stark white in the murky water. There was no obvious wound to the head or torso, no gunshot at least, but decomposition could have hidden almost anything. He could see the outline of the linoleum knife in Walsh's back pocket, so whatever had happened to him had come as a surprise.

Rollo tossed a pebble at a shattered bottle of brandy at the edge of the pond, sending ripples across the water. Broken glass glittered in the sunlight. "It's like I always told you, Jimmy, alcohol *kills*." He fired up the remains of the joint he had started in the car, inhaled, then held it out. "Take a hit, Jimmy. Kills the stink."

Jimmy turned, walking quickly now.

"Where you going?" called Rollo.

The trailer was unlocked. Jimmy stepped inside, careful not to touch anything. The lights were all on, so Walsh had probably died at night. The sink was piled high with empty cans and crusted plates fuzzy with mold—after the koi pond the stale beer smell was like fresh-cut flowers. The main room looked pretty much the way it had the last time Jimmy had been there, but it was Walsh's study that

Jimmy was interested in. He pushed aside the curtain and stayed there, surveying the small room. The bed was made, the sheets pulled tight and pillow fluffed. The two Academy Awards were back on the bookcase, and the typewriter was still on the table. But the script was gone, as was the accordion-style file folder with the investigator's raw notes. There was no balled-up paper in the wastebasket.

Jimmy barged into the room, looking for something amiss: a book askew, a piece of the fake wallboard bowed out, a ceiling panel that didn't quite fit—anything to indicate where Walsh might have stashed his precious script, his notes, his files. He rested a hand on Walsh's chair, still seeing the fear in the man's eyes as he begged for help that night, hearing his voice crack as he glanced out the window. Jimmy knocked over the chair and picked it back up, clumsy now. He bent down and checked under the mattress, felt the mattress itself, then moved into the tiny bathroom, looking behind the toilet and inside the tank. He wasn't really expecting to find the screenplay. It was a lousy thing to wish that a man had gotten drunk and drowned in a glorified lily pond, but that was what Jimmy had been hoping for: an accident.

B.K. was wiping his tongue when Jimmy walked out of the trailer. He had thrown up all over his corduroy pants. Rollo stood in front of the koi pond, staring down at Walsh, right where Jimmy had left him. He looked up as Jimmy approached.

"Give me the phone number for the Monelli twins," said Jimmy.

"They didn't tell anybody about Mr. Walsh. He said to tell Napitano that we got the Oscar from an anonymous collector, and that's what we did."

"You should give it to me anyway."

Rollo turned back to the body. "Mr. Walsh—I think he might have gotten a kick out of us finding him like this. You know, like *Sunset Boulevard.*"

Tires crunched on the gravel road, and Jimmy turned, his heart pounding way too loudly. It was a police car, Anaheim PD, and another, unmarked unit. The full treatment.

Rollo gobbled down the last of the joint.

B.K. waved feebly to the cops. He would have called 911 sometime after seeing the body and before throwing up. Guys like B.K. always called the cops when bad things happened. That's what you were supposed to do.

Jimmy had other ideas. He had no respect for rules or authority, no regard for holographic ID badges, formal invitations, or signing in at the front desk. He cheated on his taxes, trespassed when he felt like it, and broke the speed limit every time he got behind the wheel. But he never stiffed a waitress and never told a woman he loved her if he didn't—his internal compass *always* pointed to true north. If you had to think about a moral choice, wondering what you should do, then it was best to roll over and play dead, leave it to the cops or just let the bad guys inherit the earth.

The breeze kicked up and sent Walsh's body bumping gently against one of the large rounded rocks in the koi pond, one hand waving sluggishly, draped in skin like a lace glove. Walsh had been right—he hadn't killed Heather Grimm. Maybe if he had gone about his business like a good ex-con, grateful to be out, and keeping a low profile—maybe if he had shut up about working on the Most Dangerous Script in the World—maybe if Jimmy had believed him, he would be alive today.

A glossy black crow landed on the back of Walsh's head, claws brushing the scalp, then quickly flew away, trailing hair. Walsh's head bobbed in agreement.

Jimmy heard footsteps approaching.

Chapter 6

Jimmy was watching the crow fly away, trailing a strand of Walsh's hair in its claw, when he became aware of Rollo edging away and knew things were going to get ugly. He slowly turned around. Oh, *shit*. He forced a smile. "Good afternoon, detective."

Detective Helen Katz glowered at him, a big rawboned cop with short dirty-blond hair and a face like a plowhorse. She elbowed Jimmy aside and stood there with one foot on the stone border of the koi pond, wrinkling her flat nose at Walsh's bloated body. "Jesus, this bastard is *way* past his pull date."

Katz was one of those female cops who habitually wore crepe-sole brogans, shapeless suit pants, and a white shirt and tie, thinking that she had to dress like Sergeant Joe Friday to be respected. That's what she had told Jane Holt anyway, criticizing Holt's designer suits and pearls, her iridescent running shoes, as "too girly"—fine for the politically correct Laguna PD, but Anaheim was an inland PD whose officers had to face down warring gangbangers, not chase rowdy boogie boarders off the beach. In actuality, no one on the Anaheim PD would have dared treat Katz in less than a professional manner regardless of what she wore. A former army MP who regularly took top honors in the annual Southern California Peace Officers hand-to-hand combat competitions, Katz was a hard-ass who considered interpersonal skills a sign of weakness. She scared the shit out of everyone. Jimmy was always overly polite with her, complimenting her wardrobe, solicitous about her health. It drove her nuts.

"Is that a new perfume you're wearing?" said Jimmy.

"I'm in my period."

"Congratulations. You must be so proud."

Katz draped a meaty arm across his shoulders and dragged him closer, her body warm and heavy. "This floater a friend of yours?"

Jimmy could hear a camera whirling behind him, the uniforms taking Polaroids until the CSI wagon arrived. "His name is—"

"I know who he is." Katz grabbed Jimmy by the scruff of the neck, throwing him off balance, his shins butting painfully up against the rocks. One push, and he'd be headfirst into the filthy water. "What I'm interested in is what you're doing here fouling up my crime scene."

Jimmy relaxed, refusing to struggle, not wanting to give her an excuse. He pretended they were old friends out for a stroll in Venice, and that the flies floating around them were pigeons in St. Mark's Square. He could see Rollo huddling with one of the uniforms, glancing over at him. "I'm writing an article on Walsh—"

"Detective? Is there a problem?"

Katz spun around and stared at the young uniformed officer, a strapping Hispanic rookie wearing his Sam Browne belt too high. "A *problem*?" she demanded, her hand still on the back of Jimmy's neck. "You think I might have a problem that you could actually *do* something about, Commoro?"

"Yes . . . I mean—yes, sir. Yes, detective," Commoro corrected himself, his adolescent acne flaring against his dark brown skin.

"Can you swim, Commoro?" asked Katz.

"I still hold the record in the hundred-yard butterfly at Santa Ana Catholic—"

"Good." Katz tossed him a set of keys. "Go get my boots out of the trunk of my car."

Commoro looked at Walsh's putrid body, then at Katz, then back to the body. He was fingering the car keys like rosary beads.

"Move it!" Katz waited until the uniform hustled away, handcuff jingling against his belt, before letting Jimmy go, giving his neck one last painful squeeze for good measure. She blotted her sweaty forehead with her necktie. "Now, where were we?"

"I was mentally composing my police brutality complaint."

"That'll be the day," Katz snorted. "Nice photo of you and the naked bimbos in *SLAP*. I bet Jane Holt was thrilled. Why did you have your hands over your unit, though? You got something to be ashamed of?"

"I'm *sure* yours is bigger than mine, detective."

"Follow me," snapped Katz. The two of them started a slow circuit of the koi pond. Katz stopped after a few feet, chewing on a thumbnail as she studied the body from a new angle. "You said you came here to do an article on Walsh. This your first visit?"

"I was here once before, about three weeks ago."

"Walsh had a drug problem when he went into prison," Katz said idly. Something in the water had caught her attention. She seemed barely interested in talking with Jimmy. "Did—did he have one when he got out?"

"I don't know what that means."

Katz looked at him, her eyes the intense blue of an antique doll, painted on and hard all the way down. "So in your position as a professional journalist and helpful citizen, was Walsh still strung out when you last saw him?"

"He liked to mix painkillers and booze. A lot of people do."

Katz watched a blotchy gray koi nuzzle what was left of Walsh's right ear. Cartilage was the last to go. "I saw a broken bottle in the water back there. A sloppy man and a sloppy death."

"Maybe."

Katz stared at him, but he didn't back down. The collar of her white shirt was soaked with sweat, but she wouldn't loosen her tie if you threatened her with a cattle prod. "Maybe?"

Jimmy didn't offer a clarification. The trick with someone like Katz was to make her force the information from you that you *wanted* her to have—the only truth she believed was the one she extracted under duress. If Jimmy was willing to be strong-armed, he could give up a partial truth and hold back the most important parts.

Commoro clomped across the dry ground wearing thigh-high rubber boots and rubber gloves, cursing to himself, accompanied by a stoop-shouldered man with a backpack.

"I need to get my samples before you disturb the body, detective," called the stooped man, his voice reedy and eager. You'd think he was at a birthday party, ready to blow out the candles on the cake. He was a few years older than Commoro, a pencil-neck in hiking boots, khaki shorts, and a denim shirt with double-decker pockets, his hair a nest of unkempt curls.

"Just don't take all day, professor," said Katz. "Make sure you get photographs first."

The professor took a 35-millimeter camera from the backpack and started taking photos of the corpse from every angle, moving closer, leaping from rock to rock until he was right next to Walsh's body. He perched there and finished out the roll, ignoring the flies swarming around him. The camera returned to his pack and he pulled on a pair of surgical gloves, then bent down over the body, knobby knees wide, his face inches from the putrefying flesh. Sunlight flashed on the stainless-steel tweezers in his hand as he plucked something off and held it up for examination. It wriggled.

Jimmy looked at Katz.

"Professor Zarinski is a bug doc who wants to be a consultant," Katz explained. "He's a pain in the ass sometimes, but he doesn't charge the department anything, and besides he buys coffee." She nodded to where B.K. was talking to an older cop. "The doofus there says you took one look at the floater and made a beeline for the trailer." She punched him lightly in the kidneys, more of a love tap. "What were you looking for?"

"A phone. I wanted to call it in to the proper authorities."

Katz smiled. "The proper authorities—who's that, the *Drudge Report*?" She stared into the koi pond again, cocking her head to get a better look. "Hold that thought, Jimmy. Okay, Commoro, time to take a dip."

Commoro shifted from one foot to the other.

"Get in there," ordered Katz. "There's something just under the surface, right near the head. I can see it catching the sunlight. See that gray rock? *That* one. Hurry up, the fishies won't bite you—they already hit the smorgasbord." She laughed. It was a nice laugh too, a sweet laugh, a private joke on a summer day.

Commoro gingerly entered the pond, dark blue circles spreading under the armpits of his uniform. The bottom of the pool varied in depth, the scummy water rising to his knees as he made his way to where Katz pointed. He tried not to make waves, but he sent ripples across the pool with every step, banging Walsh's body against the rock the professor knelt on. Commoro stuck his hand in the water, his head turned away.

"What were you looking for in the trailer, Jimmy?" asked Katz, still watching the water.

"The things that a reporter learns from a source. That's privileged information, but at the same time," Jimmy hurried, sounding nervous, "I feel an obligation to help your investigation. We're on the same side."

Katz laughed.

Commoro fumbled around the gray rock, the water filling his rubber glove. He shuddered, trying not to breathe, as the body bobbed against him.

"A word of advice," the professor murmured to Commoro as he picked through Walsh's scalp with the tweezers, his voice barely louder than the flies that buzzed around them. "Take *deep* breaths. It will make it easier. It's called sensory overload. Once the nasal receptors fully fire, well, it's really quite tolerable."

"Take off your glove, Commoro," ordered Katz. "Okay, Jimmy, show and tell."

"Okay." Jimmy was going to tell her the truth, as much as he needed to anyway. "In exchange, I'd like a heads-up on the autopsy report before you release it. There's going to be reporters all over this story."

"Sure, Jimmy, share and share alike, you and me, we'll have a regular circle jerk. Hey, Commoro!" Katz's voice echoed off the surrounding hills. "You puke on my floater, you're going to be directing traffic at Disneyland until your nuts drop!"

Commoro was shaking as he pulled off one of his rubber gloves. He took a shallow breath, held it, and plunged his bare hand into the murky water, setting Walsh's body rolling as he reached around. He suddenly held up Walsh's sunglasses. One of the lenses was cracked.

"Bag 'em," said Katz.

Commoro's look of triumph turned to shock as what was left of Walsh's face came briefly into view.

"They go for the eyes first, the soft parts," Katz said conversationally, batting away flies. "They swim right inside the mouth going after the tongue."

"What kind of fish are these, detective?" said Commoro, hand on his pistol. "Piranha?"

"Koi, officer," soothed the professor. "Quite harmless, I assure you."

"There's not a fish alive that won't eat dead meat," Katz said to Jimmy. "These assholes who keep tropical fish—goldfish are just Dobermans with fins, if you ask me."

"Detective?" Sergeant Rollings lumbered over to them, a fleshy old-timer sweating in the sun, counting the coffee breaks until retirement. "I finished the preliminary with the two civies and checked on the meat wagon—they should be here in five or ten minutes." He hitched his pants, his blue uniform so wrinkled it looked deliberate. "Hey, Jimmy, loved the picture of you with the twins. How do I get your job?"

"How are you doing, Ted?"

"My hemorrhoids are acting up, and this heat ain't helping." Rollings watched the rookie standing in the koi pond. "Hey, Commoro, you need a license to fish!"

"Start a walkaround on the ridgeline, sergeant," said Katz. "Keep your eyes out for anything that might indicate someone had been up there watching the trailer."

Rollings looked up at the steep slope. "How about if I do a look-see inside the trailer instead? My bunions are killing me."

"Gum wrappers, cigarette butts, anything that you can find," said Katz, as though she hadn't heard him.

Rollings hitched at his pants again, sighed, and shuffled away.

"Can I come out now, detective?" Commoro sounded like he was twelve.

"A doper tries walking on water, slips, cracks his head on a rock, and drowns. That's my first impression," said Katz. "But you don't think it was an accident. What do you know that I don't?" She shifted her stance, closer now. "You don't want to make me wait, Jimmy. You really don't."

"Walsh was working on a new screenplay," said Jimmy. "We were going to have a little party today, then I was going to interview him and—"

"That's what you were doing in the trailer?" said Katz. "Getting the screenplay?"

"It wasn't there."

"Maybe you didn't look hard enough."

"He was supposed to show it to us today. That's why we were having the party."

"What was this screenplay about? Some kind of crime story?" Katz stroked her thick jaw. "Walsh writing about somebody he met in the joint? That could be dangerous. Nobody likes a snitch." She smiled again at him. "So what was it about?"

"I don't know. Walsh said he didn't give previews."

Katz stared at him with those hard blue eyes of hers, and Jimmy wondered if anyone had ever been able to look past them and see inside of her. "Commoro! Go toss that bag of briquettes onto the barbecue and fire them up." Her eyes never left Jimmy.

"Detective . . . ?" Commoro was more confused than ever now.

"Go on, Ernesto," Katz said to the uniform, gently now. She waited until Commoro splashed away, then grinned at Jimmy. "Wouldn't want those steaks to go to waste."

"I just wanted you to know about the missing screenplay," said Jimmy. "The ME does good work, but sometimes the caseload piles up and she gets behind, or she hands an easy one off to Boone, and we both know what *he's* like. I want to make sure that Walsh gets four-star treatment, that's all."

"Save your cheerleading for Detective Holt," said Katz, hands on her hips. "I don't see anything here that looks like murder, but I treat *any* suspicious death as a potential homicide. Now you show up with this missing-screenplay story, the mysterious screenplay that you don't know anything about." She closed in on him, so near that Jimmy could smell stale coffee on her breath, "I *surely* hope you're not trying to stir things up so you can get a story out of it. If I decide that's what you doing . . ."

"Walsh just said that it was a million-dollar idea. That's all I know."

"Okay." Katz held his gaze. "I'll go over Walsh's trailer myself. This screenplay—does it look like a book or a magazine or what?"

"It looks like a stack of paper. Maybe a hundred pages. He might have put it in a binder, or a manila folder—I don't know."

"Just a stack of paper?" Katz shook her head, disgusted. "I guess a million dollars doesn't buy much in Hollywood."

Chapter 7

"I have no intention of running phone numbers for you," said Jane Holt, keeping a steady pace in spite of the twinge in her left hamstring, the one that was always tight.

Jimmy didn't answer.

"I'm not going to do it," Holt repeated. Seagulls screamed overhead as she ran along the waterline. Her dark hair was pulled back, elegant somehow, even in nylon shorts and a Catalina marathon T-shirt, but her legs were too muscular for the debutante she had once been. The T-shirt was untucked, covering the .380 auto clipped to the waistband along her back, and the handgun would have been out of place at a deb ball too. "You know I can't."

"I wouldn't ask except I'm having trouble pulling—"

"Is *that* why you came this morning?" Holt stopped now, confronting him.

"I'm having a hard time pulling up Walsh's cell phone calls," said Jimmy, not answering the question. "He didn't have credit, so he had to use prepaid cards, and they're hard to trace. Rollo says you have to go through central billing, and—"

"Private citizens aren't *supposed* to trace calls. Even police have to get a court order."

"I don't think Walsh is going to complain that we violated his civil rights."

"That's not the point." Holt adjusted her weapon—a tiny callus had long since formed where it rubbed against the small of her back.

Jimmy had noticed the small roughened patch of skin the first night they made love and tenderly kissed it, guessing exactly the cause. The first lover of hers who had figured it out. Maybe if she dated cops once in a while . . . But she didn't like mixing business with pleasure. Until Jimmy. He wasn't police, but he had the same heightened survival instincts and street smarts as a good cop. Or a good crook. She sometimes thought his journalism was just an excuse to work the middle ground between right and wrong, an opportunity to keep company with the dregs and the desperadoes, the high and the mighty too. Getting involved with him was a bad career move, particularly for someone as ambitious as she was. She didn't care. She didn't have to explain things to him, didn't have to make excuses for her silences, didn't have to hide her anger and frustration with the job. Plus, he was wicked in bed—and even better, he allowed her to be wicked too. Holt started running again, wanting to change the subject. "Sergeant Leighton asked me today if you would autograph this month's copy of *SLAP* for him."

"I *told* you, I had no idea that Polaroid was going to make it into print—"

"One of the detectives posted your page on the bulletin board. They drew a crown on your head. Do you want to know what they drew on the twins?" Holt made it sound like good times in the squad room, but she knew that the other detectives lionized Jimmy only to humiliate her. "What *is* it, this thing men have about twins? Is it the challenge?"

"More like a death wish." Jimmy tried to keep up. "I need your help, Jane."

"You have to let Helen Katz work the case. You don't even know if it's a homicide or not."

"Walsh was murdered."

"It's only been four days. Wait until the coroner's report is released, *then* you'll know." Holt started running again, increasing her pace, forcing him to push himself to keep up with her. She was tan and fit, in her mid-thirties, crow's-feet starting at the corners of her eyes, and some serious vertical lines in her forehead from thinking too much about things that thinking couldn't do anything about. They had been together almost a year now. Jimmy liked her wrinkles, but a couple of weeks ago she had looked in the mirror and actually started thinking about getting botox injections. *Jane, you've been living too long in southern California.* She could hear Jimmy a couple of steps behind her, breathing hard. She ran faster.

A Rhode Island WASP with breeding and a law degree, Holt had intended to become a prosecutor, entering the police academy more for the training, an adjunct to her legal career rather than an end in itself, but after graduating second in her class, she gave up all thoughts of the courtroom. Being a prosecutor was all about making deals and taking long lunches with boring people, she had told Jimmy. If she wanted that, she would have gone to work at her father's hedge fund. Holt was a detective now, a by-the-book cop with a designer wardrobe and the best arrest-to-conviction ratio in the department.

"If it was an accident, what happened to the screenplay?" said Jimmy.

"I don't know. Neither do you."

"I know Walsh was killed for it, *that's* what I know."

"Walsh could have hidden the script where it wouldn't be found. He could have given it to someone else to read, someone he thought could help him more than you." Holt's explanations made perfect sense, but she knew that Jimmy wasn't going to give up. He never quit—it was one of the things about him that she was attracted to.

The thing about her job that never ceased to amaze her was the look of relief on so many suspects' faces when she arrested them. Some of them actually sighed when she read them their rights. There was no real pleasure in arresting them. Other suspects though, smart ones with plenty of career options, rich ones, thought the law was their servant, something to keep the little people in check and ensure that no one stole their Porsche. The smart ones were always shocked when she arrested them; they insisted that she had made a mistake, politely at first, then threatening her with lawsuits and calls to the mayor, then finally, when they realized it was really happening, happening to *them*, the fear took over. She enjoyed that.

Jimmy's brother, Jonathan—*he* had been a special case. Smarter than anyone else Holt had ever arrested, a successful plastic surgeon, handsome, urbane—and a serial killer who called himself the Eggman. He had written Jimmy an anonymous letter at *SLAP*, taking credit for his kills, taunting him. A police task force had concluded that the Eggman was a hoax, but Jimmy wouldn't be dissuaded. Those instincts of his again, those lovely instincts. Jonathan had been startled when she arrested him, but it hadn't lasted long. As she snapped on the handcuffs, he had looked at her with contempt, as though he knew something she didn't. Maybe he did. He should have gotten life without parole, minimum, but after a hung jury at his first trial, Jonathan had pled guilty to one count of homicide, *second degree* nonetheless, and was sentenced to an indeterminate stay at a facility for the criminally insane. A "facility"—that was how the judge referred to it.

Running full out, Jimmy stumbled, tumbling onto the beach.

Holt looked back, and he was already on his feet, sand stuck to one side of his face. She slowed to a walk and allowed him to catch up with her.

"The husband murdered Walsh, either by himself or by hire," Jimmy gasped, breathing through his mouth. "Killed him and took the screenplay he was working on—the screenplay and all his notes. Maybe the husband was just taking care of loose ends, but if he found out that the wife suspected him, she could be in danger."

That got Holt's attention.

Jimmy bent forward, trying to catch his breath. "A few days before he was murdered, Walsh sat across the table from me and told me he was innocent. He said that the man who had framed him was going to kill him. Walsh was an arrogant man, but he was scared that night, too scared to hide it. He begged me to save him, but I didn't believe him then. Now . . . now I do."

"Then let the authorities handle it."

"The authorities? Give me a fucking break." Jimmy stood up, still holding his side. "I clean up after myself."

Holt took his hand. "All I'm saying is that until there's an official finding on the cause of death, you're just spinning your wheels. If you're right and Walsh was murdered, then I'm sure Detective Katz is up to the task. She'll find the wife before anything happens to her. Helen Katz is a good cop." She smiled. "Crude but thorough."

"Katz doesn't know about the wife."

Holt stopped in midstride. "I beg your pardon?"

"I didn't tell her about the wife or the letter she sent. I just told her Walsh was working on a screenplay."

"You withheld evidence in a possible homicide?"

"Yes, I did, detective."

"That's not funny. It's a *crime*."

"I told her all she needed to know."

"*You* decided what she needs to know?" Holt shook her head. "I'm required to inform Detective Katz about this. Otherwise, I'm as culpable as you are."

"Let your conscience be your guide. That's what I do."

"That's not the way the law works."

"The law is written by judges, and judges are just lawyers who kissed the right ass. I don't need laws to tell me what I should do."

"Perhaps—perhaps you were just speculating about the existence of a letter. Of the wife and the husband when you told me about them."

"Yeah—perhaps."

Holt adjusted her automatic as she looked up and down the beach. It was barely past sunup. There were just a few other runners far down the strand. The hard core. Like her. She had only a few ironclad principles. One was to never have a drink before five P.M. Another was, no matter what happened the night before, get her run in the next morning. She used to have another ironclad principle, following not just the letter of the law but the spirit too. She looked at Jimmy, but he didn't flinch.

"I let Walsh down," Jimmy said. "Seven years he sat in prison, thinking he had murdered a high-school girl. Murdered his future too. I think about what it must have felt like to read that letter from the wife after all that time inside, after all the things he had seen. Just the chance that he hadn't really killed Heather Grimm—that he could reclaim everything that had been taken from him, *everything,* Jane."

Holt wanted to smooth the pain from Jimmy's face, but she didn't make a move, still angry at him for implicating her in the suppression of evidence.

"Walsh was a mess the night I met him, so loaded he could hardly stand, but he sized me up right away. I was on a scavenger hunt, but so was Walsh. He was looking for someone to change his luck, to turn the tables on the man who had put him away. Walsh had a con's instincts: Seize the advantage—that's how you survive in the joint, you don't waste any opportunity, you take your best shot because you might not get another. That's why he told me about the letter. He thought I was going to help him." Jimmy looked like he wanted to hit somebody. "I guess he was a bad judge of character."

"You didn't do anything wrong."

"I didn't do *anything.*"

"If the coroner's report rules Walsh's death a homicide, you have to tell Katz."

"Katz could get the wife killed. Cops don't have to move quietly, they just have to get results. Katz will elbow her way into people's lives, hauling them in for questioning, insisting on answers. Me, I'll move light and easy."

"Tell her what you know, Jimmy. If you don't, I will."

Jimmy looked into her eyes, slowly shook his head.

Chapter 8

"Filet mignon, bloody, baked potato with the works, asparagus tips," ordered Detective Helen Katz, the waiter scribbling to keep up. She shoved her empty cocktail glass across the white linen tablecloth. "Another double bourbon too. One cube."

"I'll have the tuna," said Jimmy. "Rare, please."

"Must be nice to have an expense account—go anyplace you want, order anything you want, and stick somebody else with the bill," said Katz. "I always wanted to eat here"—she watched the waiter hurry off—"but they don't give a police discount, and the steak costs more than a tank of gas."

"What's the ME's report going to say about cause of death?"

"Hold your horses, Pancho. You don't want to rush a lady."

Jimmy started to laugh but then thought better of it. Katz was wearing a blue suit and white dress shirt, her necktie the height of cop chic with a pistols-and-handcuffs pattern, her dirty-blond hair swept back into a ducktail. For all he knew, she considered this a working date.

"You going to finish your appetizer?" Katz grabbed the rest of his onion soup before he could answer. "You bring Holt here some-times?" Strings of mozzarella hung from her spoon. "Special occasions?"

"No."

"What's the matter, her ladyship not a meat eater?"

Jimmy wished Katz would have just told him the results of the autopsy over the phone, but she had insisted on giving him the news here. He hated the Grove. The food was overpriced, the menu was geared to induce coronary thrombosis, and the decor was Hollywood circa the time when Buddy Hackett was considered funny. At least the ancient tuxedoed waiters didn't introduce themselves. Lately the Grove had made a retro-chic comeback, frequented now by twenty-something hipsters and bitter, retired executives chewing unlit cigars and talking about how good things used to be and how lousy they were now.

"I'm just giving you shit about Holt," said Katz, picking at her teeth with a fingernail. "She's a good cop. Not my kind of cop, but a good cop just the same."

"I'll tell her she has your seal of approval."

"That supposed to be put-down?"

"Yeah, that's what it was."

Katz grinned again. "See, just when I'm ready to write you off as a scumbag with gainful employment, you go ahead and give me an honest answer. Makes me almost like you." She looked around the dark, wood-paneled restaurant from the shelter of their rolled red leather booth, her head bobbing in approval.

"So . . . what did the ME decide?"

"That's right, I almost forgot what we were here for." Katz slurped the last of the soup. "The ME said that person or persons unknown shoved something long and sharp through Walsh's ear canal." The spoon banged against the bottom of the bowl as Katz chased the last drop. "Doc almost didn't catch it." She ran a thick finger around the rim of the bowl and put it in her mouth. "You don't look surprised." Jimmy didn't respond, but it didn't seem to bother her. "Me, I was surprised, I admit it, but I'm just a big dumb cop." She barely covered a belch. "So, who do you think did it?"

"I don't know."

"I think you got an idea." Katz gently swirled her double bourbon, the single ice cube clinking against the heavy crystal as she waited for an answer.

"Walsh was afraid of someone, I know that much. When I met him at the trailer, he was jumping out of his skin, but I thought he was just hustling me for some ink."

"Guess we were both wrong." Katz looked around for the waiter.

Jimmy rearranged his silverware, not sure of how much to reveal. Maybe Jane was right. Katz was working the case as a homicide now, so there was no reason to keep information from her. No reason except he liked having an edge, liked having room to maneuver. "Walsh said he got a letter in prison. The writer suggested that Walsh didn't really kill Heather Grimm. That he had been set up."

Katz laughed. "Manson has pen pals too, all of them convinced he's innocent."

"Walsh took this letter seriously. Maybe he wanted to believe. He confessed to killing Heather Grimm, but he didn't remember doing it, so after he got the letter, he was determined to prove his innocence. He didn't really know how to do it, but he was making all the right noises. The screenplay he was working on was going to lay it all out. That's what he said, anyway."

Katz idly stirred her drink with a forefinger.

"Walsh's lawyers hired a private investigator to do a background on Heather Grimm, but his plea bargain stopped all that. Walsh had a copy of the raw notes—he was hoping to use them to find out the truth. I already contacted the attorney. They won't even acknowledge that the file exists, but if you got a subpoena—"

"I didn't find any notes," said Katz, still stirring her drink.

"Neither did I."

"A letter, raw files." Katz flicked her finger and sprayed him with bourbon. "Why didn't you tell me all this at the crime scene?"

Jimmy wiped his face. "I have a hard time sharing my toys. It's a personality defect, but I'm working on it."

"I got a few personality defects myself, but I'm not touching them—why mess with success?" Katz waited in vain for him to disagree with her. "Who wrote this letter to Walsh?"

"I don't know." There was no reason for Jimmy to keep the existence of the good wife from Katz, no reason other than the fact that he wanted to find her first. Jane said he liked saving the damsel in distress, liked playing the hero, but Jimmy knew better. "I asked Walsh, but he wouldn't give it up."

"How convenient." Katz drained her drink, banged it onto the white linen tablecloth. "Well, I searched the trailer myself, and I didn't find anything. No letter. No notes. No screenplay. Poof, disappeared. I did find nine empty prescription bottles of assorted painkillers. Found a quarter-ounce of crank taped under the bathroom sink too, but you probably don't care about that."

Jimmy leaned forward over the table. "Walsh wasn't murdered over a dope deal. If you want to find out who killed him, find out who set him up for killing Heather Grimm."

The white-haired waiter appeared at their table, and Jimmy sat back as the man laid another double bourbon and steak in front of Katz. The man moved so precisely that he didn't disturb the air molecules. He set down Jimmy's plate next, shaking out his napkin before handing it to Jimmy.

"Hey, gramps," said Katz. "Where's the Thousand Island dressing?"

The waiter acted like his pacemaker had just started sparking inside his chest. "The Grove asparagus spears are served only with soft-boiled eggs and lemon wedges, madame," he croaked. "It's one of our signature dishes."

"You ever hear the phrase 'The customer is always right'?" People at the surrounding tables glanced over, but Katz was oblivious. "Just bring me the Thousand." She shook her head as the waiter retreated, then sliced into her steak, the knife clicking on the thick china plate. "We dusted the trailer for prints, every inch of it." She brought the forkful of meat to her mouth, blood running down the tines. "Got some hits too."

"Yeah?" Jimmy forced himself to be careful. Something wasn't right.

"Yeah. *Yours.*" Katz chewed with her mouth open. "Good cow," she pronounced, washing it down with a swallow of bourbon. She took the knife to the steak again. "Rollo's too. And Walsh's, of course." The fork was poised in front of her mouth. "Last but not least, Harlen Shafer, until recently a resident at one of our fine penal institutions. Mr. Walsh's alma mater, to be exact. Aren't you proud of me, Jimmy?" Katz was having way too good a time for Jimmy's taste.

"What was Shafer sent up for?"

The waiter returned and set a side dish of Thousand Island dressing in front of her, then sidled away as Katz ladled dressing onto the asparagus.

"Do you have an APB out for him?" Jimmy said.

"An *APB*?" Katz picked up three of the asparagus spears and waved them coquettishly at him. "I just love it when civilians use police lingo. I bet that gets Jane hot too."

Jimmy didn't answer. Anything he said was going to be used against him.

"Don't get your panties in a bunch. Shafer's just a small-time dope dealer." Katz bit off the heads of her asparagus. "I do have a confession to make, though." She hung her head for an instant, crossed herself, then looked up at him, showing off those big flat horse teeth of hers. "I haven't been completely honest with you, but then, you weren't completely honest with me. What goes around, comes around." She gulped down half her fresh drink and smacked her lips. "*Nobody* shoved anything in Walsh's ear, you silly bastard. He wasn't murdered. He died from drowning, with alcohol and drug intoxication as contributing factors." She batted her lashes at him, a little bleary now. "I do hope I haven't destroyed your faith in law enforcement."

"Walsh didn't drown."

"I'm afraid he did." Katz beamed.

"Walsh's body was too deteriorated for the ME to be sure of—"

"*Deteriorated* is too nice a word. Walsh looked like month-old cottage cheese." Katz wiped her mouth with the back of her hand. "Floating in the hot sun all that time, fish chewing at his fingers and toes, and the *ravens*—it was like that Hitchcock movie. Good thing we had Walsh's prison dental records, or we couldn't have made a positive ID."

"Walsh might have been strangled, and no one would know. Any ligature marks would have been eaten away."

"Ligature." Katz chuckled, then reached over and rapped Jimmy on the larynx, suddenly solemn as he jerked back, coughing. "That's your hyoid bone. Somebody chokes you to death, you're hyoid bone is going to show it even if the flesh is mushy. Walsh's hyoid—it was just fine."

Jimmy rubbed his throat.

"Then there's the blood chloride levels." Katz started in on the steak again, gleefully masticating her meat. "Blood chloride levels on the left and right chambers of Walsh's heart were equal." She finished off her bourbon and held her glass above her head. "*Garçon!*" She grinned at Jimmy. "I always wanted to say that."

"What does blood chloride have to do with it?"

Katz let him simmer, watching the waiter hustle toward the bar. "I barely passed chemistry myself, but Doc says that if the chloride levels are equal, it means that Walsh was still breathing when he went into the water." She stopped as the waiter came by with another drink, then sipped this one now, rolling it around in her mouth; Jimmy had watched Jane do the same thing with her first drink of the evening until she noticed him paying attention. She hid her pleasure now.

"So Walsh drowned. Maybe he had help."

Katz stuck the end of her napkin in her water glass and rubbed at the gob of Thousand Island dressing that had fallen on her necktie. "You hold somebody down, he's going to put up a fight, even somebody as drunk as Walsh was," she lectured. "Those rocks in the koi pond are rough, but Walsh's hands and knees—what was left of them anyway—there were no lacerations on them. His fingertips were gone, but the fish didn't touch his fingernails—none of them were broken off. Sorry to spoil your fantasy, but Walsh just fell down drunk and drowned. The ME's issuing the report tomorrow afternoon, so consider this your heads-up—I always keep my word."

"*Somebody* took the screenplay. It just didn't disappear."

"The screenplay may be missing, but that doesn't mean somebody took it." Katz inspected her tie, smoothed it flat. "I did my job. I even had the crime scene unit take tire impressions from the ground around the trailer; we haven't had rain in what—three months? CSI got a match on standard-issue tires from Walsh's Honda, your Saab, the Ford Escort driven by Mr. Ponytail, Rollo's VW van, and one more, origin unknown. I admit I got a little interested at that point, but then we determined that Goodyear 275 R15 radials were basic equipment on 1996 Camaros, like the one currently registered to the aforementioned Harlen Shafer, the dealer who makes house calls. That's it, Jimmy—those were the only tire treads up there. Give it a rest."

"Have you talked to Shafer?"

"About what? The case is *closed*. If you don't know what that means, ask Holt."

The waiter reappeared, nodded at Jimmy's untouched plate. "Is everything all right, sir?"

"Yes, fine." Jimmy looked at Katz. "You're wrong."

"Put my date's tuna into a doggie bag, gramps," Katz told the waiter. "And drop in a few of those dinner rolls." She pushed her plate away and leaned close to Jimmy. "Thanks for the chow and the laughs. I'll keep your number in my wallet. If I ever need somebody to track down the Easter Bunny, I just know you're the guy who can do it for me."

Chapter 9

"Just a minute," the man with the high cheekbones said to Jimmy, barely acknowledging him, too busy with the girl in the chair, a blond teenager clad in a pale blue shorty nightgown, the gauzy fabric spattered with fake blood. The man hovering over her was small and slight, wearing a black, full-cut shirt and matching jodhpurs, his dark hair sculpted high, his sideburns tapered to perfect points.

"Are you Martin?" Jimmy moved closer.

"I told you, just a minute," hissed the man, delicately applying a thin gel pack to the side of the blond girl's neck with gum adhesive. At a remote signal the pack would explode, sending fake blood spurting at the camera, one of the many money shots in *Slumber Party Maniacs II*. His black cowboy boots clicked as he walked around the makeup chair, checking his work. The boot heels must have been five inches high at least, but he moved smoothly, pivoting like a ballerina. "Yes . . . I think that will do."

The shooting location today was a large house in Santa Monica. A temporary makeup room had been set up in the servant's quarters off the squash court, a small room stacked with canned goods, the few items of furniture pushed into a corner.

"It's not going to hurt, right?" said the girl, reaching up to touch her neck. She looked like she belonged in a shampoo commercial, brushing out her long blond hair while she talked to the captain of the football team on the phone—one hundred strokes a night, and none for him. "When it goes off, I mean. It won't hurt, will it?"

The man smacked her hand away. "Do I look like a fellow who would hurt anyone as gorgeous as you?"

"Is that a trick question?" The girl turned to Jimmy. Her eyes were blue as an overchlorinated swimming pool. "Is he making fun of me?"

Jimmy wasn't really paying attention. He kept replaying his lunch with Detective Katz yesterday, annoyed at himself for letting her get to him. The ME's autopsy report on Walsh had been thorough and conclusive and documented, but there was no way that Jimmy believed it. Jane said it was hard to argue with science, but Jimmy knew that anyone who could set Walsh up for murder, set him up so sweetly that Walsh himself bought it—science was no match for someone like that.

The man with the high cheekbones brushed on makeup over the edges of the gel pack that matched the blond girl's skin tone, made it almost invisible. He had a pencil mustache that matched the scimitar sideburns, and thin, arched eyebrows—a silent-screen heartthrob striding about with a makeup palette.

"Can I practice my scream on you?" the girl asked the man in black.

"Not a chance, darling," said the man, hands on his hips as he examined her makeup, deftly arranging her silky hair so that it fell naturally over the gel pack.

"What about you, mister?" the girl asked Jimmy. "Can I try out my scream on you?"

"I vote with Valentino there," said Jimmy.

"Who?" said the girl.

"You're done, darling," said the man. "Go forth and be butchered. Now shoo!" He turned to Jimmy as the girl scooted out the door of the makeup room. "I liked the Valentino line, by the way. Sometimes I get called Zorro, and I really don't appreciate that." He indicated the chair for Jimmy to sit. "I'm Martin. What am I supposed to do with you? Are you one of the maniacs?" He tapped his teeth with a forefinger. "You're a little small—most of the maniacs are total gym rats, just huge. The room positively *reeks* of testosterone when they walk in."

"I'm not in the movie. I'm Jimmy Gage." They shook hands—Martin had a firm, dry handshake. "I'm a reporter with *SLAP* magazine."

"Oh, I *love SLAP*. The producer just hired a couple of girls from the current issue. Maybe you—"

"I wanted to ask you some questions about Garrett Walsh. I know you crewed on his second film."

"If you're looking for someone to dump on Walsh, you've come to the wrong boy," sniffed Martin. "He was a monster and a prick, but *Hammerlock* was my big break, and it was Walsh who insisted on giving me the job." He smoothed his sideburns with a forefinger. "I was ever so young and had barely enough hours to qualify for my union card, but he had seen my work. He told me I did the best bruises in town."

"I believe it. The job you just did on the blonde—amazing."

"Thank you, kind sir, but bruises are much more of a challenge—more subtle." Martin tapped the side of his nose. "Here's a clue: Estée Lauder Potpourri, Blush All Day, and red dye number nine. That's just the basics of a good bruise. There are other ingredients, which shall remain nameless." He pursed his lips. "Can't expect me to share all my secrets, can you? Not even for *SLAP*."

"You said *Hammerlock* was your big break. Too bad it never got finished."

"Yes, too bad." Martin glared at Jimmy. "If it had—well, let's just say I wouldn't be working for scale on a slasher movie, and a sequel to boot. There was plenty of bad luck to go around on the shoot, but if you want someone to piss on Walsh's grave, hit the road, Jack."

"I just wanted to ask you some questions about *Hammerlock*. Makeup artists always have the best dish. You spend more time with the talent than the director, and people loosen up in the chair, they talk, and even when they don't—"

"*Hammerlock* is ancient history. Why talk about it now?"

The door to the makeup room opened, and Tamra Monelli stuck her head in. "It *is* him!" she cried, then she and Tonya rushed into the room, the twins squealing as they hugged Jimmy. They wore matching white nightgowns, the fabric so sheer you could read the tax code through it.

"Is this great or what?" Tonya said, one side of her face cut to the bone, the makeup job so realistic Jimmy could barely look at her. "The same day *SLAP* came out, we got a callback from the director. The very same day."

"So much for blondes-only," laughed Tamra, her shoulders dappled with puncture wounds.

"Was that *you* in the photo?" Martin squinted at Jimmy. "I didn't recognize you with your clothes on."

"Did you come here to do a story on us, Jimmy?" Tonya asked.

"Of course he did," said Tamra. "Why else—"

"I came to talk with Martin. I didn't even know you were working on the film."

"What's so important about him?" pouted Tonya. "No offense . . . Milton."

"It's Morris," Tamra corrected her, "like the cat."

"It's Martin," snapped the makeup artist, taking each of them by the hand and dragging them toward the door, his boot heels going clickety-clack. He was stronger than he looked. "Go away and adjust your implants or something. *Out.*"

"Just a second." Jimmy walked over to the twins. "That night at Napitano's party. Did you tell anyone the truth about where you got the Oscar?"

"Yeah, right," sneered Tonya. "We're really going to brag about how we're hooked up with some has-been perv who, like, lives in a *trailer.*"

"For a smart guy, you really don't understand how to play the game," clucked Tamra. "No wonder Rollo is always having to bail you out of trouble."

"If you want to interview us later, you can get our private phone number from the casting director," said Tonya. "Ciao!"

"That was pleasant," said Martin, as the door closed. "Sometimes I bet you feel embarrassed being heterosexual."

"Don't get your hopes up."

Martin smiled back at him. "Don't flatter yourself."

"Are you going to help me?" asked Jimmy. "Walsh is dead. I just want to know about *Hammerlock*. That was the point in his life when he had it all—the point when he lost it all too. That's the story I want to write."

Martin scrunched his face, his cheekbones sailing. He checked his watch. "Sit down. I'm now officially on lunch break." He pulled a blender out of a bag, plugged it in, then opened up a small cooler on the floor and took out a half gallon of soy milk. "Vanilla protein smoothie?"

"Ah—sure."

Martin added protein powder and soy milk into the blender, mixed in a few spoonfuls of something green, then something blue, then tossed in a handful of frozen strawberries. The small room was filled with grinding sounds as Martin cranked the blender to liquefy, and the strawberries and the green and blue powder blended with the soy milk to form a sludgy gray concoction. Martin poured half into a tall glass and handed it to Jimmy, then toasted him with the rest in the blender.

Jimmy took a tentative taste. It was delicious.

Martin must have read his expression. "Life is short. If it doesn't taste good, why bother?"

They sat beside each other on the floor, their backs against the wall. Jimmy allowed himself another long swallow before asking, "You said the *Hammerlock* shoot was jinxed. What exactly did you mean?"

Martin ran the tip of his pinkie across his pencil mustache, wiped off foam, and licked his finger clean. "It was rushed from the start. Walsh didn't even have a complete script that first day. Or that first month. I guess after he grabbed the two Oscars, the studio didn't think he needed one, but it made things difficult for everyone. The actors were frustrated, they never knew from one day to the next what scenes they were in or what their lines were going to be, and Walsh kept changing his mind, rewriting and reshooting. We went through two line producers in the first two months, and the original cine-matographer walked after waiting three days for his setups to be delivered."

"I'm surprised the studio didn't step in."

"They tried, but Walsh just ran the suits off the set, told them to go crunch somebody else's numbers. It took Danziger, the big cheese himself, to get Walsh's attention, but by then . . ." Martin shrugged. "When was the last time you heard of a studio chief visiting a shoot? Danziger hardly said a word, but you could feel the chill. Even the crew made themselves look busy, union guys with twenty years seniority."

"Danziger had been Walsh's biggest supporter. He was the one who okayed the project and gave Walsh carte blanche. No wonder he was pissed."

"He should have gotten involved sooner. Walsh was a genius, but he was in way over his head."

"A sloppy set and too much time on your hands—there must have been plenty of gossip. What were you hearing about Walsh?"

"Sex or drugs?"

"Sex."

Martin rolled his eyes. "The man was a machine, a piston-driven fuck machine. I don't know how he got *anything* done. Actresses, secretaries, models—there was even a girl on the lighting unit who would pop into his trailer after a call."

"Was there anyone special?"

Martin buffed one of his black cowboy boots with the palm of his hand. "There were a few regulars, but Walsh was a free-range hump-monkey. For a while, anyway." He shrugged. "If you're writing a general feature about sex on the set, I can give you a few names. One sitcom actress in particular makes Walsh seem like a celibate—" There was a knock on the door. "Go away!" He looked at Jimmy. "I'm not going to out anyone, if that's—"

"What did you mean, 'for a while'?"

Martin turned his boot in the overhead light, checking his reflection.

"You said Walsh was free-ranging it for a while. When did he stop?"

"I don't know—three or four months into the shoot. Suddenly the talent was turned away, and the great man's trailer declared off-limits." Martin smiled. "The crew—certain members of them, any-way—were quite happy to comfort the rejects."

"Was there one woman who still had access to the trailer? Some-one who seemed to have an ongoing relationship with him?"

"You're asking if Walsh found Ms. Right?" Martin chuckled, then shook his head. "I just assumed he decided to focus on the film. Still, I was quite busy with my job. I might have missed something."

"Did Walsh have any enemies on the set?"

"Just *everyone*."

"I mean did he exchange words with anyone? Threats or—"

"Everyone. I saw one of the *caterers* wave a knife at Walsh once, threaten to cut his balls off if he talked to her like that again, and who could blame her? The producers—you don't even want to get into that. He drove them absolutely mad. Mick Packard kicked in the door to Walsh's trailer one afternoon, one of his signature roundhouse kicks, but it was no act. The PA closed the set and told us to go to lunch, but we could hear them shouting from fifty feet away."

"That's right, Packard was the star of *Hammerlock*."

"Mr. Action Hero himself. He was hotter than Boys Town on a Sat-urday night in those days, and he wanted the whole world to know it. God, was I grateful when his career went into the shitter. Talk about karma."

"What were he and Walsh arguing about?"

"No telling. It was one of those typical Hollywood-alpha-male pissing contests from the very first day on the set." Martin took an-other sip of his power drink. "In your article I hope you don't just talk about the bad things that Walsh did—killing that poor girl. He was a very talented man. The *Hammerlock* shoot was a mess, disorganized and self-indulgent, but he shot some incredible footage. Walsh's *out-takes* were better than most of the crap that gets released today. I just hope you tell people the truth about him."

"Are you going to the funeral tomorrow?"

Martin looked pained. "I thought about it, but I can't afford to miss work, and besides—it's just kind of sad, isn't it? Drowning in a fish pond, eaten away by *koi,* for God's sake, which are just so . . . passé." He started giggling, "I know I shouldn't laugh." He laughed harder. "Forgive me, but it's this stupid movie—you spend all day making beautiful girls look like hamburger, it changes your sense of humor."

Jimmy smiled. He didn't even have Martin's excuse.

Martin drained the blender, stood up, and stretched. "Finish your shake, dearie. It's got yohimbé extract—your prostate will thank you."

Chapter 10

"You can always tell a true has-been, pilgrim—they have lousy timing," said ATM, shaking his head at the sparse turnout for Walsh's funeral. He snapped a couple of telephoto shots of a cop scratching his nuts beside a wilting floral display at the entrance to the chapel. "Walsh gets planted on the same day that a nationally syndicated talk-show queen may be getting indicted for murder, you know where the cameras are headed. Not that I blame them. Debra! caps her longtime boyfriend—that's entertainment."

"So what are you doing here, ATM?" Jimmy looked across the grassy expanse of Maple Valley Memorial Gardens, a boneyard just outside Seal Beach, with a view of the ocean from the most expensive plots, and a view of the 405 freeway from the lowlands where Garrett Walsh was being interred. "Why aren't you camped out at the Hall of Justice, waiting for the DA to announce his decision?"

"*Major* miscalculation." ATM sighed, the three cameras slung around his neck swinging gently. He was a rotund, slovenly paparazzo specializing in car crashes and Hollywood Babylon, utterly heartless in pursuit of a tabloid buck. "Not an A-list star in sight, no current ones anyway—strictly cable and movie-of-the-week-grade heat." He assessed the crowd. "No wonder the only other shooters here are amateurs who wouldn't know an f-stop if it blew them." He snorted. "Second-rate media coverage too. A couple of radio talk-show remotes and one local TV news crew. Bottom line: This funeral is a waste of film."

"Not for you," said Jimmy, looking at ATM. The photographer was renowned for staking out the rich and famous in a food-stained sweatshirt and baggy shorts, but today ATM wore reasonably clean jeans and a black tuxedo T-shirt, his tangled hair freshly washed. "I think you knew what you were doing when you came here today."

"Yeah," ATM admitted, scratching his belly. "Walsh—he was a stone genius. A snap of Debra! sneaking out the side door of County is good for a paycheck, but sometimes you have to show respect. Even if it costs you."

"Does that mean you *didn't* try to bribe the funeral director to open the casket for a shot?"

"Come on, give me some credit."

"I am."

ATM sighted through his camera. "Open-casket portrait of a floater that used to be famous? I could peddle that horror show to some European tabs maybe, but it would barely bring in what I'd have to lay out to take it." He swung the barrel of the telephoto toward the chapel. "Just for your information, never approach the funeral director—go through his assistant. It maintains deniability, and assistants have a better grasp of the marketplace."

A dozen or so demonstrators from Voices of Victims, a throw-away-the-key advocacy group, marched around the gravesite, waving their signs at a cluster of listless goth teenagers who squatted on the nearby markers flipping them the finger. Jimmy waved to Lois Hernandez, the Orange County chapter president, and she waved back. The goths were sweating in their black outfits, capes dragging on the grass, necks layered in silver crosses and ankhs, but even in the heat they remained cheerful; death of any kind was cause for celebration, but the death of a murderer was particularly festive. Every few minutes a bored off-duty cop would order the goths and the VV demonstrators to disperse. He was ignored by everyone. The cop didn't care; he was pulling down forty dollars an hour for standing around watching the freaks. The Maple Valley officials didn't care either—any kind of publicity was good for business, and they were as bummed out about the arrest of the talk-show diva as everyone else.

"I'm going to check this out," ATM said, heading toward the demonstrators. "With any luck, maybe it'll turn into a riot."

Jimmy watched him hurry down the grassy slope, then turned to see Rollo leave the chapel and walk rapidly toward him. The flowers and funeral expenses had been picked up by the Directors Guild, a legal obligation that hadn't entailed any current members showing up for the service. Jimmy had been disappointed when he found out who had paid the bill—he had hoped it would be the good wife. Or even an anonymous benefactor he could have tracked down.

"I signed the guest book," said Rollo, oddly dapper in a blue suit—Armani, it looked like, one of the latest shipments of merchandise to fall off a truck at the precise instant that Rollo was there to catch it. "You wouldn't believe some of the nasty things people wrote in the book, Jimmy. What's wrong with people?"

"They think the dead can hear them. Evidently so do you."

Rollo slipped a business envelope out of his inside jacket pocket. "I brought you a surprise. Don't open it here."

Jimmy tore open the envelope and pulled out five pages of telephone numbers with dates and time of day listed. He stared at the billing records. "How did you *get* these? Jane wasn't sure she could get prepaid records even with a court order."

Rollo blushed. It made him look about thirteen. "These are only the records for the cell phone he had when—when we found him. No way to pull up any calls he might have made from another line."

Jimmy riffed through the list. "You're amazing."

Rollo pushed back his glasses.

"How much do I owe you?"

Rollo shook his head. "I don't know what you're up to, but I know you're trying to help Mr. Walsh." He stuck a finger under his glasses and wiped an eye. "Someday people are going to realize what a great man he was."

Jimmy slipped the records into his pocket.

"I'm going home and watch some movies. This is a bad day at Black Rock, man."

Jimmy waited until Rollo disappeared into the parking lot before walking over to where Mick Packard was being interviewed. Jimmy had been on his way to talk to the actor when he ran into ATM, and he had kept Packard in sight ever since. He was interested in Packard, but he was even more interested in the woman hovering just behind him, keeping a discreet distance.

Packard was at least twenty pounds heavier than Jimmy remembered, his extra chin badly hidden by a turtleneck.

The interviewer was a freckle-faced redhead who kept thrusting the microphone at Packard's face. Packard had to pull back before he spoke. The cameraman was equally young, a well-built jock in shorts, muscle-T, and backward ball cap. The camera atop his shoulder had FULLERTON STATE UNIVERSITY stenciled on the side.

Jimmy pulled out his reporter's notebook as he approached. The woman with Packard was in her early thirties, a beautiful brunette, long-limbed and tan, wearing a slinky charcoal-gray dress and huge dark sunglasses. Packard was shorter in person than onscreen, his thinning hair slicked straight back.

Packard put his hand over the microphone. "I'll be right with you," he said to Jimmy. He acted like Jimmy should be grateful.

"Hey, this is my interview," the redhead said to Jimmy.

"Take your time," said Jimmy.

"I don't want you listening in to my questions," said the redhead.

"Don't fight, boys," Packard said beneficently. "There's plenty of me to go around. Just ask your questions," he said to the redhead. "I'm sure this gentleman will respect your professionalism." He glanced at Jimmy. "Who are you with?"

"*SLAP* magazine."

Packard brightened, then turned to the redhead. "Let's wrap this up." He smiled into the camera. "I had intended—make that, I had *hoped* that Garrett Walsh and I would have the opportunity to work together again. He was a flawed man, a haunted man, but I considered him a spiritual brother in arms, another Hollywood outlaw, just like myself." He nodded to the camera, walked over to Jimmy, and threw a mock karate chop at him. He looked annoyed when Jimmy didn't flinch, but quickly covered. "Nice to meet you. I didn't catch your name."

"I'm Jimmy Gage."

"Great. Fabulous. Shall we get started? It's Jimmy, right?"

Jimmy smiled at the woman in the gray dress and sunglasses. "We haven't been introduced. I'm Jimmy."

"Hello," the woman said, her voice soft, a little tremulous. "I'm Samantha Packard." Her eyes were invisible behind the dark glasses.

"Hey," said Packard, "are you interviewing me or my old lady?" If it was supposed to be a joke, none of them believed it. "So you want to start with my new movie, or you want me to spout off on *Hammerlock*?"

"Let's go with *Hammerlock*," said Jimmy, watching Samantha Packard as he wrote in his notebook. "That must have been an interesting shoot. Big budget, and Walsh had just won a couple of Academy Awards—"

"Those awards are just popularity contests. I was the number-one box-office star in the U.S. the year before—that's all that counts," blustered Packard. "Walsh knew that. He was a rising star, but I think I intimidated him. I get that a lot."

Jimmy dutifully entered the information in his notebook under Packard's watchful eye.

"Is this going to be a main feature in *SLAP*?" demanded Packard. "My agent said I should always insist on a cover." He patted his shellacked black hair. "What the hell, I'm doing this one for Garrett."

"Were you and Walsh friends before *Hammerlock*, or did you get close during the shoot?" Jimmy saw Samantha Packard pull a pack of cigarettes out of her tiny purse and light one up, inhaling as though it were the last breath she was going to take.

"We knew *of* each other, of course," said Packard, keeping his chin high as he looked around, checking to see how many in the crowd were noticing him. "But it was only when we got on set that things started to click. You have to remember, Walsh was still new to the big leagues. I like to think that I showed him the ropes, helped him to stand up to the studio. I don't think he would mind me telling you this, not now, but he used to ask my advice on blocking and dialogue. I was happy to help, of course."

"Of course." Behind Packard's back, Jimmy could see Samantha Packard turn away, her hand shaking as she brought the cigarette to her mouth again.

"Where's your photographer?" asked Packard. "It's Jimmy, right? You want to do something here, Jimmy, or should we arrange for a photo session later?"

"Later is fine. I'm traveling light today." Jimmy took a slow pan of the cemetery. The victims' rights demonstrators were circling more slowly now, beaten down by the heat and the lack of TV news crews. The goths had taken off their capes and were fanning themselves. At the buzzing sound of a prop airplane, everyone looked up—maybe they thought it was going to be some flyboy supporting the cause, but it was just a Piper Cub towing an AGAVE GOLD TEQUILA banner along the beach. Jimmy turned back to Packard. "I heard there were a lot of problems on the shoot."

"Studios never really understand talent," said Packard. "They understand money, that's all, and schedules and contracts—"

"I was told that you and Walsh didn't really hit it off."

"Walsh was okay. He and I—giants always bump shoulders. That doesn't mean we didn't respect each other." Packard squinted at Jimmy. It was the same look that usually preceded Packard breaking somebody's neck or throwing them down a flight of stairs. On film, anyway. "Maybe we should talk about my new movie? It's called *The Holy Killer,* and I think it's really going to change the way a lot of people in this town think about me. So far we haven't gotten an American distributor, but that's just the way it works. You buck the system, you maintain your integrity as an artist and a man—you get knifed in the back. That's why I chose to work overseas. Foreigners—they have an appreciation for integrity."

Jimmy wrote down *integrity* and underlined it three times for Packard's benefit. "My understanding is that you and Walsh had some pretty intense arguments." He sneaked a look at Samantha Packard, but she had her back turned toward them. "What did you fight about? Integrity?"

"Artistic differences, that's all. No big deal."

"I heard you actually broke down the door to Walsh's trailer."

"Who told you that?"

"Just doing my research."

Packard gave Jimmy a little shove. "Was it Danziger? That fucker hated my guts from day one. He blamed me for everything that went wrong on *Hammerlock*. Said I had bad chemistry, which was bullshit, because I was only on steroids for a few months, *under doctor's orders,* for inflammation . . . or something." He glared at Jimmy. "Is Danziger the one telling tales about me and my chemistry?"

"You have a reputation for having a temper. So did Walsh," said Jimmy, baiting him. "I don't think it's some dark secret that you might have had words on the set. I just was curious to know what you were arguing about."

"You write that I'm difficult to work with, I'm going to break your fucking face," Packard said quietly, barely moving his mouth. "Is that what you're really doing here? You writing a hit piece on me?"

"I'm writing a piece on Garrett Walsh."

"I'll take you out if you hurt my career," said Packard. "I'm the last of my kind—the last man in Hollywood that does what he promises—and I'm promising you, fuck me over, and I'll fuck you up."

Jimmy nodded as he wrote in his notebook. "How do you spell *fuck*?"

Packard stalked away.

Samantha Packard turned around, covering a smile, her eyes still hidden. She flicked her cigarette onto the grass, then slowly followed her husband toward the nearest camera.

Chapter 11

His phone was ringing again, but Jimmy still ignored it, focused on the eight-by-ten publicity photos of Samantha Packard on his desk. He'd picked up one from about eight or nine years ago, when she had a minor role in a thriller called *Bloodletting.* He barely remembered the film, and he didn't remember her being in it at all. Eight years ago . . . if she was the good wife, that was around the time she would have met Walsh. He peered at the woman in the photo. Her hair was shorter then, and even though she was beautiful, she seemed awkward, not really comfortable with the camera. Real stars bloomed for the lens. Maybe Samantha Packard bloomed in private. He laid the photo back on the desk.

After Walsh's funeral Jimmy had run a quick search on Mick and Samantha Packard. Packard was a martial artist and rumored ex-CIA operative. He had been hot box office at the tail end of the action-film era, but five consecutive flops had knocked him off the Hollywood radar screen. Now forty-five years old, no longer even a punch line on late-night TV, his screen output was limited to direct-to-video releases and Japanese commercials, where he still had a cult following. Samantha Packard was thirty-one, a marginally talented actress whose screen credits were limited to films in which her husband starred.

Jimmy straightened the publicity photos and lined them up. Mick and Samantha had been married ten years and had no children. Twice in the last five years the tabloids had done stories about their imminent divorce, but no papers had ever been filed. He was going to have to move cautiously. Mick Packard had been on full alert yesterday; if he got spooked, somebody could get hurt. Starting with the good wife. Samantha Packard looked back at him from one of the photos, her face softly lit, her eyes expectant. Jimmy had to turn away and stare out the window, but there was nothing in that clear blue sky that brought him any relief.

People worked all around him in the main editorial office of *SLAP*, chattering away, fielding calls, pounding their keyboards—they barely registered. He hadn't yet gotten started on the list of Walsh's cell phone calls that Rollo had given him at the funeral yesterday. The list was five pages of single-spaced calls without referents—just date, time of day, and duration. Jimmy was going to have to go through the reverse directory number by number, then call up and find out who Walsh had talked to, turn on the charm and the lies. He smiled to himself. It was terrible the things he was good at.

He looked at Samantha Packard's photos. If Jimmy had believed in prayer, he would have prayed that when he dialed one of the phone numbers on Walsh's list, Samantha Packard would answer. But Walsh wouldn't have been that direct, even if he knew her number after all those address changes. Jimmy whisked the photos into a stack with one sweep of his hand, slid them into his notebook, and turned to the computer. His phone rang again, but he kept typing, logging in.

Twenty minutes later Jimmy was still intent on the computer screen, scrolling through the California Department of Corrections database. Three hundred and eighty-nine Shafers had been processed through the system in the last twenty years, but only six had Harlen as a first or middle name. He accessed three files, but none of them fit the profile for the man Detective Katz said was Walsh's last visitor. Number four, Maxwell Harlen Shafer, didn't look too promising either.

"Jimmy?" Mai stood beside his desk, slim and straight as a needle, a first-generation Vietnamese immigrant, all eyes and ears and brains. No telling how long she had been standing there. "You are not answering your phone."

"That's right."

"Mr. Napitano wishes to speak with you."

"Tell the emperor that I'm busy, Mai."

"Mr. Napitano said it was important."

Jimmy tried to concentrate on the computer screen, but he could feel Mai's gaze at the center of his forehead, her intense quietude an irresistible force. He got up and followed her through the maze of desks and into the private elevator to Nino's penthouse office.

Mai punched in the proper numerical code on the elevator keypad, shielding the keys from view. (Three two nine nine five but who was counting?) She waited until the doors closed before speaking. "He was in a very good mood until you refused to answer your phone." It was a flat statement, devoid of recrimination or innuendo. "I am fluent in Italian, of course, but some of his curses—they are untranslatable."

"You don't have a dirty mind. It's a liability in dealing with Nino."

Mai just looked at him. Jimmy tried to imagine what she would look like smiling, but he couldn't conjure the image. Mai didn't smile, she didn't frown, and she didn't show surprise or disappointment. Her emotional responses were hooded—saved for someone more worthy of them, perhaps. Jimmy hoped there was someone. The elevator doors opened, and Mai walked quickly out, her footsteps silenced by the thick red carpet. She knocked once on the door to Napitano's office and strode away. Jimmy followed her with his eyes—for a small woman, she walked tall.

Jimmy opened the door and strolled into the office. The carpet and drapes were white as hoarfrost, Napitano's desk was cut from a single gigantic piece of polished ebony, and the sofas were covered in buttery black leather. The only vibrant bit of color in the room was a tiger skin draped across the back of Napitano's desk chair, ensconcing him in stripes.

Napitano greeted him with a wave, his bare feet up on his desk as he talked on a speakerphone, voice booming. He was a soft little man, barely five feet two, wearing pink cashmere pajamas, an autocrat with an oversize head and languorous eyes. His mouth was stuffed with tiny sharp teeth.

Jimmy sat down on the sofa nearest the desk, and hung one leg over the side.

"Just do what I tell you to," Napitano said to the phone, breaking the connection with his big toe. "Jimmy," he said, drawing out the word to obscene length, "so glad you could honor me with your presence." He held up a dark-gray, irregularly shaped rock the approximate size of a golf ball. "Do you know what this is?"

Jimmy shrugged. "Lava?"

"It is a moon rock. From the Sea of Tranquillity, to be exact."

"Sure it is."

"No, for true." Napitano cradled the rock in the palm of his hand. "This was torn off the craggy surface of the moon and brought back millions of miles to earth. Now it is mine."

"Did you get that from Rollo?"

Napitano nodded. "A gift."

Rollo and Napitano had become close a year ago after Jimmy had introduced them. Rollo had been hiding out and needed someplace safe to stay for a few days, and Napitano was eager to show off his new armored limousine. They were a good match. Both of them were smart and funny, with no respect for protocol or the common man, and Rollo, like Jimmy, wasn't intimidated by Napitano's wealth and power. Rollo was a free agent, a quality Napitano respected above all others.

Napitano caressed the lump of rock with his fingertips, his face glowing, probably imagining himself the lord of the moon. "Try to imagine where this has come from, the tales it could tell: the bitter chill of the lunar surface, the bombardment of meteor showers, the steady rain of cosmic rays—"

"Where would Rollo get a moon rock, Nino? All of them have been catalogued. They're either at the Smithsonian or on display at museums. Maybe the White House."

"Such naïveté." Napitano carefully replaced the rock on his desk, then leaned back in his chair, his enormous head lolling against the tiger skin. "The more precious the cargo, the more likely that some percentage will be lost in transit. A tax of desire. That is what I wanted to talk with you about." He crossed his bare feet, the pink cashmere pajamas softly rustling. "I want you to do a story on sacred objects, objects of disputed provenance, things that don't belong in private hands."

"Looted artworks? Biological oddities? Necklaces of gold teeth and eagle headdresses? How about a vial of anthrax?" Jimmy shook his head. "I'm working on something, Nino."

Napitano caressed the underside of his soft throat, then thumped the underside of his double chin. "Put it aside."

"No."

"No?" Napitano wiggled his pink toes, soft baby toes that had never touched a bare floor or anything rougher than glove leather. "This project of yours, this secret thing—it must be quite important."

"It is."

"Dangerous too, perhaps?"

Jimmy didn't like Napitano's expression.

"I ask because the editorial receptionist has been receiving some very ugly phone messages for you."

"What else is new?"

"This man keeps calling. His threats have been quite explicit— and quite vulgar." Napitano ran a hand through his oiled locks, rearranging them across his forehead. "He won't leave his name, but this gentleman always calls from a phone booth, a *different* phone booth each time, which would indicate a certain seriousness on his part."

"It just indicates he's got a pocket full of quarters."

"Ah, Jimmy's vaunted cowboy sangfroid."

"I'll do what I always do, Nino. Walk light, watch my back, and hope for the best."

"How deliciously optimistic of you, dear boy."

Chapter 12

"The place don't usually look like this." Rita Shafer picked up the dirty clothes, tossed them behind the sofa, and sat down. She patted the cushion beside her, beckoning. "Darn kids. They'd live like pigs if I let them."

"Thanks for seeing me, Ms. Shafer," said Jimmy, iridescent Froot Loops crunching underfoot as he crossed the carpet and sat down beside her on the swaybacked sofa.

"Rita," she corrected him, pulling one leg up so her bare knee touched him. "And it's *Miss*. I'm free and easy. That Ms. shit—I never got the point of it."

A TV blared from the back bedroom, the channels changing every few moments, accompanied by the outraged howls of children. Rita Shafer's stucco one-bedroom apartment was part of a fourplex just north of downtown Long Beach. Unopened mail was strewn on the floor, utility bills with overdue stamped on the outside in red letters. Shutting off your lights and gas wasn't enough—first the city wanted to embarrass you. Through the security bars on the side window of the living room, Jimmy could see the *Queen Mary* docked in the harbor, shimmering in the afternoon sun, the former luxury liner now a floating mall for tourists.

"You here for Harlen?" asked Rita.

A Nerf football landed in Jimmy's lap, startling him. He smiled and picked it up off the floor, standing now. "Go out for a pass," he said to the sullen eight-year-old in the doorway, cocking the football behind his ear. "Go long, I'll hit you."

"Just give me the fucking ball, mister," said the boy, scratching the seat of his Scooby Doo underwear.

"Axyl Rose Shafer, you apologize right now to the nice man," said Rita.

Axyl Rose gave his mother the finger and turned away. Jimmy bounced the foam football off the back of his head before he took a step. "Hey!" howled Axyl Rose, angry, not hurt.

"Don't talk to your mother like that," said Jimmy.

Axyl started to flip Jimmy off, then thought better of it, scooting away into the back bedroom.

Rita pulled Jimmy back onto the couch. "Thanks. I need a man around to keep Axyl in line." She snorted. "'Course, that's not the only thing a man's good for."

Rita Shafer had started out pretty, taut and slender, with high sharecropper cheeks and large eyes, but she was exhausted now, beaten down, her skin sallow, her eyes dull. All the makeup and caked-on mascara didn't hide the damage. There had been three kids running around the cluttered living room when he arrived: Axyl and a couple of younger ones, four or five years old maybe, skinny blond girls with skin like cream and sad blue eyes. The girls stopped what they were doing when they saw Jimmy, suddenly on their best behavior. Three kids, and Rita was still slim-hipped and high breasted, sexy in short-shorts and Harley-Davidson tank top. Only her face showed her mileage.

"You got kids?" Rita asked.

"Never had the courage."

"None that you know of." One of Rita's front teeth was chipped, but it was a good smile.

"I think I'd know. I hope so, anyway."

"That's a sweet thing to say." Rita turned it over, like a pretty pebble. She held up her beer can. "Get you a cold one?"

"I'm fine, thanks."

"You're better than fine," cooed Rita. "Me, I could use another one." She headed for the refrigerator, turning around partway there to see if he was watching her ass.

Rita Shafer was the sister of Harlen Wilson Shafer, and her apartment was his last-known address. According to the Department of Corrections, Shafer was a small-timer with two convictions for sales of a controlled substance, a high-school dropout who had recently finished a five-year pop at Vacaville, Walsh's alma mater. Jimmy had read through Shafer's jacket on the computer at *SLAP* and *known* he was the one—Walsh's last date. No history of violence with Shafer; he was more likely Walsh's dealer than his killer, but Jimmy still wanted to talk to him.

Rita came back from the kitchen and popped a beer, delicately cupping her hand over the top to shield herself from the spray. It was a curiously ladylike gesture that made Jimmy want to scrub her clean.

"You were right before. I *am* looking for your brother."

"I figured that's why you were here," nodded Rita, plunking herself down beside him. She killed half the beer in one long swallow.

"No, it's nothing like that."

"Lucky you." Rita took another hit of the beer. "Harlen stayed with me about a week when he got out of prison, emptied my purse when he left." She edged closer to him. "He left me some pot and some pills, like some pack rat, thinking it was a fair exchange. I still got most of the pot. Good stuff too." She plucked at the hair on his arms. "I don't smoke so much anymore. It makes me too horny." She turned toward the bedroom doorway. "Turn down that goddamned TV!"

"Do you know where he's staying?"

"Harlen's not bad. He's just got bad luck," said Rita. "Been like that his whole life—he calls tails, heads come up."

"Does he have a job? I really need to get in touch—"

"A *job*?" Rita threw back her head and showed Jimmy her fillings.

"Rita?" The two little blond girls were standing in the doorway, holding hands. "Rita, Axyl Rose won't let us watch *Sesame Street*. He says it's for babies."

"You tell Axyl Rose if I have to come in there, I'm gonna whip his ass," said Rita. "He should be in school anyway. His damn earache got better as soon as the bus left."

Jimmy watched the girls run back into the bedroom, giggling.

"Harlen said he loved me, but he just couldn't stand it here," Rita said to Jimmy. "He said it was louder than prison and the food wasn't as good, and I kept ragging on him because I don't like drugs around my kids. You got a cigarette?"

"Sorry."

"That's all right, I done quit anyway." Rita smiled, her breasts shifting in the tank top. "You don't smoke, you don't want a beer— you have *any* vices, handsome?"

"I've got a few left. My girlfriend is working on them though."

Rita played with her white-blond hair. "Me, I'm a broad-minded person." She turned again to the bedroom. "I *told* you, turn that thing down!" She looked at Jimmy and smiled, drawing her long legs up. "Now, where were we?"

"Did your brother ever mention someone he knew in prison named Garrett Walsh?"

"Harlen didn't talk much about prison." Rita shrugged. "If he did, I weren't listening."

"Garrett Walsh was a filmmaker," Jimmy said helpfully.

"Porno?" Rita sat up. "I don't go for that, mister."

"No, real films."

"I don't know what you heard, but I don't do that no more."

"I'm just trying to get in touch with your brother. If he calls you— if he comes by, I'd appreciate you letting me know where he's staying." He handed her his business card. "My cell phone number is on here. Call me anytime."

"*SLAP* magazine?" Rita pondered the card. "I heard of that. What's Harlen done now?"

"Probably nothing. He was one of the last people to see Garrett Walsh alive. I'd like to ask him some questions, that's all."

Rita shook her head. "I don't think Harlen would like talking to you." She stared at the business card. "Is Harlen going to jail again?"

"I doubt it."

"Harlen called me a stupid whore when he left. He's my brother and I love him, but he shouldn't call me names in front of my kids. You think that's right?"

Jimmy looked her in the eyes. "No."

"How come I never meet guys like you?"

Jimmy smiled. "Just lucky, I guess."

Rita shook her head, not returning the smile. "No, I ain't lucky. I'm just like Harlen that way." She took a deep breath. "He comes by for more money, I'll give you a buzz. You got a brother, Jimmy?"

"Yeah."

"I bet you get along fine. I bet you're a real family."

"You'd lose that bet. My brother and I—we're not close."

"Got to be his fault."

Jimmy handed her the mug shot of Harlen Shafer he had down-loaded from the Department of Corrections database. "Is this accurate?"

"What do you mean?"

"This photo was taken when Harlen went into prison. Does he still look the same?"

"Pretty much." Rita rapped the photograph with a finger. "His hair is longer now. I don't like it so much, but he don't care what I think. His face is different too, harder. I guess prison does that."

"Do you have a more recent shot of your brother? One that I could make a copy of?"

Rita shook her head. "I got something I want you to see." She pulled her purse out from under the couch and fished out her wallet. The red leather was worn smooth, the sides bulging, the seams split. She flicked through the photo section, pulled a black-and-white out of the yellowed glassine, and handed it over.

Jimmy stared at two underfed kids standing there, holding hands. The boy's jeans had a hole in one knee; the girl's dress was well worn but pressed. They both looked scared, but the boy was trying hard to hide it.

"That's me and Harlen. I was nine, he was eleven. Our mama had just died, and we were being farmed out to kin, separated. I know you're looking for Harlen. I just want you to know what he was like before—before things changed. He was a good big brother once. I want you to remember that."

"I'm not out to hurt him."

"Life changes people. They start out one way, then things happen and they're not the same afterward."

"I know," said Jimmy. "I just need to talk to him."

"I believe you." Rita took the photo from him and tucked it carefully back into her wallet. "I don't know why, but I feel like I can trust you."

Jimmy stood up and shook her hand. "It was nice meeting you, Rita."

"Nice meeting you too." Rita pumped his hand, not wanting to let go. She waited until he was almost at the front door. "I think he's staying at one of them . . . motels, you know, a no-tell motel. I don't know where, but I know what Harlen likes."

"Thank you."

"That doesn't really do much, does it?" Rita looked embarrassed. "There's only probably about a million of them motels around. I just wanted to help."

"I appreciate it."

"You find him, tell him no hard feelings about him ripping me off. Tell him to come by sometime. There's always a beer waiting for him." Rita turned away so she wouldn't have to see the door close behind him.

Chapter 13

Rollo glanced out into the twilight before scurrying inside Jimmy's third-floor apartment, a laptop computer clutched to his chest, the rain falling warm and clean behind him, one of those summer storms that didn't cool anyone off.

Jimmy stood in the doorway. "Come on in, Rollo!" he shouted over the rain, calling to the row of apartments across the courtyard, his hands cupping his mouth like a megaphone. A fatigued pigeon resting on a phone wire cocked its head. "You bring the drugs and donkey porn?"

"Very funny." Rollo unzipped his windbreaker as he walked inside, taking handfuls of cell phones out of the inner pockets, clattering them down onto Jimmy's kitchen table. He headed for the refrigerator. "You got any Mountain Dew?"

Jimmy sat down at the table and spread out the papers Rollo had given him at the funeral, listing over two months of Walsh's prepaid phone calls. Like a lot of ex-cons freed from the system's rigid phone restrictions, Walsh was an inveterate talker. The record contained hundreds of brief calls, touchstone calls rather than conversation. Jimmy had barely started checking them out. He picked up one of Rollo's cell phones. "Clones?"

"Just like you asked for." Rollo cracked a can of Mountain Dew and sat beside him, opened his laptop. Now that everyone and his cockatoo had Caller ID, the only way to run Walsh's numbers without being tagged was to use untraceable clone phones, their ID and billing codes identical to a legitimate unit in use somewhere else. Rollo cracked his knuckles, loosening up his fingers. "Hundred bucks a dozen, but no guarantee on how long they're good for. The phone company is getting smarter all the time."

"Boo-hoo."

"Hey, man, people put in a lot of time and effort scamming the system, then some supercomputer steps in and ruins everything." Rollo dragged a few sheets of crumpled paper out of his pocket. "You're lucky Walsh didn't have a clone, or you'd be shit out of luck. These are the last calls he made—my inside guy at the company couldn't pull them until this morning. That's what he said, anyway. I think he was holding out for a big-screen TV." He glanced around the apartment. "Speaking of which, isn't it about time you joined the modern world? That Trinitron is a joke. My Game Boy has a better picture."

"TV looks better small. If I want big, I'll go to a movie."

Rollo looked at his reflection in the computer screen, tugged at the soul patch under his lower lip. "You think I should grow back the goatee?"

"Everyone needs a hobby."

"This girl I met yesterday said I have a weak chin. A goatee might help cover it up. Or I could grow longer sideburns." Rollo nodded, tilting his head. "Yeah. Distract attention from my chin."

Jimmy fumbled with the cell phone. "Could we leave the makeover for later?"

"I'm looking for an opinion here. I trust your judgment, man."

"I think you should quit eating burgers and fries every night. I think you should get outside more. Work on your tan. Play in the ocean. I think you should go out with women who don't tell you about your weak chin or your skinny legs or your sunken chest. At least on the first date. I think—"

Rollo gingerly touched his pectorals. "What do you mean, sunken chest?" He grabbed the phone from Jimmy, pressed some numbers, and handed it back. "The access code on all the clones is six six six. Cool, huh?"

Jimmy pushed a few pages of numbers to Rollo as he listened for the dial tone, keeping the most recent ones for himself. "We're going to have to share the reverse directory."

"Books are old tech. I don't mess with them," said Rollo, hooking up one of the clone phones to his laptop, establishing his wireless Internet connection. He punched numbers into another phone while he waited for his computer to load. "Hi," he said into the receiver, "this is Richard Burns, from Travel Associates, and I'm pleased to inform you that you're the lucky winner of an all-expense-paid trip to Reno, Nevada. For legal reasons, what is the correct spelling of your first and last . . . Hello? Hello?"

Jimmy looked down his own list of numbers, making notations. "Before you start randomly dialing, you might try scanning the sheet for recurring numbers. No way Walsh could camp out in that trailer for a few months without calling the good wife." He ran a finger down the list. The last two entries were identical, although made a day apart. He flipped through the reverse directory and found that the number was the main switchboard at the California state prison at Vacaville, Walsh's last-known residence before the trailer in Anaheim. Jimmy worked his way backward up the list and checked the next number in the directory, then reached for one of Rollo's phones.

A woman answered on the first ring, her voice sultry. "Wild Side Spa, can I help you?"

Jimmy was poised over his legal pad. "This is Garrett Walsh, W-A-L-S-H. I'm concerned that someone has been using my credit card at the spa. Could you tell me the last time it was—"

"I don't do billing," said the woman on the other end, annoyed. "Take the matter up with your credit card company." She hung up.

"What was that all about?" asked Rollo.

"One of Walsh's last calls was to a spa in Santa Monica. A massage parlor, maybe, or a phone-sex joint."

"Maybe he knew he was going to get smoked," said Rollo, clicking away on his laptop. "One last jerk-off before the long walk. That's what I would do. I wouldn't have to spend seventy-five dollars to do it, either."

"Interesting you have the price right at your fingertips," said

Jimmy, going back to the list. "Cross-check your databases and see if you can find the home number of Mick and Samantha Packard. I haven't had any luck on my own." He peered at the list. There were more calls made to Vacaville, plenty of them over the last couple of months—Walsh was probably leaving messages for old cellmates. Released cons always had a list of requests from buddies still inside: families to contact, girlfriends to remind to visit, lawyers to prod into another appeal. Most requests went forgotten as soon as the con hit the city, but Walsh had evidently followed through on his promises.

Rollo's fingers flew over the keyboard, the sound like a host of maniac woodpeckers beating their brains out. "Sorry, nothing listed or unlisted for Mick Packard." He looked up at Jimmy. "You have the wife's maiden name? They use that sometimes."

"I'll ask around tomorrow. Let's keep going."

"Where *are* we going?" said Rollo, bent over the keyboard again. "I mean, if you think Mr. Walsh was murdered, that's good enough for me. But what's in it for us?"

"Nothing."

"That's exactly what I mean. *Nothing.*" Rollo's eyes never left the computer screen as he tapped away. "This lady you're worried about—the good wife—what do we care what happens to her? We don't know anything about her. She could be somebody who bakes chocolate chip cookies for shut-ins or sets puppies on fire when she's bored."

"You don't have to help."

"How can you care about somebody you don't even know? That's all I'm asking. You read about a bus going off a mountain road in Pakistan, do you give a shit?"

"I care about finding who killed Walsh. I care about finding the good wife. If you're not interested, I understand. I'll let you know how things turn out."

Rollo pushed back his glasses. "All I'm saying is that I'd feel a lot better if there was some payoff."

"Other than maybe saving somebody's life?"

"That ain't no payoff."

Jimmy smiled. Rollo was a crook, but he was honest. "How about the satisfaction of finding the man who murdered Walsh? The same man who murdered Heather Grimm."

Rollo pushed back his glasses again, his watery brown eyes as sincere as a bridegroom's. "Mr. Walsh and Heather Grimm—they don't care what we do."

"Just think of this as doing me a favor."

"I can live with that." Rollo went back to the computer screen. "Mr. Walsh put a lot of calls in to pizza joints and Chinese take-out restaurants. Can't blame him. The idea of a genius like him sweating over a stove—where's the justice?"

"Try under the J's." Jimmy punched in another number on his cell phone.

"Universal Pictures, Mr. Duffy's office," said a woman.

"Thank you, wrong number." Jimmy clicked off, then continued through his list, making notes beside the three other times Walsh had called the studio. Like Walsh had said, he had tried every major player in Hollywood. Every studio had been called at least five or six times, every major production company and talent agency. Walsh had been passed along from office to office, starting at the top and working his way downward. He probably got stalled at the assistant to some powerless VP, some Hugo Boss smoothie who was forever "in a meeting" when Walsh was on the line.

Jimmy imagined Walsh sitting around that stuffy little trailer in the afternoon heat, drinking beer and waiting for a callback that never came, ordering pizza and listening for the sound of tires on gravel. Paranoia hadn't helped him. The ME had found no skin under what was left of Walsh's fingernails, no bruises, no signs of a struggle. Walsh had been taken by surprise, taken by a professional, someone who knew how to make a killing seem like an accident. With Walsh's luck, the call for his big meeting, the lunch that would turn everything around, would have come in while the fishies were nosing around his fresh corpse, the cell phone ringing until the battery ran down.

"Did I tell you I got a call from a new reality TV show?" said Rollo, his nose practically touching the computer screen. "Not another *Survivor* clone, either. I told the assistant producer, 'Rollo don't sweat, Rollo don't eat rats'—"

"Rollo keeps talking about himself in the third person, Jimmy's going to throw his ass out the door."

"I'm saying that winning the scavenger hunt made me famous. I'm trying to thank you."

"The Monelli twins got some work out of it too. I saw them on the set of *Slumber Party Maniacs II.*"

"No wonder those two stiffed me," said Rollo. "I asked them out for a date last week, told them I didn't care which one, they could decide. You would have thought I had a sign on my forehead, 'Warning: Anal Warts!'"

"Women—you flatter them, and they turn on you. It's not fair."

"Exactly." Rollo got up and grabbed another Mountain Dew. "You should get one of those refrigerators with an automatic ice-maker."

"Let me know if you find any calls made to a motel," said Jimmy, still going through his list. "I don't know the name of it, but it's probably not the Peninsula."

"Nino has an ice-maker in his limousine," said Rollo, his head in the refrigerator.

"Which reminds me, what are you doing passing off a chunk of lava as a moon rock? Nino isn't the kind of guy you fuck around with."

Rollo turned from the refrigerator with a can of Mountain Dew in one hand. "I didn't hustle him."

"You gave Nino a real moon rock?"

"Duh."

"Where did *you* get a moon rock?"

Rollo popped the can of Mountain Dew. "There was this NASA engineer, a regular mission-control kind of guy." He gestured with the can. "I guess things were different in the early days—space, Jimmy, the final frontier. Why shouldn't this guy bring home a little chunk of history from the office?" He took a long drink. "This engineer, he died last year, but he had a kid, smart kid too, fix anything electronic, but you know how it is—bad grades. High school, man, it should be illegal the shit teachers get away with." He took another drink, and the Mountain Dew foamed out and down his hand, dripping on Jimmy's carpet. Rollo idly rubbed it in with the toe of his shoe. "This kid. I kind of went into his high-school computer system and fixed his grades. Got him a scholarship to Caltech." He sat down at the computer. "So he gave me the moon rock."

"And you gave it to Nino?"

"I kept it for a while. It was fun. You know, holding it, thinking about it—like green cheese. But Nino, he's into possessions, and I thought he'd really like it. I mean, it's not like I was going to lay it off on the Smithsonian." He tapped at the keyboard. "Hmmmm."

"What?"

"I've got one, two, three, four, five calls to a motel just off Sunset, the Starlight Arms. According to AAA online, the Starlight is not one of your high-quality establishments. No phones in the rooms, no pool, no bathtubs, just showers. A fine selection of triple-X videos on cable, though."

"What's the number?" Jimmy looked up as Rollo gave it to him. "I've got it on my list too. Three days before Walsh died." He reached for a phone.

Somebody took his time answering. "Yeah?" The man sounded like it hurt to talk.

"Is this the Starlight Arms?" asked Jimmy.

"Yeah. So?"

"Is Harlen Shafer one of your guests?"

The manager or whoever he was laughed so hard he coughed up a couple of chunks of lung tissue. "We don't got *guests* here."

"Is Shafer still checked in?" asked Jimmy. Silence on the other end, then a dial tone.

"Who's Harlen Shafer?" Rollo asked as Jimmy hung up.

"What's the address for the Starlight Arms?" Jimmy waited while Rollo jotted it down. "Shafer was in prison with Walsh. He used to visit him at the trailer, probably copped dope for him. Katz said his fingerprints were all over the place."

"Let's go over there now," said Rollo. "I'm tired of playing phone tag, and this motel—I know that area. There's a great Thai restaurant not far from there—" He jerked at the knock on the door, ready to bolt.

Jimmy beckoned him quiet, walked to the door, and checked the peephole. He smiled, then opened the door.

Chapter 14

A jumpshot from Kobe Bryant at the buzzer, and the Lakers and Houston were in double overtime. Yes! The Butcher sat in his car, pumping his fist as he watched the lady climb the stairs of the apartment complex, the cheers of the crowd reduced to a fuzzy whisper through the blown speakers of the radio. The rain was gusting, and he followed the lady's progress through the rain that was spattering the windshield, wondering what a finely dressed woman was doing in surfer and secretary heaven. Jimmy's apartment was just past the Huntington Beach oil field, close enough to the oil patch to hear the grasshopper derricks creaking away, close enough to the beach to catch the salt air when a storm was rolling in.

The fancy lady had parked just down the street, walking to the building with a controlled swivel, her purse held close against her hip. All the thong queens and high-school honeys flashing it for free on the beach, but this lady with her power suit and self-control got him stoked. He had been tempted to turn on the wipers to get a better look at her as she crossed the street, but he didn't want to give away his position.

Shaq got fouled taking a three-point shot, which bounced around the rim before rolling out. The air went out of the arena—the Butcher could feel it as acutely as if he were really there. He pounded on the steering wheel, the heavy plastic vibrating with the blows. Shaq was a dominating center but a brick foul-throw shooter.

The lady kept climbing, caught for a moment in a stairwell light.

The Butcher checked out her tight ass for a moment until she moved higher, into shadow.

Shaq's first foul shot was an airball. The arena crowd was silent. The Butcher had to resist the impulse to tear the steering wheel off and beat someone to death with it.

The lady reached the third-floor landing, looked around, and then turned right. Unbelievable. She was knocking on Jimmy Gage's front door. Up until that moment the Butcher had been considering going one on one with the lady, but that ruined it for him. Chalk it up as one more thing Jimmy was going to have to answer for.

The rain beat down suddenly on the roof of the car, and the Butcher jerked. When he peered through the windshield again, the lady was gone. *Inside.* The Butcher adjusted his seat, trying to get comfortable, the busted springs groaning under him. Ridiculous for someone his size to be stuck driving around in a junked-out Geo Metro anyway. Twenty-nine years old, and the Butcher was driving a toy car. The best gas mileage on the market and every penny counted, but it still added up to shit car, shit life. Do the math.

The Butcher—that wasn't really his name, it was just something Jimmy Gage had stuck him with. No matter how much the Butcher tried to ignore the name, threatening those who used it, the tag had stuck. Soon enough he was going to take his real name back. Take his life back too.

Shaq bounced the ball prior to taking his second foul shot. *Bounce bounce bounce.* The announcer was so tense he sounded like he was going to cry. *Bounce bounce bounce.* Take the fucking shot, Shaq!

Shaq did. The Butcher closed his eyes, seeing that perfect arc. The radio squawked, and the Butcher opened his eyes. *"Nothing but net, ladies and gentlemen!"* The Butcher watched Jimmy Gage's front door, hearing the crowd cheer over the radio, feeling the blood pounding in his temples. Lakers up by one. That was sweet, but for the kind of money Shaq was paid, he should have made them both.

Chapter 15

"I'm not interrupting anything, am I?" Holt looked from Jimmy to where Rollo sat at the kitchen table. The two of them together always appeared guilty.

"Just the usual felonies and misdemeanors." Jimmy kissed her, lingering for a brief moment, and she hated the fact that she noticed how long their kisses lasted, trying not to compare the way they were now with the way they had been a few months ago. "Come on in. This is a pleasant surprise."

Holt hoisted her package, the brown-paper wrapping rustling as she handed it to him. "I hope this is too."

Jimmy pretended to shake it. "What have I done to deserve this?"

"Not a thing. Open it anyway."

Jimmy tore at the wrappings.

"The DA has decided to present the Strickland case to a grand jury," Holt said lightly, pleased that the news immediately got his attention.

"That's *great!*" Jimmy looked as happy for her as she had felt nailing that son of a bitch. If Holt had her way, serial rape would be a capital offense—a point of view that would have shocked her before she became a police officer. Now she knew better.

Her parents had been appalled when she had decided to enter the Academy, to the point of getting the mention removed from her alumni newsletter. Her father said he knew he should have put his foot down when she opted for criminal law instead of corporate at Stanford. He had barely gotten used to the idea of a federal prosecutor or a district attorney in the family, but a *police officer*? "*Our sort don't get their hands dirty, Jane,*" her father had intoned. "*I do, Daddy,*" she had responded. Her mother said her father would get over it, but they both knew better.

Jimmy kissed her again. "If the jury indicts Strickland, I hope the case gets put on Cheverton's docket. Hang-'em-high Cheverton—that would be sweet."

"I'd like that too. The lieutenant gave me the afternoon off after the DA gave the go-ahead. He acted as if was a reward for a job well done, but we both knew he just wanted the TV cameras all to himself. I called you at the office, but they said you were on assignment. You have *no* idea what you missed."

"I have a vivid imagination," said Jimmy, warming her with his eyes. He broke contact just long enough to tear apart the wrapping paper and pull out a framed photograph. He was smiling so hard now that it had to hurt.

Out of the corner of her eye, Holt saw Rollo quietly shut down his laptop and disconnect it from the cell phone. He had either been accessing a porn site or hacking into someplace he shouldn't be.

"This is . . . wonderful." Jimmy stared at the photograph, an eleven-by-fourteen black-and-white casual portrait of the young Elvis, sensual and full lipped, gazing into the camera. The future King was sprawled in a lawn chair outside a mobile home. He held a bottle of Pepsi-Cola in one hand. A teenage boy with a bad haircut and a man sat nearby, looking surprised that anyone was taking a picture.

"What is it?" asked Rollo, craning his neck to see, his hands working independently, tucking telephones inside his jacket.

"I thought you would like it," said Holt. "I was at an auction, and it reminded me of you somehow. I don't know why. It just seemed so . . . unposed and authentic."

"I love it."

"I hate to interrupt this magic moment, but do *I* get to see?" complained Rollo. He squinted as Jimmy showed him the photo. "Who is it?"

Jimmy laughed. "It's *Elvis*, you fucking cultural illiterate."

"I don't think so," said Rollo, completely serious. "Elvis was fat, and he wore spangly jumpsuits with belt buckles the size of peanut butter sandwiches. This dude looks like he belongs pumping gas at an Esso station off the interstate."

"This is the way Elvis *used* to look," explained Jimmy, more patient with Rollo than Holt ever saw him with anyone else. "This photo was probably taken around 1957, before he hit it big, but close enough that he could smell it coming." He turned to Holt and kissed her. "Thank you." He kissed her again. Longer this time.

It took an effort for Holt to separate herself from him, flustered by Rollo's presence. "I don't know who the boy and the other man are," she said, pointing to the photograph. She could feel perspiration along the back of her neck.

"The kid is Elvis's cousin Donny, and the man who looks like he just came from checking the still in the woods, that's his dad, Vernon," said Jimmy.

"You know the names of his relatives?" Jane was astounded.

Jimmy tapped the photo. "Check out Elvis, Jane, just *look* at him. This was taken before Colonel Parker took over his career and cleaned him up, made him presentable to Ed Sullivan and Dick Clark and the rest of those white-bread motherfuckers. The Colonel let Elvis keep the hip swivel, but those hungry cracker eyes were too scary for prime time. No telling what nastiness that boy was thinking as he looked at the bobby-soxers on *American Bandstand*. This picture was taken at the last moment, when Elvis was still himself and unashamed of it, when he was still pure."

Rollo stood up, phones falling out of his jacket and clattering onto the floor. There must have been a dozen of them. "I got to go," he said, hastily retrieving the phones, not sure what to do with them, finally placing them in the sink. "Jimmy and I—we were doing an experiment, Jane," he said, hurrying for the door. "These phones, I found them in a Dumpster behind a Radio Shack. I was going to see if I could fix them up and donate them to some homeless shelter. Or maybe a battered women hideout."

"Here I was thinking they were stolen," said Holt. "I'm ashamed of myself."

Rollo pushed back his glasses, not sure if she was serious. He was intelligent but a bad liar, which meant that lying still bothered him—he was still salvageable. As Rollo shifted from one foot to the other, Holt got a glimpse of what Jimmy saw in him.

"Good night, Rollo," said Jimmy.

"Right." Rollo's eyes darted from side to side. "I'll work on that stuff we talked about."

Holt watched the door close after him, then turned to Jimmy. "*Stuff?*"

"It's code. You'll never crack it."

"I'll just have to guess." Holt took off her jacket and neatly folded it across the back of a chair. "I hear you've been calling around trying to locate the lead detective on the Heather Grimm homicide. Evidently you're still looking into Garrett Walsh's death," she said, trying not to make it sound like an accusation, almost succeeding.

"The cop's name is Leonard Brimley. He's retired, and nobody knows where he's living. His retirement checks are directly deposited into a bank in Oxnard, but that's as close as I can get."

"Why would Brimley help you reopen a case that he already got credit for clearing?"

"Maybe he's more interested in getting it right than getting credit." Jimmy smiled. "Or maybe he's not going to know that I want to reopen the case."

"Why turn this into a crusade? The autopsy report was conclusive: 'accidental death, precipitated by drug and alcohol intoxication.' Why isn't that good enough for you?"

"I never had much faith in the official version of events. It's not a matter of conspiracies or evil intent. Human error, Jane, it's everywhere."

Holt couldn't disagree with that, but she wasn't about to admit it to him. She wandered over to the kitchen sink and took a look at the jumbled phones, smiling at the thought of Rollo donating them to a homeless shelter.

Jimmy leaned against the table, not bothering to hide the paperwork spread out there.

"Quite a collection of phone logs you have here." Holt shook her head at the computer printouts, the legal pads filled with notations, knowing immediately what he had been up to. "How lovely not to need court orders or due process to get information."

"Walsh was murdered."

"Not according to Helen Katz. I'm not a fan of her methodology, but she runs a tight investigation. She says it was an accident. Dr. Boone says it was an accident. You're the only—"

"Boone?" Jimmy looked angry. "Katz told me she was going to make sure that Rabinowitz did the autopsy. I read the report—it had her signature on it."

"Rabinowitz is chief medical examiner; she signs off on all official documentation. But I got a look at the autopsy notes, and Dr. Boone did the actual work. Don't worry, he's a good pathologist."

"Not nearly as good as Rabinowitz." Jimmy slowly smiled, and Holt knew she was in trouble. "You looked at the autopsy notes, didn't you?"

"Just a glance."

"That Walsh case wasn't in your jurisdiction. You wouldn't even run a phone number for me when I asked—you said it was a violation. Now you tell me you're checking out Boone's raw notes?" Jimmy eased closer to her. "Had to be a reason."

Holt picked up the Elvis photograph. "Let's see how this looks in your room."

"You're not getting off that easy." Jimmy was right behind her. "You believed me, didn't you? You thought I was right and Katz was wrong."

"Not at all." Holt held the photograph on the wall opposite the bed, set it down on the dresser, and stepped back to check it out. "It was a slow day at the office. I thought I'd make some calls."

"I don't think so." Jimmy was right behind her now.

"I was talking to a friend of mine in the ME's office about a blood-spatter seminar he's leading. The autopsy report just happened to come up." Holt led Jimmy over to the bed. "This is probably the best place to view your new photo. What do you think?"

"I think you believed me."

Holt kicked off her shoes, lay down, and stretched. "I think you should get a bigger bed."

Jimmy joined her on the bed, nuzzled her neck. "You *believed* me," he whispered.

Holt unbuttoned his shirt and slid a hand against his bare chest, pinching his nipple hard enough that he jumped. "I was curious, that's all." She undid his jeans. Mr. Up and Ready. "You've actually been right once or twice before. I thought you might be due."

"I'm *overdue*." Jimmy eased his hand up her skirt and played with the lace of her panties, higher now, caressing her. "I'm right about Walsh, Jane." He kissed her as he gently slipped two fingers inside her. His hands were strong, but his touch—it was silk. "I'm right, and you know it."

"Shut up while you're ahead," gasped Holt, and Jimmy did as he was told. This time, anyway. She never knew what he was going to do the next time. She rocked gently against his grip for a long time, just long enough, then eased away, kicking off her panties, unhooking her skirt. She watched as Jimmy peeled off his shirt, then helped him out of his jeans, the two of them moving faster now, all bare arms and legs, kisses and bites.

"Be right back," said Jimmy, getting up and crossing the room, his white ass stark against his deep tan. He turned the photo of Elvis to the wall and slid back into bed beside her.

Holt bounded over to the dresser and turned the photo back so the King could get a good view, his pompadour and knowing smirk lending just the right tone to the action. A couple of bad boys and a bad, bad girl. She took her time returning to bed, giving Jimmy a little show as he lolled on the sheets, enjoying his reaction. "I was never a big fan of Elvis," she said, straddling him, "but I just *know* I'm about to change my mind."

Chapter 16

The radio exploded in static, the crowd at the arena cheering so hard it must have felt like an earthquake inside the building. Laker girls bouncing, balloons and confetti drifting down from the rafters . . . the Butcher switched it off in the middle of the echoing victory chant. The Lakers had won in double overtime by eleven points, but it felt anticlimactic. Houston had just given up and played loser-ball, letting the Lakers run the court, destroying the poetry and ferocity of the game. The Butcher stared through the rain-spattered windshield, his long legs cramping in the tight confines of the Geo Metro. The Lakers might be champions, but *he* hadn't won anything.

He shifted in his seat. The lady was still up in Jimmy Gage's apartment. Some four-eyes had stumbled out about fifteen minutes ago, looking around before he scampered down the stairs like a rabbit. The lady though—she was probably making a night of it.

Must be nice writing for that fancy magazine, getting your pussy home-delivered, and fucking with people's lives for fun and profit. The Butcher had been shadowing Jimmy Gage off and on for a few weeks, still not sure what he was going to do when he cornered him. This morning the Butcher had waited near the exit of the *SLAP* security garage, waited for hours until Jimmy had driven past in his black Saab. The Butcher remembered the car from the first time they met, but of course big-shot Jimmy Gage didn't recognize the Geo Metro with the dented door. He didn't know what the Butcher drove. Didn't care either. The Butcher had followed the Saab, but lost it on the freeway. Fucking Geo.

The Butcher turned the key in the ignition, listening to the starter grind, cursing it, threatening it, until the engine finally turned over. It sounded like a coffee grinder, metal clanging against metal. Yeah, life was fair. The Butcher got to drive through the rain to his nowhere job on the graveyard shift, hoping that the Geo didn't throw a rod on the freeway or the bald tires didn't blow. Meanwhile, Jimmy Gage got to bone the lady with the nice calves.

The Butcher slipped it into first gear and pulled away from the curb. He turned on the wipers and bent forward, trying to see as the old rubber blades left streaks across the windshield. He wiped at the condensation on the inside of the glass. It was almost the last fucking straw.

Chapter 17

"Twenty-eight bucks for a room; same rate for an hour or for a night." The man in the wheelchair didn't even look at Jimmy, his attention on the television.

Jimmy rapped on the thick glass that separated them. "I don't want a room."

The man in the wheelchair glanced over at him, then went back to the TV. Paperback books were haphazardly stacked on the counter of the tiny office, next to an open liter bottle of Evian. A cigarette smoldered in an ashtray shaped like a tiny tire, smoke wafting through the air like nicotine incense.

"I called you a couple days ago. I asked you about a . . . guest you might have had."

"A *guest*?" The man in the wheelchair cackled, then choked, spit into a wastebasket. "I remember you now."

"Harlen Shafer." Jimmy slid the photo of Shafer through the security slot of the window.

The man in the wheelchair made no move to retrieve it. "Pleased to meet you, I'm Christopher Reeve."

Jimmy looked around the tiny lobby of the Starlight Arms Motel, the orange carpet stiff with years of street grime, pintoed with undetermined stains. Fly-specked publicity photos of dead movie stars were taped next to the door. The wall next to the pay phone was dotted with tacked-up business cards, most of them dog-eared and greasy:

cards for bail bondsmen, taxi companies, escort services, take-out Chinese food and pizza, drug and alcohol counseling services.

"You're blocking my doorway," said the man in the wheelchair, eyes on the television. He was probably in his forties, thin-faced, his hair shot with gray, pulled back into a ponytail, his legs lost in desert-pattern surplus cammies. He was oddly dapper in a white shirt and clip-on tie, but his upper body was caving in on itself, the tie falling to one side. His hands were in half-gloves, his fingers wiggling. "Take a hike. You're killing my walk-in trade."

Jimmy shifted closer to the window, curious to know what the man was watching. The small color set showed a man standing at a podium with a screen behind him showing an operation in throbbing pinks and reds. Jimmy took a twenty-dollar bill out of his pocket and pressed it against the glass. "Twenty bucks for an honest answer." No response. "Would bumping it up to fifty make a difference?"

The man in the wheelchair kept watching the TV, his fingers stitching along with the surgeon on screen. "What do you want with him?"

"Is he here?"

The man in the wheelchair looked over at Jimmy. "Are you Harlen's supplier?"

Jimmy shook his head.

"Harlen peddled painkillers and other pharmaceuticals. Real sweet stuff too. He wasn't averse to passing out samples once in a while. How about you? You feeling generous?"

"I can't help you."

The man in the wheelchair scooted over to the glass. "That's *good*, mister, because they don't make dope that helps what ails me. I just wanted to make sure you weren't coming by to collect from him."

"So he skipped out?"

The man in the wheelchair picked up the photograph Jimmy had left on the counter, smiled at the mug shot. "That's right, Harlen is no longer a *guest*." He grinned at Jimmy. His teeth were too big for his emaciated face. "What do you really want with him?"

"A man named Garrett Walsh made at least five phone calls to your office in the last couple of months. He probably left messages for Shafer. The two of them were in prison together." Jimmy glanced around the shabby office and checked the street. "I'm sure you remember the calls. Short-term place like this, no luggage required—anyone staying for weeks at a time would have to feel comfortable here."

The man in the wheelchair started coughing, arched a gob of phlegm into the wastebasket, and shook a cigarette out of the pack on the counter. He narrowed his eyes at Jimmy as he lit up, taking shallow drags.

"I'm not looking to hurt Shafer. I just want to talk with him." Jimmy slid his business card through the slot in the window. Added fifty dollars. "Have him call me. There's another hundred in it for you. A hundred in it for him too, just for calling."

"Well, well—I always wanted to meet a fool with some money." The man in the wheelchair sank deeper into his chair, ashes tumbling past the buttons of his white shirt. He picked up the card. Left the money.

"Garrett Walsh was murdered a few weeks ago. I think Shafer was the last person to see him alive."

"Harlen didn't kill him."

"I didn't say he did."

"Harlen was no saint, but there is no violence in him. Anyone who says different is a liar."

"Walsh and Harlen were buddies: yard buddies, drinking buddies—dope bodies. Walsh kept things close, but if he talked to anyone, he would have talked to Harlen. I'd like to ask him what got said, that's all."

The man in the wheelchair swiveled back to face the television, his eyes on the medical channel again. "Most of the street trash walk through that door, it's 'Hey, Ironsides?' or 'Yo, wheels?' Harlen—the very first time he came in, he asked me for my name. Never used anything else afterward, either."

Jimmy felt himself flush.

"Amazing how many John Does and John Smiths and Johnny Wadds there are in the world," mused the man in the wheelchair, "and all of them checking into my motel. The ones who *truly* piss me off, I stick in room number five." He smiled to himself. "I gave Harlen room seventeen. Peaceful, and the hot water never runs out. He stayed almost three months. I gave him a rate, but I never had to remind him to pay his bill. Always paid cash." He remained focused on the television, his fingers deftly mirroring the surgeon's movements onscreen. "I had an accident one time—problem with my personal plumbing. Harlen helped me out and acted like it was no big deal. He said he had seen worse. I guess he had. Harlen. He was the only one I ever took messages for. I *did* take a few from this Garrett Walsh. Harlen was proud that they were friends, told me he was some famous movie director. Me, I never heard of the man before."

"Do you have any idea where he is now?"

"He left a few weeks ago, just cleaned out his room and disappeared. Had two more days on his prepaid too." The man in the wheelchair stared at the TV. "He didn't even say good-bye. That's why I thought you were his drug supplier come to collect. I thought maybe that's why he skipped out so sudden like."

"Walsh was worried that someone was going to kill him. Harlen may have seen something. I just need to talk to him."

The man in the wheelchair kept watching television—it looked like he was knitting. "We have pay TV in the rooms. All kinds of channels, all kind of options: gay, straight, tranny, rough, lesbo, fetish, B&D, and you'd be surprised at the choices some people make. You'd never guess to look at them. I study these things. Psychology is a hobby of mine." He glanced at Jimmy. "Glad you didn't laugh." He went back to the television. "Harlen. His taste in movies ran to *Anal Fever, Anal Coeds, Bend Over Baby.* Always the same. No variety whatsoever." He nodded to himself.

"Harlen—was he still driving a white Camaro?"

The man in the wheelchair nodded. "He loved that car."

"You said Harlen took off suddenly. I'd like to talk to whoever cleaned up the room afterward."

The man in the wheelchair picked up the cigarette from the ashtray and took a tentative puff. "Her name is Serena. Room eighteen." He put the cigarette down as though it might explode. "If you find Harlen—*when* you find Harlen—tell him to stop by sometime and say hello."

Jimmy started to leave, stopped. "What's your name?"

The man in the wheelchair turned back to the television. "Too late for that now."

Room 18 was right beside Shafer's old room 17, both of them set back from the street, a short walk from the parking lot of a twenty-four-hour liquor store but away from the street noise. Jimmy knocked, waited, then knocked again.

A woman's voice called out, muffled by sleep.

Jimmy knocked again, and the door finally opened, a woman peeking out through the security chain. "Serena? The manager said I could talk to you for a few minutes, if it's all right with you."

Serena rubbed at her eyes with her fists, a chubby woman in an extralarge Mickey Mouse T-shirt. "I don't do that oral thing—I'm Catholic. And the intercourse thing, that's out too, because my husband may come back, no matter what Ronald says, and I don't want to have to lie to him." She yawned. "So if that's what you're interested in, there are plenty of ladies on Sunset who will help you."

"That's not—"

"I will pleasure you with my hand for ten dollars," said Serena, yawning again. "That is not a sin. Not a sin for *me*," she corrected herself. "For you, it is a sin, but that is between you and God."

"How about twenty dollars just to answer a few questions?"

Serena stared at Jimmy, confused, her round face bisected by the security chain. "I don't do that dirty talk thing either."

"I just want to ask about Harlen Shafer. The manager said you cleaned out his room when he moved out."

A ripple of awareness crossed Serena's placid face. She fumbled with the chain and opened the door, shuffling toward the rumpled bed, her squishy hams jiggling as she walked.

Jimmy entered the room cautiously, checking the corners before stepping into the twilight of the single room. Brightly colored dresses hung neatly in the open closet, shoes lined up below. The television was in a cage of steel, bolted to the dresser, a 3-D postcard of Christ on the cross taped on the wall over the set. A large Styrofoam cooler sat on the floor beside a round table, a bag of mangos beside it. In the corner the wall air-conditioner rattled away, not making much progress against the heat and humidity. The room smelled of orange blossom perfume and overripe bananas.

Serena opened the nightstand drawer beside the bed and took something out, then closed it. "This is what Mr. Harlen sent you for," she said, approaching him with a Gideon Bible in her hand. "You tell him I touch nothing. I do not steal."

Jimmy stared at the Bible.

Serena rubbed her fingers together.

Jimmy handed over the money and took the Bible from her. He opened it up and saw that a compartment had been cut out of the pages, the space filled with four quarter-ounce Baggies of pot, assorted vials of pills, and a large Baggie filled with a sparkling white powder—crank or coke, it didn't matter.

"You tell Mr. Harlen Shafer that I do not approve of cutting up the word of God," chastised Serena. "You go now."

Jimmy closed the Bible. "Serena, Harlen Shafer didn't send me. I'm trying to find him."

Serena shook her head. "You asked me if I cleaned the room."

"No, I was hoping . . ." Jimmy checked the Bible again, closed it. Shafer might have been in a hurry when he left, but no way a dealer leaves his goods behind. "This was all you found in the room?"

"Only that." Serena nodded. "When I clean, I always make sure that the Bible is in the top drawer of the left-side nightstand." She yawned, and Mickey Mouse on her T-shirt seemed to yawn too. "That way you reach for the Word with your right hand."

Jimmy nodded. It made as much sense as anything else. "Room seventeen is right next door. did you hear anything when he left?"

"The walls, they are thin," said Serena. "It was very late, but the walls are thin."

"Did you see him?"

Serena sat down on the edge of the bed as though the conversation was exhausting. "I heard noises in Mr. Harlen's room, clothes being pulled off hangers, very fast, and a glass breaking in the bathroom."

"Did you *see* him?"

"Why so many foolish questions? I am sleepy."

"Please?"

Serena shrugged. "I heard noises in his room and footsteps past my window toward the parking lot. Who else could it have been?"

Jimmy fingered the Bible as though the answers were in there. In a way they were. Harlen Shafer hadn't cleaned out his place and left his stash; somebody else had emptied his room. Somebody who didn't know about what was hidden in the Good Book. "Thanks for your help. I appreciate it."

"You are taking the Bible?" asked Serena, as Jimmy turned toward the door. "What do I do if Mr. Harlen comes back for his drugs?"

"Harlen Shafer isn't coming back."

"I do not want Mr. Harlen to think I am a thief."

"Shafer isn't coming back." Jimmy fumbled in his wallet and handed her his business card. "If anyone comes around asking about him, tell them to call me." Serena was still staring at the business card as Jimmy closed the door behind him.

Chapter 18

Helen Katz was on one knee by the curb, lifting the sheet that draped a body. The draping was unusual for the big rawboned detective, who didn't care enough about spectators to shield them from the sight of death. A bicycle lay in the street near the body, a new red mountain bike with a bent front rim. Bright yellow police tape ringed the crime scene. Two units had blocked off the street, light bars flashing, one of the uniforms redirecting traffic. "Just another drive-by," the dispatcher had told Jimmy when he called looking for Katz. Another drive-by, not even worth a TV news crew.

Jimmy inched his way through the crowd of onlookers to the edge of the crime scene tape, surrounded by tourists on their way to the nearby entrance to Disneyland, and locals caught up with curiosity. A fat man with mouse ears had a camcorder out, documenting the moment, whispering commentary into the built-in microphone. Closer now, Jimmy could see that the victim was a Hispanic boy with the top of his head torn away, his shiny black hair matted with brain tissue. He watched Katz work, noticed the care with which she examined the body, her pink surgical glove flecked with blood. She glanced at the street, then at the surrounding apartments, trying to gauge where the shooter had been and who in the vicinity would have had a clear line of sight from the front window. She was good.

Katz looked even angrier than usual. Her face was flushed, and her thick jaw clenched whenever she spied the two women across the street: an older Hispanic woman wearing a supermarket clerk's uniform, and a teenager in orange soccer shorts and a white jersey, the two of them clutching each other. Standing on the grass behind them was a huge glowering young man, his arms folded across his chest. He wore knee-length cutoffs and a buttoned-up Pendleton, his neck and forearms laced with tattoos.

Jimmy had decided to find Katz as soon as he left the Starlight Arms Motel, sitting in his car, working it out. Time to call in the professional. Shafer had probably been used as a stalking horse, a decoy to gain access to Walsh. The two of them would have been murdered shortly thereafter, Shafer's body dumped somewhere like a bag of rotten oranges. A murder to cover up a murder, to cover up a murder—an infinite series, backward in time. Perhaps forward too. Jimmy was going to keep looking for the good wife, but he needed Katz's help. Somebody had to find her before she disappeared too or drowned in her bathtub.

Katz stood up, peeled off her gloves, and tucked them into the back pocket of her trousers. She beckoned over the photographer and directed him to take pictures, barking out which shots and angles she wanted. Her short dirty-blond hair was limp from the heat. She caught sight of Jimmy on the fringe of the crowd and brightened, then walked over to him. The people beside Jimmy took a step backward as Katz ducked under the police tape, and he knew just how they felt. "Glad to see you," Katz growled. "A stringer from the *Times* showed up, took a look around, and drove off. How did you catch the call?"

"I need to talk with you."

Katz noticed the tourist with the mouse ears videotaping their confrontation. "Excuse me, sir," she said to him, "but if you don't cease your taping, I'm going to have to confiscate your equipment as potential evidence. It should be returned to you in three or four months."

The tourist gulped, put the camera down, and retreated back into the crowd.

Katz took Jimmy by the elbow and led him back under the tape, the two of them walking toward the body.

Jimmy's whole arm was numb in her grip. "Ouch," he said quietly.

Katz looked at her hand as though she hadn't realized her own strength. "Sorry," she said, releasing him. "I'm in a bad mood. I knew this kid."

A uniform walked up to Katz, a full-gutted veteran keeping his head tilted so he didn't have to look at her directly. "Beaners don't know nothing," he said, jerking a hand toward the nearby apartments. "Ten to a room, but they don't see nothing, they don't hear nothing. '*No hablamos inglés,*'" he singsonged.

"I wouldn't talk to a *puto* like you either," Katz said. "Relieve Simmons on traffic control, and send him over to talk to me. He's better looking than you, and he doesn't slur the people he's asking for help."

"Hey, *detective*," sputtered the uniform. "I know my job better—"

"You don't know shit, Wallis. That's why I just told you to send Simmons over."

Wallis slunk off, cursing softly. *Dyke, cunt, bitch* floated on the breeze like dandelion seeds.

Katz bent down beside the body again. "Take a look, Jimmy."

"I think there's a misunderstanding." Jimmy bent down beside her. This close he could see a single gold hoop in the boy's ear, the earring gleaming in the sunlight; it made him seem even more innocent. "I'm not here because of—"

"Meet Luis Cortez." Katz gently closed the boy's eyes, her fingers lingering on his smooth brown skin. "Luis was thirteen years old. Good kid, never in trouble, a solid student. He played third base on the Boys Club team. Lousy player, but he loved the game. He just . . . loved it." She glanced over at the bike lying broken a few yards away. "Police Athletic League bought him that bike not a month ago. You should have seen his face." She chewed on her lower lip. "He hardly got a chance to break it in." She looked at Jimmy. "You put that in your article. He hardly got a chance."

"I'm sorry."

Katz glared at the sullen homeboy watching them from across the street, arms crossed. "That's his big brother, Paulo." She gently pulled the sheet over the boy's head. "Killing Luis was supposed to send a message to Paulo. If you ask me, they should have delivered it direct and smoked his gangbanging ass." She stood up, and Jimmy stood up with her. "You know the thing I hate the most about my job? The wrong people die."

Jimmy looked in her eyes. "That's what I hate about my job too."

"Why aren't you writing this down?"

"Detective?" A young uniform hustled over. "You wanted to see me?"

"Go ring some doorbells, Simmons," said Katz. "They've already been asked once, so try it with a smile. And take off your hat when you talk to the *señoras*."

"Yes, detective."

"Wipe you feet before you walk inside," she called as Simmons took off at a dogtrot. She stared off into the distance. The tip of Disneyland's Matterhorn ride was visible over the jacaranda trees, the mountain's fake snow glistening in the heat. "The happiest place on earth, my *ass*."

"Detective, I'm not here to write a story about Luis."

Katz turned to him, her face frozen.

"You told me at the restaurant that you had pulled Harlen Shafer's prints off Walsh's trailer. I followed up on him."

"Luis Cortez isn't worth your time, but Garrett Walsh is?" Katz scowled. "A thirteen-year-old kid gets blown away riding his bike, and it's who-gives-a-shit. A convicted killer drowns in a fishpond, and you treat it like the Kennedy assassination."

It was a good question, but Jimmy didn't have an answer. Instead, he pulled the Gideon Bible out of his jacket and offered it to her.

Katz didn't touch the book. "It's a little late in the game for me to get religion."

"Take it."

Katz took the Bible and flipped it open. One of her eyebrows raised.

"I ran down Shafer to a motel off the Strip. He moved out just after Walsh died. Cleared out in the middle of the night and left the Bible behind."

Katz moved around the Baggies of pot and pills with a fingertip.

"You ever hear of a small-time dealer who loads up his shirts and underwear, his socks and toothbrush, but forgets to take his stash?"

Katz closed the Bible, her expression impenetrable.

"No one saw Shafer scoot," said Jimmy, standing close, not afraid of her. "The motel manager and he were friends. The man was disappointed that Shafer didn't stop by to say good-bye. Detective, I don't think Shafer cleaned out his room. I think he's dead, and whoever killed him wanted to make it look like he had run off."

Katz didn't answer, waiting for more. Like good reporters, good cops knew when to be quiet.

"Walsh was paranoid, listening for the sound of a car on the gravel road, but Shafer made regular visits to his trailer. Walsh wouldn't have thought twice seeing his Camaro driving up some evening. He would have figured the two of them were just going to sit around the koi pond getting loaded and talking about bad times in the joint. I think on that last visit Shafer had company. That's why the crime scene unit didn't find any tire tracks they couldn't account for."

Katz waved the first uniform over, tapping her feet as the paunchy sergeant took his time. "Make sure that Paulo doesn't leave the scene," she told him when he finally arrived. "I want to interview him after he's stewed a while, after he's gotten a chance to see his baby brother's blood leaking into the storm drain. Not yet, sergeant," she ordered, as the man turned to go. "Have someone bring the mother and sister a cold drink, a *female* officer. Tell Morales to drive to McDonald's, pick up some lemonades, then come back and hold their hands. *Now* you can go."

"Whoever killed Walsh used Shafer to help with the job," said Jimmy, trying to regain her attention. "Shafer got him so high he could hardly move. That's why the coroner didn't find any defensive wounds on Walsh's body, no signs of a struggle. Just dope and alcohol. Shafer probably thought he was saving his own life by cooperating, but all he was doing was buying a little time."

Katz checked her watch. "Maybe it was just Shafer and Walsh getting high that last night, so wasted they both passed out." She shook the Bible and set the pills rattling, "Only Shafer was lucky—he passed out in the dirt. Walsh stumbled into the koi pond and drowned."

"Walsh didn't drown."

"A few hours later Shafer wakes up, sees Walsh floating, and he panics," continued Katz, paying no attention to Jimmy's protests. "Shafer knows the drill—*he's* the one who supplied Walsh with the drugs, *he's* looking at manslaughter. So he drives back to the motel, grabs his gear, and splits. Unlike you, though, Shafer isn't a deep thinker. He forgets his dope, and by the time he remembers it, he's too scared to come back."

"Boone did the autopsy on Walsh. You told me you were going to make sure that Rabinowitz handled the job."

"Rabinowitz was on vacation when we brought in Walsh, not that it's any of your business." Katz patted him on the cheek; to a bystander it would have looked almost affectionate, but it rattled Jimmy's teeth. "Walsh was a rapist and a murderer, and he drowned with a mouth full of fish shit."

"*Somebody* took Walsh's screenplay," said Jimmy.

"Maybe Shafer took it."

"Shafer's dead."

Katz laughed.

"The letter Walsh got in prison," said Jimmy, wanting to convince her, needing to convince her, "it was from a woman he had been having an affair with when Heather Grimm was murdered. A *married* woman. She wrote him, said she had found out that her husband knew about the affair the whole time they were together. She suspected that her husband set Walsh up for the murder."

Katz shook her head. "Your story just keeps getting better and better."

"It's the truth."

"The truth is, we have a missing screenplay you never read. A missing letter you never saw. Written by a married woman whose name you don't know."

"I've got some possibilities on that."

"I'm sure you do." Katz patted his cheek again, and he tasted blood in his mouth. "I did a little follow-up myself after our lunch date. I called around to a few studios, and what do you know? Walsh had hit them all up about his new screenplay. He actually described it as 'the most dangerous screenplay in the world.' You believe that? I'm surprised the studio execs could keep a straight face. Strange thing, though—Walsh wouldn't let any of them read it, either. Not a word. Said it was a work in progress." She grinned those wide, flat horse teeth at him. "See where I'm heading?"

"I believed him."

"Of course you did—that's *your* job." Katz cocked her head, hearing a siren approaching. "So here's Walsh, getting nowhere with the studios, and suddenly you show up, and he pitches this wild story about a prison letter and a wife and a jealous husband, and you can see the headlines already. Walsh isn't a loser who murdered a young girl, he's an innocent artist wronged by the system. Too bad he died before you resurrected his career." She leaned closer. "The only thing I can't decide is whether he really fooled you, or if you knew it was a scam and were using him too."

A crime scene van approached, the siren turned off now as it moved past the police line.

"What are you afraid of?" Jimmy said quietly, so furious he didn't trust himself to raise his voice. "Did you get all weepy about Luis Cortez because he was an innocent kid, or because it's an easy case? Putting away gangbangers, how hard is that? They don't even try to hide what they've done. They *brag* about it."

Katz waved to the van. "Go home, Jimmy. Go home, get stoned, get laid, go do whatever it is you do when you're not playing boy detective."

"Whoever killed Walsh knew how to get away with it. He was smart enough to get away with killing Heather Grimm. Smart enough to—"

Katz jabbed him in the chest with a forefinger. "Shoo."

"I'll throw you another steak. Maybe that will get you to do your job."

Katz poked him with the Gideon Bible, poked him hard, a vial of pills falling out and rolling across the street. "We're done here."

"You are. I'm not."

Chapter 19

Jimmy climbed over the NO ADMITTANCE WITHOUT PERMISSION gate, then started down yet another long dock at the Blue Water marina, checking names on the sterns of the boats parked there, past seventy-foot oceangoing yachts and four-masted schooners, and—fuck it, Jimmy didn't know what he was talking about. His knowledge of boats began with Captain Hook's pirate ship in *Peter Pan* and ended with the doomed fishing boat in *A Perfect Storm*. And, oh yeah, those fat rich guys who hired fit young guys to race their yachts every few years for the America's Cup, while sportscasters desperately tried to get the rest of the country to give a shit. All Jimmy knew was the marina was filled with boats, lots of boats, some with inboard engines, some with sails, but all of them big and beautiful and costing way too much money, even before you got to the tricked-out electronics sprouting from their rigging. If Detective Leonard Brimley really was living here, he had retired in style.

Jimmy had been walking up and down the docks for the last half hour looking for Brimley's boat, the *Badge in a Drawer*, without success. He had tried the main office, but according to a note taped on the door, the harbormaster was home sick with flu. Jimmy had stopped at two or three boats asking for directions, but he had gotten nothing but blank stares and misinformation.

Leonard Brimley had retired after twenty-five years on the Hermosa Beach PD, a mostly unremarkable career marked by a few commendations, a few community service awards, and not one civilian complaint. Not one. Brimley had evidently been a low-key cop who didn't go looking for trouble and kept his emotions in check. His most notable achievement in the twenty-five years was arresting Garrett Walsh for the murder of Heather Grimm, and even that had been mostly accidental. According to the news accounts, Brimley had been off duty, driving home from his shift, when he heard a call over the police band to investigate a disturbance at a beach cottage a few blocks away. The nearest cruiser reported they were already involved in something else, and Brimley, the good soldier, had broken in and offered to take the call. Like the queen of England said, better to be born lucky than smart.

Jimmy reached the end of the dock, then started back, wondering if Jane had been wrong. There *had* to be a first time. Jane had called him this morning and said she had gotten Brimley's address. Jimmy hadn't even known she was looking, which was Jane's style—she'd argue with you, say that you were wasting your time, then go behind your back and help you out.

Holt had gotten a copy of the Police Guild newsletter from the month that Brimley retired and taken down the names of the people in the party photo with him. One of them, a woman working the switchboard at his station house, said that Brimley had bragged to her at the party that he was moving into a fishing boat, going to be living the good life in a marina just north of the city. It had taken fourteen phone calls before a secretary at the Blue Water Marina in Ventura had confirmed that Leonard Brimley was a live-in.

It had been three days since his conversation with Katz; her dismissal of his theory about the death of Garrett Walsh didn't surprise him, but Holt agreeing with her—*that* stung. Not that Jane would ever admit that she agreed with Katz—she was too diplomatic for that. But when Jimmy told her what had happened at the gangbanging crime scene, Holt had just looked at him and asked, "What did you expect?" There was more, of course; Holt explained basic police logic to him as they sat on her patio, half naked, half drunk, watching the sun set into the ocean. Holt said that when there were two equally logical explanations, a good cop always chose the interpretation that had a coroner's report to back it up. He told her it didn't sound like Pythagoras to him. Holt just sipped her drink, one bare leg perched on the balcony railing as she looked out over the waves.

Jimmy scampered back over the security fence and onto the public sidewalk, hot and tired, his shirt sticking to his back. He should have worn shorts. Not sure which direction to go in, he took a right. Behind him he could hear a faint, steady thumping—it sounded like someone beating on a drum. He glanced around, still walking, then spotted a soft drink machine and hurried over. He fumbled in his pocket for change as he scanned the options, his throat dry. No Coke, no Pepsi, no root beer or RC Cola. Instead there was iced tea, fake-sweetened and unsweetened, four different brands of mineral water, and two sports drinks that promised to replace his electrolytes. Jimmy put his quarters back into his pocket. If it didn't rot your teeth, he wasn't interested.

Jimmy turned toward the next dock when something hit him on the side of the head, slamming him into the pop machine. He clung to the machine, clung to it like they were dancing, when something hit him again, knocking his head into the glass front of the machine. Jimmy slid slowly down to the sidewalk. He could hear the thumping sound again, louder, getting closer. He got to his knees, bleary now, blinking at the sight of a tall, muscular white man in Lakers shorts and tank top a few feet away, the silky material billowing in the breeze. He looked familiar, but Jimmy couldn't focus. The man nimbly passed the basketball from hand to hand, round and round his body. Jimmy started to rise, when the man whipped the ball from around his back and threw it into his face. Jimmy's nose exploded with blood.

"Fouled in the act of shooting. Two free throws," said the man.

Or maybe Jimmy just imagined it. He could barely hear anything with the pain and the roaring in his skull. He had fallen down again, slumped against the pop machine. He pushed himself up, trying to stand. You stay down, it was too easy to get used to it.

The basketball player stood over him, holding the ball in two hands. Set shot. He bounced the ball, once twice, three times, and Jimmy heard the pounding of drums. The natives are restless . . . he smiled, and then the ball smashed against his right eye, snapped him back to where nothing was funny anymore. "One point," said the player. "The crowd goes wild."

Jimmy groaned. Monotonous game. Every time he tried to get up, he found himself on the pavement again. Breathing made red bubbles, which was not a good sign.

The player was doing the round-the-world move again, the ball a blur. He acknowledged the cheers of the crowd with a goofy smile, then let loose, just as Jimmy slid down the pop machine and the ball slammed into the metal, just inches from his head. The player looked disappointed. "Off the rim," he said, his eyes filled with hate.

Jimmy watched the player take the ball back a few yards, dribbling rapidly, the ball bouncing through his legs effortlessly, keeping up a steady tom-tom beat. Jimmy knew him from *somewhere.* He tried to push himself off the sidewalk, but he was shaking too hard and it was raining blood. Time to stay inside, stay right where he was until the storm blew over. Jimmy shook his head. No, he couldn't stay here.

The player dribbled closer, then backed away, moved in again, then back out, a regular matador. His baggy shorts and tank top were flapping in the wind. Or maybe it was the pennants on the yachts nearby—every one of those tubs had a dozen flags on it. The player dodged left, then right, trying to attract Jimmy's attention, the ball bouncing louder now, BAM BAM BAM.

Jimmy held one hand out.

The player smiled, the ball beating against the pavement. "That's good, Jimmy. You *try* and block my shot."

Jimmy squinted, but his eyes kept tearing over. *Who is this asshole?*

"Think fast, Jimmy," said the player, dribbling closer now. "Here it comes." BAM BAM BAM. "Here it comes." BAM BAM BAM.

Jimmy watched the player, helpless. It seemed to him that the player was uncertain now, taking too much time dribbling, hesitant to take that final shot.

"You ready?" said the player, louder now, trying to convince himself. BAM BAM BAM. "You ready for it? BAM BAM BAM. "I'm going to do—"

A beefy arm reached out from behind the player, grabbed his ball hand, and jerked it behind his back, bending him forward. The player howled as an older man planted a knee in his back and drove him into the sidewalk, then deftly pulled the other hand beside the other. The older man wasn't as tall as the player, but he was a lot broader, and he moved with confidence and certainty, his takedown so fluid that it was over before Jimmy or the player realized what was happening.

The basketball bounced free, rolled over against Jimmy's foot, and stopped.

The older man snapped a pair of handcuffs around the player's wrists and dragged him over to the security fence. He glanced over at Jimmy and smiled, and it was a good smile, then he grabbed the player at the waist and lifted him high, hooking his handcuffed wrists over the top of the fencepost. The player was left suspended, his toes just touching the ground. As long as he didn't struggle, he could keep from dislocating his shoulders with his own weight.

Jimmy stared at the player up there on the post, utterly amazed.

The player was equally stunned. His mouth moved, but no sound came out.

The man walked over to Jimmy, a fleshy old bear with cropped reddish blond hair, built like a wine vat, wearing plaid Bermuda shorts and a pink short-sleeved shirt with crossed nautical flags on the breast pocket. He peered down at Jimmy. "How are you, son?"

Jimmy licked his lips. It hurt.

The older man knelt down beside him. He had an easygoing round face with a peeling nose and lively blue eyes. A man who liked a good joke. "What did you do to that fella I hung up to dry, anyway? First time I ever saw a basketball used as a lethal weapon."

"I didn't do anything to him." Jimmy stirred, winced.

"Don't move. I'm going back to my boat and call the police. And an aid car."

"Aren't *you* a cop?" Jimmy pointed at the player hanging on the fence. "The handcuffs . . . ?"

"I used to be a cop," said the older man. "I'm retired now, but I keep an eye on things, and the marina gives me a break on the slip fee. Only way I could afford a place like this."

"Are you—you Leonard Brimley?"

The older man looked surprised. "That's me. Who wants to know?"

"I'm Jimmy Gage. I came here looking for you. I'm a reporter."

Brimley scratched his head. "It's been a while since anyone wanted to talk with me."

"Hey!" shouted the player. "What about me? You're tearing my fucking arms off."

"Hush now," Brimley said without rancor. "I'll get to you presently."

Jimmy pulled himself to a sitting position. "Forget the ambulance."

"Are you sure?"

"I've been beat up worse than this."

"You're *proud* of that?" Brimley grinned.

"Just let me sit here for a while," said Jimmy, sounding tougher than he felt. Something about Brimley made him want to sit up straighter, not give in to the pain.

"That's always a good idea." Brimley patted him gently on the shoulder. "I'm going to put a call in to the locals. They're good boys; they know me."

Jimmy watched Brimley saunter down the sidewalk to the next gate, open it with a key, then continue down the dock. He was still impressed at the ease with which the older man had handled his attacker. Jimmy felt blood dripping from his nose. He looked over to the fence and saw the player struggling, dancing on his tiptoes. "Who *are* you?"

"You don't even recognize me?" The player spit at him, missed. "Perfect. Just fucking perfect."

Jimmy pulled out his shirttail, lightly wiping at the blood on his face. His right eye was swelling up, but he didn't think his nose was broken. "Tell me your name. You owe me that."

"I owe *you*?" The player's voice cracked. "You're the one who owes *me*."

"What did I do to you?" Jimmy carefully pulled himself upright, then had to bend over, resting his hands on his knees until the world stopped spinning. He hobbled closer to the fence and stared at the player. The man's arms were powerful, lumped with muscle, his face all rough edges and thick brow ridges. Jimmy squinted. "Butcher?"

The man on the fencepost kicked at Jimmy, howling as his full weight tore at his bound wrists.

Jimmy had to sit down again.

"My name is Darryl Seth Angley, you *fuck*," snarled the Butcher.

Jimmy's head throbbed so loudly he thought someone was dribbling another basketball. It must have been five or six months since he had written the article about the Butcher. It was no big thing, just a short piece on the regular two-on-two pick-up basketball games at Venice Beach. Napitano had held it for a few issues, printing it only last month. Jimmy had almost forgotten about it.

"You turned me into a joke," moaned the Butcher. "The ballers just laugh at me now."

Jimmy had spent the afternoon courtside, taking notes, doing a few interviews. The Butcher had owned the court, playing with a succession of partners, always winning. The Butcher played a hyper-aggressive game, even for street ball, elbows flying, bumping, and thumping, forcing even bigger players to back off. Better players too. The Butcher wasn't the best one out there, but he made up for it with a ferocious, full-contact game, even knocking aside his own teammate going after a rebound. Jimmy had named him "the Butcher" in his notes, giving all the players nicknames: the Butcher, Stringbean, Ghettoblaster, the Phantom.

The Butcher went limp on the post, sweat rolling down his upraised arms.

The Butcher had ruled the court all day, driving away his last partner an hour earlier, challenging the waiting players to a little one-on-one, bouncing the ball as he called them out. They stood up, one after the other, and one after the other he sent them away bleeding. No one could beat the Butcher. Until the Waiter showed up.

"What did I ever do to you?" wailed the Butcher.

Jimmy had been ready to leave when the Waiter first walked onto the court, but there was something about the new guy that made him stay. The waiter was a tall, skinny white guy wearing black trousers and a white dress shirt with the sleeves rolled. A black bow tie was tucked into his shirt pocket. He wore street shoes. The Butcher tossed the ball to the Waiter, giving him a few minutes to warm up, then walked over and drank from his water bottle. One of the bikini girls who had been hanging around all day tried to speak to the Butcher, but he ignored her, his eyes on the Waiter shooting jumpers. Jimmy sensed something interesting was going to happen, and the other players must have too—they drifted over from the other courts to watch, whispering among themselves.

"You're not even a player," the Butcher said to Jimmy. "You just run down people who are."

The matchup between the Butcher and the Waiter got off to a fast start, the Waiter bringing the ball into play, hip-faking the Butcher, then blowing past him for a slam dunk. The backboard hummed with the force of it. The crowd was silent. No cheers, no jeers. Silence. The Butcher took in the ball, bullied the Waiter aside, and dove for the basket, but as he went for a lay-up, the Waiter plucked the ball from his grasp and buried it. The crowd stirred. The Butcher took the ball in again and swung an elbow at the Waiter's head, but the Waiter ducked under the blow, stole the ball again, and hit a fall-away from almost midcourt. The crowd shouted their approval, whooping it up now.

The game continued like that for the next twenty minutes, the Waiter scoring from all areas of the court, outjumping, outrebounding, outplaying the Butcher, just *scorching* him. In response, the Butcher became increasingly violent, tripping the Waiter when he went up to dunk, flagrantly fouling him, cursing and arguing with him. The Waiter stayed cool, even as the knees of his pants were torn; he just quietly kept making shot after shot. When he won the first game, the Butcher insisted on making it two out of three, and when he won the second game, the Butcher said he meant best of five. When the Waiter won the third game, the crowd booed the Butcher off the court, catcalling, mocking him. Jimmy had written it up just that way.

"I used to be somebody," said the Butcher. "People respected me. You took it away. It wasn't losing to that Waiter, that was a fluke, but you turned it into something important."

"I just wrote an article—"

"You and your fancy job. People listen to you, even if you get it all wrong. Well, I got a nothing job and nobody cares what I think. I clock in five minutes late, I get docked a half-hour. I got to ask permission to take a crap. That's *my* job." Tears rolled down the Butcher's cheeks. "You fuck. You fucking fuck. The only place people paid attention to me was on the court."

Jimmy heard whistling, turned around, and saw Leonard Brimley approaching.

"Local cops should be here soon," Brimley said. "You doing okay?"

"Yeah." Jimmy stared at the Butcher, remembering the near misses, the basketball slamming into the soft drink machine inches from his head. Most of all he remembered the indecision on the Butcher's face. He turned to Brimley. "Why don't you call the cops. Tell them we don't need them."

The Butcher's head jerked up.

Brimley rubbed his jaw. "Assault and battery. That's a serious charge."

Jimmy pulled himself up hand over hand and hung on to the fence to support himself. "Darryl and I—we were just practicing our b-ball moves. I guess we got a little out of hand."

"I saw the whole thing," said Brimley, as if he were in on the joke. "You weren't practicing for anything other than getting your brains beat out."

"Let him go, Mr. Brimley," said Jimmy. "I'll talk to the cops. Darryl and I just had a little misunderstanding, but we got it straightened out. Right, *Darryl*?"

The Butcher nodded slowly. "Yeah, we're all straightened out."

Brimley shook his head, stepped over to the fencepost, and lifted the Butcher down. He checked with Jimmy one more time, then unhooked the cuffs.

The Butcher stood there, rubbing his raw wrists.

Brimley waved the Butcher away with the back of his hand. "Go and sin no more."

Jimmy watched as the Butcher picked up his basketball and slowly dribbled back to the parking lot. He kept waiting for him to look back, but he didn't.

Brimley put an arm around him. "Let's go to my boat. I'll call off the locals and clean you up. You better get some ice on that eye, or it's going to swell shut on you."

Jimmy was going to argue, but it sounded like a good idea. Besides, he still wanted to talk to Brimley about Garrett Walsh. "Thanks, detective."

"No need to call me detective," said Brimley, helping him. "I'm retired and glad of it."

"Leonard, then."

Brimley chuckled. "The last person to call me that was Miss Hobbes in eighth grade, and I hated it then too. Leonard sounds like someone who starches his underwear. You're probably the same way—that's why you go by Jimmy instead of James."

Jimmy gasped as they went down a step. "What do you want me to call you?"

"Call me what my friends do." Brimley nestled Jimmy closer. "Call me Sugar."

Chapter 20

Jimmy leaned against Sugar as he hobbled down the dock, his ribs throbbing with every step. Seagulls floated overhead, screaming, and the sound cut right through Jimmy's skull.

"You doing okay, son?"

"Yeah," Jimmy gasped, and kept walking, the gray concrete dock stretching out before him. He focused on the next few steps, one foot after the other. The yachts bobbed gently on either side of him, the blue water shimmering with pools of oil and gasoline. Dizzy again, he clutched at Sugar and felt hard muscle underneath a cushion of blubber. The big man smelled of suntan oil, reassuring him somehow. He stared at the nautical flags patterned across Sugar's pink shirt, wondering what they meant—clear skies or storm warnings. "Thanks for what you did back there with . . . Darryl." He still had to work to remember the Butcher's real name.

"No problem." Sugar supported him, fitting his pace to Jimmy's. "That boy sure wanted to get your attention."

"It was my own fault."

Sugar chuckled. "Usually it's the man that got the worst of it who throws the blame."

"Darryl *did* get the worst of it."

"If you say so."

"I'm sorry if I caused you any trouble with the police. I'll make sure they know it was my idea to cut him loose."

"Don't worry about it." Sugar shifted his weight and drew Jimmy closer. "Besides, I like a guy who doesn't run to the cops with every little cut and scrape. Most cops won't admit that, but I'm retired, I can tell the truth. When I was in uniform, half the calls I used to get were strictly nuisance beefs: *He hit me, she hit me, he called me names, his stereo is too loud.* Total waste of time. Even when I became a detective, you'd be amazed at the cases I had to blue-sheet."

"Not Heather Grimm, though. That one wasn't a waste of time."

"No." Sugar shook his head. "That one broke my heart." He cradled Jimmy against his chest. "I *thought* that's why you were here."

"I'm doing a piece on Garrett Walsh. Sorry, I'm messing you up." Jimmy's nose had opened up again, and blood was dripping onto Sugar's Bermuda shorts.

"Heck, I been bled on before." Sugar brushed off his shorts, grinning as Jimmy disengaged himself, walking on his own now. "Besides, plaid hides everything."

"How—how much farther?"

"Almost there."

Jimmy glanced around at the sleek ocean cruisers on either side of the pier, waxed teakwood and chrome gleaming in the sun. "Nice neighborhood. Yacht city."

Sugar laid a hand on Jimmy's shoulder and caught him as he stumbled. "*Yachts*—that's a term only we commoners use. The people who pay the luxury taxes call them boats." He had a good laugh, deep and resonant; hearing it made you feel as if you were in on the joke with him, just a couple of old friends out for a stroll. "Here we are," he said, indicating a thirty-foot cabin cruiser, a solid but slightly shabby vessel, paint peeling, the chrome rails flecked with rust. He took Jimmy's arm, guiding him up the gangplank. "Careful. You trip, I'm going to get sued."

"*Hello,* Sugar!"

Jimmy looked over, saw three girls in bikinis stretched out on the deck of a large yacht—boat, whatever. It was at least an eighty-footer, with three decks and enough electronics gear to signal the Mars lander.

"What happened to your friend?" called a redhead in a polka-dot bikini, her sunglasses pushed up onto her forehead.

"Sports injury." Sugar gave Jimmy a wink.

Seeing the redhead's sunglasses, Jimmy thought of Walsh . . . remembered the last time he had seen him, the director floating facedown, maggots wriggling in his hair . . .

Sugar caught Jimmy as he fell and carried him up the gangplank in his arms while Jimmy mumbled apologies. Sugar told him it was no bother at all and laid him down in an aluminum chaise longue. "You rest. I'll be right back."

Jimmy closed his eyes, drifting . . . then jerked alert and saw Brimley hovering over him.

"Take it easy, I'm not going to hurt you." Brimley's eyes twinkled as he bent down beside Jimmy carrying a basin of water and an ice bucket, a clean white cloth slung over one shoulder, a couple of long-neck beer bottles poking out of his pockets. He pulled up a chaise, ignoring Jimmy's protestations, and began cleaning his face, gently working the edges of the cloth against Jimmy's nose, dabbing at his split lip. The water in the basin reddened as he wrung the cloth out over and over, his movements tender. When he was finished, Brimley emptied the basin over the side, then filled the cloth with ice cubes and handed it to Jimmy. "Keep that against your eye, otherwise it's going to swell shut on you." He opened one of the beers and gave it to Jimmy, then opened the other. He toasted Jimmy with the bottle and stretched out in the warm sunshine on his own chaise, the nylon webbing groaning with his weight. "Life is sweet, huh?"

Jimmy took a tentative sip. The beer burned his torn lip, but it was cold and soothing and he finished half of it in one long swallow. The taste of blood lingered.

"Those are the Whitmore girls," Sugar said, nodding toward the nearby yacht. "They just moved into Daddy's boat for spring break."

Jimmy looked around at the other boats, the sunlight shimmering off the water.

"Not bad for a retired cop, eh?" Sugar grinned at Jimmy, reading his mind. "Like I said, the marina cuts me a deal. Everybody hates to see a cop in their review mirror, but they love living next door to one." He sipped his beer. "What newspaper you work for?"

"Magazine," Jimmy corrected him. "*SLAP.*"

Sugar lifted an eyebrow. "Never heard of it."

"We do lifestyle coverage mostly. Movies and movie stars, TV, fashion."

Sugar puffed out his chest, his teats jiggling slightly against his shirt. "You want to do a fashion spread on me? You should have warned me—I would have gone on a diet."

"Keep eating. I'm doing a retrospective on Garrett Walsh. I thought I'd look you up and see if I could get a new angle. You were—"

"A new angle? Like what? You going to write a happy ending for the son of a seacook?"

"Little late for that." Jimmy squinted in the sun, trying to keep Sugar in focus. "I've read through Walsh's bio, but there's not much information on the crime itself. His plea bargain short-circuited the coverage, so I thought I'd ask you about—"

"How did you find me?" Sugar scratched his belly. "I'm not trying to hide, but I keep a low profile. You must be a real bloodhound."

"Not *me*. We have people at the magazine who specialize in locating subjects. I don't know how they do it—I just put in a request."

"Wow . . . put in a request for something, and there you have it." Sugar worked on the beer, smacking his lips. "I thought you might have needed some stitches under that eye, but it doesn't look too bad. You take a pretty good punch."

"I think the idea is to *throw* a pretty good punch, not take one."

"That's the idea all right." Sugar pulled out an aspirin bottle from his Bermudas and shook a few into his hand. "Four enough? I'll get you some water."

"No, thanks." Jimmy chewed the aspirin, careful to keep them away from his swollen lip. "How did you get the name Sugar? You have a sweet tooth?"

"I *do* have a sweet tooth, but my mama was the one who gave me the name." Sugar's gaze shifted to the surrounding boats, the distant walkways—not as a series of jumpy glances but as a steady scan of the surroundings, barely moving his head. Brimley might have retired, but he still had cop eyes. "Mama always said you catch more flies with sugar than with vinegar, and she was right about that, like she was right about everything else." He grinned at Jimmy, but Jimmy was drifting on the soft rhythms of Sugar's voice, the boat rolling under them. "Most instructors at the Academy didn't think I had what it took to be a cop—too easygoing, they told me, not aggressive enough. But I knew it wasn't a matter of being a tough guy, throwing your authority around. I got better results with a friendly smile and a sympathetic ear than most of the other uniforms did with a billy. 'Course, me being the large economy size helped, but—" He suddenly grabbed Jimmy's sore shoulder, making him howl. "Hey, stay awake."

Jimmy shook him off and sat up, blinking.

"Falling asleep with a head injury can be fatal. I should take you to the emergency room."

"I'm fine."

"You could have a concussion. I'm a damn fool for giving you alcohol."

Jimmy put down the ice pack. "Why don't we just get out of the sun? That way I could drop dead in the shade." Sugar tried to help, but Jimmy waved him away and followed him into the cabin. Jimmy looked around the main cabin before sitting down on one of the two armchairs. He wanted to get out of the sun, but he also wanted to get into Sugar's living space. He needed the retired cop's cooperation, and for that he needed to get inside the man's head.

The main room was small and compact—if Sugar stood on tiptoes, his head would graze the ceiling. But it was clean and neat, with recessed lamps, hardwood floors, and a flat-screen television. The small galley contained a stainless-steel two-burner and a built-in mini-fridge, an espresso maker, and a microwave. A bowl of ripe mangoes was on the counter, next to a half-eaten, store-bought apple pie with a fork resting inside the aluminum pie plate.

He had expected to see the usual career memorabilia on the walls: badges and commendations, framed news clips and photographs of himself taken with the chief or the mayor, maybe a movie star, but there wasn't anything like that. Either Sugar didn't have much of an ego, or he wanted to forget all about his former career. Or maybe he had simply moved on to better things. The decor confirmed that impression. The walls were covered with framed photographs of Brimley holding up fish: bone-fishing near Key West, standing with a near-record tarpon off the Gulf Coast, small fish, large fish. His grin remained goofy and thrilled, and his nose was perpetually peeling. The biggest photo showed him standing beside a nine-foot sailfish hanging off a yardarm.

"Nice-looking black marlin," said Jimmy. "Baja?"

"You know your fish and your fishing holes," said Sugar, pleased. "Seven hundred and eight pounds." He tapped the photo with a thick forefinger. "Hooked him at dusk, and it was nearly midnight before I landed him. A real fighter. Thought I was going to have a heart attack out there on the Sea of Cortez."

Jimmy looked toward the interior of the boat, wondering if Sugar had a wall big enough to mount the marlin.

Sugar shook his head. "Taxidermist lost it," he said, reading Jimmy's mind again. "You believe that? I kept calling and calling for three months, and all I got was 'Sorry, *señor*, next week, *por favor*.' Maybe I *am* too easygoing for my own good. Probably sold it to some rich *norteamericano* who wouldn't know a marlin from a mackerel."

"Every fisherman has a story about the one who got away. At least you have proof."

"Never thought of it that way. I *like* that." Sugar sat down in the other armchair and turned it to face Jimmy. His skin was ruddy from the sun, his shanks freckled—he was one of those big white guys who would never tan, only blister, but loved the outdoors anyway. "You ever been to Brazil? I hear the fishing's great down there."

"Never had the pleasure."

"They say you can live off the land—fish in the ocean and fruit on the trees." Sugar nodded. "With my pension . . . a man can dream, I guess. You sure your head's okay?"

"I read that Walsh actually answered the door when you rang the bell. Did you identify yourself as a police officer first?"

"I guess you're well enough to ask questions."

Jimmy smiled back at him, a couple of grinny-Guses knowing how the game was played. "I'm doing okay. It feels good in here, Sugar. Cozy."

"Thanks. I don't get many visitors, but it suits me. By the way, I did ID myself to Walsh. Standard procedure. I may not be smart, but I know enough to follow the rules."

Jimmy stretched out, his feet almost touching Sugar's well-worn deck shoes. "Walsh opened the door anyway? Covered with blood—"

"He was a mess. Blood . . . everywhere."

"But he opened the door to a cop. You didn't find that odd?"

Sugar beamed. "I'll tell you a story. True story. My first month on traffic duty, fresh on the job, I make a stop on Pier Street, Mustang convertible driving erratically. It was a Thursday night, streetlights just coming on. I walk up to the car, ticket book in my hand, the full weight and authority of the city of Hermosa Beach behind me, and I see that the driver is . . . well, he's having a sex act performed on him by the young lady in the passenger seat. Driver just hands me his license. The lady—she doesn't even come up for air. I fill out the ticket, my hand shaking I'm writing so fast. The young lady is sitting up now, checking her lipstick in the mirror like I'm not even there. I tell the driver to watch where he's going in the future, and he promises me he will. Then he drives off." Sugar shook his head. "I learned right there that some people don't have the same respect for the law that police officers do. The night I came knocking on Walsh's door, he was messed up pretty bad on drugs. I think he was in a state of shock, but I wouldn't have been surprised if he had been cold sober opening the door for me, showing me what he had done. That's just the way it is. If people act the way you expect them to act, there wouldn't be any need for police." He winked at Jimmy. "*Or* reporters."

Chapter 21

Helen Katz rapped on the front door of the Cortez home, a firm knock but not her usual triple-bang that sent the residents scrambling to answer. Deaf, dumb, and blind, you knew that there was a cop at the door when Katz came calling. Right now though, she was feeling kindly toward Mrs. Cortez and didn't feel the need to jump-start her heart. The woman had been through enough, and it was only going to get worse.

"*Sí?*" Mrs. Cortez peered through the steel webbing of the security screen, a short, stocky woman with neatly pinned gray hair and a long-sleeved black dress—mourning clothes for her younger son. Katz's first partner had told her that if she ever wanted to get rich, she should go into business selling funeral dresses to the barrio *mamacitas*. The paunchy twenty-year vet had looked over at her, grinning. Even fresh out of the Academy and needing a good report, she had looked right through him until he turned away, muttering.

"I'm Detective Katz, *señora. Hablas inglés?*"

Mrs. Cortez turned away, said something to someone inside, and a teenage girl joined her at the door. Her daughter—Katz recognized her from the drive-by crime scene of Luis Cortez last week. She had been wearing bright orange soccer shorts at the time. This morning she wore a more subdued beaded peasant dress with a black woven choker around her slender brown neck. Her dark eyes were older than her years. "May I help you?" Her voice was soft as flowers.

"I'm Detective Katz. I was the officer—"

"I know who you are," said the girl, opening the door. "Please come in. My name is Estella." She nodded as Katz stepped inside. "Mama!" She conferred with her mother for a moment, then Mrs. Cortez smiled at Katz and disappeared into the kitchen.

"Please, detective, make yourself comfortable." Estella indicated a worn blue-leather sofa, then waited until Katz had sat down before sitting down herself, smoothing her dress as she did so. "We are very glad to see you."

Katz looked around, confused, but the house was quiet—only the sound of water running in the kitchen disturbed the silence. The living room was clean and organized, with a sofa and two matching leather chairs that faced the television, a new thirty-one-inch Panasonic. An ornate wooden crucifix hung on one wall, next to a velvet painting of Cesar Chavez waving in triumph. On the opposite wall was a velvet painting of a muscular Aztec warrior holding an obsidian lance, his expression proud and threatening. In the far corner of the room was a small round table with a framed photograph of Luis Cortez flanked by two flickering votive candles. Luis was thirteen when he was murdered—the photo was recent, his seventh-grade portrait probably, Luis at his desk, hands folded, a mischievous smile on his face, his eyes silky.

"He was a beautiful boy, yes?"

"Yes," said Katz.

"Yes." Estella nodded. "We thank you for coming to the funeral."

"I'm sorry." Katz felt tongue-tied in the girl's presence, wishing that the mother would return. "I'm looking for Paulo."

"Paulo is here last night," Mrs. Cortez said from the doorway, a tray of cookies in her hands. *"Toda la noche."*

"Mrs. Cortez . . ." Katz turned to Estella. "I didn't mention anything about last night. Your mother is giving him an alibi before I even asked for one."

"Paulo here *toda la noche*," Mrs. Cortez repeated, setting the cookies on the coffee table in front of Katz.

"Last night three Latin Princes were shot to death while sitting in their car outside a *taquería* in East Anaheim. These men—we believe they were the ones who killed Luis."

Mrs. Cortez crossed herself as she walked back into the kitchen.

Katz took a bite of a cookie. It was a plain biscuit covered with colored sugar. "The man who killed the three Latin Princes . . ." She wiped crumbs off her lips, remembering the last time she had seen Luis's older brother, Paulo, a huge nineteen-year-old in knee-length cutoffs and Pendleton. He had glowered at her from across the street at the crime scene, arms folded across his chest, his powerful neck and forearms laced with tattoos. "This man—his description fits Paulo."

"As my mother said, detective, Paulo was home all last night."

"I'm glad to hear that." Katz finished the cookie, reached for another. "It was a nasty shooting. The Princes were drinking beer in their Buick when someone pulled up, leaned out the driver's side, and emptied the clip on an AK-47." She chewed with her mouth open. "Armor-piercing rounds. Swiss-cheesed the Buick something awful."

"I am sorry for their families," said Estella.

"*Qué lástima*," agreed Mrs. Cortez, setting a tray on the table. She poured red hibiscus tea into a cup, dropped in a couple of sugar cubes without asking, and handed it to Katz.

Katz put the cup down without tasting it and reached for another cookie. "You say Paulo stayed home last. That's good to hear." She took a bite. "So . . . where is he?"

Mrs. Cortez sipped her tea, then spoke to her daughter, who translated.

"My mother says Paulo left early this morning. She does not know where he went. To look for work, perhaps."

"I don't think so." Katz licked her lips, sugar granules drifting onto her lap. "After the shoot-up at the *taquería,* I had a unit parked down the street watching this house. They were there all night, and they didn't see anyone leave."

Estella listened to her mother. "Paulo sometimes sneaks out the back. He is worried about being"—she searched for the word—"ambushed by the Latin Princes. He must have gone out through the back alley."

"I had the alley watched too."

Mrs. Cortez spoke again. She didn't raise her voice, but her eyes watching Katz were small and hard.

"My mother says your fine police officers must have fallen asleep and missed seeing him. She hopes you are not too harsh with them. It was a warm night."

Katz brushed crumbs off her lap. "It would be better for Paulo if the police found him before the Latin Princes."

Mrs. Cortez spoke rapidly as she stirred her tea, the spoon clinking against the cup.

Estella blushed. "My mother—she thanks you for your concern. She will tell Paulo that you wish to speak with him."

Katz stared at the photograph of Luis Cortez and wondered where that shy knowing smile had come from. "Estella, you know what's going to happen to your brother if he doesn't turn himself in. Make your mother understand that you two could also be in danger."

"God will provide."

"What happens if the Latin Princes don't believe in God?"

"*Everyone* believes in God, detective."

Katz shook her head, then laid her business card on the table. "Call me if you change your mind. My pager is always on." She grabbed a couple more cookies as she stood up.

Mrs. Cortez stood up too and spoke to Estella.

"My mother thanks you very much for sending Señor Jaime to talk with us. It—it was a very rare occasion for us."

Mrs. Cortez took Katz's hand and squeezed it between her two palms, ignoring the cookies crumbling onto the carpet. *"Gracias."*

"I don't understand," said Katz, feeling the heat of Mrs. Cortez's hands.

"Muchas gracias." Mrs. Cortez let her go.

"Mr. Jaime—he said you sent him. He asked about Luis. He wanted to know everything. We spent the whole afternoon together.

All of us cried. Me, my mother, Mr. Jaime. Even Paulo, who pretended it was the dust in the air making his eyes water."

"I didn't send anyone to talk with you."

"Mr. Jaime said he was a writer for a magazine—"

"*SLAP.*" Mrs. Cortez acted like it was funny. She lightly slapped her own cheek. "*SLAP.*"

"Jimmy's writing about Luis?"

Estella nodded. "He said he wanted people to know who Luis was. To put a face on the killing, to show what the world had lost." She was crying again. "He said he wanted everyone who read about Luis—he wanted them to feel what we feel—to feel the weight of a stone in their heart."

Mrs. Cortez nodded, her eyes ferocious. She had cried herself dry. Katz might as well take her card back—no way they were going to turn in Paulo.

"Mr. Jaime—we can trust him, yes?" asked Estella.

Katz turned over the idea of Jimmy tracking down the Cortez family, facing off against a desperate and grieving Paulo to write a story about a boy who was just a statistic, a kid whose death didn't even make the local TV news. "Yes, you can trust him."

Chapter 22

"Where's your bathroom?"

"First door on the left," said Brimley, pointing. "And it's called the head."

"Aye-aye, captain." Jimmy was still unsteady on his feet, but he made it into the narrow corridor, one hand on the wall, closing the door behind him. There was no lock. He ran cold water in the small sink and gingerly splashed his face. His reflection wasn't pretty—his right eye was swollen and purple, and dried blood was crusted over his eyebrow. He rinsed his mouth out and spat into the basin. He hadn't come in here to wash his face or use the toilet, though; he was interested in what Sugar's bathroom looked like. Private zones revealed more than a mirror.

Brimley said he had been greeted at the door of the cottage by a disoriented Garrett Walsh. The director had been wearing an open purple robe and was clutching a gold statuette caked with blood. Brimley hadn't even recognized the statue as an Oscar. He had quietly taken it away from Walsh, peeling away the man's fingers while Walsh mumbled apologies. Jimmy had already read that in the official transcript, but a few minutes ago Brimley had added that Walsh had wiped his hands on his robe and offered to do a PSA warning kids against using drugs. Brimley had shaken his head when he told Jimmy, still amazed after all these years.

The room was small and wood-lined, just a sink and commode, a stall shower with a bathing-beauties curtain. A single rectangular window was slightly propped open, looking out at the furled sails of the boat next door. The rack next to the commode contained recent issues of *Deep Sea Fishing, Power Boating, Travel and Leisure, Playboy,* and *Gourmet.* He glanced at the door, then carefully opened the medicine cabinet, coughing to cover the squeak. Colgate toothpaste, a toothbrush with wild boar bristles, mint-flavored dental floss, aspirin, Pepto-Bismol, eyedrops, a double-edged razor, and Aqua Velva after shave. No hair dye. No denture cream. No prescription bottles. Nothing that would indicate high blood pressure, ulcers, colitis, diabetes, rickets, or scurvy. Sugar was healthy as a bull elk.

He checked the window again—it was small, but there was room enough to wiggle through. He instinctively checked for ways in and out of places, marked exits and unmarked ones. His first job in journalism had been at a free rock magazine; without press credentials or credibility, Jimmy had learned how to bypass concert security, regularly sneaking backstage, sitting in on closed soundchecks. A conservative three-piece suit and a briefcase allowed him to blow past rent-a-cops; Jimmy simply declared himself the band's attorney and kept walking. He enjoyed the subterfuge more than the music. Jimmy flushed the toilet and opened the door. He smelled coffee.

"Thought you could use this," said Brimley, handing him a mug. "You look like a black coffee type to me."

"Good guess." Jimmy blew steam off and took a sip, favoring his lip.

"My personal blend—half Hawaiian, half French roast." Brimley drank from his own mug. "You talked to anybody else about the case?"

"Not yet."

"The assistant DA could probably tell you more than I can. He was looking over my shoulder before I even finished my report. Can't blame him; from an investigative standpoint, it was pretty open and shut."

"I'm more interested in the crime scene itself—what you saw, what you did. Even though it was open and shut, forensics still got a workout, right?"

Brimley stared at him. "What are you getting at?"

"I'm just asking questions, Sugar, trying to get a sense of things—an immediacy that was missing from most of the newspaper accounts. You were hardly quoted at all."

Brimley leaned against the counter. Backlit from the window behind him, tiny red hairs were visible at the edges of his ear canal. "I was under orders to run all requests through the public information officer and the DA's office. Bosses were afraid I was getting too much attention, and to tell you the truth, that was fine with me. I was never a glory hog."

Jimmy sat down, dizzy again. "The man who called in the noise complaint that night—the screams—I was hoping to interview him, but I couldn't find his name in any of the news accounts."

"You find him, let me know—I'd like to buy him a prime rib dinner."

"He never came forward?"

Brimley shook his head. "Sometimes an anonymous tip wants to remain anonymous. The tabloids put out a reward for him to come forward and tell his story, but all they got was crackpots and phonies."

"Hermosa Beach has Caller ID on their 911 system, don't they?"

"Call came in from a pay phone a couple blocks away. We figured it was somebody out walking their dog—jogging or roller-skating maybe." Sugar eyed the apple pie on the counter. "I canvased the area, but nothing came of it."

"Interesting that a jogger heard screams from the house but not the neighbors."

"You did your homework, I like that. Neighbor on one side was out of town, people on the other side had their air-conditioning turned up. I never cared much for air-conditioning myself. Not natural. Besides, a little sweat never hurt anybody."

Jimmy carefully sipped his coffee, biding his time. Getting beaten up had given him an advantage; there was no way Brimley was going to rush him now, and Jimmy had learned that letting someone help you was one of the best ways to ensure their cooperation. He often started difficult interviews with a simple request: a glass of water, an aspirin, a pen to use in place of his own, which had "suddenly" gone dry. Brimley was easy; he was helpful by nature. Jimmy crossed his legs, winced.

"You all right?"

"I'm not going to be dancing the tango for a few days, but I'm fine."

"Tango—that's the national dance of Brazil. Gosh, I'd love to see Rio."

"Argentina," Jimmy corrected him. "Brazil is more like the samba, bossa nova."

" 'Blame it on the bossa nova,' " Brimley singsonged, snapping his fingers, his voice light as he danced around the kitchen, holding an invisible partner around the waist.

Jimmy had to laugh at the big man's smooth moves and his self-assurance in showing them off, not caring what anyone thought. It made him like the old cop. "You should take a trip to Brazil. A friend of mine was born and raised in Rio—she's a travel agent. I could put you in touch with her. She'll get you there cheap, find you a hotel on the water, and line you up with some great fishing. She knows every-body."

"I might just take you up on that. Brazil. They have fish down there I've only read about, game fish that put my marlin to shame." Brimley sat down, beaming now. "What's your name again? Jimmy who?"

"Gage."

"Jimmy Gage. I know that name. You did something a while ago— I remember seeing you on TV." Brimley stared at Jimmy, nodded. "You saved a cop's life. That was it. I don't remember what you did exactly, but it was a big deal."

"Right place, right time, that's all."

"That's plenty." Brimley patted Jimmy's knee. "Sorry you had to take your lumps, but meeting you sure turned out lucky for me. I don't usually get to meet a genuine hero."

Jimmy let the hero crap pass. "You must have been born under a good sign, Sugar. 'One Lucky Cop'—that was the headline in the

News-Herald the next day. They said you were on your way home after your shift change when the call came."

"We still used two-way radios back then. Now calls come in to squad cars on the computer. Whole new world."

"I just thought it was strange for a detective to follow up on a noise complaint himself."

"Hermosa is a small department; we covered for each other whenever we could, and I've never been one to stand on ceremony. The nearest squad car that evening was investigating a report of gunshots fired, and I was in the area." Brimley shrugged. "Don't think those two uniforms didn't rub it in; they should have been the one getting the commendation and their picture in the paper, not me. 'One Lucky Cop'—gee whiz, I thought I'd never live it down."

Jimmy laughed along with him, but not too hard. His head *did* hurt.

"Maybe I should take you home. We can get together when you're feeling better."

"Just let me sit here a few more minutes."

"Stay as long as you want."

"One thing I never understood. Was what Heather Grimm was doing in Hermosa, anyway? She lived in Whittier. Why didn't she go to Huntington? It's closer, and it's a better beach too."

"If you want help figuring out the mind of a fifteen-year-old girl, you're on your own."

"That's what I mean, she was fifteen. She wouldn't go to the beach by herself. She was too young to drive. So who drove her there?"

"I asked her mother the same thing myself. She said Heather drove herself to Hermosa Beach that day. It wasn't legal, but neither is tossing a gum wrapper on the sidewalk. Mrs. Grimm was raising Heather on her own, working double shifts as a waitress, doing her best. Heather used to drop her mama off at the restaurant around eleven, then pick her up again at ten that evening. Mrs. Grimm said most days Heather went to the beach, she took a girlfriend or two along for company. No boys, Mama was adamant about that—no boys in the house when she wasn't there, no boys in the car."

"Did you talk to any of her girlfriends?"

"Mrs. Grimm is dead now. Less than a year after Heather was killed. Officially she overdosed on her prescription medicine, but if you ask me, she died of a broken heart. That girl was her whole world."

Jimmy remembered the crime scene photos of Heather Grimm, her skull shattered, bone and brain matter on the carpet. Mrs. Grimm would have had to identify the body too. *Yes, that's my daughter.*

"You okay, Jimmy? You don't look so good again."

Jimmy cleared his throat. "You said forensics gave the scene the full treatment."

"We're back to forensics?" Brimley chuckled. "I need a scorecard with you."

Jimmy put the ice pack against his face again. "Did they find any prints that didn't belong to either Walsh or Heather Grimm?"

"Plenty. Cleaning lady, furniture movers—some of the actors working on that film of his, the last one, whatever it was called. I guess they had a party one time. The crime scene detail said they hoovered enough cocaine out of the rugs to—"

"What about Mick Packard? Did you find his prints there?"

Brimley did a mock karate chop. "Marvelous Mick? I don't remember. I like that guy's movies. Whatever happened to him?"

"I may be seeing him in a few days. If you want, I'll get his autograph for you. He'd probably be thrilled."

"That's all right. After the Heather Grimm case . . . let's just say I lost my respect for Hollywood. All those pretty faces getting interviewed, talking about what a talent Walsh was—it made me sick."

"The crime scene report just said the prints of 'persons known and unknown' had been found in the cottage."

"You say you're writing a story about Walsh, but you keep asking questions about fingerprints and Mick Packard, and did I do this and did I do that." Brimley scratched his head. "I guess I'm confused. What's going on?"

Jimmy loved the head-scratching routine, the prelude to the amiable old cop asking for help. "I know I'm not making a lot of sense."

He shifted the ice pack slightly. "Maybe we can talk more when I'm feeling better. We could get together at Walsh's beach house. You could take me on a walkaround. I'd really appreciate—"

"I'd like to help, but I got no special pull with the new owners. A few years ago one of those *True Police Stories* TV shows was going to do a reenactment, but they couldn't get permission to film inside the cottage. Not for love or money. The people who owned it said any kind of publicity just drove down their property value. Can't blame them—no one wants to be reminded that they're living in a slaughterhouse."

"We could do it *outside* then. Just being there with you, talking about what happened that night—you've got a perspective that no one else does."

Brimley was looking out the window again, lost in thought.

"I want people to know what you saw when Walsh opened the door, what you saw when you walked inside."

Brimley turned to face him, and Jimmy glimpsed the other side of the sweetness, the weight and power held in check. "It's all in my report. Isn't that good enough for you?"

"I trust a cop's memory more than any report he wrote for the brass. The question is, Sugar, do you trust *me*? Do you trust me to do right by you? And do right by Heather Grimm too? I wouldn't blame you if you didn't. I'm sure you've been burned by reporters before— everybody has. I could sit here trying to convince you that I'm worth your time and your trust, but I'm going to go home, lie down on the couch, and watch a ball game. When we get together again, I hope we can do it at the beach house."

Brimley chewed it over and finally nodded. "Don't pin me down on a time and date, though. The bluefin are running off San Luis Obispo, and I promised myself I'd get me one."

"You call the shots. Oh yeah, one more thing."

Brimley's eyes narrowed, his instincts sharp enough to know he wasn't going to like it.

"When we do the walkaround at the beach house, would you mind bringing your notes?"

"You can get them from legal affairs. Just put in a written request."

"I meant your field notes."

Sugar laughed. "You want to see my tax returns and high-school transcript too?"

"I'm trying to get it right, Sugar. You don't have to show me the notes. Having them along might help put you back to what you saw, what you *felt* that night, the little details that didn't make it into the official report. You don't have to commit yourself now. Just bring them along. You can decide then if you trust me with them."

"I bet most folks have a hard time telling you no."

"Look who's talking."

Brimley shared a tiny smile with him. "I'll give you a call in a week or so, but don't get your hopes up about the notes. Hero or no hero."

Jimmy left his card on the coffee table and stood up. "Call me anytime, day or night." They shook hands, Jimmy feeling lost in Brimley's grip.

"Let me give you a ride home."

"I'm okay to drive." Jimmy had to hang on to the counter. He had stood up too fast.

"I'll take you home. You can get a buddy to bring you back here tomorrow and pick up your wheels."

Jimmy sat down again and rested his head in his hands.

Brimley patted him on the shoulder. "Don't worry. I'll keep an eye on your car for you. What are you driving?"

Chapter 23

"I don't know how you found me, but make it snappy," said Lashonda, pacing, a black wireless microphone dangling from her earpiece. All twelve phone lines on her board were blinking. "You got five minutes, and that's only 'cause you say you going to write something nice about Sugar."

Jimmy followed her as she walked her spacious living room in Pacific Palisades, the house a half-acre view property with a swimming pool and a tennis court. "You were the police dispatcher who took that 911 call on the Heather Grimm homicide."

"Weren't no homicide call." Lashonda listened to her earpiece as the board switched lines again. It was on a thirty-second interval—Jimmy had timed it. "It was a four one five domestic disturbance call. Wasn't till Sugar got there, it turned into a homicide call."

"Right."

"What happened to your face? You ask somebody a question they didn't like?"

Jimmy smiled, and it hurt. One side of his face was still swollen from his pick-up basketball game with the Butcher, his eye blackened. "The reason that Sugar took the call that night—"

"'Cause lazyass Reese and Hargrove was on another call and wasn't in no hurry to take a four one five. Sugar broke in, told me he was in the area. Everybody knows that." Lashonda peered at Jimmy over her half-glasses, a well-dressed, smooth-skinned black woman with four-inch nails and a turban of hair rising high above her head. "You wasting my time."

"Sugar was off shift. Did he jump in like that very often?"

"Teresa, you blowing it," Lashonda said, talking to someone on the end of the microphone. "The client wants to talk about himself, and you keep bringing up your own damn aura." She looked at Jimmy. "Why you asking how many times Sugar grabbed calls after he went off shift?"

"I told you—"

"Don't you *ever* say you sorry, Marvin," said Lashonda. "If you say her daddy on the other side, wants to let her know he's fine, and she tell you her daddy is driving an Oakland city bus, you don't say you made a mistake. You say, sometimes you see things before they happen, but that don't make them less true. Lashonda's Spiritual Hotline *never* wrong. You got it?" She looked at Jimmy again. "I know what you told me, mister. If I was stupid, I'd still be answering police calls instead of working for myself." Her face flattened out with anger. "This about Sugar's pension? You trying to get him in trouble after all this time, just 'cause he grabbed a little overtime once in a while?"

"No."

"Sugar's a good man, he don't talk down to a body. Not like some of them police, looking down on woman, making cracks, thinking he was high and mighty because he carried a gun and a badge. Sugar—" Lashonda wagged a finger at someone who wasn't there. "Deborah, you being too specific. Not France. *Travel.* Not quit his job. *Experience life changes.* Another thing, girl, you talking too fast. At four-ninety-nine a minute, don't be in any hurry." She looked at Jimmy. "Sugar was real people. He didn't hold himself any better than the rest of us."

"Lashonda, I don't care if Sugar got paid overtime or not. I just want to know if he freelanced calls on a regular basis. Just to help out."

"Sugar Brimley was one fine policeman. Most of them, when they clocked out, they was gone. Not Sugar. He was always ready to fill in.

You need help, Sugar was your man." Lashonda pressed the ear-piece, listening, waving Jimmy away.

Jimmy headed for the front door. He was grateful to Brimley for saving him from the Butcher, but the idea of an off-duty cop grabbing a call, a detective no less—it had made him wonder. His hand on the doorknob, he looked back at Lashonda overseeing her network of psychic counselors, impressed at the way she could keep a dozen calls going in her head, orchestrating the give-and-take, the need for reassurance. For answers. Jimmy could use a few answers himself.

Chapter 24

Jimmy found Samantha Packard's red Jaguar—license plate number 863 YSA, according to the DMV—in the parking lot of the Santa Monica Pro Sports Club. He drove right past it and eased into a slot in visitors' parking.

Jimmy had called Packard's agent that morning hoping to get a home phone number, but Packard had been dropped two years ago, according to the receptionist. She directed him to a smaller agency. The agent there was giddy at Jimmy's interest, suggesting that the three of them sit down for lunch and talk about Packard's next project. Jimmy had told her that he was just quote-checking for a piece on Garrett Walsh's funeral. The agent shook off her disappointment after a suitable grieving period and gave him the number.

The two calls Jimmy made to Packard's house were a bust. The housekeeper answered both times, and when he asked to speak to Mrs. Packard, he was told to leave a name and phone number for a return call. He declined. Miss Chatterbox, the society editor at *SLAP*, had been more help, telling Jimmy that Samantha Packard worked out regularly at the Pro Sports Club.

"Can I help you, sir?" The tanning-bed Adonis behind the front desk looked like he had come out of some breeding program that had succeeded beyond its wildest expectations. His white polo shirt had *Sandor* written in small letters above his heart. "Sir?"

"I'm considering joining. I'd like a tour of the facility."

"Do you have an appointment?"

"No."

"You should have made an appointment."

"I feel bad about that too."

Sandor didn't react. He stared at Jimmy and finally came around the back of the desk, replaced by a female of the same perfect species who appeared from a nearby alcove. For all Jimmy knew there were hundreds of them stacked up back there, an army of glorious beings in white shorts and polo shirts programmed to say "May I help you?" without really meaning it.

"Thanks," said Jimmy.

"You should have made an appointment," Sandor repeated as he sauntered past the marble entryway. He glanced over at Jimmy. "I can see why you're interested though. You have decent muscle bellies, but you're not doing anything with them."

"I know." Jimmy had no idea what a muscle belly was.

"The initiation fee is ten thousand dollars. Dues are four hundred a month," said Sandor. "You still want the tour?"

"Absolutely."

"Good for you. Fitness is the best investment a person can make."

They walked through the men's locker room, Sandor reciting statistics in a dry monotone: four single-sex Jacuzzis, two saunas, a private aromatherapy spa, and three hundred individual lockers. Jimmy noted four TVs in the waiting room, all of them tuned to business channels. No sports. He commented on that, but Sandor said he didn't understand what Jimmy's point was.

Sandor pushed open the doors to the locker room, almost knocked down an older man in a three-piece suit, and walked on without apologizing.

"This is the coed weight room," said Sandor, leading Jimmy through the large, well-lit, immaculate room filled with Nautilus, Hydro-Press, and every other form of resistance equipment made. The floor was deeply cushioned, and all the walls were mirrored. Jimmy showed interest in everything, looking around while Sandor continued his spiel. There were plenty of people in the weight room, most of them beautiful fit women in skimpy, high-fashion breathable fabrics, but he didn't see Samantha Packard.

They toured the tennis courts, the squash courts, the four swimming pools, and the six aerobics studios. No Samantha Packard. Jimmy was just about to ask Sandor if he knew her when he spotted her through a large widow, doing yoga asanas in a room full of other women. She was sweating. They all were sweating. The yoga mats were covered with thick towels, and the window dripped with steam. From the moment he walked into the Pro Sports Club, Jimmy had not seen anyone sweat—the air-conditioning was frigid. So why was Samantha Packard sweating?

Sandor tapped the glass. "Thermal yoga," he explained. "Thermostat in the room is set at a hundred and ten degrees. Keeps the muscles limber and pushes out the toxins."

"Must be a regular Love Canal in there."

"You need to bulk up more than you need yoga," said Sandor. "Let me show you—"

"I'd like to stick around here for a few more minutes and see what's going on."

Sandor checked his watch. "I wanted to show you the virtual-reality stationary bike stations. You can bicycle across the Alps or twenty different cities in the world."

Jimmy watched Samantha Packard bending backward, hands clasped over her head. Her leotard was soaked, her dark shoulder-length hair lank against her neck. He remembered his brother, Jonathan, doing yoga exercises in the ocean off Newport Beach early one morning, the water so cold Jimmy could barely feel his feet after walking out to him.

"We should move along," said Sandor.

"That's Samantha Packard," said Jimmy, pointing. "I think I'll stick around until the class lets out. I'd like to talk to her about the club, see how she likes it."

Sandor seemed uncomfortable. "That's not a good idea."

"It's all right. Samantha and I have met before."

"Then wait and meet her again off premises. We can't afford the liability."

Jimmy waved to Samantha Packard through the steamed glass. She pretended not to see him, folding her hands in front of her chest. Praying for a cool breeze, maybe.

"I wouldn't do that if I were you. Her husband shows up as soon as the class is over. He's very . . . protective. I try to stay out of his way. We all do."

"Really?" Jimmy pretended surprise. "Mick seems pretty relaxed to me."

"You know Mr. Packard?" Sandor squinted. "I don't think so. If you knew Mr. Packard, you wouldn't be waving at his wife."

Chapter 25

"You are early." The man's disapproval was evident even through the intercom.

"Traffic was light. If you want, I can circle the driveway for fifteen or twenty minutes, but I have to warn you, I need a new muffler."

The intercom was silent. Then Jimmy heard the elevator descending. The doors opened, and he stepped in. He could see the Pacific Ocean sparkling as he rode the glass elevator up eighty or ninety feet to Michael Danziger's house, an ugly modernist assemblage of planes and cubes perched atop the highest of the Malibu Hills. He stood in the center of the private elevator, watching the ground rapidly fall away under him as he rose into the morning sun. When the doors slid open, he was still blinking.

A slim man cinched into a red jacket glared at him as the doors slid open, but Jimmy didn't apologize. He liked being early for interviews. Sometimes he would be asked to wait, but usually he got ushered in, and the time dislocation slightly tilted the emotional playing field in his favor. The man in the red jacket turned on his heel.

Jimmy followed him along the outside of the house and out onto a huge redwood deck. He could see almost to Santa Barbara to the northwest, the dry brown hills shimmering with heat. L.A. was spread out across the southeast, wrapped in freeways, half hidden under a haze of smog, but Danziger's house was serenely above the carcinogenic fog. West was the Pacific, dark and deep and teeming with cold-blooded life.

The man in the red jacket bent down on one knee, seeming to speak into the deck.

Closer now, Jimmy could see a twelve-foot-long rectangular jet-pool built into the redwood. A man was hanging onto the side, water churning around him.

The man flipped a switch, and the water stopped. He pushed his swim goggles back onto his forehead. "You're early," he said to Jimmy, smiling. "I hope you don't mind if I finish my workout. Raymond will bring you orange juice or coffee. We can talk over breakfast when I'm done."

Raymond tugged his jacket, shot Jimmy a dirty look, then headed toward the house.

Danziger hit the switch again. Powerful jets pushed him to the back of the pool. He trod water, tugged his goggles back into place, and started swimming against the artificial current.

Jimmy sat down at the patio table nearest the pool. Danziger was a strong swimmer, with a powerful kick and an economical freestyle stroke—his mouth barely cleared the surface of the water to take a breath. Raymond came out after a few minutes with a glass pitcher of fresh-squeezed orange juice and two thick cut-crystal tumblers, leaving as silently as he had come. Jimmy sipped at his juice, watching Danziger; he knew the jet-pool was an efficient way to get a workout, but Jimmy didn't like treadmills. It made him feel like a gerbil. Not that the thermal yoga class at the Pro Sports Club was any more appealing—he could still see the water droplets running down the inside of the glass, Samantha Packard avoiding his gaze through the steam. He had waited in the parking lot, hoping that she would come out to her car alone, but Mick Packard had accompanied her, swaggering, one hand clasped on her arm. Jimmy thought he saw Samantha glance around as she eased into the car, but he couldn't be sure. Maybe Michael Danziger could tell him what he needed to know.

Danziger had been head of production at Epic International, the studio chief who had hired Garrett Walsh to make *Hammerlock* after he won those two Academy Awards, the man who had greenlighted the film and okayed the budget—the man who had ultimately taken the fall for that debacle and several other high-profile failures. Danziger had been eased out five years later in a bloodless coup, given a cushy severance package and an independent production deal with the studio. He had produced three pictures since leaving EI, none of which had made money.

Jimmy finished his orange juice, slowly chewing the pulp. Restless now, he got up and walked to the edge of the deck, leaning against the railing. A hawk drifted overhead, riding the thermals, and Jimmy could see a woman horseback-riding along a nearby ridge, riding easily in jeans and a creamy white shirt, her long, dark braid flopping against her shoulders. Horses scared the shit out of him. They were too big, too strong, and just smart enough to sense that he was intimidated. He watched the woman until he heard the jet-pool suddenly stop, and turned back.

Danziger put his hands on the edge of the pool and easily launched himself onto the deck. He stood there dripping in the sunshine, goggles pushed back, water glistening across his tan. His bio listed him as fifty-three, but he was still broad chested, lean and muscular, an aging preppy, handsome as any of the stars of his recent flops. Raymond appeared with a white terrycloth robe and held it out while Danziger stepped into it, then knotted it insouciantly around his waist. "Nothing like a swim to get the blood flowing. You look like you work out yourself, Mr. Gage."

"It's Jimmy, and yeah—I play a little basketball."

"I'm not much for team sports myself." Danziger waved at the patio table. "Shall we?"

Raymond ferried a carafe of espresso to the table, poured Danziger orange juice, then set a half-papaya dabbed with nonfat vanilla yogurt before each of them.

"If there's anything you'd like, just let Raymond know," said Danziger, spooning out papaya, stopping halfway to his mouth. "Did you get your invitation to the press screening of *My Girl Trouble*?"

"I did."

"There's been some negative buzz. I don't know who starts these things, but I hope you'll approach the film with an open mind."

Danziger smiled. "That sounds rather desperate, doesn't it? In fact, I'm quite confident that the film will find its audience. We tested very well among single women aged twenty-two to thirty-six." He blotted his lips with the napkin. "Still, anything you could do to help would be appreciated."

"I'm not reviewing many films these days, but I'd be happy to mention it in my article."

Danziger scraped the last of the orange-colored flesh away from the rind. "This article you're doing . . ."

"It's about *Hammerlock*. I'm using the production as a metaphor for the grand ambition and ultimate destruction of Garrett Walsh."

"*Hammerlock?*" The water beaded along Danziger's eyebrows gleamed in the sun. "Why would I want to rehash one of my worst failures?"

"I thought you got a bad rap on that."

"Tell that to the board of directors of Epic International." Danziger looked off toward the ocean, and Jimmy followed him.

Fishing boats bobbed in the far distance, heading out toward Catalina, and Jimmy thought of Sugar Brimley, wondered what he was catching today. Jimmy had called a couple of times in the last few days, checking in, hoping to prod the retired detective into sharing his files, but his calls hadn't been returned. He watched the boats shimmer at the edge of his vision, losing definition until they were indefinable from the water.

"I'd be happy to help you with your article," said Danziger. "I'll have my office send you a press kit on *My Girl Trouble* too. Just in case."

"Sounds good." Jimmy pulled out a mini-recorder and set it on the table between them. "I've talked to some of the crew. They say the production was in trouble early on, and most of them blame the fact that the cameras started rolling before there was a completed script." He looked at Danziger. "Wasn't that a bit—optimistic of you? Okaying a ninety-million-dollar film without a script?"

"Optimistic?" Danziger shook his head. "It was *insane*, but after the success of Walsh's first film, every studio in town was eager to hand him a blank check. He actually got better offers than mine from some of the majors, but Walsh and I hit it off. He said he thought he could work with me." He leaned toward Jimmy. "And for your information, *Hammerlock* was originally slated for sixty-five million. It was supposed to be a six-months shoot; Walsh was arrested during the tenth month, and it *still* wasn't finished."

"I met Walsh just once. It was after he got out of prison, and he was pretty messed up, living in a rusty trailer, strung out on pills and booze. What was he like before?"

"Ambitious, egotistical, demanding, volatile, insecure." Danziger stirred his espresso. "Brilliant, insightful, generous, and *funny,* God, he used to make me laugh. Garrett was the most talented individual I ever met. I'll never forgive him for throwing it all away."

"Were you aware that he was using when you signed him to direct *Hammerlock?*"

"If abstinence from drugs were a prerequisite, Hollywood would be run by Mormons." Danziger shrugged. "I thought he had it under control. *Garrett* thought he had it under control. We were both wrong."

"His arrest cost the studio millions, but you stood up for him at his sentencing. That took a lot of courage. I read the editorials afterward. The papers mocked you for pleading for leniency; they said you were hoping to salvage *Hammerlock.*"

"I stood up for Garrett because I believed in his talent. He wrecked my picture, he put my job in jeopardy, and he killed a young girl, but he was a great artist. The film business is filled with hacks who consider themselves artists, but Garrett was the real thing."

"Walsh was working on a screenplay after he was released. Did he contact you about it?"

"Right after he got out. I told him he'd have to try someplace else."

"I'm surprised."

"So was he. I told him that even if I still ran a studio, I'd have a hard time selling a Garrett Walsh project to the executive committee. Not because he killed that girl. You know this town; we believe in second chances, as long as you put enough asses in the seats. No,

Garrett committed the one unforgivable sin: he cost the studio money." His eyes were cool, still faintly ringed with red from his swim goggles. "Maybe if I were still running EI, I could have thrown him a bone, a low-budget feature or a direct-to-video for the foreign market, but I don't work there anymore. When I left the studio, I got a three-picture, first-look deal with them. That's over now. I don't even have a production office on the lot anymore. I had to raise the capital for *My Girl Trouble* from Europe."

Jimmy looked around at Danziger's mansion. "I guess the secret of being an independent producer is never to tap your own bank account."

"One of them." Danziger had a great set of choppers, white and flat, fakes so perfect that they looked natural.

"During the shooting of *Hammerlock*, the papers were filled with stories about the rapport between Walsh and Mick Packard. They supposedly liked going out together after work, street racing their Ferraris, and hitting the joints. I heard a different story from people who worked the shoot. They said the set was toxic, that Walsh and Packard hated each other."

Danziger looked at Jimmy, amused.

"You can be as off the record as you want. I just want to know what happened."

"Let's just say that the publicist assigned to the project was paid six thousand dollars a week, and she was worth every penny of it."

Jimmy picked at his plate, allowing the silence to sit there.

"The package looked good when we first were negotiating," explained Danziger. "Mick had box office, but no credibility with the critics; Garrett had credibility, but had never worked on a big-budget film before. At first things went well." His laugh was warm and confident. "But by the second day . . ."

"Did they have differences about the direction of the film, screen time?"

"Oh, there was more than enough ego to go around, but that's true of any shoot. You *expect* the talent to butt heads. In fact, the most maddening aspect of the failure of the film was that Mick had never done better work. I got involved about midway through the shoot, and the dailies were incredible. Who knew Mick could act? *Garrett* did— the only chemistry between the two of them was *bad* chemistry, but Garrett got things out of Mick that no director had done before or since." Danziger turned his face into the breeze from the west. He had a great profile. "The problem was tying all the footage together. Garrett kept reshooting scenes that were already perfect. It wasn't that he was displeased with the performances—he just kept changing his mind about the plot. There were so many twists. I don't think even *he* knew where it was going."

"Is that why you started showing up on set? A studio chief that makes house calls—that doesn't happen very often."

"I had no choice. Garrett ignored my memos and barely spoke to me when I got him on the phone. I should have fired him, but we were in too deep by that point. When I showed up, I found all these useless people, Mick's entourage, Garrett's entourage. That software fellow who bankrolled his first feature—*he* was there, for God's sake, and don't ask me why. Eyeballing the starlets, probably. Garrett had so many of them lined up, he should have assigned them numbers—except that would have taken away the pleasure of playing them off against each other. Garrett and his little intrigues."

Jimmy hadn't heard about the software entrepreneur being on the set. "The women. Was there anyone in particular?"

"With Garrett? You must be kidding." Danziger massaged an acupressure point at the base of his skull with a knuckle. "Are you referring to the coke whore?"

Jimmy had no idea what Danziger was talking about.

Danziger allowed himself a slight frown. "One of Garrett's dealers had a girlfriend, a spectacular woman from what I heard. Evidently Garrett got a little frisky with the lady in question at a party, and the lady was . . . receptive. Shortly thereafter Garrett alerted studio security to double-check the passes of anyone wanting access to the set."

"Are you sure she was the dealer's girlfriend? Could she have been his wife?"

Danziger chuckled. "I don't know. Do drug dealers have wives?"

"Did Walsh mention the dealer's name?"

"Hardly."

Jimmy didn't like the way Danziger took pleasure in telling him no. He was probably a real thrill in a pitch meeting, getting a pedicure while some screenwriter crawled. "Walsh was pretty up front about his escapades. It sounds like he enjoyed his reputation. But did you ever hear of him having any *secret* affairs?"

"I didn't keep track. I only know that he wasn't fucking the blonde playing Mick's sister, because *Mick* was already fucking her."

"Is that why Samantha Packard wasn't working on the film?" Jimmy tried to ignore Danziger's amused expression. "I went over the call sheets for *Hammerlock* and couldn't find any record of her."

"You went over the call sheets?" Danziger applauded. "I wish my assistant were as thorough as you are. If you ever need a job, give me a call."

"Did Samantha Packard know that her husband was screwing his costar?"

Danziger allowed himself a thin smile. "Samantha knows how the game is played."

"She didn't care?"

"Wives *always* care. The smart ones know better than to make too much out of an on-set romance, and Samantha was smart. She was supposed to have a small part in *Hammerlock,* but shortly after Garrett started filming, she was written out."

"Whose idea was that?"

"I don't know, but it was no great loss to cinematic history, I can assure you." Danziger checked his watch. "I have to leave for my office shortly, but if the thrust of your article is sexual tension on the set, you might consider a sidebar on *My Girl Trouble.*" He inclined his head—it was supposed to look conspiratorial, but it came out wolfish. "Just between the two of us, Jimmy, I liked it better in the old days, when people were either hetero or homo and never the twain shall meet. Try getting anything accomplished with a cast of switchhitters. The permutations are dizzying."

Chapter 26

Jimmy waited outside the side exit of the Pro Sports Club, bent over, pretending to tie his tennis shoes. About ten minutes later, his back aching, the door swung open, and a florid man walked out, already on his cell phone, his squash racket under one arm. Jimmy caught the door before it closed and slipped inside, his gym bag slung over one shoulder. "Left my keys in my locker," he said to an attendant restocking the juice machine, walking purposely toward the locker room he remembered from his visit two days earlier.

He walked through the locker room, grabbed a clean towel from the stack, and took the stairs to the second floor. Samantha Packard's thermal yoga class was supposed to start in a few minutes. He checked out the hallway. Sandor, the attendant who had given him the tour, said that Mick Packard was always on hand when the class let out; Jimmy wanted to make certain that he didn't drop her off too. Women in thin, baggy cotton pants and tops were filing into the room, and warm moist air drifted out into the hallway.

Samantha was in the back corner of the room, just where she had been before. She was standing on a mat doing slow neck rolls, sweat rolling down her face. No Mick.

Jimmy slipped through the door. The warmth of the room made him gasp, the air so hot and thick that breathing it felt like breathing through a wet towel. Soft music burbled over the sound system. Every pore in his body was wide open, his workout clothes were already soaked, and the back of his hair was dripping.

A slender middle-aged woman looked at him. "Try breathing through your nose."

Jimmy edged toward the back of the room, trying to follow her suggestion. It still felt like there wasn't enough oxygen in the place. He could see Samantha standing on one leg, her eyes closed, her other leg tucked behind her. She was a long-limbed brunette with full lips, and her deep tan looked like beaten bronze in the heat.

Most of the people in the class were fit women in their thirties and forties, barefoot and without makeup, their eyes clear and enthusiastic as they went through their warm-up routines, some of them meditating. The teacher, a tall, skinny man, chatted with two of the students, checking their posture.

"Nice to see you again," Jimmy said to Samantha.

Samantha opened her eyes and jerked back, losing her poise. She stood on two legs now, breathing hard. Scared.

Jimmy spread his towel on the floor, sweat stinging his eyes as he bent down. "I wanted to give the class a try, but I don't know now. Isn't this what it's supposed to be like on the surface of Venus?"

"Are—are you a member here?"

"I'm Jimmy Gage. We met at Garrett Walsh's funeral."

"I know who you are," Samantha said, her voice so soft that it barely disturbed the air molecules in that stifling room. "My husband didn't like the way you were looking at me. I didn't like it either."

"I need to talk to you."

Samantha glanced toward the hallway window. "I don't think it's a good idea." She blotted her forehead. Her diamond wedding ring flashed in the dim light.

"I know about you and Walsh." Jimmy could see a vein at the base of her neck throbbing. She smelled as healthy and steamy as a racehorse, her face glowing, nervous as a racehorse too. "We have to talk. Can we get out of here for—"

"There's nothing to talk about." Samantha glanced again at the window.

"I'm not trying to hurt you."

"Then *don't*. Garrett and I . . . that was a long time ago. I don't want to see my name in print."

"This isn't about an article. I'm here because I want you to know that it wasn't an accident. No matter what you read, his death—he didn't drown."

Samantha stared at him.

There was a clap from the front of the room. Class had started. Everyone was on their feet now, facing the yoga teacher, his voice deep and mellifluous as he ordered them to stretch for the stars in search of their center.

"*Please go,*" said Samantha. "You're going to get me in trouble."

"I'm trying to help you." Jimmy moved closer to her, whispering. "I know about the letter you wrote to him. I know about the tapes—"

"I didn't write Garrett any letter."

"Listen to me. It was no accident. Walsh was murdered."

Sweat streamed down her arms as Samantha stretched toward the ceiling. "I haven't cared whether Garrett was alive or dead for a long time."

"I know better, Samantha."

"It's *Mrs. Packard.*"

"The good wife—that's what Garrett Walsh called you. I spoke with him a few days before he was killed. He loved you."

Samantha Packard shook her head. "No, he didn't. I wish he had, but—"

"Speech is a distraction," intoned the teacher. "Ego is a distraction. Pay attention only to the emptiness within."

Jimmy moved closer to Samantha Packard, not caring who saw them, wanting her to admit what he already knew. He felt claustrophobic in the heat, the moist air closing in on him. "He loved you, Samantha. It cost him everything, but it didn't stop him."

"Love is not a term Garrett ever used in my presence. Not once. Not *ever.*" Samantha Packard managed to speak without moving her facial muscles. In tandem with the rest of the class, she slowly bent forward, back flat, her arms pointed backward. "Now get out of here."

"I think you're in danger."

"You're the one who's *putting* me in danger."

"I'll leave my card at the front desk."

"Don't do that."

"Call me at the magazine then."

The yoga teacher stalked over to Jimmy. "You're upsetting the harmonics of the class." His hands waved in the air, and Jimmy thought of machetes hacking at jungle undergrowth. "Be silent, or be gone."

Jimmy reached for his towel. "Call me," he said to Samantha, but she didn't look at him.

Chapter 27

The shot was always the same: interior, Walsh's beach cottage, moderate-wide angle. The camera lens was tiny, and you lost a little resolution because of it, but he didn't mind—the images had their own awful clarity. He preferred watching through half-closed eyes, dreamlike, led along by the sound of their voices, imagining them before the camera started, winding their way to the rendezvous. Walsh would have parked in the cottage's single garage, of course, while *she* parked a few blocks away, off the main streets, window-shopping on her way over perhaps, making sure she hadn't been followed, then a hurried dash across the street and inside, home sweet home away from home.

He sat back in the chair as the footage ran, eyes closed now, listening. He could hear Walsh blustering about the day's shoot, and she was telling him she didn't care. Walsh liked that—her disinterest excited him almost as much as the fact that she was another man's wife. *His* wife. She sounded slightly out of breath now, saying something about not having much time, not nearly enough time, but she couldn't stay away, and Walsh groaned, and if the two of them had been closer to the microphone, he might have been able to hear the slide of a zipper. On some of the recordings he heard sounds like that—zippers and shoes dropping, sometimes even the tearing of fabric, along with the grunts and groans, the cries, the desperate urgency, the whole fucking symphony.

The audio on this particular recording didn't pick up such small details. There was only a single surveillance camera in the one-room cottage, a miniature camera/microphone seamlessly fitted into a wall sconce that faced the bed. It was a remarkable piece of equipment, the high-resolution lens the size of a BB, the lovers' sounds and images digitally captured and transmitted instantly to his recorder across the city. No tapes in the cottage to change, none to retrieve. A sound technician on one of his films had installed the remote camera for him in a single afternoon. The man was a Russian on a temporary visa, a former KGB drone probably, eager to curry favor. He was sent packing when his visa expired just the same.

His wife's voice was louder now. In a moment he would hear the sound of Walsh opening a bottle of champagne. He didn't need to open his eyes; he knew the recordings by heart. Every sound. Every image. He had had the original tapes transferred onto forty-seven DVDs so the images would never degrade. Not ever. Forty-seven separate incidents of adultery, each one identified by the date. A time capsule of deceit. He had had seven years to memorize the recordings. To savor them. To torture himself with them. He heard a champagne cork pop. Right on schedule. Popping champagne was déclassé, a waste of the natural effervescence, but Walsh was a prole with a two-picture deal, a janitor blessed with a vivid imagination. Walsh whooped, pouring, and his wife laughed.

On some of the DVDs their voices were eager, in some they were playful, and in some, particularly the early ones, they were circumspect, nervous even. Always though, *always,* on each and every one, there was a tumescent ripple of guilt in their voices, the titillation of betrayal in their whispers. Sometimes he even heard his name mentioned. Yes, even that.

He opened his eyes. His timing was perfect. Onscreen his wife was splayed nude on the leather sofa, her back arched, her legs wide as Walsh grazed at her vagina. One of her legs was thrown over his shoulder, her foot against the back of his neck, driving his face deeper into her.

Chapter 28

"Say *star.*" Chase Gooding cocked her head against Jimmy, impaling him with her smile. *"Staaaaar."*

"Star." Jimmy blinked as the Polaroid flashed and spit out a photo.

"Thank you," said Chase Gooding, taking the photo and the camera from the boy. "Back on stage now." She clapped her hands. "Wings on your feet, fly, fly!" She watched him scamper down the aisle of the tiny theater, one eye on the developing photo. "Vegetables, from the top! Broccoli, with feeling this time!"

Rows of children dressed as broccoli, carrots, and asparagus marched raggedly across the stage, singing about vitamins and beta-carotene, and all Jimmy could think of was that he hadn't dropped acid in years, but his daily life had become increasingly psychedelic. "Your mother sounded strange when I asked if Chastity was there," he said.

"That's the name she and my father came with up. *Chastity.* Yuck. I changed it to Chase when I went into show business."

"Like the bank?"

Chase beamed. "Most people don't pick up on that. Not consciously anyway, but my name works on their subconscious. They associate me with money and power."

"It worked on me. I saw you, and I wanted to take out a loan."

"Is that a joke?"

"I guess not."

The two of them sat in the back row of the Little Stars of Tomorrow theater, a 120-seat auditorium in a strip mall just off the freeway in Whittier, the lobby dotted with photographs of kids dressed as pirates, flowers, and elves. Chase was currently directing a play for the local elementary school on healthy eating and nutrition, which meant that all eight food groups were wearing Velcro sneakers and braces.

It had been a couple days since he had confronted Samantha Packard, and she still hadn't contacted him. He didn't blame her. There was no way to prove she was the good wife, not *yet*, but that didn't mean he couldn't start looking into Heather Grimm, find out how she had ended up on Walsh's beach that day.

Jimmy had had gone through an old Whittier High School yearbook at the library and found a photo of the Thespians Club at the time of her murder. There were twelve girls in the club. "Such a waste," Mrs. Gifford, the Whittier drama teacher, had said when he asked her about Heather. According to the teacher, Heather and Chastity had been best friends, smart and pretty and always in contention for the lead in the school play. She said the last she had heard, Chastity was still living at home with her parents. Jimmy had checked; her parents' number appeared on Walsh's phone records. Jimmy had called immediately; he had introduced himself and said he was working on an article about Heather. He offered to meet with her after work, but she had insisted he attend today's rehearsal.

Chase was twenty-four now, but she hadn't changed much from her yearbook photo, the classic California girl: long-legged and tan, a slim, fresh-faced blonde. She wore white shorts and a man's white dress shirt, with the tails loosely knotted around her midriff. It had probably taken her a half-hour to get the knot to lie so perfectly above her belly button. The Monelli twins would have hated her.

Chase reached under her seat, pulled out a thick scrapbook, and put it on her lap. An *Entertainment Weekly* cover had been pasted on the front of the notebook, with Chase's face superimposed on Julia Roberts's as she accepted the Academy Award. She tapped her photo with a fingernail. "See it, dream it, *be* it—that's my motto."

"You got my vote." Jimmy wasn't humoring her—you had to bet on long shots to have any hope at all. If you ever considered the odds against you, no one would get out of bed in the morning—the whole world would be hiding under the covers.

Chase checked the Polaroid of her and Jimmy as she flipped through the scrapbook, stopping at a section titled "Chase and VIPs." She swiped the back of the photo with a glue stick and carefully affixed it next to a Polaroid of herself standing beside Hugh Hefner in a nightclub, the bunny king waxy and cadaverous, his fake teeth blinding.

"I feel honored."

"I recognized your name as soon as you called. I have a subscription to *SLAP*." Chase turned the pages, showing off photos of herself with Erik Estrada, Heather Locklear, the Channel 13 weatherman, Regis Philbin, Vince Vaughn, Ronald McDonald, Johnnie Cochran, and the woman who played Buffy the Vampire Slayer. "I have subscriptions to twenty-three magazines, although actually they're in my dog's name." She laughed. "That way when the bills come, I just throw them away, and they can't do anything about it."

"Clever."

"Do you know Tom Cruise?"

"Ah, no."

"How about John Travolta?"

"Afraid not."

"Oh, *poo*." Her perfect mouth grimaced for just a moment. "I'm a born-again Christian, but I've heard that Scientology is the most popular religion in Hollywood. I wanted to know if it would be worth it for me to convert. Career-wise speaking, I mean."

"Maybe we could talk about Heather. I can ask around about Scientology for you when I get back to the office, see if it would be a good career move."

She touched him on the wrist, the scrapbook sliding across one bare leg. "That would be so *sweet*." She glanced toward the dancing vegetables. "Junk food! Enter stage left!" She waited until a group of candy bars and chocolate chip cookies had trundled onstage before turning back to him. "Now, where were we?"

"You were going to tell me about you and Heather. Mrs. Gifford said that the two of you were best friends."

"The *very* best." Chase patted her heart to prove it.

"You have a lovely tan. Did you and she used to go to the beach together?"

"Even though you don't know Tom Cruise or John Travolta, I bet working at *SLAP* you still must meet lots of famous people."

"A few."

"That's what I thought. You know, it's *so* interesting you calling me up about Heather after all these years. You won't believe who I got a call from just a couple of months ago. Take a guess."

"Garrett Walsh."

She slapped his knee. "You cheated." She growled for him. It was kind of cute. "Can you believe that man actually called me up and wanted to get together? After what he did to poor Heather? Can you believe that?"

"Did you get a photo of the two of you?"

Chase slapped his knee again, harder this time. "I'm going to have to watch my step with you—you're a smart one." She flipped through the scrapbook to a section titled, "Chase's Brush with Death," and there was a Polaroid of her touching heads with Walsh, the two of them preening for the camera. "I thought he was making a comeback, but look at those clothes of his. He smelled bad too." She brushed the photo with a finger. "I look good though, don't I? You'd think I was having a grand old time with him, but you'd be wrong. That's acting. I have an associate degree in theater arts from Orange Coast College. Four-point-oh average too." She smoothed the page of the scrapbook. "Garrett Walsh asked if I used to go to the beach with Heather, just like you did. He wanted to know if we had ever gone to Hermosa before, and whose idea it was."

"What did you tell him?"

She looked at Jimmy, and her eyes were clear and sweetwater blue. "I told him to fuck off and die." She glanced at the stage. "Junk food!" Candy bars bumped into each other, startled. "I don't feel the danger! Threaten me! I want to feel it!" She turned back to Jimmy. "I saw the picture of you in this month's *SLAP.* I like a good scavenger hunt myself. What does a girl have to do to get invited to one of those parties?"

"I'll talk to Nino."

"Just like that? I always knew it was just a matter of meeting the right person." Chase smiled at him, and it was a shy smile, innocent as milk, but he could see her earlobes flush with blood. She riffed through the scrapbook, stopping at the "Chase and Heather" section. "As you can see, Heather and I were a couple of regular beach rats," she said, pointing out the two of them posing astride the bronze Seal Beach seal. "That last summer anyway." The following pages were filled with snapshots of the two girls lying on the sand, playing Frisbee, and frolicking in the waves. Chase looked younger, but Heather could have passed for eighteen easily—no wonder Walsh had been fooled.

"Where was that one taken?"

"Sunset Beach. We used to hit Sunset regularly. The best boys were there."

"What about Hermosa?"

Chase glanced at the stage, then back at Jimmy. "Couple weeks before—before she died, we started going there. Heather said she was bored with Sunset. I wasn't, but Heather, she always knew best."

"You must have seen Walsh's beach cottage on TV after she was murdered. Is that the area where you used to go?"

Chase nodded. "You wouldn't think such a small house could cost so much money. Do you have a house on the beach too?"

"How did you end up in that particular spot?"

"I don't know. Who remembers things like that? We just parked the car and started walking until we found a place for our towels." Chase tightened the knot in her shirt. "Heather probably was the one who decided. She was very selfish."

"You and Heather went to the beach together all that summer, but not on the day she was murdered."

"We were *supposed* to go to there together, but at the last minute Heather called up, said she was staying home. Just like that. Didn't even apologize. Like my feelings didn't count. Then she goes to Hermosa without me."

"After she was murdered, did you tell anyone about her changing plans?"

"Does Tom Cruise ever show up at those scavenger hunt parties?"

"Did you talk to the police about her changing plans?"

"No, but some man in a nice suit came by the house, said he heard that Heather and I wanted to be in show business. I thought he was an agent or a producer, but my father confronted him, and the man admitted that he was working for one of Walsh's lawyers. My father almost hit him." Chase shook out her hair, and Jimmy smelled her perfume. "Do you believe in guardian angels? Well, if it wasn't for my guardian angel, it would have been *me* murdered in that beach house that day, not Heather."

Jimmy stared at her.

Chase flipped through the scrapbook, her fingers knowing just where to go, right to the section titled "Chase's Beauty Pageant." The first page showed a younger Chase wearing a short evening gown and a bright yellow sash. "I was in the Young Miss Whittier pageant with Heather. She won, and I was first runner-up. I *would* have won, but my face broke out the night before, a real Vesuvius, and all the makeup in the world couldn't cover it up." She touched Jimmy's face. "Men—you can have a black eye, and it makes you look kind of sexy. But for a girl, any imperfection—forget it." She stared at her runner-up photo. "If it wasn't for those zits, *I* would have won, not Heather. Then it would have been me in the beach house with my head broken into pieces."

Jimmy was confused. "You think winning that contest got Heather killed?"

"We prefer *pageant*." Chase turned the page, scanning the photographs of herself and Heather, arms around each other, hugging for the cameras. "Why else would Garrett Walsh have made love to her? She was beautiful, but without that gold crown, she would have been a nobody."

"Chase, how would he have known she was Young Miss Whittier?"

"She would have *told* him, silly. That would have been the first thing out of her mouth." Chase turned the page, distracted now. Most of the photos in this section were of Heather. "I know that's what I would have done."

Jimmy had a headache. The Butcher—Darryl—beat him up with a basketball, Chase did it with conversation. "That last week did Heather seem different? Did she talk about anyone new that she had met?"

Chase shrugged, turned the page. "These are some bathing suit shots I had taken at a sportswear show. A lot of actresses got their start modeling."

"Was she more excited than usual? Buying lots of clothes, full of big plans?"

"You should have heard her going on about her new agent." Chase turned the page, smiled at her own photograph. "An *L.A.* agent. I got so tired of hearing her brag—"

"When did she get the agent?"

"Right after she won the pageant. You believe that? Nobody else ever got an agent for winning, not for Young Miss Whittier anyway. Like maybe you got a job modeling sportswear at the Tustin Mall or—"

"What was the agent's name?"

Chase tapped a photo of herself modeling lingerie, a wispy red bra and panties set. "Do you think I need breast augmentation? Be honest."

Jimmy could feel his heart pounding. "The agent. What was her name?"

"You think Heather would tell *me*? Probably afraid I'd steal her away. The only thing she told me was that her agent was a size twenty-four with big hair and lots of flashy rings. Heather thought that was *so* Hollywood." Chase smoothed down the corner of a curling photo. "She should have been *my* agent. If my face hadn't broken out—"

"Did Heather tell anyone else about this woman with the big hair?"

"Just her mother. It was like a big secret. She only told me so she could rub it in." Chase smiled to herself. "I guess I got the last laugh. That agent of hers never even came to Heather's funeral. I looked all over for a woman with a helmet head and lots of rings; I stopped a few that looked like they might be in the business and said I was seeking representation, but they looked at me like I was crazy. What a waste. I brought my portfolio and everything."

Jimmy stared at her.

"What? Like you wouldn't, if you were me?"

"Was this agent at the beauty contest? Maybe the organizers would—"

"I told you, it wasn't a beauty contest, it was a *pageant,* and no, the agent wasn't there. Heather said it was the photographer at the pageant, the one taking the official shots, who lined her up with the agent. If I had known that at the time, I would have been nicer to the little creep. And no, I don't know his name either. The way he was looking at Heather made me feel like I was just a porker in a dress standing next to her. Don't think she didn't love it too."

Jimmy reached for the scrapbook. "Please?" He turned back to the first photo, the eight-by-ten of Chase with her first-runner-up smile. "This is the official photograph, isn't it?"

"Yeah."

"May I?" Jimmy had already started pulling off the photo, being careful not to tear the backing. COPYRIGHT BY WILLARD BURTON was stamped on the back.

"Geez Jimmy, what are you so happy about?"

Chapter 29

Helen Katz was already hammered by the time Holt walked into the Blue Grotto. She had staked out a prize booth in the corner farthest from the street and was slouched there by herself, smoking a cigarette under the no smoking sign. Her table was strewn with beer bottles and a near-empty bowl of salted peanuts. None of the other cops in the place came near her, clustering in twos and threes at the long bar, mostly men, but a few women too, the uniforms pounding on each other's shoulders as they watched the game on the overhead TV, or sitting in the other booths bitching about the day, the bosses, the gangbangers, the stupid civilians, the squad car with the busted springs. Katz was hammered, but she spotted Holt immediately. She wasn't the only one.

Holt surveyed the dingy saloon, then walked over to the bar and edged herself in beside a couple of boozy retired narcs. She said something to Rufus but had to repeat herself a couple of times before he nodded. There was something about the sight of Holt leaning against the bar in her designer suit, taking in the fishnet hanging across the fly-specked backbar mirror, a gold mermaid and carved wooden fishes caught in the net—it pissed Katz off. Holt didn't belong here. If she wanted to talk to Katz—and what other reason would she have for walking into a strip-mall Anaheim cop hangout?—she could have called, left a message, sent a fucking carrier pigeon. Heads turned, following Holt's progress across the crowded room, and that didn't improve Katz's mood either.

"I hope you don't mind a little company, Helen," said Holt, sliding into the booth.

"I don't like pretty women."

"I can understand that."

Katz felt her cheeks flush. "Jimmy sent you to ask a favor? He think I'll cut you more slack than I'll cut him?"

"Jimmy doesn't know I'm here." Holt turned as Rufus brought over two glasses and a bottle of blue agave tequila. "Thank you."

Katz waited until Rufus lurched away. "Is it my birthday?"

"I remembered that's what you were drinking at the wake for Mack Milner."

"I drank it because it was free and I can't usually afford the good stuff. That don't mean I like it," said Katz.

Holt poured herself a double and downed it in one smooth movement, her eyes on Katz the whole time. "Then drink your beer."

Katz smiled and filled the other shot glass. The tequila was as warm and smooth as she remembered, burning all the way down. She topped up her glass and did the same for Holt, noticing how small the other detective's hands were, smooth and white. Katz's thick-knuckled hands seemed like paws in comparison. So what? Let Holt try to take down a tweaked-out biker with those manicured hands of hers. She checked the bar and saw Wallis watching the two of them; he turned away, taking a sudden interest in the beer tap in front of him. Good idea. Wallis still had a hard-on at Katz for sending him packing at the Luis Cortez crime scene, but not enough to try staring her down.

"You have an admirer," said Holt.

"It's a lonely job, but somebody's got to do it." Usually Katz would have bit Holt's head off for a remark like that. The good booze must be making her mellow. "You think the grand jury is going to indict Strickland? Courts officer told me some of your witnesses were going south. I'd hate to see that bastard walk."

"So would I." Holt sipped her second drink, watching Katz. "I heard you were involved in an altercation at the coroner's office."

"I don't have *altercations*, lady."

Holt covered Katz's drinking hand with her own. "It's *Jane*. Or *detective.*"

Katz stared at Holt's hand, but Holt didn't remove it. Katz liked that.

"There was an argument," said Holt, sitting back now, taking her hand with her.

"I get in lots of arguments. What's the big deal about this one?"

"Jimmy thinks Dr. Boone make a mistake on Walsh's autopsy. Actually he thinks a lot of things, but none of them follow unless the forensic report was wrong, and—"

"And when you heard about me getting in Boone's face, you thought maybe Jimmy was on to something?"

Holt nodded and finished off her drink. The woman could put it away. Katz liked that too.

"He's a hardhead," said Katz.

"He's a pain in the ass," said Holt.

They clinked glasses. Katz savored her drink, reveling in the slow sensuality of the agave. Holt looked tired. Close up there were wrinkles at the corners of her mouth and dark circles under her eyes. "You worried about him?"

Holt stared right through her.

Katz lit another cigarette. "Jimmy told me about a love letter Walsh got in prison and a script he was writing." She exhaled a plume of smoke. "A real cock-and-bull story about an angry husband who had it in for Walsh, angry enough to frame him for murder, angry enough to drown him in a fishpond and make it look like an accident. Knowing Jimmy, I'm sure there's other things he didn't tell me." She blew a perfect smoke ring, a halo drifting over Holt's head. "I don't know if Jimmy is really on to something. I just figured I'd give him the benefit of the doubt."

Holt raised an eyebrow. "Why?"

"Why?"

"Why would *you* give Jimmy the benefit of the doubt?"

Katz shifted her weight. Her limp, wrinkled gray suit fit her like a hippopotamus's skin, and she knew it. "He did a good deed, a favor for a dead kid I knew. Didn't even bother telling me about it. Got me to thinking maybe I had been wrong about him."

"Maybe you have."

"Don't worry, it's not like I'm going to ask to wear his letter sweater."

Holt cracked up at that one, but she wasn't laughing at Katz. She just thought it was funny, and Katz laughed along with her.

"So what happened at the coroner's office? *Did* Boone blow the autopsy?"

Katz shook her head and stubbed out her cigarette on the side of the countertop. "All I know for certain is he doesn't like having his work questioned. He's going to dislike a lot more things before I'm done with him." She suddenly leaned across the table. "Just for curiosity's sake, who does Jimmy think the angry husband is?"

"Jimmy's not sure either."

"He's got an idea though," said Katz. "Guy like Jimmy, he would *have* to have an idea."

"Yes, Jimmy has never lacked for ideas." They bumped hands reaching for the bottle, and Katz deferred, let Holt pour. "Do you know who Mick Packard is?"

Katz squinted, her head throbbing from the tequila on top of the beer. "The actor? Mr. Macho? *He's* the angry husband?"

"Jimmy thinks so."

Katz watched her. "But you don't."

Holt shrugged. "Jimmy talked to Packard's wife, Samantha. The woman admitted that she and Walsh had an affair way back when, but said that she had never written Walsh a letter. She also said Walsh never even told her that he loved her."

"So what? I'd lie too if I thought it would get me off the hook. Mick Packard's supposed to have a bad temper and not be afraid to show it."

Holt circled her glass with a forefinger, around and around. "Jimmy said the same thing. Samantha thought he was writing an exposé, and she was scared. She knew what her husband was capable of—that's why she lied."

"Makes sense to me."

Holt looked up from her drink. "Not to me. A woman lies about a lot of things. She lies about her age, her weight, even her sex life. But denying that a man ever said he *loved* her?" She shook her head. "A woman doesn't lie about that."

Katz stared at her and finally nodded. Holt knew what she was doing.

Holt checked the room, then inclined her head toward Katz. "Jimmy might be wrong about Mick Packard, but if he's right about Walsh being murdered"—her eyes were unwavering—"if he's *right* about that, then whoever killed Walsh isn't going to like Jimmy asking questions."

"You're worried about him?"

"Jimmy takes too many chances."

Katz stifled a belch. "I consider that one of his few good qualities."

Holt laughed, clicking glasses with Katz, and the two of them downed their shots.

Katz could barely hold her head up. "Let's not get ahead of ourselves. I don't know if Walsh was murdered. I doubt he was. I just don't like Boone coming on like an asshole when I ask him a few questions."

Chapter 30

Jimmy leaned against his car, watching the kids in bathing suits shuffle past, carrying coolers and boom-boxes as they headed toward the beach. He had parked on the Strand, the street paralleling Hermosa Beach, parked right across from Garrett Walsh's cottage, one of a string of million-dollar shacks built right on the sand, butted up against each other and separated from the street by a narrow alley.

A truck horn beeped at a Rollerblader racing down the Strand, keeping pace with the morning traffic, oblivious in his headphones. A trio of high-school-age girls cut through the alley and started down a beach-access path, their voices high pitched and eager, birdlike. That was the route Heather Grimm would have taken that day. One of the girls was blond like Heather, with a Hawaiian Tropic sun visor and folds of baby fat edging out of her thong. She carried a folding beach chair, stumbling slightly now as she shifted it to the other shoulder, then looked around, afraid that someone had noticed her awkwardness. He wanted to call out to her, remind her that it was Friday and she should be in school. He shook his head. Getting old, Jimmy.

Brimley should be here anytime now. He was back from his fishing trip and probably tired but was making the drive down from Ventura anyway, saying he felt he had promised Jimmy. It was a kind thing to do. Yeah, Sugar was a real angel, always ready to lend a hand—that's what Lashonda had told him as she fielded calls to her psychic hotline. That should have been good enough for Jimmy, but it wasn't.

There was just something about an off-duty detective grabbing a disturbance call that bothered him. He hadn't caught Brimley in any lies. The man had told the truth about how he afforded living at the Blue Water Marina: The management did waive half his moorage fees and all his utilities. The boat itself carried a sixty-eight-thousand-dollar mortgage. Maybe Lashonda was right, but yesterday, after turning in his profile of Luis Cortez, Jimmy had driven over to Brimley's former apartment.

The old neighbors said Brimley had kept his TV down and moved his trash cans back off the street as soon as they were emptied, and he liked passing out fish that he had caught. Detective Wonderful. It was only on the drive back to the office that Jimmy realized that Brimley's apartment was north of the Hermosa Beach police station, and Walsh's cottage was *south* of it. The newspaper accounts of the murder all said Brimley was on his way home when he heard the noise complaint over his radio, said he had been just a few blocks away. So what was Brimley doing in Walsh's neighborhood when the call came in?

"Sorry. I'm late," Brimley said from behind him, hurrying along a the path that cut from Hermosa Avenue to the Strand, flip-flops rustling with every step. The beefy man was wearing shorts and a faded Bimini Tarpon Derby T-shirt. Instead of his field notes, he carried a box of Kreamy Kruller doughnuts, grinning. "Had to stop for supplies. You got to try one."

"No, thanks."

Brimley handed him one anyway, the doughnut the size of a bath sponge. "Go on."

Jimmy took a bite, and warm maple cream squirted into his mouth. It was delicious.

Brimley pulled out a doughnut for himself. "They don't have any Kreamy Kruller stores in Ventura. Probably a good thing too—I'd be the size of a walrus." He glanced at Jimmy's car. "Keep track of your time. The meter maids here got no heart."

Jimmy took another bite. He tried to see Brimley as he was—not as an amiable retiree but as the man who might have helped frame

Walsh for murder. Who better to use for a setup than the arresting officer? "How was your fishing trip, Sugar?"

"Didn't catch a thing. Guess they saw me coming." Brimley squinted. "Your mug looks pretty good. You heal quick. That must come in handy in your line of work."

Jimmy darted across the street as the traffic broke, and Brimley humped along after him.

"There it is." Brimley pointed at Walsh's old beach house, a wood-frame cottage with a sagging front porch. "Walsh turned it over to Mrs. Grimm in a civil suit, if I remember right."

"She had to split it with his attorneys. It's been sold and resold since then." Jimmy nodded at the thick bushes circling the house. "Was the hedge that high at the time of the murder?"

"Higher. It was technically a code violation, but we're pretty kick-back around here. Unless there's a complaint."

"So the hedge would have muffled the noise from inside the cottage. Makes me wonder how somebody walking past would have heard anything."

"You and me, we think alike." Brimley licked his fingers. "When nobody stepped forward to take credit for the nine-one-one, I came back here a couple days later, same time as the original call came in. Early evening. Traffic was light. Loud music might have been ignored, but the caller had said there was a woman screaming inside. I stood there, and I figured you *could* hear that from the sidewalk."

Jimmy started toward the beach, Brimley beside him, the box of doughnuts tucked under one arm, the two of them trudging through the soft sand. Jimmy stopped after a few steps and took off his sneakers, barefoot now. The beach was dotted with groups of people lying on towels, high-schoolers mostly, a few families too. Frisbees arced across the sand. Teenagers paraded along the waterline, toes splashing, checking one another out. A volleyball game was in progress, and a hunky guy was doing a chestplant in the sand trying to get a hard serve. His girlfriend brushed him off as he got back up.

"Pretty, aren't they?" said Brimley. "I don't think I was ever that young."

Jimmy stopped on the surf side of the cottage, trying to see what Heather Grimm had seen that day. The deck extended out from the house about ten feet, surrounded by a waist-high wall.

"That wall is new," said Brimley. "Walsh liked an unobstructed view from the deck. He had a couple of lawn chairs out there, so he could check out the action."

"It would have worked both ways. From the beach you could see right into his place."

"Long as the curtains were open. They were pulled tight when I got there that night." Brimley felt around in the open box. "I made a few phone calls," he said idly, then finally selected a doughnut and looked up at Jimmy. "Turns out you weren't completely honest with me back at my boat. I'm a little hurt."

Jimmy's stomach felt like he was in Danziger's glass elevator again, riding it straight to the bottom.

Brimley took a big bite, red filling oozing onto his chin. "Remember when I said I had read about you, something about you saving a cop's life, and you waved me off, said you were just in the right place at the right time?" He flashed a raspberry grin. "Horsefeathers. You didn't just save a cop's life—you killed a man to do it. Huge fella too, almost three hundred pounds of pure meanness, from what I heard." He put his arm around Jimmy. "I never even fired my weapon in the line of duty. Not once. Only discharged it on the police range, and even then I only managed minimum competency, and here you are saving a cop's life."

The breeze off the ocean kicked up sand. Jimmy looked around, avoiding Brimley's gaze. "These cottages are close together. In your interviews, did anyone mention seeing anyone hanging around Walsh's house that night? Someone who didn't belong there?"

"Like who?" Brimley rooted around in the doughnut box but didn't pick one. "You think someone was checking out the house from the beach? A witness that I missed?" He thought about it. "I guess it's possible, but, I don't know if it matters." He plucked another dough-nut out of the box. "We didn't need witnesses. Heck, we hardly needed forensics the way Walsh kept confessing. I read him his rights, and he kept talking anyway. Told me how sorry he was all the whole way to the station."

"I'm not criticizing. I give you a lot of credit. You had just finished a full shift when you heard the dispatcher on your radio. You must have been eager to get home and kick your shoes off. Most cops would have just kept driving. It wasn't your call. So don't worry, Sugar—you're not going to be the bad guy in the piece."

A glob of chocolate cream dripped from the doughnut onto Brimley's T-shirt. "Can you keep a secret?"

"Some of them."

"Heck, a man who saved a cop, I guess I can tell you—just don't put this in your article." Brimley leaned closer, his forehead shiny with sweat. "I *wasn't* on my way home that night. Not directly, anyway. I lived clear on the other side of town in those days, but I used to swing by here first just about every day." He bit into a chocolate doughnut. "It was the Kreamy Krullers. Good, aren't they? Well, the store on Hermosa Avenue was the only one in the area in those days, and I was hooked on the butternut eclairs. Used to grab a half dozen after work, and by the time I got home there wasn't more than one or two left." He patted his ample belly. "Can you imagine the fun people would have had with that if the papers had found out? Cops and doughnut shops—Jay Leno would have been making jokes at my expense for a month."

"*That's* what you were doing here that night?"

Brimley drew a forefinger to his lips. "Shhhhhhh."

Jimmy felt the ache draining from his shoulder blades. He hadn't realized how tense he was until Brimley's doughnut confession, the explanation offered up without being asked. It was almost always a mistake to like a potential suspect, to want to believe them. He was still glad that Brimley had offered up a rationale for his behavior—and not to make himself look good but to avoid looking foolish.

"What is it, Jimmy?"

"Nothing. I'm just *really* glad to hear about your love affair with Kreamy Krullers."

Brimley scratched his head. "I'm never going to figure you out."

"If you trust me with that kind of damaging information," said Jimmy, recovering fast, "that means you're probably going to let me see your field notes."

"You never quit."

"Never."

Brimley popped the last of the doughnut into his mouth. "I got my notes in the trunk of my car. Just don't gloat." He closed the lid on the box. "That's all for me. You want to come get the notes? I don't know what else there is do out here except sweat."

"Not just yet." Jimmy scanned the beach. "Take a look around. The girls are all in groups, lying around on their blankets, talking, oiling up, and checking out the boys from behind their sunglasses. That sort of thing never changes. So why was Heather different? Why did she come here alone that day?"

"You asked me that on the boat. I told you I didn't know, and neither did her mama. The way you keep asking makes me think you must know the answer."

"No, I just have the question." Jimmy was tempted to tell Brimley about his conversation with Chase Gooding, tell him about the photographer who cruised teenage beauty contests, and Heather's new agent who hadn't bothered to attend her funeral. He kept quiet though. The good husband wouldn't have killed Heather himself—he would have farmed the job out. Jimmy wondered if the man who had done it had come this way, come in off the beach, a towel draped around his neck. Jimmy took in the whole scene and scanned the shoreline. He wondered how long the man had been out there, imagined him with his nose in a paperback, waiting for the crowd to drift off and the darkness to come. Most of all, he wondered where the man was now.

"You got cop eyes, Jimmy. I mean that as a compliment."

"I take it as a compliment."

"It's a mixed blessing, seeing things clear, noticing what other folks miss." Brimley hunched his broad shoulders, his bare arms burned from the sun. He might love the sun, but the sun didn't love him. "The Heather Grimm homicide was the biggest case of my career, but I wish I had never taken the call. I should have let the uniforms handle it. She was dead already. Wasn't like I did her any good." He shook his head. "Hermosa is a small department, we probably didn't get more than one or two murders a year. I had seen things before, bad things, but nothing like what was in that little house."

Jimmy had only seen photos of the crime scene; they were bad enough.

Brimley shook his head. "I thought it was going to be just another domestic disturbance call. Tell them to keep it down, and I'd go on about my business. Instead, the door opens, and Walsh is standing there holding that stupid gold statue, blood everywhere, *everywhere*, and lying next to the fireplace—this pretty blond girl with her face caved in. I tried CPR, that's what you're supposed to do, but her teeth were all over the carpet, and the whole time Walsh is crying like *he's* the one hurt."

"I'm sorry, Sugar."

Brimley's expression hardened. "I'm a gentle person, but it took everything I had that night not to shut him up for good."

"The nine-one-one disturbance call—I haven't been able to get a copy of it."

"I'm not surprised, the way they keep things. Not that it would do you much good anyway. Call came in from the street. Too much traffic noise in the background, if you were hoping to recognize the voice." Brimley started toward the street. "Come on, you can borrow my notes. Maybe they'll do you more good than they did me."

Jimmy kept pace with him as they slogged through the soft sand.

"I think you were pulling my leg back on my boat," said Brimley. "I asked how you found out where I lived, and you said you just handed the job off to someone else, but I bet you didn't. You're a bird dog, that's what you are." He walked slower now, the two of them side by side. "I've known a few cops who were the same way. We'd get a heads-up on a skinny hooker or a car prowler with braids, some description that would fit half of L.A., but by the end of the shift, the bird dog would drag in the bust, acting like it was no big deal. Never could figure out how they did it. Instinct like that—it's a gift."

Jimmy kept walking.

"Me, I never had a gift," said Brimley, a little out of breath now. "I always said the only reason they made me a detective was because I didn't have enough street smarts to stay in uniform. Even so, once I had the bad guys in custody, well, they'd tell me what I needed to know, without me ever having to get nasty in a back room. I hate that rough stuff, smacking a man with a phone book or planting a knee in his privates. That's not police work. Me, I'd settle back in my chair and break out a candy bar, a Baby Ruth maybe or a Butterfingers, and I'd take a nibble, looking across the table at the bad guy. Then suddenly I'd catch myself, apologize for my poor manners, and offer him a bite. Heck, couple of candy bars later, we'd be old friends, and the hardest con would tell me anything I wanted to know."

Jimmy wanted to laugh. The rap was total bullshit. He had seen the look that crossed Brimley's face when he thought no one was looking. Brimley's gift was that he was the good cop and the bad cop all in one, a terrifying combination. No wonder suspects were quick to spill their secrets. Jimmy was just glad he didn't have anything that Brimley wanted.

Chapter 31

"Happy now?" Sugar didn't introduce himself. Old buddies like the two of them didn't need introductions.

Silence on the line.

"I told you not to do anything, didn't I? Let sleeping dogs lie, that's what I said. Now they're up and yapping."

"Who is this?"

"Yeah, okay, this is a wrong number." Smart. At least the man still had his wits about him. "You didn't do the job on your own, I know that much. You always need help. Now I got this fellah showing up at my place unannounced, asking questions. Somebody else to worry about. Somebody else needs quieting down."

"I didn't do anything."

Sugar looked out across the Pacific, the waves the color of blood. "'Red sky at morning, sailors take warning, red sky at night, sailor's delight.' The question for you, my old friend, is what time is it? Morning or night?"

"Listen carefully. Please. I didn't do—"

"Morning or night?"

"I didn't do anything. I give you my word."

"It was an *accident*?" said Sugar. "That's what you're telling me?"

"Accidents—accidents do happen. Some men invite misfortune upon themselves . . ."

Sugar held the phone lightly, watching the sunset. It was his favorite time of day, the stillness filling his chest, quieting his heart.

"The dogs you spoke of—I'm concerned too. I trust you can put them back to sleep?"

On the edge of the horizon, Sugar watched a fishing boat caught in the setting sun, its rigging on fire as it headed home.

"Hello? Are you still there?"

Sugar broke the connection. Let *him* worry for a change.

Holt winced as the dog's howling undulated up from somewhere below. "I thought you said your building didn't allow pets."

"The kids in two-eleven just got a puppy," said Jimmy, not looking up from the papers spread across the kitchen table. "Looks like a dachshund and collie mix. Wish I had been there for the conception."

Holt shut the window, then sat down beside him. She opened one of Brimley's notebooks. "I still can't believe Brimley loaned you his raw notes."

Jimmy flipped through another one, skimming now. He had to strain to read the handwriting. It was a routine interview of one of Walsh's neighbors, a banker who hadn't heard anything the night Heather Grimm was killed. Hadn't seen anything either. There had been a football game on that evening, and he liked listening with the volume turned way up to catch the crowd noise. Brimley must have been bored with the banker—the margin of the notebook was covered in doodles, rods and reels and sailing ships. A sketch of a hooked marlin wasn't half bad, the marlin leaping in the air, an odd smile on its face. Fisherman humor or cop humor, Jimmy couldn't decide.

Holt chewed her thumbnail as she stared at the page. "Helen Katz. She got into an argument at the ME's office with Dr. Boone. Right in the middle of an autopsy. Helen may be the only person in the world to confront a man holding a stainless-steel blade."

Jimmy looked up.

Holt kept reading. "I didn't get any specifics, just that it was something about his findings in the Walsh case. A cop from Anaheim PD said Boone tried to pull attitude, and Katz came back at him so hard he dropped the liver he was weighing."

"How did this cop know to contact you?" Holt didn't answer, but Jimmy saw her smile anyway. "Thanks, Jane."

"Thank Helen Katz. I think she's got a crush on you."

Jimmy laughed.

Holt tapped the open page with her forefinger. "No wonder Brimley didn't like your suggestion that Heather went to the beach to seduce Walsh. This is his second—no, his third meeting with Mrs. Grimm. She had gotten a visit from Walsh's attorneys the previous day. They were intimating the same thing. Mrs. Grimm was very upset, weeping. Brimley jotted down that she was on medication. Tranquilizers." She squinted at the page, tilted it slightly. "Looks like Valium."

"She overdosed on Valium a few months later. Valium and a pint of vodka."

"Brimley was a good detective," said Holt. "A lot of cops wouldn't have noted the medication his subject was taking. You can tell he's angry—the attorneys' business card is clipped to the pages, with a note to himself to call them."

"Since when do defense attorneys pay attention to the investigating officer?"

"You'd be surprised. Sometimes a cop, just by making it clear that he or she is not going to slack off until the verdict comes down, can cause an attorney to shift his strategy. You'd think a DA would carry more weight with a defense team, but it doesn't necessarily work that way, because all a prosecutor has to work with is what the police uncover. A good cop, a *dedicated cop*, can make a difference."

Jimmy looked at her. He knew why she had a law degree but had never practiced, why she had gutted her way through the Academy, taking flak for her finishing-school manners and accent, finally earning the grudging respect of her colleagues by working harder and longer. She just liked scaring the shit out of bad guys, whether they wore three-piece suits or gang colors. "I love you, Jane."

Holt pretended she didn't hear him, but she was blushing as she went back to the notes. "Remember those transcripts you showed me a few weeks ago? Walsh's defense team had deposed a couple of Heather's classmates who hinted at drug usage and some sexual activity too. They were going to go after her hard, but something dissuaded them, made them come to the bargaining table. I think Brimley paid them a visit."

"Maybe he made them realize that he wasn't going to allow Heather to be victimized again." Jimmy riffed through the stack of notebooks until he found the one he wanted. "Right here. His first interview with the mother, he did a walk-through of the house. He listed all the posters and photographs on Heather's walls, the books on her bookshelf, the stuffed animals on her bed, even the *names* of them. I passed right over it before, but now I see what he was doing."

"Exactly. Those are the kinds of details that the DA's office loves to present to the jury. It makes the victim flesh and blood again, shows the jury who she really *was,* not the image that the defense team wants to present. Brimley did right by Heather."

Jimmy read through the mother's first interview again. He could almost hear her voice crack as she told Brimley about the last time she had seen her daughter. Mrs. Grimm had been in a hurry, had been late for work. She didn't kiss her daughter good-bye, didn't even tell her to drive carefully. She always did that too. Not that day.

"Are you okay?" Jane touched his hand. "Why don't we finish this up later?"

"Last week I talked with a woman whose son had been murdered in a drive-by, a kid, barely thirteen. I sat in her living room, and she told me about her boy while her daughter translated. The woman's voice never wavered, never broke, but she kept dabbing at her eyes with a tissue. You would have thought she was made of steel, except for her tears, and when I looked into her eyes, the grief—it was bottomless. Nothing was going to fill the hole inside her." Jimmy fumbled a piece of folded paper out of the notebook. "Now I read Brimley's notes, and I know Mrs. Grimm had the same hole inside her, only she was all alone, without any family to help her through it, just herself, day after day in that house with Heather's things everywhere and TV crews camped out on the sidewalk. Just herself and her memories." He stared at a photograph of Heather Grimm, an eight-by-ten that Brimley had copied and tucked into his notes, her face creased down the middle, right through her beautiful smile.

Holt took the photograph out of his hands and put her arms around him.

Jimmy leaned into her, felt her heart beating against him. "How do you do it, Jane?"

"What?"

"You know what I mean. How do you do it?"

"You get tough, or pretend you have." Holt held him tighter. "Then you go home, have a few drinks, and cry by yourself. Or with someone you trust."

Jimmy drifted, feeling Holt's warm tears on his neck.

Chapter 32

Desmond pulled a driver out of his golf bag and sighted down the shaft. "Watch your mouth with Trunk."

"What does that mean?" said Jimmy.

"Trunk doesn't like reporters, he doesn't like wiseasses, and he doesn't like white boys. You're three for three."

Jimmy and Desmond Terrell waited on the first tee of the Golden Wedge Country Club, the most exclusive golf course in southern California, members only, strictly enforced. The fact that Napitano was a board member wouldn't have been enough to get them on the premises, but last year Nino had bid thirty-seven thousand dollars at the club's charity auction for the right to play a round of golf with three nonmembers. Nino didn't ask why Jimmy needed entree to Golden Wedge, he just knew it had something to do with the article Jimmy was working on. Nino didn't ask about the article either. *Surprise me, dear boy. You haven't disappointed me yet* was all he said, perched behind his desk, slurping oyster shooters, his eyes bright and orgasmic at the possibilities.

Jimmy wished he was as confident as Napitano. Brimley's field notes hadn't given him any breakthroughs, but after Sugar had warned him about the meter maids yesterday, Jimmy had spent a few hours searching the traffic records of Hermosa Beach. No vehicle registered to Mick Packard or his production company had been ticketed the day Heather Grimm was murdered. Not that day or any other day. If Packard had been watching the beach house, he kept the meter fed.

The sun peeked through the surrounding trees. It was barely 6 A.M., and the fairways were shimmering with dew, the air crisp. Desmond picked infinitesimal bits of grit out of the grooves of his driver with a tee. He was a gray-haired black man of medium height, smooth skinned and fit, wearing light brown trousers and a matching polo shirt. His golf shoes were shined bright. A former cop, Desmond looked more like a tenured college professor, soft spoken and serene. Jimmy would have trusted Desmond with his life, and with the truth too—as much of it as he knew, anyway.

Desmond bent down and grazed a hand across the grass. "Look at this. Not a weed, not a sign of crabgrass, no brown spots. I bet the White House lawn isn't as well taken care of. I should ask the groundskeeper what he uses on it."

It was a beautiful course, but Jimmy didn't care about golf. He just wanted to talk to Trunk about Willard Burton. His attempts to locate Burton had failed; the pageant photographer's business license had lapsed eight years ago and had not been renewed, his last known address vacated the day after Heather Grimm was murdered. According to Desmond, Abel "Treetrunk" Jones had worked vice all over L.A. Trunk had arrested Burton once, said he had stories to tell, but he wasn't telling them—not even to Desmond—without a round of golf at the Golden Wedge, the "whitest course in the West." Desmond thought it was pretty funny.

"Where is he?" asked Jimmy.

"He'll be along presently."

Jimmy pulled out one of his own thrift-store clubs, swung it like a baseball bat, and almost hit himself in the head. Stupid game. He put the club back into his bag before he hurt himself. "Heather Grimm's agent sent her to Walsh's beach house to seduce him. I'm sure of it. I just don't think Heather knew what she was getting herself into."

"I doubt she did." Desmond stood just back of the first tee, adjusting his grip on the driver. "The way you described her—young girl, full of vanity and ambition—I expect she thought Walsh was going to fall for her. Make her a star."

"The agent knew what was happening. That nine-one-one call from a phone booth had to be part of the setup. No way someone makes a call like that, then doesn't step forward to tell their story. Or *sell* their story."

"It happens. Not often, but it happens. Some folks have enough money, or they just don't want the attention."

"That's what Brimley said. I think you're both wrong."

"I've been wrong before. I expect Detective Brimley has also."

"The agent wasn't working for Heather, she was using her. She was working for someone else. Someone who wanted to set Walsh up, maybe for statutory rape, maybe for murder. But the agent is the only one who knows what really happened."

"Not exactly." Desmond cocked his hips, taking a half-swing in slow motion. "There's the husband." He took a full swing, and the clubhead grazed the ground, sending wisps of grass skyward. "And there's the man who killed Heather Grimm." He looked at Jimmy. "Unless you think it was really Garrett Walsh who killed her. You said he didn't remember. Drugs make people do crazy things, things they couldn't imagine themselves doing. Maybe he *did* kill that girl."

"Walsh didn't do it."

"You sure of that?"

Jimmy glanced back toward the clubhouse again. "Where *is* he?"

"Throwing up probably."

Jimmy looked over at him.

"Trunk is sick." Desmond wiped the clubhead with his hand. "He's on disability leave. Pancreatic cancer."

"Jeeeeeeeeeemy!"

Napitano hurtled toward them in a golf cart, a tall emaciated black man beside him, hanging on for dear life. The cart skidded up to the first tee, missed Jimmy by inches, and pulled up beside their cart. "*Buon giorno,*" chirped Napitano, dressed in white shorts and a white dinner jacket.

"How are you doing, Trunk?" said Desmond.

"Better, now." Trunk stared at Jimmy. His skin was a deep black, his hair in patches. His head and hands were enormous—no way they belonged with his pipe-cleaner arms and hollowed-out torso. He wore a Raiders football jersey and baggy paisley knickers, the waistband cinched with a belt that had been shortened, new holes punched in. "What are you looking at, motherfucker?" He still had a big man's voice.

"Good to meet you too," said Jimmy.

"How are you and Nino getting along?" asked Desmond, stepping in.

Trunk grinned, his teeth as incongruously large as his hands. He clapped Napitano on the back. "This little fella puked right along beside me. Everybody else cleared out when they heard me unloading in the shitter, but Nino just walked over, grabbed the next stall, and let loose, the two of us going at it in stereo. You believe that, Desmond?"

"Vomiting is an ancient Roman tradition." Napitano smoothed his dinner jacket. "It is a healthy thing, to make room for more eating."

"You hear that, Desmond?" said Trunk. "Maybe I'm I-talian."

Desmond just smiled.

"Where's your clubs, Nino?" asked Jimmy.

"I do not play golf. I joined the club because at first they did not want me. Now I just come to drive the carts and to hear the cursing of the other players. Their frustration—it is a symphony to me."

Trunk clapped Napitano on the back again.

"We should get started," said Jimmy. "The foursome behind us is getting antsy."

Trunk looked over and saw four short white men in designer outfits, the leather bags in the back of their carts stuffed with titanium clubs. "They'll wait." He got out of Napitano's cart slowly, carefully—he seemed so frail that if he moved too quickly, one of his arms would snap off. "Nice course, eh Desmond? They always keep the best for themselves, don't they?"

"You've got the honors, Trunk," said Desmond.

Trunk pulled his driver out and bent down on one knee to tee up his ball, not resisting when Desmond had to help him up. He stood over the ball, adjusting his hips, taking his time, looking around to see who was watching, enjoying himself. The air smelled clean and green. His first shot dribbled about ten yards. He didn't leave the tee but reached instead into his pocket. The next ball went a little farther. The third one landed almost a hundred yards away; a weak shot but straight and true. He must have been good when he still had some muscle to go with that frame. "I'll take that one." No one argued.

Desmond was up next. He took a practice swing, then uncorked a deep drive, two hundred and fifty yards at least, but hooking into the rough.

Jimmy reached for his club.

"Put that back," growled Trunk. "I didn't come here to play golf with *you*. I'll talk with you, but I'm only playing with Desmond."

"Fine." Jimmy shoved his club back into his bag and jumped behind the wheel of the cart. Desmond started to climb in beside him, but Trunk stopped him.

"Ride with my man Nino, Des. Whiteboy's going to caddy for me this eighteen."

Desmond smiled at Jimmy, grabbed his clubs, and put them in Nino's cart.

"What are you waiting for, whiteboy?" said Trunk. "Go fetch my clubs."

Jimmy flipped the finger at Napitano and Desmond, who were enjoying the show, then transferred Trunk's clubs for him. He slid into the cart and started the engine.

"Pick up my mulligan," said Trunk.

Jimmy stopped the cart, got out, and picked up Trunk's first ball. He got back in, drove another thirty yards, and did the same thing with the second ball.

Trunk held out his hand for the ball. "You should run. I don't like being kept waiting."

"Yaz, boss."

Trunk looked at him hard but didn't say anything.

It went like that for the first four or five holes. Trunk hit two or three or four balls before he liked his lie; Jimmy drove and chased down Trunk's mulligans. On the third hole Napitano opened a wicker picnic basket and pulled out a bottle of champagne and some fried egg and bacon sandwiches. Jimmy was sent to bring Trunk a taste. Then sent back to bring him refills. Then stood by waiting while Trunk threw up again, handing him a towel when it was over.

"Don't feel sorry for me," Trunk said softly, as Jimmy helped him back into the cart. He fished a fat joint out of his knickers, hands shaking. Desmond and Napitano had pulled over about fifty yards ahead, talking as they waited for them to catch up. Trunk fired up the joint, took a deep drag, then slowly exhaled. "This is strictly medicinal."

Jimmy plucked the joint from him, took a hit himself, and passed it back. "An hour of being your caddy, and I could use some medicine too."

Trunk laughed.

"How long have you and Desmond been friends?" asked Jimmy.

"From the first minute I met him. How about you?"

"Same."

Trunk watched him. The whites of his eyes were yellowed. "Let's you and me just drive to the seventh tee and wait for Desmond. I'm tired. I thought playing here would be good for me. I mostly played public courses, rocks and divots and scalped greens. This country club—it's nice, but I'm tired." They drove in silence, Trunk puffing the joint, passing it over when he felt like it. "You ain't asked me anything," he said finally. "I keep waiting, but you don't get to it."

"I figure it's up to you."

"That's a first. Never met a reporter yet who wasn't in a hurry to get in and get out."

Jimmy parked the cart on a grassy slope off the asphalt track and parked under a large tree, where it was cool and shady. He took the remnant of the joint from Trunk's thick fingers and held it up to his lips so Trunk could get the last of it.

"Thanks," said Trunk, exhaling. He wiped his forehead. They waited, watching Desmond far down the fairway, sauntering toward his ball. "Desmond says you're looking for some heavy-tonnage pageant hawk wears lots of rings." He kept his eyes on Desmond. "She don't come to mind, but all that means is she was smart enough not to get caught." Desmond's shot hooked left, and Trunk shook his head. "I keep telling him not to drop his shoulder."

"Good luck telling Desmond anything."

Trunk looked over at Jimmy, then went back to Desmond. "I popped Willard Burton once—kiddie porn. Must have been ten years ago." He stopped to listen to a crow squawking overhead, breathing heavily but smiling as though he were listening to his favorite tune. "Slimebag beat the bust. I had him dead to rights, but he had a hot-shot attorney who argued that Burton had a constitutional right to take nudie pictures of little girls. Lawyer even brought up *Alice in Wonderland* to prove it. Did you know the guy who wrote that book was a perv too?" He rested his hands on his knees. "Makes makes me almost glad I never had kids."

Jimmy noted the *almost* but didn't say anything.

"Burton getting a walk like that pissed me off. Police work is more personal than most cops will admit, but I got nothing to lose now. I kept an eye out for Burton, that's all I'm going to say. I would see him sometimes hanging around junior high football games, scoping out cheerleaders, passing out his business card. I heard he worked the beauty contest circuit for a while too, but I never nailed him again. I think he knew I was watching, because one day he was just gone."

"Gone?"

"Just dropped off the face of the earth. Must have been eight or nine years ago."

"Right after Heather Grimm was murdered."

Trunk considered it and nodded. "I just figured good riddance. Then Desmond calls me a few days ago and says you're looking for him. Says maybe Burton's involved in a homicide." He lifted his head up with an effort and locked eyes with Jimmy. "I had to sit down, I was so happy. Getting a second chance at him *now*—"

"If I had known that, I could have saved Nino thirty-seven thousand dollars. You probably would have settled for a nine-hole course off the Pomona Freeway."

Trunk smiled. "I'd have settled for a round of miniature golf, you dumb cracker." His head drooped, his neck too weak to support it.

Jimmy looked away, now wanting to embarrass him. He watched Desmond on the sixth green, lining up his putt. "Do you know anyone who can help me find Burton?"

Trunk raised his head again and sat up. "Don't—don't I count?"

"You said you had lost track of him."

"I bumped into him a couple years ago." Trunk peered at the sixth green. "I didn't even recognize him at first. He'd cut off his beard, dyed his hair, got rid of his glasses too, but it was him. He calls himself Felix Watson now, which ain't much of an improvement if you ask me, but I guess it's a name without a history. . . . *Sweet*."

Jimmy followed his gaze and saw Desmond walking over to the cup to retrieve his putt, heard Napitano applauding from his nearby cart.

"Sixteen footer," said Trunk. "Desmond always was steady."

"Where did you run into—"

"Warehouse district, but don't expect to find him there—he moves around like a Mexican jumping bean. Felix Watson shoots porn films. That's how I bumped into him again. He's smarter now though, strictly three pieces of picture ID for the talent, and all his permits in place. Couldn't touch him." Trunk grinned, and Jimmy glimpsed again the man he had once been. "You should have seen his face when he saw me walking into the warehouse. It was almost worth having to cut him loose."

"I'm going to find him."

"He's a freelancer. I asked around—nobody at the department has a line on him."

"I'll find him."

"I believe you just might." Trunk watched Desmond and Napitano approach. "Desmond showed me that picture of you and the girls in the magazine, all of you naked as jaybirds. You know, when I started out working vice, that magazine would be strictly under the counter. Now it's on display at the supermarket, just fun and games." He turned to Jimmy. "Good thing I'm dying. I live much longer, I'd be out of a job."

Chapter 33

"Hey, I know this guy." Rollo leaned his head out the window as Jimmy parked. "Wayne! Dude!"

Wayne looked up from his magazine, a crew-cut muscleboy sitting on a steel equipment crate, catching rays in a tank top and shorts. He waved at Rollo and stood up.

"Lucky break, Jimmy," said Rollo, as they crossed the street. "Wayne's cool."

The house was in an upper-middle-class section of the San Fernando Valley, a two-story job on a cul-de-sac, a rental van in the driveway. Every house on the block had a swimming pool in the backyard, with high fences and hedges to guarantee privacy. It was a mind-your-own-business street, sunny and safe and clean, just like every other street in the Valley—one of the reasons this area just over the hill from L.A. had become the porn-production capital of the universe. Rollo had never heard of Willard Burton, or his new name Felix Watson either, but he had crewed plenty of porn flicks, shooting cutaways and facials. It didn't take too many calls before he got the address of today's shoot.

Wayne tossed down the current issue of *Honcho* as Jimmy and Rollo walked up, a six-packed stud on the cover. Wayne was shorter up close, with a hyperdeveloped torso, veins snaking across his biceps and innocent Bambi eyes. "Hey, Rollo, they didn't tell me you were crewing today."

"I'm not," said Rollo. "Social call. What about you? They got you doing security now?"

"Nah. I'm driving the gear, running errands, whatever. I like the goatee, by the way."

Rollo tugged at his new facial hair. "Thanks. This is my friend, Jimmy."

They shook. Wayne had a small hand, but Jimmy could feel the lifting calluses across his palm, right under the fingers. "Felix working today?"

Wayne nodded. "You know Felix?"

"I need to talk to him."

"You're not police, are you?" Wayne pulled a carefully folded sheaf of papers out of his back pockets. "I got all the paperwork—"

"I told you, Jimmy's with me," said Rollo. "You heard anything about Nikki Sexxx? Somebody said she moved to Maui with an investment banker."

"He wasn't a real banker," said Wayne. "She's back on the circuit."

Rollo brightened.

"All she got out of Maui was a tan," said Wayne.

"Don't give me that look, Jimmy," said Rollo. "I *miss* her."

"Of course you do. She stole your passport and traveler's checks, left you in the middle of Costa Rica, and ran off with a guy in white Guccis. If she had shot your dog too, you'd probably want to marry her."

"I feel your pain, Rollo," said Wayne. "My ex was competing at the Natural Bodybuilding Championships last weekend. I watched him start his posing routine, and I just started bawling. I had to turn the TV off."

"Love's a bitch," said Rollo. "I still got one of Nikki's Anabolic box covers, even though they spelled her name wrong."

"Too many consonants," said Jimmy.

"No," said Wayne, "Nikki don't mess with that stuff anymore. Strictly girl-girl scenes."

Jimmy stared at him.

"Girl-girl?" Rollo pushed back his glasses. "I could live with that."

Wayne opened the door. "They're out by the pool. I really admire your camerawork, Rollo. The shooters Felix uses are pathetic. Half the time they miss the money shot, then the talent has to do it again, and it's never as good the second time around."

"Do you know what Felix looks like?" Jimmy asked Rollo as the door closed.

"He'll be the asshole with the big mouth, just like every other porn director I ever met."

They made their way through the house, following the noise, stopping in the kitchen. Through the sliding-glass doors they could see a three-man crew—two video cameras, and a single lighting/sound tech—hovering around a fourway on the steps of a small kidney-shaped swimming pool. A pudgy man with a ponytail and a safari jacket stood on the pool apron, fingering the gold chain around his neck as he gave orders.

Rollo looked at Jimmy. "I rest my case."

The fourway on the steps consisted of three skinny women with fake breasts and a compact man with an enormous penis. The cameraman shooting close-ups kept bumping the actors with the camera lens as he circled in, a lit cigarette jutting from the corner of his mouth. The actors straddled each other, looking at the director for instructions, their feet slipping on the wet sides of the pool. It looked like a drunken game of Twister.

"You bring the Snapple?"

Jimmy turned and saw a nude woman next to the open refrigerator, chewing gum like a pile driver, a bottle blonde with huge breasts and no pubic hair. A large black widow spider tattoo walked down her flat belly, its legs reaching her hipbones, its jaws just above her vagina.

"We're supposed to get Snapple on the set, but all they have is diet." The blonde cracked her gum. "I don't drink diet." The gum popped, louder this time. "Hey! Quit looking at my cunt. You got the Snapple or not?"

"Ah . . . no," said Jimmy.

"Tell Felix I'm not doing my scene without my Snapple," said the blonde, stalking out.

"That was *scary*," said Rollo.

"Definitely." Jimmy heard a splash on the other side of the glass, and cursing. He saw one of the women and a cameraman floundering in the pool, while the male star was climbing the steps, howling, holding his penis with both hands. The director shrieked at them. Jimmy slid open the glass door. "Hey, Felix?"

"Who wants to know?" said Watson.

"Bitch broke my dick!" shouted the male star, bent over, still clutching himself.

"Put some ice on it." Watson pointed at the cameraman wading up the steps. "Careful with the equipment, douchebag. You cost me my damage deposit, it's coming off your salary." He turned back to Jimmy and Rollo. "Who the fuck are you?"

Jimmy smiled. "Relax, *Willard*."

Watson jerked, his second chin jiggling. The three-carat chunk of cubic zirconium in his right earlobe sparkled in the sunshine. "Ten-minute break," he said, staring at Jimmy.

Jimmy watched the male star holding a handful of ice cubes under his swollen purple penis, while the three women hovered nearby, stifling giggles.

"Dude's johnson looks like a Japanese eggplant," said Rollo, half in awe, half in sympathy.

Watson's face was smooth and pink as a pig's ass. "You must have me confused with someone else."

"If you say so," said Jimmy.

Watson shoved his hands into his safari jacket. "I'd like the opportunity to clear up any misunderstanding."

"Smile." Rollo took Watson's photo with a small digital camera, then took another one for insurance, catching Watson's shock and fear.

"Give me that," Watson said as Rollo slipped the camera back into his pocket. He actually snapped his fingers.

Jimmy laughed. "That's okay, Willard. We'll send you some prints when they come back from Fotomat."

"Take five," Watson called to the crew, following Jimmy and Rollo inside. "Wait! Don't go. What do you want?"

"World peace," said Jimmy.

"I'd like to be six inches taller," said Rollo.

Watson faked a smile. "Either of you ever had a porn queen?" He nodded toward the swimming pool, his eyes the color of dirty ice. "It'll change your life. They do things no normal woman would even think of."

"What do you know about normal, Willard?" said Jimmy.

"I—I would appreciate it if you wouldn't call me that," Watson said softly. He beckoned Jimmy and Rollo into the living room. "Let's get comfortable. No sense talking where the whole world can listen in." He sat on a plastic-covered sofa, the plastic squeaking. "Willard Burton is ancient history, dead and buried. My name is Felix now. Felix the Cat."

"I know who you are." Jimmy sat next to Watson, close enough to smell his sweat and bad cologne. "I know what you did too. I know that you turned Heather Grimm over to a talent agent—"

"Heather who?"

Jimmy grabbed the gold chain around Watson's neck and pulled him forward so he hit his face on the granite coffee table.

Watson sat back up, stunned. "What—what did I do?"

"Tell me the name of the talent agent," said Jimmy.

Watson gingerly touched the gash over his eyebrow, stared at the blood on his fingers. "*Look* at this."

Jimmy yanked the chain again, not hard enough to bang Watson into the table again, just hard enough to let him know he was considering it.

Watson waited until Jimmy let him go. "Please don't hurt me. I have a heart condition."

"No shit," said Jimmy.

Wayne opened the front door and peeked inside. He waved to Rollo, then closed it again.

"Maybe you didn't know what was going to happen to Heather." Jimmy let it sink in. "That's as sympathetic as I'm going to get,

Willard. I know this big old cop—he sweet-talks people into telling him what he wants to know. Never raises his voice, never raises a hand—that's what he tells me, anyway. But me, I haven't got his patience. So the next time I ask you a question and you don't answer, I'm going tear off that earring of yours."

"Really cheap zirc, dude," said Rollo. "You should invest in a better fake."

Watson looked from one to the other. "I—I don't even know who you are."

"That's Rollo, he's the sensitive, artistic one. I'm Jimmy, the troubled loner with a bad temper. Does that help?"

"Jimmy killed a man once," said Rollo. "It was self-defense, but a thing like that changes a person. It *did*, Jimmy, it changed you."

"Yeah, Felix, it's too bad you didn't meet me a couple years ago. I was a sweetheart then. I would have brought cake and cookies, asked you pretty please."

"I see." Watson squirmed. "Well, you were right before—I *didn't* have any idea what was going to happen to that girl. It was just an innocent business transaction. I mean, who knew Walsh was going to smash her brains out? A man with that kind of money, and fame—why not just beat her up?" He looked at Jimmy and decided he wasn't going to get an answer to that last question. "The agent's name was April McCoy."

"I want to talk with her."

"You'll have to shout." Watson laughed, then thought better of it. "She's—uh—dead."

One of the cameramen came in from the kitchen. He looked at Jimmy, then turned to Watson. You okay, Felix? Your lip is bleeding."

"What *is* it?" hissed Watson.

"T-Bone's salami is swolled up awful. He wants a ride to the emergency room."

"T-Bone can wait," said Watson. "Go get Wayne and tell him to saddle up."

"Wayne don't like tunafish—"

"I don't care what Wayne don't like. Give him a couple Viagra and tell him to do it for the home team." Watson waited for the cameraman to walk away, then turned back to Jimmy. "The night Heather was murdered, the same night, April took a swan dive out the window of her office. Eight stories, straight onto the sidewalk. TV said it was suicide, but I packed my bags and hit the road, Jack."

"Who were you afraid of? Walsh had already been arrested."

Watson felt at the gash over his eyebrow with a forefinger.

Jimmy sat beside him on the couch. "It wasn't April's idea to send Heather to the beach house. It was someone else's. *That's* who you were afraid of."

Watson nodded. "I saw Heather's face on the nightly news, and I *knew* it was a disaster. Then when I read about April the next day . . . Suicide? I knew her better than that. Whoever paid for Heather wanted to make sure it didn't come back on him. Tossing April onto her face was a smart move." He looked at his pure white Keds. "I should have kept going. My problem is I really like L.A. The sun and—"

"Who paid for Heather?"

"How should I know?"

Jimmy grabbed the chain again, the gold links cutting into Watson's soft neck as he tried to pull away.

"You think April was going to tell *me*?" groaned Watson. "We were strictly cash and carry. She had a legitimate agency, teenage talent mostly, actors and singers nobody ever heard of—"

Jimmy cut him off with a light tug, watching his eyes. Out on the front porch, he could hear Wayne arguing with the cameraman. "As soon as you saw Heather's face on TV, you knew it was a disaster. What was *supposed* to happen that night?"

Watson fidgeted. "Most of the girls I sent to April were strictly fun and games. A few promises, maybe a shopping spree at the Galleria or a trip to SeaWorld, and everyone has nice memories afterward. I have a good eye. April respected that. No one ever got hurt."

"Heather got hurt."

Watson didn't know what to do with his hands. "Heather was different." He peered up at Jimmy. "What are you picking on me for? Walsh is the one who killed her, not me."

Wayne and the cameraman came inside, then headed out to the pool.

"Good luck, dude!" called Rollo.

Jimmy gave Watson's necklace another tug. "Did April ever brag about her contacts in the movies?"

"All the time, but it was just talk. April always had some excuse why her kids lost out on the big part." Watson blinked "Could you *please* let me go? I've already got whiplash from an auto accident last month. My chiropractor says I have nerve damage."

Jimmy released him. "Did she name names?"

Watson rubbed his neck. "What names?"

"Did April ever talk about knowing Mick Packard?"

"Packard?" Watson shook his head. "Is he still alive?"

Jimmy could see that he was telling the truth. "What did you mean before, 'Heather was different'?"

Watson leaned forward, proud to share now. "There's wolves and lions and then there's the cute and cuddly animals that get ripped to pieces. Most of April's private clients were vanilla—they preferred cute and cuddly. You know, cheerleader outfits, Little Bo Peep."

Jimmy held his temper. "I've seen Heather's photo. She was no victim."

Watson nodded. "You got a good eye yourself. The malls are filled with cute and cuddly, but Heather was a special order. April wanted young but able to pass for legal. Someone *experienced* and smart, someone who wouldn't melt under pressure."

"You believe this guy, Jimmy?" said Rollo. "He's pimping out little kids, but he acts like it's somebody ordering a laptop with extra RAM and a CD burner. What's *wrong* with you, man? I'm no Boy Scout, but you—I've stepped in fresh dogshit I liked more than you."

"I'm a professional, and I was good at my job," protested Watson. "That's why April worked with me. It took me almost a month to find Heather. I must have hit every two-bit beauty contest and charm school in a hundred miles." He cracked his knuckles one at a time, wriggling his stubby freckled fingers. "Heather was worth it. Got fifteen hundred dollars for her, triple my usual rate." He shook his head. "Should have asked for more. I was too easygoing back then."

Jimmy stood up. If he didn't leave now, he was going to break the man's jaw.

Watson got up from the couch, grunting with the effort. "I got to get back to work myself. Wayne's Viagra should be kicking in soon, and I want to block out some cutaways." He spit onto the carpet. "Glad I could be of help. Just so you know, I don't mess with that chicken-hawk thing anymore. I've got a career now."

Almost at the front door, Jimmy turned around. "April must have had a secretary."

Watson snickered. "If that's what you want to call her."

"What was her name?"

"Stephanie something. I don't know her last name. She was a cow. April only kept her around to make herself look good."

"Describe her."

"What do you care about her for?" Watson shrugged. "Mid-twenties, fat ankles, lousy hair. Like I said, she was a cow."

"Was Stephanie involved in the business—the special assignments?"

"Stephanie was too stupid to do anything more than answer the phone and refill the candy dish on her desk with jellybeans and M&M's. Diet Pepsi and candy, and she wondered why she was fat." Watson followed them out the door, scuffing along in his tennis shoes, boneless as a tapeworm. "I was wondering—how did you find me?"

Jimmy kept walking.

"You have to tell me," said Willard, voice cracking. "You have to play fair!"

Chapter 34

In Jimmy's dream there was thunder, a pounding on heaven's gate, growing louder and more insistent . . . he woke up in darkness and heard someone knocking on his front door. He checked the clock, then eased out of bed and pulled on a pair of shorts. Before checking the peephole, he picked up the baseball bat he kept beside the door.

Sugar Brimley waved back at him.

Jimmy set the bat against the wall again, unlocked the dead bolt, and opened the door. "My building better be on fire, Brimley."

Brimley held up a red plastic cooler like it was the holy grail. "I come bearing gifts."

Jimmy stepped back as Brimley edged past him. He wrinkled his nose at the smell of the retired cop, a combination of salt, sweat, fish, and beer.

"I don't know why you're so grumpy. It's Wednesday morning, not the weekend. You should be up anyway. What's the fun of being retired unless you working stiffs got your shoulders to the wheel?"

Jimmy yawned.

Brimley set the cooler down on the kitchen floor, then bent down beside it. His light blue trousers were soaked, stained dark with fish guts, the fabric glistening with iridescent scales, a sheath knife on his belt. His hooded blue sweatshirt was equally grimy, the neck torn. He dug into the cooler and scattered crushed ice across the floor as he pulled out a couple of yellow-striped fish, holding them up by their tails. "This one's about five pounds," he said, jiggling it, "and this little beauty is over seven."

"Congratulations."

"See how clear their eyes are? Hooked not more than a couple hours ago, one right after the other, just when I was about to give up and go home. No gaff. *Netted.* Just plucked from the sea, not a mark or a bruise on them. Look at them, Jimmy. Yellowjack is the best eating on earth."

Jimmy yawned again. "I'll make us some coffee."

"Now you're talking." Brimley laid the fish back into the cooler.

Jimmy filled the teakettle and pulled mugs and a jar of instant coffee out of the cupboard. "You want a Band-Aid?"

"What for?"

"Your cheek."

Brimley wiped at the scratch and looked at the blood on his fingers. His eyes were exhausted and wild, his hair sticking out.

"You okay, Sugar?"

"Never better, but thanks for asking. You don't mind me dropping in unannounced, do you?"

"No, I did the same thing to you."

"That you did. By the way, were my notes any use? You find anything I missed?"

"I'm still going over them."

"Well, if anybody can catch me, it's you. I asked around about you. Lot of people don't like you, but they all say you know your stuff. I think you can tell a lot about a man by the quality of his enemies."

"You sure have a way with a compliment." Jimmy turned away as the kettle started to whistle, then poured water into the mugs, stirring up the coffee crystals. "Black, right?"

Brimley blew on his coffee and took a sip. "One of those Kreamy Kruller doughnuts would hit the spot right about now, wouldn't it? Wish I had thought of it on the drive over. They got an outlet in Newport Beach." He slurped the coffee. "I drank plenty of lousy java in my time. Some even worse than this."

"Thanks." Jimmy put a couple of extra spoonfuls of instant in his cup. It was bitter and sludgy, but it goosed the brain cells. He had made a few calls after leaving the porn shoot yesterday. Trunk Jones said he had never heard of April McCoy, but he promised to ask around at vice. His voice was so soft and weak that Jimmy was sorry he had called. A search in the county records had been more fruitful; Jimmy found a business license in April's name for an office in Paramount. He was going to drive over there later today, see if anyone knew what had happened to April's secretary, Stephanie. Office gossip was more reliable than the headlines.

Brimley set his mug down onto the counter—he had a strange smile on his face, weary and excited at the same time. He pulled a wadded-up black plastic trash bag out of his pants pocket and shook it out. "Thanks for the java. Time for me to get down to business." He whipped out his knife, the curved blade flashing, and if he noticed Jimmy tense, he didn't show it, reaching into the cooler. He set the fish down gently into the sink and rinsed them off under cool running water. "I got an urge just after sunset last night. Decided to head out toward Catalina and see what happened." He lightly held the smaller fish, his knife rasping across it, scales flying. "Didn't get a nibble all night. Then about an hour before dawn, these two beauties introduced themselves. Yellowjack—they're not just good eating, they're *fighters*. They make you earn it."

Jimmy leaned against the counter and watched the big man rake the flat of the knife across the fish, working from the tail up, scales flying, iridescent in the morning light.

"Figured I'd share these yellowjack with an old buddy of mine who lives in Balboa," said Brimley, head bent, concentrating on the task. "Got him a place right on the water. Did that guy ever hit the jackpot! Married some rich dame already gone through three husbands, thought she'd try an ex-cop now that she didn't need money anymore. I docked my boat next to his and rang the bell for five minutes before the maid answered." Brimley shook his head. "Arnie Peck with a maid. I seen it all now. Arnie walks out from the master suite scratching his rump, and I hear his wife yelling at him from the other room. What a sound. Voice like that should be a felony."

Jimmy enjoyed the knowing movement of Brimley's hands, the blade an extension of him as he scaled the fish. A guy changing a tire or laying brick, Jane Holt going over a crime report, her eyes alert— watching someone who knew what they were doing, really knew—it was better than going to a museum and checking out the dead art.

Brimley put one hand in the fish's gills and lifted it over the sink, then plunged the tip of the knife into the belly, just below the head. The blade worked its way down toward the tail. "Arnie said he didn't want any fish. Man used to live to throw a line in the water. Now he says if he wants fish, he just tells the cook. Doesn't even use his boat anymore, just lets it sit there collecting cankworm. I got out of there as fast as I could. Then I thought of you. I wasn't sure I could find my way back to your place after taking you home that one time. I dearly hate to see fresh fish go to waste." He looked at Jimmy. "You like fish, don't you?"

"Yeah, sure."

The yellowjack trembled in Brimley's grip, as the knife sliced a perfectly straight line down its midsection. "Arnie—he loaned me his car. I'm not saying he was happy about it, but he did it. Made the maid cover the seat with plastic trash bags, though." He put down the knife, spread the fish open with one hand, and deftly scooped out its guts with the other, a dark mass flopping into the sink. He looked up at Jimmy. "I tell you, a woman will ruin a good man faster than cancer. The wrong woman anyway. Head on or head off?"

"On."

"Good man." Brimley set the cleaned fish onto the counter.

"How about a beer?"

"A beer? Don't mind if I do." Sugar waited while Jimmy took a couple longnecks out of the refrigerator, opened one with a twist of his wrist, and handed it over. Waited while Jimmy did the same for himself. They clinked bottles, and neither of them came up for air until the bottle was half-empty. Sugar wiped his mouth, leaving a single fish scale glistening on his upper lip. "You can always tell a bachelor. He's the man not afraid to have a cold one first thing in the morning. He's the one who doesn't have to answer to anyone." He took another long swallow. "You ever been married?"

"No."

"Girlfriend?"

"Yeah."

"Is she the right one, Jimmy?"

"I don't know. Maybe."

"Maybe? I think you'd know if she was the right one."

Jimmy shook his head. "I'd have better luck explaining the theory of relativity than why a woman is right or wrong for me. I found a *good* woman, but don't ask me if she's the right woman."

Sugar finished his beer and set it down hard on the counter. "A good woman—you *are* a lucky man."

"So far."

Brimley chuckled. "If you found a good one, don't let her go. That's my advice. Free advice is worth what you pay for it, but that's the best I got. You find a good woman, you hang on tight. There's better things in life than standing around drinking beer in your skivvies, chasing any wild hair that comes along. What's your girl's name?"

"Jane."

"Jane. I like that." Sugar nodded. "Jane. If I had ever found a good woman, I tell you, Jimmy, I'd have never let her go. I'd have kept a grip." He turned away, embarrassed, and started in on the other fish, his movements jerky now.

"What's wrong, Sugar?"

The knife tore roughly at the flesh. "Here I am, talking your ear off like some old fart can't get anyone to listen to him." He kept his face averted. "I haven't been myself lately."

"What's really bothering you? Did something happen?"

"You happened, Jimmy." Sugar forced himself to slow down, the knife gentler now, smoother. "That's what happened."

Jimmy put down his beer. Standing there in his own kitchen, the first warm light of dawn easing in through the curtains, Jimmy felt a shiver run through him.

"I had a pretty sweet thing going on until you showed up looking for me," said Brimley, working away. "Puttering around on my boat, fishing when they were running and fishing when they weren't, store-bought pies and football games on satellite TV. Then you come along and dredged up a lot of bad memories. I haven't been sleeping so well. I wake up and I'm not rested." He looked up at Jimmy and tried to smile. "Man like me needs every minute of his beauty sleep. Otherwise he ends up in a strange kitchen spouting off about love and marriage, making a fool of himself."

"You didn't make a fool of yourself, Sugar, and I'm not going to apologize for trying to find out the truth."

"No apologies, huh? I like that. Me, I'm the exact same way. No wonder I took a shine to you." Brimley gutted the fish with one swipe of his hands, rinsed out the cavity with cold water, and set it down on the counter beside the other one. "I just hope this project of yours, this story or profile or whatever it is, I hope it's worth what you're stirring up."

"It's worth it."

"If you say so." Brimley rinsed off his hands. "You got some newspaper I can use?" he waited until Jimmy fetched him yesterday's paper, then wrapped the larger fish, tucking the ends in before slipping it back into the cooler. He wrapped Jimmy's fish equally carefully and put it into the refrigerator.

"Any tips on how I should clean my floors or iron my shirts?"

Brimley didn't answer, still bothered by something. He cleaned out the sink, put the innards and scales into the plastic garbage bag, and rinsed the rest down the sink. Then he hit the garbage disposal, watching Jimmy as it churned away, and flipped it off. The silence echoed. "You think Heather was targeting Walsh the day she was killed, don't you? That's where you're going with this. Just like Walsh's lawyers." He washed his hands with soap and water and worked the lather under his nails. He tore a paper towel off the roll, almost tearing the roll off the wall. "You think she tried to flirt her way into the movies?"

"I'm not sure." Jimmy liked Sugar, and Sugar had helped him, but he wasn't about to tell him what he had found out about Heather and April McCoy. The only people he trusted with the truth were Jane and Rollo, and even with them—well, "The truth, the whole truth and nothing but the truth"—that was just courtroom bullshit, something judges and lawyers used to fool the rubes.

"There's plenty of girls would have sex with a kid popping popcorn in the cineplex because they think he's in show business, but that don't mean Heather was one of them." Brimley's eyes hardened. "Even if she was, it don't change that fact that she's dead and that Garrett Walsh killed her."

"I'm not trying to insult her memory or step on your work, Sugar. I appreciate all the help you've given me. I know you didn't have to. It's like I told you at the beach house, you're not the bad guy here."

"Then how come I feel like the bad guy?"

"You had evidence and Walsh's confession. No one could fault your work."

Brimley balled up the paper towel in his big hands and tossed it into the garbage. "You want to do justice to that yellowjack, rub it inside and out with kosher salt and crushed black pepper, then slip a half-lemon and a dab of butter inside, maybe a pinch of fresh tarragon. Put it in a hot oven, a very hot oven, and roast it until it's crispy. Angels in heaven don't eat so well."

"Why don't you sit down for a while? We'll have another beer."

"No, I got to get going, but thanks." Brimley gently laid a big hand on Jimmy's shoulder. "After I found Heather Grimm . . . after that I had to see a shrink. I didn't want to, but it was departmental policy, so I went. I was glad I did." He gave Jimmy a squeeze. "You find out I messed up, you tell me. I can take it."

Chapter 35

The Healthy Life Café smelled of lentil soup and carrot juice and roasted garlic. Men in short-sleeved dress shirts were hunched over the small wooden tables, gobbling down soy burgers while they read the sports pages. An emaciated woman with bulging eyes and bright red lips sipped at a green milkshake—she reminded Jimmy of a dragonfly. Handmade banners on the walls proclaimed FREE TIBET! and MEAT IS MURDER and DEATH BEGINS IN THE COLON! He wondered why vegetarians always used so many exclamation points.

"Table for one?" asked the hostess, a clear-skinned young thing in a paisley sarong.

"I'm looking for some women from the McMahon Building. I was told they ate here."

The hostess waved a hand toward the back patio. "Smoker's gulch."

Jimmy heard laughter as he opened the door to the patio. He made his way through the haze to a table at the rear of the deck, where three women were puffing away over their salads, large women in loud dresses, their eyeglasses big as scuba masks. They quieted slightly as he approached. "Do you ladies work in the McMahon Building?"

"Who wants to know?" said a matron with a Kool Light bobbing at the corner of her mouth.

"I bet he's the guy Barbara talked about," said a younger, henna redhead, dropping ashes onto her enormous salad. "Barb said he walked sexy."

"You the one's been asking all over about Stephanie?" said a busty blonde with black roots, her eyes undressing Jimmy. "Why don't you walk for us, let us decide?"

"I like to hold back, maintain a little mystery." Jimmy pulled a chair up to the table, smiling. "I'm Jimmy Gage. I'm looking for Stephanie Keys."

"Not Keys anymore," said the bottle blonde, dipping pita bread in the dip. " 'First comes love—' "

" 'Then comes marriage,' " said Kool Light.

" 'Then comes Steffy with a baby carriage,' " singsonged the bottle blonde, grabbing Jimmy's leg.

Jimmy howled along with the three of them.

"What do you want with Stephanie?" said Kool Light. "She's a good kid."

"Not like me," said the bottle blonde, blowing smoke in Jimmy's face. "My old man works nights, and I'm sick of making love to my pocket rocket."

"Angie, you're awful," said Kool Light. "Is Stephanie in some kind of trouble? She run up her credit cards?"

"I just want to talk to her about her old boss, April McCoy."

"That was so sad," said the henna redhead.

"No, it wasn't," sneered the bottle blonde. "April treated her like crap."

"April was *depressed,* that's why she killed herself," said the henna redhead. "My brother is the same way. He's on Prozac now."

"Everybody is on Prozac now," said the bottle blonde. "That don't mean you can treat people like crap."

"Suicide is a sin." Kool Light stubbed out her cigarette in the hummus.

"Stephanie took it hard when April killed herself," said the henna redhead. "She changed overnight. In some ways I guess it was good, because Stephanie had been in a real rut, overeating and letting herself go. April's suicide was a wake-up call for her soul."

"Like on Oprah," said the bottle blonde.

"Like holy communion," said Kool Light.

Jimmy rocked in his chair, listening to the conversational rhythm they had going. The three of them had probably been having lunch together for the last ten years, working on their moves, graceful and fluid as double Dutch street champs. Jimmy could watch them eat and smoke and talk all afternoon. He wondered if Stephanie had been part of the group. He hoped so. She would be honest then too, and straightforward. She would tell him whatever she knew.

"You got a nice smile, mister." The henna redhead bit a carrot in half. "Don't he have a nice smile, girls?" She chewed noisily. "Anyway, after April did her thing, Stephanie went to work for this home-care-products distributor on the second floor and lost just a *ton* of weight. What was Stephanie on? Jenny Craig? Herbalife?"

"Weight Watchers."

"Slim-Fast."

"Whatever," said the henna redhead, "she lost a lot of weight. It seemed like every time she came back to visit, she had dropped another ten pounds."

"She's not working on the second floor anymore," said Jimmy. "Her last employer said she moved in with her boyfriend and that was the last he saw of her."

"The boyfriend didn't last six months. I *told* her he was all wrong for her," said the bottle blonde, "but she didn't want to listen to me. I've only been married three times—what could I possibly know about the male of the species?" She flipped her cigarette over the hedge surrounding the patio. "The boyfriend was some kind of sweaty sex machine or something from the way she talked."

"That gets old," said the henna redhead.

The three of them burst out laughing. Jimmy pretended to be embarrassed.

"Stephanie dumped the sex machine and found a hard worker

willing to marry her," said Kool Light. "She said he was a hard worker, anyway."

"I couldn't find a marriage license issued in her name," said Jimmy. "I checked."

"Aren't you the eager beaver?" Kool Light narrowed her eyes. "Stephanie got married in Mexico. She showed me pictures of the ceremony. It was beautiful. The water there is bluer than ours. At least in the pictures."

"I got married in Vegas," said the bottle blonde. "Dipshit lost five hundred dollars shooting craps, and we had to come home the next day."

"Do you know where Stephanie is living now?" said Jimmy.

The henna redhead shook her head. "Someplace out in the desert, I think. She sent me a Christmas card a couple years ago. Her little girl was dressed as an elf. Even fixed her ears so they looked pointed."

"Did you write down the address?" said Jimmy.

"No, sorry." The henna redhead brightened. "I might have kept the card, though. I got a big box full of pictures and photographs that I'm saving for this big decoupage project. I want to do all my kitchen cabinets in pictures of little kids. My husband's sterile—at least he says he is—but I like kids."

"Decoupage is so over," said the bottle blonde.

"Could you check your box of pictures and see if you kept the Christmas card?" Jimmy asked the henna redhead.

The bottle blonde picked up the check and fished a calculator out of her purse. "Okay, I had the potato blintzes, the hibiscus iced tea"—her manicure flew across the keys—"and the eggplant appetizer, which we split three ways."

"I hardly touched the appetizer," said Kool Light. "Eggplant gives me gas."

"What's Stephanie's married name?" asked Jimmy.

"I had the hummus, the wheatgrass surprise—" The henna redhead glanced at Jimmy. "Something Spanish, I think. Or Jewish. One or the other."

"Jews don't move to the desert," said the bottle blonde.

"Moses led the children of Israel into the desert for forty years," said Kool Light, watching the bottle blonde add the bill. "My hearts of palm was three ninety-nine, not four ninety-nine."

"My second husband was a Jew," the bottle blonde said, "so don't go telling me about the children of Israel."

"Your Christmas cards?" Jimmy reminded the henna redhead. "Will you see if you have Stephanie's address?"

"You're *sure* you're not from a collection agency?" asked the henna redhead.

"Yeah, like he'd tell you the truth if he was," said the bottle blonde. "You need to stop trusting everything in pants. Okay, your share, with tax and tip, make it eight twenty-five."

"I'm a reporter," said Jimmy. "I'm writing a story on April McCoy. I just want to talk to Stephanie—"

"Let me see the bill," the henna redhead said to the bottle blonde.

"What, you think I'm cheating you?" asked the bottle blonde.

"I had a *small* wheatgrass surprise," said the henna redhead.

Jimmy plucked the check from the bottle blonde and pulled out his wallet.

"Look girls, we got a real strongman here," said the henna redhead. "He picked that check up like it was nothing."

The women laughed so hard that people at the other tables turned to see what had happened.

Chapter 36

An emerald tree boa and a brown-and-red-striped Burmese reticulated python placidly watched Jimmy as he walked into Santa Monica Exotics. The snakes were piled in the front windows, draped across fake tree limbs, ten and twelve and fourteen footers, their wide flat heads draped across their coiled bulk. Two black-clad goth kids stood outside, holding hands as they stared at the snakes. The girl, draped in silver ankhs and crucifixes, eyes blackened like a raccoon, flicked her tongue stud at the python.

A two-toned colobus monkey screeched, its black and white fur looking like formal attire, but Jimmy ignored it, looking for Samantha Packard. A caged red-green macaw followed his progress as he passed the gekkos and iguanas. A West African dwarf crocodile, an ugly beast no larger than a dachshund, opened wide its mouth as Jimmy walked past, its teeth like sharpened dice. A small boy pressed his face against a glass front, and the tarantulas inside waved back. A nearby cluster of black Mexican scorpions clicked their claws against the glass. The sound gave Jimmy the creeps.

Samantha Packard had called him at the office this morning, sounding out of breath, her voice little more than a whisper. "Santa Monica Exotics—do you know it? Three o'clock."

The store was a collection of nooks and crannies, narrow aisles leading into large open areas like clearings in the jungle. A saleswoman in black leather pants was showing a gold chinchilla to a middle-aged couple, brushing out its fur before handing it over to the wife, who cuddled it like a child. The chinchilla had tiny black eyes, a silky yellow pelt, and the face of a sewer rat.

Jimmy turned the corner and saw Samantha Packard at the end of the aisle, staring into one of the cages, her shoulders slumped. She was wearing a lively orchid-colored dress and her hair was coifed, but her posture gave her an air of fatigue and defeat. He came up behind her, moving so quietly that she jumped when he spoke her name.

Samantha pressed her back against the glass wall of the cage, terrified. In the dim recesses a ring-tailed lemur dangled from a tree limb, sleeping.

"It's okay," said Jimmy.

"You're—you're a little early."

Jimmy could see a small bruise on the side of her jaw, barely covered by makeup. "I'm glad you called me. Does he know?"

Samantha blinked. "Know what?"

"About the letter?"

Samantha glanced away, then back. "I'm sorry."

"It wasn't you, it was me. Walsh tried to tell, but I didn't believe him."

Samantha acted like she hadn't heard him, turning back to the cage, watching the lemur snooze, a silvery marsupial with bony humanoid hands. "They sleep sixteen hours a day, eighteen hours sometimes, dreaming their life away. They're very intelligent. They're so much smarter than us—" She jerked as Jimmy touched her shoulder, flinging off his hand, still watching the lemur, her dull eyes reflected in the glass.

Jimmy heard something behind him.

Mick Packard acted startled that he had been caught, his surprise turning to anger. "I *told* you to stop bothering my wife." He was a lousy actor.

Jimmy glanced at Samantha, who maintained her vigil on the lemur cage.

Packard advanced, looking tough in black turtleneck and black pants, hands poised in martial arts readiness. "You picked the wrong woman to harass."

"I think there's been a mistake."

"*I'm* not the one who made a mistake."

"You gave me the idea when we met at Garrett Walsh's funeral. I'm doing a profile on action stars and their wives. I wanted to interview Mrs. Packard first—"

Packard did one of his signature spin-turns, and Jimmy dodged, the kick just grazing his head. Packard looked surprised again. He had slowed down since he was a top box-office draw, but even the near miss almost tore Jimmy's ear off.

Jimmy backed away, fists cocked, watching Packard's eyes as the man closed in.

"Running away?" Packard was talking too loudly.

Jimmy glanced around and saw a video cameraman shooting from the far end of the aisle. The sight distracted him for a moment, long enough for Packard to attack again, his roundhouse kick slamming into the wall next to his head. Jimmy grabbed his outstretched foot and twisted, sending him to the ground bellowing.

Packard got quickly to his feet, limping slightly. "You've had training."

"I told you, this is a mistake." Jimmy backed up, looking for an exit.

"Hey, don't you want to play?" The question had been the oft-repeated tagline of Packard's last box-office hit.

Jimmy edged into the main corridor. Halfway down the middle-aged wife nuzzled the golden chinchilla. The cameraman stepped into the aisle from behind her, still filming. Jimmy feinted, then threw a punch at Packard, a hard left hook.

Packard swatted the blow aside, hit Jimmy twice on the side of the head, and knocked him down. Packard mugged for the camera, beckoning Jimmy to rise to his feet.

Samantha Packard faced the lemur cage, her hands clenched at her sides.

Jimmy got up, his ears ringing as he rocked on the balls of his feet. He never saw the blow coming.

Packard moved in, low-kicked, then drove the heel of his left hand into Jimmy's chest and sent him stumbling back against a wall of glass cages.

Jimmy heard the scorpions scuttling behind him but kept his eyes on Packard. It hurt to breathe. He was scared.

Packard bounced forward, dodging and weaving, a smug little smile on his face. He was right where he wanted to be: in a big-screen moment.

Jimmy kept trying to box him, but Packard slipped past his punches, smacked him and retreated, then smacked him again. Jimmy was fast, faster than Packard, but Packard's timing was perfect.

Packard hit Jimmy again and again, hit him in the exact same place each time, smiling broader now as Jimmy got angrier and more desperate. Packard stuck his head forward, daring Jimmy to take a shot.

Jimmy lashed out, and his fist grazed Packard's chin before he got nailed again. The side of his head was numb now, and blood trickled from his ear. He backed up, gasping for breath. The middle-aged wife was right behind him now, asking her husband if they were filming a movie, her voice echoing, sounding like she was speaking from inside a seashell.

Packard grinned at him, easing forward.

Jimmy grabbed the golden chinchilla from the wife and tossed it to Packard.

Packard deftly caught the squealing chinchilla, then, confused, looked at the camera.

Jimmy punched him in the face, catching him good. The chinchilla clawed its way free and scampered down his leg. Jimmy hit him again, just below the nose this time, a pressure point where all the facial nerves gathered—right where Jane had taught him. Packard grunted, and Jimmy tripped him, drove him to the ground.

Packard got halfway up, cursing.

Jimmy kicked him, sending him sprawling. Packard tried to stand, but Jimmy didn't give him a chance. No marquess of Queensbury bullshit, no time-outs, no Geneva Convention, no director calling

"CUT!" Jimmy kicked Packard's knee out from under him, kicked him when he struggled up, and punched him in the throat when he tried to explain. When Packard stopped trying to get up, Jimmy stopped hitting him.

The cameraman caught every moment of it.

Samantha Packard hadn't moved. She was still slumped against the glass, watching the sleeping lemur.

"Samantha?" Jimmy's voice was raspy.

Samantha pressed her hands against the thick glass, moaning, but the lemur didn't move, lost in some solitary rain-forest reverie where the light was cool and deep and green and the trees were heavy with fruit. If the lemur heard Samantha's soft cries in his dream, he didn't respond.

"Turn around, buddy."

Jimmy ignored the cameraman.

"You a stuntman or something, buddy?"

Jimmy shook his head. "Samantha, you have to get away from him."

Samantha Packard didn't move. "I'm sorry."

"This was for real then?" The cameraman zoomed in. "So could you please tell us why you're stalking Mick Packard's wife?"

Packard coughed and curled up on the floor. The macaw screamed at them, fluttering its bright wings.

Jimmy stared at Samantha Packard. He felt sick. "You're not the good wife, are you?"

Samantha Packard hung her head. "I've tried—I've tried to be."

Chapter 37

The footage from Santa Monica Exotics led every local newscast that evening, with endless replays of Mick Packard getting punched out, the chinchilla clawing at his turtleneck. It was a great TV moment. Now Jimmy understood why Samantha had picked three P.M. for the meeting: Mick Packard wanted to make sure they were able to make the broadcast deadline. He just hadn't counted on getting his ass kicked.

Jimmy had been standing around for the last half-hour at Napitano's monthly scavenger hunt party watching the action on the widescreen in the media room. Everyone was having a good time, cheering and hooting. Rollo did a perfect Howard Cosell impression, and Nino danced around in his peacock-blue pajamas throwing mock punches with his tiny fists. Jimmy felt nothing but disappointment.

He had cast Mick Packard as the angry husband from the moment he saw him at Walsh's funeral. Cast Samantha as the good wife too. It had been more than a leap of faith; Samantha had admitted having an affair with Walsh, and Packard was a jealous control freak, rumored to be ex-CIA, with the cunning to orchestrate a setup. Jimmy had been wrong. Samantha's affair with Walsh hadn't made her special. When he had asked her about being the good wife in the pet shop, she hadn't understood—she had taken him literally. If Mick Packard had been the husband Jimmy was looking for, he would never have pulled the stunt in the pet shop. The man who had framed Walsh would have been more subtle; Jimmy would have a fatal accident or just disappear.

"Jimmy!"

Jimmy felt arms around him and a sweet-smelling woman kissing him, the pain stabbing through his face from where Packard had hit him. He pulled away and saw Chase Gooding in gold lamé hip-huggers and a belly shirt, blond hair cascading across her bare shoulders, cold as granite and pink to the bone.

Rollo's eyes were bugging out of his head looking at her.

"Jimmy!" Chase kissed him again, the tip of her tongue banging against his teeth. "You got me on the guest list, just like you said you would! I didn't think anybody kept a promise anymore, but you did."

Jimmy disengaged himself from her. "You meet any Scientologists yet?"

"Mission accomplished. Me and Zed somebody are partnered up for the scavenger hunt," Chase said. "Zed goes to the downtown temple or church or whatever they call it. He doesn't know Tom Cruise personally, but I tell you, Jimmy, Zed's so clear and connected, it's scary." Chase's miniskirt showed off the striated muscles of her inner thighs. "Are you with anybody?"

"Aren't you going to introduce me to your little friend, Jimmy?" asked Napitano.

"Nino, this is Chase Gooding, an actress. Chase, this—"

"I know who Mr. Napitano is, silly," said Chase, air-kissing the publisher.

"A pleasure to meet you," Nino said solemnly. "Good luck in the scavenger hunt."

"Gosh," said Chase, flustered now. "I gotta go, or I'm going to blow it for the team. Ciao!" She winked at Jimmy and dashed off.

"What lovely breasts," said Napitano, watching her run across the marble floor, high heels clippity-clopping. "I hope she wins."

"You really got a thing with scavenger hunts, huh, Nino?" said Rollo.

"The scavenger hunt is uniquely American—dynamic, creative, *forceful*," said Nino, blue silk pajamas rippling with every gesture. "It is Manifest Destiny writ in the search for treasure real or imagined, the cultural detritus begged, borrowed, or stolen. You and Jimmy played the game magnificently, as I knew you would."

"Thanks, man," said Rollo. He glanced around and tapped his coat. "I got it."

"Wonderful." Napitano nodded at the current rerun of the fight at the pet store. "I've seen enough of our brave gladiator's exploits. Let us adjourn to my study for a screening, *molto privato*."

"Walsh's rough cut?" said Jimmy.

"Fucking-A *Hammerlock*, dude," confirmed Rollo.

Napitano led Jimmy and Rollo through the house, parting the crowd with an imperious flick of his hand. Purchased from a child actor whose brilliant career had flamed out a few years after puberty, the mansion was thirty-six thousand square feet of fun and offered two swimming pools, a poker room, an ice cream parlor, a full gym, a batting cage, and a video game center. Nino used almost none of the sports facilities, considering physical exercise a waste of time, but the ice cream parlor was fully utilized, the chocolate syrup flown in weekly from Switzerland. The study was in the farthest wing, where sounds from the party still echoed. Napitano punched in his entry code, shielding the numbers from view, then looked into an aperture on the wall. Retina scan complete, the door clicked open. "Please make yourself at home," he said as they followed him inside, the gimbaled door closing after them with a slight hiss.

Napitano waved to the red leather sofas facing a flat-screen television and the one-kilo tin of black Iranian caviar within its nest of crushed ice. He poured champagne for all of them.

Rollo slipped a DVD out of his jacket and into the player.

"This movie should be a most useful addition to this article on the late Garrett Walsh that you've been spending so much time on, Jimmy." Napitano sipped his champagne. "I trust it *will* be finished sometime in the foreseeable future?"

"Depends on how far you can see."

Rollo ignored the champagne Napitano had poured and pulled a can of Mountain Dew out of the small refrigerator built into the wall.

"*Hammerlock*'s not finished, but I think you guys are really going to like it. I've watched it about twelve times, and I still don't know where Walsh was going. I was supposed to get a copy of his script notes today from my source at the archives, but B.K. is paranoid."

Jimmy sat down on the couch. He really *was* interested, not just in seeing a rough cut by a master filmmaker but because Walsh had been having an affair with the good wife while he was making the movie. Maybe there was something in the footage that would give him a sense of who she was.

"Here we go," said Rollo as the movie started, no titles, no credits at all, just a close-up of Mick Packard's face, blood trickling from his nose. He looked almost the same as he did on tonight's newscast. "Packard is really good in this, Jimmy. I was surprised."

Hammerlock was the story of a clinically depressed, tough cop, played by Mick Packard, who is manipulated by a shy, seemingly ineffectual killer, sent down blind alleys, chasing his tail in pursuit. The rough cut had major continuity problems—the transitions between scenes were often jumpy and awkward—but Packard was utterly convincing as the desperate cop, gobbling pills, slapping around suspects, a strong man unraveling, trying to cover his fear with bravado, talking out his troubles only with his sister.

The cop's best lead was a beautiful woman, a waitress who had heard the killer's gloating voice after he killed his fourth victim, even saw his retreating back when she looked out her window. The waitress and the cop had real chemistry—the actress was Victoria Lanois, and like Walsh, she never did such good work again, but she was the perfect mixture of strength and vulnerability in *Hammerlock,* the attraction between her and Packard's character made even more powerful by never being consummated. An hour and a half into the movie, drunk and desperate, the cop stops by her house with a droopy bouquet of flowers and finds her dead in the kitchen, the TV blaring.

The scene didn't work; it was too graphic, particularly for a character the viewer had come to love. Multiple shotgun blasts had blown her head to pieces. Walsh let the camera drift across the blood-sprayed walls, finally coming to rest on her shattered skull.

Jimmy shook his head. Walsh had an ugly imagination.

"Oh my," said Napitano as the screen went to gray.

"That's it?" said Jimmy.

"That's it," said Rollo. "The last act was never shot. I checked three earlier versions of the screenplay, but they're completely different. The cop is more of a straight-arrow type, and the waitress doesn't die—the cop uses her for bait."

"Was there much of a change in the waitress character from the earlier drafts?" said Jimmy, wondering if Walsh's deepening affair with the good wife during filming had been reflected in the female lead.

"Not really." Rollo got up, ejected the DVD, and slipped the case into his jacket. "She was a blonde up until the second rewrite, but that's—"

"You're sure about that? She wasn't a brunette in the first draft?" said Jimmy.

"I'm sure. I remember thinking it was a weird decision. Blondes usually get a rise from the suits, and the—"

"I want to look at every version of the screenplay you've got," said Jimmy.

"The scene of the waitress taking a shower—that was new too," said Rollo, thinking. "I checked the production notes. It was one of the last things Walsh shot. Gratuitous, maybe, but that blue tile with the mermaids looking over her shoulder as she's washing her hair—it was kind of hot."

Jimmy nodded. The scene *was* hot, but it was more than that: It was loving and appreciative too, almost too intimate. He was sorry that Sugar Brimley hadn't been able to get them into Walsh's old beach house. If the new owners hadn't remodeled, Jimmy was certain, absolutely *certain*, that the bathroom would have had a blue tile shower with decorative mermaids.

Chapter 38

"I already left three messages with his service," said Jimmy. "Do you have *any* idea when he's coming in to the office?"

"Felix the Cat better not show his face. That twitch blew off two gangbang scenes yesterday and didn't even bother calling, so if he thinks he's still got a job here, he's out of his fucking mind."

"It's really important I talk to him."

"If you got the clap, I have a list of preferred providers." The Intimate Ecstasy Productions talent wrangler's voice hardened. "If you got the bug, you didn't get it on one of our movies, so forget suing—"

Jimmy clicked off his cell phone.

"Still can't find Felix?" said Rollo.

Jimmy chewed his lip. Felix had been scared at the porn shoot, but he didn't talk like he was ready to run. Now he was AWOL. "I wanted to ask him some more questions. I'm still trying to locate Stephanie, the agent's secretary."

Rollo dropped the VW van into first gear, the engine whining as they drove up the winding road toward the crest of Orange Hill. "He must have gone underground again."

"Maybe."

"What's that mean?" Rollo glanced over at him. "Should I be scared?"

Jimmy didn't answer.

Rollo edged away from Jimmy, as though that would help.

It was an overcast morning, the sun not making much headway against the haze.

"Screening the rough cut of *Hammerlock* for Nino was the smartest thing I ever did." Rollo pushed back his glasses. "I just wanted to bring something special to the party—I didn't expect Nino to bankroll a documentary about the last days of Garrett Walsh. How cool is that?" He hunched over the wheel, trying to see through the dirty windshield. "First time I ever made a movie without having to move a load of laptops." He glanced at Jimmy. "I can still upgrade that crappy Trinitron of yours. It's not like I'm retired."

"That's a comfort."

"I got a question, and I want you to take your time answering. Ready?" Rollo took a deep breath. "You think I should bleach my hair?"

"No."

"You're sure?"

"Oh, yeah."

"What if I got a sports car? Gerardo says he can make me a deal on a slightly warm Porsche. Can't you see me in a red turbocharged nine twenty-eight?"

"I see you on the way to hairplugsville, grinding the gears all the way."

"I need *help*, man. You see those women at Nino's on Saturday night? I was in play a couple times, but as soon as the pussy saw my wheels, good-bye, Rollo. Winning the scavenger hunt helped, but that was last month. You're good with women. I still don't know how you nailed Jane Holt."

"She said I was the only man who could beat her at Scrabble."

"So I have to beef up my vocabulary if I want to get laid?"

Jimmy shrugged. "I cheated."

The car crested the top of the hill. An ancient Volvo with a peeling Greenpeace bumper sticker was parked next to Walsh's trailer. Yellow police-tape streamers rippled listlessly in the breeze. The windows to the trailer were broken, and the door was torn off its hinges.

Past the trailer Saul Zarinski waded in the koi pond, a bony intellectual wearing rubber boots, khaki shorts, and a denim shirt.

Rollo parked next to the Volvo and set the handbrake. He reached for his digital video camera, but Jimmy was already out of the van.

The inside of Walsh's trailer had been trashed, the cheap furniture smashed to splinters, the refrigerator overturned, the cupboards empty, the mattress cut open, stuffing clumped on the floor. Graffiti had been sprayed on the walls: pentagrams, gang slogans, profanity, even a call for the Anaheim High School football team to "go all the way!"

Rollo moved around Jimmy with his camera, making a slow smooth pan of the main room, one knee bent, muttering, "Perfect, perfect," as he took in the crushed fish crackers and Ding Dongs smeared into the carpet.

Jimmy walked out of the trailer and headed toward the koi pond. He could see the main house higher up the hill, still vacant, its shutters closed, but the lawn was green and freshly mowed. The smell got worse at he neared the koi pond. "Professor Zarinski?"

Zarinski looked up, blinking. He wore surgical gloves, the breast pocket of his shirt was stuffed with pens, and hair was curling around his ears.

"I'm Jimmy Gage. We met—"

"I remember you." Zarinski wet a pencil in his mouth and wrote in a small notebook.

Jimmy was closer now. A metal screen dangled from the tripod. Something gray and amorphous rested on the mesh, its skin swollen to bursting, maggots wriggling across the surface. Blackflies drifted overhead, their buzzing like static. The stink burned his nostrils, and breathing through his mouth just made him taste it. "What *is* that?"

"Pig." Zarinski cranked a handle, lowering the pig back into the water. Flies walked through his hair and marched across his eyebrows. "Domestic pig." He made another notation in his book. "Twenty-four point seven grams less pig than yesterday."

"Waste of good barbecue." Jimmy watched a gold-streaked koi poke at the bloated carcass. "This is an experiment?"

"It's not sadism, I can assure you." Zarinski splashed out of the koi pond and over toward some thornbushes. He reached into the brush, slid out a hidden stainless-steel device, and checked the dials. "Hydrothermograph," he said, answering Jimmy's unspoken question. "Measures ambient air temperature and humidity."

"What are you trying to prove?"

Zarinski kept writing. "Finally. Someone who realizes that the purpose of an experiment is to *prove* something. You have no idea the foolish questions I've had to deal with. 'Do earwigs nest in your ear when you sleep?' he mimicked. 'Do scorpions sting themselves when they're cornered?'" He looked up at Jimmy. "Entomology is the most disrespected specialty in science."

"Not by Katz though."

Zarinski smiled.

"I heard that she and Boone got into an argument in the forensics lab. One of the techs told me it had something to do with you."

"Detective Katz has been very supportive of my research. I wish I could say the same for Dr. Boone."

"That's what you're doing? You're challenging the Walsh autopsy?"

Zarinski pursed his lips. "Let's just say that the man is a very sloppy scientist."

Helen Katz backhanded the fly in midair, bouncing it off the wall and onto the bird's-eye maple floor. Then she stepped on it.

The realtor dropped to one knee, wiped up the squashed insect with a pink tissue, and tucked it into the pocket of her navy blue suit with white piping. "Detective, I have a prospective client for the house coming by any moment now."

"This shouldn't take long." Katz saw the realtor glance at her watch and wanted to backhand her too. Skinny-ass broad wearing a thousand dollars worth of clothes on her back—don't get Katz even started about the woman's shoes, some matching blue lizard job with an open toe. Regular pedicures on those dainty toes. They probably didn't even make shoes like that for Katz's splayed feet. Not that she would wear them anyway. She wouldn't. "I wanted to ask you about the last time you saw Walsh."

"I already gave you my statement right after poor Mr. Walsh's body was discovered—"

"Tell me again."

"As *previously* stated, it was on the sixth. I checked my Day-Timer." The realtor sprayed air-freshener around the living room, a vanilla-cinnamon potion intended to make spending a million dollars on a fixer-upper with no backyard seem like a smart idea. "I was showing the Orange Hill house to a nice Brazilian family. It's an over-priced property, and there hasn't been much interest—"

"You're certain it was Walsh you saw?"

"Who else would it have been?"

Zarinski dangled the white maggot in front of Jimmy's face. "This is a first-stage blowfly larva, *Chrysomya rufifacies.*"

Jimmy stared at the maggot squirming between the thumb and forefinger of Zarinski's pink surgical gloves. "Vermicelli."

"I beg your pardon?"

"Vermicelli—the pasta. It's Italian for 'little worms.' "

"I didn't know that." Zarinski looked at the maggot like he wanted to kiss it. "Vermicelli." He nodded. "Thank you for that delightful factoid, Mr. Gage."

"I've always been interested in bugs."

"Insects."

"Right." Jimmy watched the fat white maggot bending back and forth in Zarinski's delicate grasp. The grub reminded him of a tourist doing sit-ups.

"Most laypersons find my research disgusting."

"Sometimes you have to get down and dirty to know what's really going on in the world."

Zarinski beamed.

"So you and Boone disagreed over the results of the autopsy?"

"Dr. Boone is an ignoramus." Zarinski cleared his throat. "Medical examiners depend on data like lividity, organ deterioration, and rigor mortis to estimate time of death, but those measurements are questionable at best with a body half-immersed in water." He held up the maggot to Jimmy. "This *vermicelli* is the single most precise method of establishing time of death. If Dr. Boone had even a basic understanding of entomology . . ." He leaned over the koi pond and tenderly replaced the maggot on the pig. "Within ten minutes of death adult blowflies are on the scene, feeding on blood or other body fluids, depositing eggs into the body cavities, either wounds or natural cavities like eyes, ears, nose, and mouth. The blowflies start the clock. Understand?"

"I'm listening."

Zarinski nodded. "During the mean temperature range at this time of year, egg-laying on the corpse would continue for approximately eight days. The life cycle of the blowfly—egg to maggot to pupa—takes eleven days. When I arrived on the scene with Detective Katz, I found discarded pupa cases floating in the koi pond. So eight plus eleven—death occurred at least nineteen days prior to your discovery of the body. *That's* our baseline. The flesh flies arrive three to four days after the blowflies, as soon as the body begins to putrefy. Local weather conditions are critical to determining the onset of flesh flies. This gives us another temporal line for our calculations. Where those two lines intersect is crucial to determining time of death. Are you with me?"

"I'm tagging along as best I can."

"Good chap. I wish I could say the same for Dr. Boone, but he was threatened by my theory. He actually revoked my privileges at the crime lab."

"What exactly was your theory?"

" 'Forget the fieldwork, Saul, get to the hypothesis.' I've heard that before." Zarinski pulled out his notebook and tapped a line of figures. "I presented Dr. Boone with my research, and he wouldn't even discuss adjusting his report. That's when I redid my experiment." He pointed at the bloated gray mass bobbing in the koi pond. "One thirty-kilo pig, drugged with the same narcotic mixture found in Walsh's toxicology results, the dosage proportionate to body weight—"

"Professor, what was your disagreement with Boone?"

"Dr. Boone *estimated* time of death as sometime on the seventh, but my *research* establishes that time of death occurred no later than the fifth."

"So how does that discrepancy affect Boone's findings? How does that prove that Walsh didn't drown, that he was murdered?"

Zarinski looked confused. "It doesn't prove anything of the kind."

"You said you and Boone disagreed—"

"Not over cause of death. Cause of death isn't my area of expertise." Flies hovered around Zarinski, but he ignored them. "Postmortem interval is my subspecialty. *Time* of death. Boone's estimate was wrong by at least forty-eight hours."

"What about Boone's conclusion that Walsh had drowned?"

"I don't speculate outside my area of expertise."

Jimmy stared at the rotting pig bobbing in the koi pond. Zarinski might not speculate outside his expertise, but Katz did. Speculating was her job, and it was Jimmy's too. She must have figured that if Boone fucked up the time of death, he might have been wrong about the *cause* of death too. He looked over at the professor. "Your time-of-death theory must have impressed Katz. That's why she got into an argument with Boone last week, wasn't it?"

"Detective Katz is a fierce advocate of the scientific method. Dr. Boone kept backing up until he tripped over a chair." Zarinski peeled off his surgical gloves with a snap. "I believe the argument also had something to do with you. Detective Katz kept mentioning your name. She's quite fond of you."

"Yeah, I could tell by the way she almost broke my face."

"Aggressive action on the part of the female is quite common before mating."

"If you're a praying mantis maybe, but—"

"Female behavior is remarkably consistent across the phyla," Zarinski said idly, scooping a black beetle out of the koi pond.

"Jimmy?" called Rollo, coming up behind him. "Whoa, dude. What's *that* in the pool?"

Jimmy's phone rang.

"Is this Jimmy Gage?"

"Hi, who's this?" Jimmy watched Rollo filming the floating pig.

"Carmen. We met at the Healthy Life Café."

Jimmy heard her cough and imagined the henna redhead with a cigarette propped in the corner of her mouth. "Hey, Carmen, how are you?" He tried to contain his excitement. "Did you find that Christmas card from Stephanie?"

"You sure you're not a bill collector?"

"Cross my heart."

"Well, you got a nice face." Carmen hacked into the receiver. "Went through ten shoeboxes full of cards and magazine clippings before I found it. Stephanie's address is right there on the back, just like I remembered. Three years ago and it seems like yesterday. Makes you realize how time flies." She cleared her throat. "I'm thinking of starting some decoupage projects next weekend, getting right on it, no more excuses. You think if I decorated a lampshade for you that you'd use it?"

"At our first interview, you said you saw Garrett Walsh. Now you're not sure?"

"The person I saw was quite some distance away." The realtor rooted in her purse. "I—I was showing the view from the second-floor bedroom when I saw him at the far edge of the property. I just assumed it was Mr. Walsh. I never saw anyone else there."

"You *assumed* it was him." Katz wasn't really annoyed—she was pleased. The realtor's assumption fit in with Zarinski's theory. She would never have thought to contact the professor if it hadn't been for Jimmy's doubts about Boone, so score one for the reporter. She didn't understand half of what Zarinski was talking about—all she knew was that the professor said that Walsh had died at least two days *be-*

fore Boone did. There was a problem with that. Her initial interview with the realtor had merely corroborated Boone's findings—she had seen Walsh on the afternoon of the seventh, the same day that Boone pegged his time of death. According to Zarinski, however, Walsh had already been dead two days when the realtor spotted him.

If Zarinski was right, the realtor had seen *someone* on the property that day, but it wasn't Walsh. It wouldn't have been Harlen Shafer either—that two-bit ex-con would have been gone as soon as he realized Walsh was dead. It wouldn't have been kids—they would have trashed the place then, not later. No, the realtor had seen someone else strolling the grounds, someone who had unfettered access to the trailer, someone who had plenty of time to look for the screenplay and notes that Jimmy was so interested in.

"Detective?" The realtor tapped her foot on the hardwood floor. "Are we finished?"

Katz slammed the door on the way out.

Chapter 39

The street sign at the intersection had been knocked down and lay half in the street. Jimmy got out of his car, walked over, and checked the sign. The broken stump gave no indication which of the streets was N.E. 47th Court; he got back into his car and picked one, checking addresses on the houses as he drove slowly past. Heat waves rose from the pavement, blurring the numbers.

Jimmy glanced at the Christmas card tucked above the car's visor. He saw a tired woman in a Rudolph the Red-Nosed Reindeer sweater and a little girl dressed as an elf standing beside a blue Christmas tree.

Victorville was a small windblown town on the edge of the Mojave Desert—about ten years ago it had been touted as a bedroom community for L.A. and Orange County, the two-hour commute a trade-off for clean air and affordable housing. The town had boomed for a while, tripling in population as housing developments with names like Desert Rose, Sunset Estates, and Tumbleweed Valhalla were thrown up as fast as nonunion carpenters could work. The recession changed everything. When business soured, Victorville's eager commuters were the first fired, their hours cut or outsourced to Mexico. The new housing developments were ghost towns now, whole blocks foreclosed and abandoned, the yards reverting to sand and weeds.

Jimmy peered through the windshield, checking numbers, when a bee bumped against the glass. He thought of Saul Zarinski and his flesh flies and beetles at the koi pond. To the entomologist, the over-lapping life cycles of the insects that had made a condominium of Garrett Walsh's corpse were a marvel of precision. Jimmy was impressed with the man's research, but bugs still creeped him out. He glanced at his files on the floor of the Saab, notes to himself strewn across the seat, with Zarinski's postmortem timeline highlighted in yellow. There was something there, something nagging at him. Right now, though, he wanted to talk with Stephanie Panagopolis.

Jimmy slowed. The blue rambler across the street had a Barney pup tent on the dry lawn, the bright purple fabric flapping in the constant wind. It was the only sign of children he had seen since he got off the freeway. The address on the house matched the Christmas card.

The doorbell rang the theme from *Zorba the Greek.*

The woman who answered the door looked like the one on the Christmas card, wearing jeans and an untucked white blouse instead of a reindeer sweater. She was even more tired-looking now than in her photo, her skin sallow, her dark hair dry and flyaway. She peered out at him from the far side of the security chain. "Can I help you?"

"Mrs. Panagopolis, my name is Jimmy Gage. I'm a reporter." Jimmy showed her his photo ID from *SLAP.* "I'd like to talk with you for a few minutes, if it's all right."

"I see. Well, I'm busy now. Maybe you could come back—"

"I need to talk to you about April McCoy."

She nodded. "Of course you do." She didn't move.

"I've come a long way to see you." Jimmy waited while she slowly slid the chain off the door, then followed her into the small living room. "Were you expecting me?"

"Yes . . . for a very long time." Stephanie sat on the sofa, knees together, and placed her hands in her lap. She was plain, with a long face and the wrong shade of makeup, but her eyes were pretty, and she had a generous mouth. Photographs of her daughter hung on one wall: pictures of her in a Brownie uniform, in a bathing suit hurtling down a water slide, in pajamas. The daughter looked just like her mother. The yellow floral-print couch was faded, but the arms were covered with bright knitted squares, and there was a knitted afghan across the back too. The house was clean and quiet, the only incongruous bit of decor the cardboard boxes stacked in the far corner of the room. No radio, no TV, no stereo—just the sound of the wind outside. "Can I get you a glass of water? It's filtered."

"Ah, sure."

She didn't move. The question had been mechanical, and his response didn't trigger any action. "I sell water-filtration systems. The unit screws right into the faucet. It's more economical than bottled."

"Mrs. Panagopolis—"

"Call me Stephanie. There's no Mr. Panagopolis anymore, there's just me and my daughter—and that stupid doorbell. I hate that song. It was my husband's idea. Only thing he ever did around the house was install that doorbell." She plucked at the collar of her blouse. "I sell Amway products. Business used to be better. If you need laundry detergent or hand cream or shaving lotion, if you need anything, you just ask me."

Jimmy glanced at the cardboard boxes.

"The bath gel, the apricot bath gel, is quite nice. I carry a full line of vitamins too. You can never get enough vitamins. Our food is dead. They don't tell you that, but it is."

"I'm here to talk to you about Heather Grimm."

"You said you wanted to talk about April."

"You'll be an unnamed source. You have my word."

Her eyes focused on him, and she saw him clearly. "An unnamed source? Oh my, *that's* a relief. That will fix everything."

"I talked to a man—he used to be a photographer. His name then was Willard Burton." Jimmy saw Stephanie grimace. "Burton told me about April McCoy's sideline."

"Sideline?" She tugged idly at her hair, a few strands drifting toward the carpet.

"Burton said he used to steer underage girls and boys to April."

"How is Willard Burton? Is he well? Has life been kind to him?"

"Heather Grimm was one of April's clients."

"I get a mammogram twice a year. I feel myself for lumps every day. My mother used to say that cancer was God's judgment. Do you think that's true?"

"No, I don't."

She smiled, and her relief made her pretty. "I think you must be right, Mr. Gage. If Willard Burton is alive and well . . . you *must* be right."

Jimmy moved onto the couch beside her. "Heather Grimm didn't end up at Walsh's beach house by accident—April sent her. But it wasn't April's idea. Whose idea was it?"

Stephanie shook her head.

"You worked for April McCoy for years."

"I worked at a desk." Stephanie's whole body was shaking. "I sat behind a desk. I answered the phone. I made coffee and went out for sandwiches. That's all."

"Maybe sitting at your desk you saw something. Maybe answering the phone you heard something. I'm just asking for your help. I'm not trying to blame you."

"If I had known what she was doing, if I had known for sure—"

"What did you see?"

"Willard Burton was an *awful* man. I knew that the first moment he showed up in the office, digging his hands into my candy dish on his way into April's office, not even waiting for me to announce him."

"When did he first start coming around?"

"It was a few years before—before Heather Grimm became a client. He didn't come in very often after that first time. I think April must have said something to him."

"So when he stopped coming by the office, he called?"

"Yes."

"You handled the incoming calls."

Stephanie fidgeted. "That was my job."

"If it was *my* job, I would have listened in once in a while."

"I could have gotten fired for doing that."

"A man like Burton calling my boss—I would have done it anyway. I would have worried for her, wondered what she had gotten herself into. I think you're the same way."

Stephanie stared out the picture window at an empty Bucket-o-Chicken blowing down the street. "This used to be a lovely place to live. Lots of young families, plenty of kids for my daughter to play with. Some of the fathers put up a playground in a vacant lot down the street—slides and swings. It just sits there now. When we had block parties, everyone turned out. People used to love my pasta salad. They would ask me for the recipe, and I always gave it to them. Some women don't share recipes, or they deliberately give you the wrong ingredients, but I can't do that."

Jimmy put his hand on her wrist and felt her pull back.

"Pimentos, that was the secret to my pasta salad. Pimentos and Del Monte tartar sauce."

"I bet Burton flirted with you when he called. I've met him. He calls himself Felix now, Felix the Cat. He thinks he's a charmer."

"He used to call me Porkchop. *Porkchop.*" Stephanie watched the brown grass across the street. "Burton talked in code to April. 'I've got a guppy for you,' he would say. I didn't even know what he was talking about for a long time. Not until it was too late. I had read somewhere that there was a black market for tropical fish. The article said that collectors paid big money for rare ones, fish that were endangered; sometimes for fish that weren't even pretty, just dangerous. That's what I thought he was doing."

Jimmy didn't argue with her. "So Burton supplied guppies to April; I already know that. What I'm interested in was who April sold the guppies to. Who paid her to send Heather Grimm to the beach house?"

Stephanie twisted a strand of hair between her thumb and forefinger. "Heather wasn't a guppy."

Jimmy stared at her. "What was she?"

Stephanie twirled her hair faster now. "A goose." She nodded. "A goose that laid the golden egg. There were plenty of guppies, but Heather was the only goose. She was *very* special."

Burton had described her the same way to Jimmy at the porn shoot.

"My daughter is seven years old now. I look at her sleeping sometimes, and I wonder how I could have been so stupid." Strands of hair floated in the quiet room. "I *was* stupid, wasn't I? Not something worse?"

"You just didn't put it all together until it was too late, that's all. It's happened to me before. You think you know what's going on, but you don't."

"You're a kind man."

"No, I'm not. I just know what it's like to fuck up."

Stephanie clasped her hands. She looked like she was trying to catch her breath. "I sell ozone generators that are supposed to reduce stress. I can't . . . I can't guarantee—"

"You never overheard April on the phone talking to someone about Heather?"

Stephanie shook her head.

"You never heard Garrett Walsh's name mentioned?"

"I left the office at six o'clock, but April always stayed late. I don't think she liked going home. Whoever you're looking for, they must have called after I left."

Jimmy sat beside her for a long time thinking. "What exactly made April special? Because she was so young, and yet so mature—"

"Heather was the only one April ever put under contract. *That's* why she was special."

"I don't understand."

"The other guppies, I never even met them. I would hear April and Burton talking, and a week or two later April would have a new designer outfit, something from Rodeo Drive. She was a big girl, but she was a clotheshorse. Stylish. I admired that."

"You never met the guppies. Did you meet Heather?"

"Heather was a goose." Stephanie smiled at the memory. "April was so proud. She kept telling Heather about this big part she had locked in for her, a 'star vehicle' she called it, not just a walk-on, a real break-out role."

"April never promised a specific part to one of her clients?"

"Oh my, no."

"What was the part April had locked in for Heather? It's very important."

Stephanie concentrated, then shook her head.

"April was *sure* that Heather had the part nailed?"

"She said it was a done deal."

Jimmy nodded. April had never expected Heather to be killed that night; Heather's rape was to ruin Garrett's career, and his arrest would make Heather a household name, a player. A high-profile film role could turn Heather into a star, and a contract would guarantee that April got taken along for the ride. Even Mick Packard at the height of his power couldn't have opened that many doors to Heather. Neither could a jealous coke dealer or a software king. No, that took *real* juice.

Stephanie sniffed. "You okay?"

"It's like I said before, sometimes it takes a while to put things together, and when you finally do, you wonder what took you so long."

"Don't be so hard on yourself. It's not healthy. I think that's why April committed suicide—she must have blamed herself for what happened to Heather."

"You think April committed suicide?"

"April—underneath it all, she was a very spiritual person."

"Willard Burton thinks she was murdered."

Stephanie was very still, a rabbit trying to blend into the background. "Willard Burton is a man who doesn't understand guilt," she said at last. "April knew about guilt. Just like me. That's why we both overate." She looked at Jimmy. "If the thing with Heather had worked out the way it was supposed to, April wasn't going to have anything more to do with Willard Burton. I'm sure of that. She disliked that man as much as I did." Her eyes were downcast now, remembering. "The afternoon Heather signed with the agency was *such* a good day. Heather was going on about buying a Corvette, a pink Corvette, and April was talking about getting a new office, and maybe one of those ergonomic chairs for me. A wonderful day. My hand actually shook when I notarized the contract."

Jimmy stared at her. "How could Heather sign a contract? She was a minor."

"Her mother was there. She signed too. We were all so happy, and then Garrett Walsh ruined everything. Me and Burton, we're the only ones left alive. It kind of makes you wonder, doesn't it?" She looked at Jimmy. "That sounded bad, didn't it? Should I be worried?"

"Just stay put. I'll be back in touch soon. If you remember the name of the movie April had promised Heather, let me know."

Stephanie glanced out the window and checked the street. "I knew I shouldn't have answered the door."

Chapter 40

Darn it. Sugar slowly pulled the splinter out from the tender flesh between his thumb and forefinger, then flicked it out into the weeds surrounding the playhouse. He sucked at the wound and tasted copper. He smiled at the double entendre.

The playhouse was a small structure with a peaked roof about ten feet off the ground, with a ladder on one side and a long slide on the other. It was built of raw boards painted to look like logs, blistered by the sun now. FORT APACHE was stenciled onto the sides. There was room for about four or five kids, but Sugar filled it up, lying there on his belly, his legs sticking out the back as he peeked out the front entrance. Down the street he could see Jimmy Gage standing on the front porch of the blue rambler, talking to a woman in jeans and a white blouse. She looked familiar.

Sugar had followed Jimmy all the way from Huntington Beach to this godforsaken bump in the road, keeping fifteen or twenty miles back. He didn't even play the radio, listening instead to the beeping from the locator-receiver on the passenger seat. The transmitter attached to the undercarriage of Jimmy's car sent out a steady signal.

One of Sugar's old cop buddies had retired and gone to work for LoJack, an electronic tracking service that retrieved stolen cars equipped with the device. Last year Sugar had traded Vince a cooler full of bonita for one, and a demonstration of how to use it. Vince had winked, asked if Sugar had a girlfriend he thought was fooling around on him. Sugar had winked back, said you never knew when fancy gear would come in handy. It *had* come in handy too. After saving Jimmy's bacon that day at the marina, then driving him home when he was too beat up to drive himself, Sugar had hooked up Jimmy's car.

Sugar had been keeping tabs on Jimmy ever since. He just had to turn on the receiver in his own car and follow the blinking light on the map readout to know where Jimmy was. Following Jimmy over hill and dale, from one end of the county to the other was too much like work, though, and Sugar was *retired.* Catching those yellowjack a few nights ago, well, it was just flat-out relaxing hooking that first fish, hearing the line spool out as it headed off to freedom. Particularly after dealing with that Felix the Cat fellow.

Sugar adjusted his position, making sure that he stayed in the shadows, careful of splinters now. The playground was deserted, the basketball hoops bent, the swings rusted. Half the houses on the block were empty. He had spotted Jimmy's car parked in front of the blue rambler, made a U-turn, and parked on the next street, taking up his position in the clubhouse, where he had a good view and privacy. The houses on either side were boarded up. He didn't have to wait long until the front door opened and the two of them came out, dragging out their good-byes. Sugar rested his chin in his hands. He just *knew* he had seen the woman before.

Chapter 41

"Danziger residence."

Jimmy drove with one hand on the wheel, thinking.

"Danziger residence, may I *help* you?"

Jimmy disconnected the call. He wanted to talk to Danziger's wife, but not enough to go through the butler or whatever the hell Raymond was. He punched in the main switchboard of *SLAP,* then the extension for the magazine's gossip columnist.

"This is Miss Chatterbox, talkee-talkee."

"Hi, Ann, it's Jimmy." He kicked the Saab up to eighty-five and passed the silver Toyota 4x4. The kid behind the wheel was in a backward Lakers hat and toasted Jimmy with a beer. "Do you know anything—"

"I know you're in heap big trouble. Napitano has been looking for you all day."

"Yeah, I got a couple of his messages."

"He's been cursing in Italian."

"Ann, do you know anything about Michael Danziger and his wife?"

"Film producer, right? Used to be somebody?"

"Used to be head of Epic International."

"Oh, yes, I remember him now. Got canned five or six years ago. *Taurus Rising* finished him, if memory serves. Budgeted at eighty million and did less than five million at the box office. Sayonara, Mikey."

Jimmy could hear Ann flipping through her Rolodex. She was one

• 263

of the old-school gossip columnists who preferred card files to computer directories. There were plenty of Hollywood big shots who April McCoy could have been working for, plenty of executives who could have promised a film career for Heather Grimm, but Michael Danziger was the one who had hired Walsh, the one who showed up on set halfway through the shoot. He'd been keeping an eye on the production, he had told Jimmy. Maybe. Jimmy remembered Danziger swimming against the jets in his lap pool, swimming hard and steady, his workout routine precisely calibrated. Yeah, there were plenty of suspects, but like Jane said, when your investigation stalls, start with what you have in front of you.

"Michael and Brooke Danziger," Ann must have been reading it off the card, "married twelve, no make that thirteen years ago. No children. The usual charities, Cedars-Sinai, AIDS America, Lupus, Parkinson's. I see them at parties and fund-raisers once in a while. He's a smoothie, handsome as the day is long, always shaking hands. Perrier drinker, vegetarian . . . Oh, this is interesting. I made a note to myself a few months ago. Seems Michael's last two—no, three charity pledges haven't been honored. I was going to run it, but I decided to wait until he had another hit. How *is* his new movie? *My Troubled Girl, Trouble with My Girl,* something like that. Can I run with my item?"

"You're going to have to keep waiting." The Saab's steering wheel vibrated in his grip, and Jimmy slowed slightly. The road was nearly empty going back to the city, but he backed off the gas. The Highway Patrol had radar units and helicopters, and he didn't want to waste another Saturday in traffic school. "What about the wife?"

"Ummmmm, Brooke's not really part of the business. I remember seeing her at the Academy Awards a few times, but she seemed a little out of place. She always sticks close to Michael. Oh, she was evidently an equestrian champion before she was married. Rode in the Rose Parade for several years—a real Dale Evans."

"Do you have a photo?"

"I smell a scoop here, Jimmy. I told you where Samantha Packard worked out, and the next thing I knew you're on TV being attacked by that jealous ass of a husband. Now you want to know about Brooke Danziger. If you're on some Hollywood wives scavenger hunt, I want an exclusive."

"You overestimate me." Jimmy checked his rearview mirror. The Toyota pickup was a silver speck in the distance. He thought of Stephanie Panagopolis miles away now, with her memories of guppies and the goose that was going to lay the golden eggs. He should have bought something from her, apricot bath gel for Jane, or a water filter. He could have put it on his expense account, see what Napitano said about that.

"What's this all about, Jimmy?"

"Just a minute, Ann, I've got another call. Hello?"

"Jimmy? Michael Danziger here. You just called the house but didn't say anything. I was wondering if there was some kind of problem?"

Jimmy hated Caller ID. He was going to have to find another way to contact Brooke Danziger. "Thanks for following up, Michael. The battery in my cell phone is running low and kept cutting out. Just wanted to ask, when is the premiere of *My Girl Trouble*?"

"How *lovely*," said Danziger. "This Friday at the Regency. I'll messenger you over some VIP passes."

"I'm cutting out here," said Jimmy, switching back to the other line. "Sorry, Ann. One last question. When you saw the Danzigers at parties, did you get any sense of trouble between them?"

"Darling, there's *always* trouble between man and wife in this town. What do you really want to know?"

Jimmy jerked as a green dragonfly slammed into the windshield, disintegrating, one lacy wing caught for a moment under the wiper. He thought about the professor back at the koi pond and wondered if he would have been able to identify the exact species of dragonfly in the instant before it was blown to pieces.

"Jimmy? What's going on?"

Jimmy glanced over at the accordion file-folder on the floor of the car, the worn cardboard file bulging with his notes on the Garrett Walsh story. "I'll let you know as soon as I figure it out," he said, accelerating.

Chapter 42

Jimmy set down the beer, and the bottle fell over on the uneven ground, bubbling toward where his notes were spread. "Son of a *bitch*." He picked up the printout of Walsh's phone records and shook them off. He knew there was something important about the professor's reconfigured time of death, something that set off bells without him knowing why. He turned away from the printout, looking down at the distant koi pond. He had a headache from thinking.

The midafternoon sun was hotter than the morning, but he didn't notice. He sat in the shade of a scrawny lemon tree safely upwind from the stink, alone with his unfocused suspicions. Rollo and the professor were long gone. Just Jimmy now. He watched the bloated pig carcass bob serenely in the brown water and thought of Michael Danziger swimming against the tide in that little pool of his, never reaching the far side.

Sugar pressed the buzzer and heard some Greek melody. Nice. He had probably rung as many doorbells as any cop—a little personal touch was appreciated. He squared his shoulders. He had brushed off the dirt from the playhouse, then gotten in his car and driven to the nearest mall, stolen a license plate from one of the cars parked outside the movie theater, and stuck it on top of his own plate with a couple dabs of Super Glue. The Super Glue would keep the fake plate in place, but he could remove it on the way home with a strong tug, The

LoJack indicated that Jimmy was well on his way back to L.A.—that boy better be careful, the Highway Patrol was hell on speeders. He rang the bell again. That Greek tune could grow on a fellow. He adjusted his navy blue sport coat, the one he always kept in the trunk of the car, for official purposes. He smiled at the peephole.

The door opened, the security chain taut. "Yes?" The woman was suspicious, which he thought was an attractive quality in a female, and she was wearing a frilly blue apron, which really won his heart.

Sugar flipped open his wallet and let her take a good look at his gold shield while he took a good look at her. "Detective Leonard Brimley." He left the wallet open, like he was holding open the Red Sea with it. He grinned at her. "You can call me Sugar, Stephanie. Everybody else does."

Stephanie glanced at his car parked in the driveway, a five-year-old Ford with a little salt corrosion on the chrome. "Do I know you, officer?"

"Not yet, but we'll fix that." She had lost a lot of weight. They had never been introduced, but Sugar had seen her leaving April's office on three or four different occasions, watching her from the darkness of the stairwell as she trudged down the hall toward the elevator. She must have lost fifty pounds, but she still slumped. "I need to talk to you about your gentleman caller earlier today."

Stephanie slowly unchained the door. "My daughter gets home from school at three. I like to meet her at the bus stop."

"You're a good mama, but don't you fret, we'll be done by then." Sugar sniffed. "Something good's cooking."

Stephanie wiped her hands on her apron. "I just finished making cookies."

"Let's talk in the kitchen then." Sugar beamed. "Nice to see that there's still women out there who bake from scratch instead of opening up a bag of store-bought."

Stephanie clutched the apron. "I'm not much of a cook. I just wanted to whip up something my daughter could bring to class. The other kids have been picking on her."

"Kids can be so cruel. Nothing like passing out cookies to make everyone your friend."

"That's just what I was thinking."

Sugar followed her into the kitchen. It was small but neat and clean, real shipshape. A carton of eggs was on the counter, next to open bags of flour and sugar and a stick of butter. The mixing bowl was almost empty. Crayon drawings were magneted to the refrigerator. Two batches of cookies were cooling on a wire rack. The stove was gas.

"Can I get you some water, detective?" Stephanie let the tap run while she got out two tall glasses. She handed him his glass a moment later, ice cubes clinking. She looked surprised, noticing his thin leather gloves for the first time.

"Eczema," explained Sugar, taking a long drink. "Ah." He smacked his lips. "Nothing like cold water on a hot day."

"Filtered water." Stephanie took a demure sip from her own glass and wiped her lips with a pinky. "I used to drink five or six cans of soda pop a day, but now I just drink water." She blushed. "I used to have a weight problem. My whole metabolism was out of kilter."

"I find that hard to believe." Sugar ran the spatula around the rim of the mixing bowl and tasted it, gauging her reaction. "Ummm, chocolate chip—everybody's favorite." She didn't look annoyed, she looked pleased.

"I limit myself to just one cookie per batch. They used to be one of my trigger foods. Chocolate of any kind is my weakness." Stephanie broke a corner off one of the cookies and surreptitiously placed it into her mouth. "Do you take vitamins?"

"Can't say as I do."

"You really should, detective."

"Call me Sugar."

"You really should, Sugar. I'm a distributor for some of the best chelated vitamins on the market. No sugars, no starches, no fillers. They boost your energy level *naturally*."

"I guess we could all use a little more energy." Sugar leaned against the oven. It was warm but not hot. "You're a real good busi-nesswoman. I like that. Shows character."

"It's not really a choice." Stephanie broke another piece of cookie off. "I'm a single parent. Somebody's got to pay the bills."

"Maybe I'll pick up a couple bottles of vitamin C when we're done here. I don't know much about vitamins, but I heard that's good for colds."

"I have a very good thousand-milligram time-release C available. If you buy two bottles, the third one is free. I also have some aloe vera gel that will help that eczema of yours."

Sugar grinned at her. "Looks like this is my lucky day. I almost hate to have to talk business with you, but I have to." She took a longer drink, and he watched her white throat shiver as she swal-lowed. "This gentleman you were talking to"—he flipped through his notebook—"Jimmy Gage. What exactly did he ask you about?"

Stephanie drooped like a week-old daisy. "I'm not in any trouble, am I?"

Sugar patted her arm. "I've got the inside track with the district at-torney. Not to brag, but if I say you're a friend of the department, that will pretty much settle things."

"I really never knew what was going on. Not until it was too late. Could you write that down?"

Sugar wrote it down in his notebook, while Stephanie leaned over to watch. "You told that to Mr. Gage?"

"Yes, I did. I certainly did."

"You said you didn't know what was going on until it was too late. So later you *did* realize what was going on?"

"Well, yes, but by then—"

"By then it was too late. Not your fault." Sugar wrote that down too.

"Jimmy said I was going to be an unnamed source. He *promised* me."

"Jimmy Gage is interfering in a police investigation. He can't promise you anything."

"I see." Stephanie's hand shook. "You meet someone, you think you can trust them . . . It's my own fault. As I said, I used to be mildly obese. A fat girl, she always trusts a man who smiles at her. I guess, deep down, I'm still a fat girl."

"Stephanie, I need to know exactly what you told him. The whole investigation could be compromised. I'm sure he mentioned a photographer that April McCoy used."

"Willard Burton. Yes, Jimmy knew all about him."

Sugar looked up from his notes. "Would you mind pulling the drapes? I'm getting a wicked reflection off the window." He waited until Stephanie had closed the drapes and returned to the sofa. The room was darker now, cooler.

"Jimmy wasn't really that interested in Willard Burton," said Stephanie.

"No, I expect he was interested in Heather Grimm. He thinks somebody put her up to going to Garrett Walsh's beach house."

"Well, actually he knows that *April* sent her there." Stephanie drank the last of her water, the ice cubes tumbling against her upper lip. She looked pleased with herself. Nothing nicer than being able to correct a police officer. "What he wanted from me was who it was put April up to it."

Sugar took it all down. "And who did put April up to it?"

"I have no idea. That's what I told him."

"Was that the truth?"

"Yes, sir, it was."

"I know this Jimmy Gage, Stephanie. He doesn't take no for an answer. I'm sure you must have told him something he could use."

"Well, I told him that April put Heather under contract. He seemed excited by that. April said Heather had a real career in front of her. She had her lined up for a big part, a real movie, with stars and everything. Then she got killed."

"Did April ever tell you what the movie was?"

"That's just what Jimmy wanted to know." Stephanie shook her head.

"What did you tell him?"

"I told him I couldn't remember. It was the truth too."

It didn't matter. If Jimmy asked the question, he was already halfway to the answer. Sugar saw her glance at her watch. "What time does your daughter get off the bus?"

"Quarter to three."

Sugar closed his notebook. "I'd like some of that fancy vitamin C."

Stephanie beamed and headed toward the back of the house. "How about some aloe vera too?" she called over her shoulder. "No reason you should have to wear those hot gloves all the time."

"Sold." Sugar followed her into the hallway and waited until she disappeared, then went back into the kitchen. He stared at the child's drawings taped on the refrigerator: a stick-figure picture of a girl and a woman riding bicycles under a smiling, yellow sun. It made his stomach hurt. He turned away, opened the stove, slid out the wire shelves, and laid them against the wall. On one knee now, he blew out the pilot light and closed the oven door. He thought for a second, then snagged a small cushion off one of the kitchen chairs, laid it in the bottom of the oven, and closed the door again. He turned on the gas full blast, listening to it hiss. "Stephanie? Make it *two* tubes of that aloe vera gel."

"You got it, detective," Stephanie called from the rear of the house.

Sugar listened to the hissing oven for a few more minutes, then strolled back down the hallway and saw Stephanie coming out of a bedroom holding a paper bag.

"I put in a few skin-care samples. I know a big strong man like you doesn't care about things like that, but the lady in your life will appreciate it."

"There is no lady in my life."

Stephanie cocked her head. "Really?"

Sugar smiled. "I've never been much of a ladies' man."

"I find that hard to believe, detective."

Sugar looked inside the bag. "You really think these pills and potions will help me?"

Stephanie sniffed. "I smell gas."

Sugar followed her into the kitchen and found her holding the door to the oven open, waving at the rank air. He stopped her as she went to turn off the gas.

"What are you doing?"

Sugar closed the door. "We have to talk."

Stephanie lunged again for the stove dial. "The pilot light must have gone out again."

Sugar held her tightly against him, felt her struggle, and the heat and friction aroused him. "Listen. Just listen. Stephanie, *listen.* That's better," he said, as she stopped for a moment. "I want you to know, this is not my fault."

"What's not your fault?"

"What's going to happen next."

"Detective, you're scaring me."

"Not as bad as I scare myself."

Stephanie moistened her lips. "I want you to turn off the gas."

Sugar shook his head. "I'm sorry."

Stephanie bolted for the back door, but Sugar caught her, She kicked and struggled, screaming now, her voice high-pitched and shrill.

Sugar pushed her face against his chest as she screamed, his flesh muffling her cries. He patted her head, endured her kicks, and kept on talking, his voice soft and soothing. "I don't blame you. It's a lousy thing to happen to a good woman like you, coming out of the blue like this, but that's the way it's got to be."

Stephanie pulled half away from him, howling for help, but there were no neighbors to hear her, they both knew that.

Sugar drew her closer and wrapped his big arms around her. "Shh-hhh."

Stephanie kneed him, but he had been kneed by experts, and it hadn't stopped him.

"We haven't got time for this," said Sugar, his lips brushing against the pink shell of her ear. "Your little girl is going to be home soon. You don't want me to be here when she comes in through the door." He felt her shudder. "She's going to walk in, call your name, maybe ask why you weren't there at the bus stop—and then she's going to see me, and I'm not going to be able to stop myself."

Stephanie whimpered and pulled away. She was stronger than she looked. "Why are you *doing* this?"

"Don't concern yourself with that. It's your little girl you should be worried about."

"Please don't hurt her."

"I'm not a monster. It's Jimmy you should be mad at, not me."

Stephanie scratched at him, but he turned his face away and held her close.

"You keep that up, you're just going to make it worse." Sugar's voice was calm and steady. He had taken a course in hostage negotiation once; the instructor said he had the perfect voice, reassuring and nonthreatening. "If you keep fighting, you're going to bang yourself up, and you're not going to make a believable suicide. That changes everything. Then it's got to be a break-in; I'll have to spend time rifling the house, going through your purse, and when your daughter walks in and finds me here—"

Stephanie sagged. Please—please, don't." You would have thought someone had pulled a cork in her belly and her insides had poured out onto the floor. It never ceased to amaze him how it worked sometimes. "Please don't hurt her."

"That's up to you." The gas smell was stronger now, even with the oven door closed. His head was throbbing. "If your little girl comes home when I'm still here—well, it's going to give me indigestion for the rest of my life. Don't do that to me."

Stephanie's fists beat against his chest. She might as well be hitting him with flowers.

"You're a good mama. I could see that the moment I walked into the house."

Stephanie was sobbing now.

"I'll make sure I leave the doors locked. I won't let your little girl walk in and see you. There's someplace she can go if she can't get in, isn't there? Some friend down the street?" Sugar felt her nod. "It won't be so bad. You just lay your head down on the pillow, take a few deep breaths. You'll just go to sleep and dream forever."

"What did I ever do to you?"

"Not a darned thing." Sugar rocked her and felt her heart fluttering against him as the oven hissed away. The room was heavy with gas. "Not a blessed thing."

"Please—"

"You want to blame someone, blame Jimmy Gage. *He's* the one responsible."

"Jimmy? I—I hardly talked to him. A half-hour, that's all."

Sugar lifted her off her feet. Stephanie lay limply in his outstretched arms as he carried her toward the stove. "Lady, once upon a time it took just five minutes to turn my life upside down. Five minutes." He flipped open the oven with a fingertip. "A half-hour is *forever* in my book."

"I'm just tired," said Jimmy. "No, I'm fine, Jane, I'll see you tonight." He snapped the phone shut and tucked it away. The breeze shifted, and he wrinkled his nose, catching a whiff of the koi pond. He finished the beer, hefted the long neck, and considered standing up to make the throw, see if he could bounce it off the little piggy fifty or sixty yards below. Then he remembered Walsh's body floating in the same spot, swollen like a zeppelin, the skin blistered and split, pecked by crows. Katz had needed dental records to make a positive ID, but Jimmy had known it was Walsh as soon as he saw the devil tattoo on the corpse's shoulder.

Jimmy riffed through the phone records on his lap. He ran a finger down a column of Walsh's phone calls, wanting to remind himself of the last call that Walsh had made. Vacaville. Of course. Phoning home. He stopped and checked the notes he had written earlier after talking with the professor. He stared at the phone log again, not believing it.

The last two calls had both been to Vacaville, the state spa where Walsh and Harlen Shafer had done time together. Jimmy hadn't thought much of it when he and Rollo first went over the records; Walsh had called the prison every few weeks since he first got out, short calls to the main switchboard, forwarded to some paid-off guard probably. No way to trace that. Walsh was just contacting his cellies, leaving word that he had kept the promises that most cons made when they got kicked: checking up on wives and girlfriends, maybe taking a kid to the zoo in place of his three-strikes daddy. That's what Jimmy had thought at the time. Not anymore.

If the professor was right about the time of death, those last two calls had been placed *after* Walsh was already dead. Somebody else had called Vacaville while the fishes were fighting over Walsh's soft parts. Jimmy considered the possibility that Boone's time-of-death estimate was the right one, but he didn't consider it for long.

Flies floated over the koi pond, a dark cloud in the distance. Jimmy sipped his beer, thinking, glad that he couldn't hear the buzzing from where he sat. He had enough noise in his head.

Walsh had been murdered. Jimmy had been right about that, but the good wife's husband wasn't behind it. Those regular calls Walsh had made to Vacaville weren't to his bunkies—he was playing for time, tap-dancing for some O. G. with a grudge, somebody who could reach out through the bars and touch him. Touch him dead. It wasn't love or jealousy that did Walsh in. He had gotten whacked over an unpaid carton of smokes, or for talking during *Baywatch,* or maybe just for looking at the wrong guy the wrong way. With Walsh's mouth it was a wonder he had lasted seven years inside without getting shanked.

The last two calls made from Walsh's phone had been placed by his killer, the first one passing on the news that Walsh was dead, the second one—it had lasted barely a minute—confirming that the message had been received. This prison honcho had probably used Harlen Shafer to set up the hit, used him as a stalking horse, getting Walsh so stoned he couldn't fight back. Shafer himself had probably been killed for his trouble.

Jimmy wanted to be wrong, because if he was right, all his efforts trying to find the good wife and the husband—none of it mattered.

Walsh had been in a panic that night in the trailer, full of tales of love and vengeance, his bravado collapsing with every noise outside. There was a jealous husband all right, there was *always* a jealous husband with a guy like Walsh. Whether it was Danziger he was afraid of, or his prison karma catching up with him, at the end all Walsh had left was his fear. Leave it to Walsh to think that a screenplay would save him. To be white hot once again. Untouchable. The return of the golden boy.

Jimmy tipped the bottle to his lips. The beer was warm and bitter now. Why did the killer wait around so long afterward? Do it and go, run away, that's what Jimmy would have done. But the man who had killed Walsh had been in no hurry to leave. Probably took a shower afterward, went through Walsh's refrigerator. He owned the place. He had waited two days to make that second call, searching the trailer, seeing if there was anything he wanted, cleaning out the rest of the dope and booze. Showing his yard cool.

Jimmy smacked the beer bottle on the ground, angry at himself. *That's* what had happened to Walsh's screenplay. Jimmy had been convinced that the missing screenplay proved that the husband had been behind the killing, but the killer had taken it. Grabbed it as a souvenir. Or maybe, knowing Walsh had once been famous, he thought it *had* to have value. Helen Katz was going to laugh her ass off when he told her. He could hear her now, telling him to leave the police work to the police, that amateurs always made crime more complicated than it really was.

Jimmy stood up and hurled the beer bottle at the koi pond, putting everything he had into the throw, but it landed short.

Chapter 43

"Thanks for coming tonight." Holt cracked the window of Jimmy's Saab. The evening was cool, but it was steamy inside the car. She sat in the passenger seat, shaking her hair out, checking the sideview mirror. "I didn't give you much notice."

"No big deal. I was just sitting around a crime scene drinking beer and beating up on myself." Jimmy felt Jane's gun bump his knee as she leaned over to kiss him. "Besides, it's these romantic moments that make it all worthwhile."

Holt nipped at his earlobe, her hand with the gun resting on his thigh now, tap-tap-tapping. "I thought you liked dangerous women."

"I don't like them with a nine-millimeter near my dick. You have the safety on, right?"

Holt kissed him again, not answering.

They were parked in an isolated lovers' lane, on a ridge overlooking the lights of downtown Laguna Beach, a cul-de-sac where a plat of luxury houses lay uncompleted, the contractor bankrupt, the property involved in lengthy litigation. The skeletal homes shimmered in the darkness. Most had their roofs up, but their sides were just barely framed out. The half-built houses offered more hiding places than refuge.

"What crime scene?" asked Holt.

Jimmy was still thinking about Walsh, wondering how much of what he had told Jimmy was a lie.

"Were you back at Walsh's trailer again?"

Jimmy looked over her head. He thought he had seen a shadow move in the nearest house, darkness among the darkness.

Holt moved closer. "I thought you had finished with the Walsh case."

"I think it's finished with me." He felt the automatic graze his knee. "You know, I'd feel better if I had a gun too."

"I wouldn't." Holt changed position, still keeping watch. Waves of curly blond hair covered half her face. "You don't have a permit, and I've seen you on the firing range. You close your eyes when you shoot."

Jimmy caressed her breasts. "I think the blond wig is a little much, by the way. You sure you're just not trying to get me hot? Add a little variety—"

"Shut up." Holt leaned back, enjoying his touch, her eyes checking the side mirrors for signs of movement. "I'm going to get this son of a bitch."

"I believe you."

"I am going to get him," Holt said quietly. "Maybe not tonight, but soon, and when I do, I hope he resists arrest." She was breathing hard, and Jimmy couldn't take any credit.

"You sure this isn't entrapment?"

"I know what I'm doing."

"Okay."

"*Okay.*"

Last week the grand jury had failed to indict Henry Strickland for multiple sexual assaults. Holt had been the arresting officer, nailing Strickland for a series of lovers' lane attacks. The assailant's MO was to charge the parked car from the underbrush, smash in the man's window with a baseball bat, then beat him senseless before raping the woman. He preferred blondes. The assailant was careful, wearing a ski mask, surgical gloves, and a condom. But Holt had pulled out all the stops and finally found a jogger who remembered a partial license plate on a car parked near one of the assaults. Holt had made the arrest with a single female uniform as backup and forced him to his knees with wristlock when he argued with her, tightening the handcuffs until Strickland howled.

The arrest had been the high point of the case. The female victims were ineffective on the stand, unsure, unable to make eye contact, still terrified. The men were either hospitalized or unable to make a clear identification. After the grand jury gave their findings, Strickland had passed Holt in the courthouse hallway and told her he was going to sue her and the city. He undressed her with his eyes as he spoke.

The day Strickland walked, Holt got a call from another woman. She wouldn't give her name, but she said she had been raped by him too, months earlier, at an isolated spot overlooking the city, a cul-de-sac filled with half-built homes. Her boyfriend had dodged the baseball bat and run off, leaving her alone with the rapist. They had never reported the crime. Strickland's usual hunting grounds were too dangerous for him now, but Holt knew that sooner or later he would hit the cul-de-sac again, thinking it was safe. The Laguna PD wasn't interested in staking out the site, wasn't interested in paying overtime; they accepted the grand jury's decision. Holt didn't care about overtime. She had Jimmy, her sense of outrage, and her 9-millimeter.

The crescent moon didn't shed much light on the cul-de-sac—it merely lit the edges of the houses. The wind rustled in the surrounding trees. Jimmy found himself checking the side mirrors and the rearview every few seconds, listening for the crunch of footsteps on the gravel. Jane straddled him, grinding slowly against him. He wasn't sure how much her actions were for his benefit and how much to make Strickland buy the scenario. He felt the heat of her pelvis, and he didn't care, working back against her, making her eyes flutter.

Holt changed position and pulled away slightly, trying to clear her head. "Don't *do* that."

"Don't *you* do that."

Holt rested against him, listening. Crickets sawed away in the moonlight. Both of their doors were unlatched—Jimmy had unscrewed the interior lights so they wouldn't give it away. Now they just needed Strickland to hit the bait. They sat there tangled up for another ten minutes, sometimes pretending to kiss, sometimes not pretending, waiting for the sound of footsteps.

"How much . . ." Jimmy shifted his erection. Amazing the situations that turned him on. Forget Viagra, just sit around making out with the woman you love while expecting to have to fight for your life. A real Discovery Channel moment, the mating instinct kicking into high gear under stress conditions. "How much longer do you want to stay here?"

"Until he shows up."

"What if he doesn't show up?"

Holt checked her watch. "If he's going to hit, it will be soon. He likes to be back in his own bed by midnight. Bastard thinks he's Cinderella. Kiss me."

"Yes, ma'am." Jimmy kissed her neck, pushing aside the blond hair. "We can always come back tomorrow."

"Just keep your eyes open."

They sat there, lightly touching, on full alert. A twig cracked, and the two of them jerked, listening so hard their heads hurt.

"I think I know who the good wife is. Her and her husband."

"Uh-huh." Holt checked the mirrors.

"I put it together today. Woman named Stephanie gave it to me on a silver platter." Jimmy shook his head. "She didn't even know what she knew."

Holt shifted slightly, not really paying attention to him.

Jimmy didn't blame her.

Holt cocked the automatic. "I saw something in the house, the second one. Just a shadow, but it's getting closer."

Jimmy forced himself not to look. He moved one foot against his door, ready to kick it open as soon as Strickland got close, needing to time it so he caught the man just before he smacked the glass with the baseball bat.

A piece of wood clattered nearby, and Holt laughed. "False alarm."

Jimmy turned and saw a raccoon atop one of the bare rafters of the nearest house, peering at them. Its black-circled eyes made it look like one of the Beagle Boys from the *Uncle Scrooge* comics. Jimmy exhaled. He hadn't realized he had been holding his breath.

Holt backed off the hammer of the 9-millimeter, still laughing at herself. She wiped sweat off her forehead, took off the blond wig, and tossed it onto the seat between them.

"That's probably what the raccoon was after. I think he was in love with your wig."

"He's welcome to it. That thing was too hot." Holt raked a hand through her own dark hair and shook it out. "I forgot to tell you, I got a copy of *SLAP* today. That was a wonderful article you wrote on Luis Cortez. Made me want to cry."

"Thanks."

"So sad. We don't get too many drive-bys in Laguna, but I've seen the names in the crime stats from Anaheim and Santa Ana and just passed over them. I don't think I'll be so quick to turn the page in the future." Holt put the wig back on and was on watch again. She couldn't help herself. "Did you see the layout of the article? It was striking."

"No, not yet." Jimmy kept thinking about Danziger and the smug look on his face when Jimmy had interviewed him. The man who knew the secrets. Jimmy still didn't know if the secret was setting Walsh up for a statutory rape charge or for murder. Walsh hadn't known either.

"The art director must have had all these gangbangers come into the studio to be photographed. You couldn't see their faces, just their tattooed arms. Their right arms bordered the whole article. It was really powerful. You got the sense of Luis being encircled, both in love and danger by the gang, unable to break free."

"Yeah, Robert Newman, the art director, he's brilliant." Jimmy shook his head. Even at the end Walsh still wasn't sure he hadn't killed Heather Grimm. It had bothered him, genuinely bothered him.

"The *vatos* must have all been in the same gang." Holt watched the woods. "Their arms all had a tattoo of an Aztec warrior, same spot too, right across their biceps. Very unsettling, but strong."

"Yeah, that's the idea. You want to sport your colors, not just as an individual." Jimmy could feel the world start to shift. "You want— you want to be part of something bigger, so you get a measure of protection." Jimmy stopped. The poles had reversed, and suddenly there were monarch butterflies in the Antarctic, caribou grazing in the Amazon, and all the loose ends, every one of them, slid smoothly into place.

"What's the matter?"

Jimmy kissed her, and it wasn't a decoy, some phony kiss, the two of them distracted, pretending to be lovers. He kissed her, and she went with it, all the way.

"What's—what's going on?" said Holt. "Not that I'm complaining."

"Nothing. I'm just happy to be here." He held her close so she couldn't see his eyes. He knew now what had really happened at the koi pond.

Chapter 44

Rita Shafer followed Jimmy to the front door, keeping the pink terrycloth robe closed with one hand. The morning sun was harsh on her
face. She looked exhausted, dark circles under her eyes, and he
thought of the raccoon at lovers' lane last night. "You think Harlen's
dead, don't you?"

"I've been wrong too many times to say for sure."

"I saw the way you looked when I told you about Harlen's l'il devil
tattoo. You think he's dead."

Jimmy nodded. "I'm sorry."

Rita clutched at her robe. "I shouldn't be surprised." She wiped at
her eyes. "Was it painful the way he died? Don't bother—I know you
wouldn't tell me if he died hard. You're too good a man to tell me the
truth."

Jimmy wanted to go. He needed to be in Malibu in a couple hours,
by eleven or so, and there were things he had to do first.

"Somebody paid my utility bills." Rita blew back a strand of hair
away from her face. "I called up the electric company to ask them for
some more time, and they said it had been taken care of. Same thing
with the phone company. That was you, wasn't it?"

"I have to go."

"*Had* to be you." The kids were fighting in the apartment, bouncing on the sofa, but Rita ignored them. "I thought at first maybe it was
Harlen done it, but now, well, it couldn't have been him, could it?"

Jimmy patted her shoulder. She was all bones and sharp edges. "I just did it to try and balance out the bad shit I pull."

Rita smiled. She deserved the medal of honor for it. "That's just the kind of thing Harlen would say. The first time he sold a pound of skunkweed—couldn't have been older then fifteen—he bought me a pair of red shoes and a Max Factor lipstick."

"That's a nice memory. You should hang on to that one."

"You got to go, don't you?"

Jimmy hugged her, and she hugged him back so hard, he thought he was going to be wearing her imprint on his chest.

Sugar leaned over the side of his boat, one hand keeping the line taut, the other one scooping up the tarpon with a net, cradling the steel-gray fish as he lifted it out of the water. It was a beauty, still thrashing in the netting, black eyes bright. It had taken him almost a half-hour to land the tarpon. They weren't such good eating, but they were ferocious fighters. An honorable creature.

He felt the same way about Stephanie. Killing her yesterday had been hard, hard for him, hard for her, but they both had done their duty. She was a good mama. If there were more like her, the world would be a better place. He didn't like doing it, but now the killing was over and done with. *All* of it. No witnesses left now. Those barking dogs could go back to sleep again, and Sugar could get back to his fishing.

The tarpon shuddered and snapped at him. Sugar clipped the line with a pair of needle-nose pliers, set down his rod and reel, and hefted the net, careful not to damage the scales. Twelve pounds at least. It was a beautiful morning, the sun high, the sky clear and blue, the deck gently rolling under his feet. He was bare-chested, wearing baggy shorts and deck shoes that any sane man would have replaced months ago, but he liked the feel of familiar things. He winked at the tarpon and carefully removed the hook in its mouth with the pliers. It was almost noon now, time to release the fish and head back home for lunch. The two of them would live to fight another day.

The phone in his pocket was ringing.

Sugar had a moment of indecision, then finally flipped open the phone, still holding the fish in the net. "Hello?"

"Detective Brimley?"

Sugar started at the phone. He didn't recognize the woman's voice. "That's what they tell me. Who am I speaking to?"

"Katz. Helen Katz. I'm a detective with the Anaheim PD."

Jimmy waited until the horse and rider had crested the top of the slope and started down the rugged path before peddling the mountain bike up toward them, wanting to make sure that they were out of sight from the mansion on the hill.

The rider pulled the horse back, giving Jimmy plenty of room to pass, but he stopped a few feet away and flipped back his helmet so she could see his face. He had watched her for the last ten minutes, paralleling her movements on the network of trails that crisscrossed the Malibu hills. "Mrs. Danziger?"

Brooke Danziger eyed him warily as the horse snorted, sidestepping on the path, the two of them dappled with fine gray dust.

"I'm Jimmy Gage."

"How nice for you."

Jimmy stared at Brooke. For weeks now he'd been searching for the good wife, trying to figure out who she was, trying to imagine what she would look like. He wasn't sure what he was expecting. The passionate ravishing beauty Walsh had risked his career for and thought it a good bet? The all-devouring Kali with a blue dress who had cost Heather Grimm her life? Jimmy hadn't expected the good wife to look like Brooke Danziger.

She was attractive, beautiful even, but southern California was filled with beautiful women, true heartbreakers, women who honed their looks, used them as weapons. Brooke was no beach bunny or fashion queen. She was a warm one, an outdoors type with creases around her eyes and a wide full mouth, a woman who looked at home in jeans and cowboy shirt. She sat astride the horse now, aware of his scrutiny without being bothered by it, the reins loose in her hands, her hair in a thick braid. Walsh had had his pick of any starlet in Hollywood, but he loved Brooke. Too bad Michael Danziger had married her first, married her and then maybe killed to keep her. Jimmy still wasn't sure about that.

"I've seen you on television recently, Mr. Gage. You beat up that Mick Packard at a pet store. My husband said it was a publicity stunt, but I thought it was real."

"You win."

"Good for you. Are you looking for my husband? He doesn't ride."

"No."

The horse sneezed, but Brooke didn't react.

"I called the Wild Side Spa and asked for you. I told them I was with your husband's production company. I was half-expecting the receptionist to hang up on me, but she said you had your weekly appointment yesterday. That's when I knew for sure what really happened at the koi pond."

Brooke continued to watch him, one hand lightly holding the reins, slightly amused. She was a deeply tanned brunette wearing well-worn boots and faded jeans, an embroidered denim shirt with the sleeves rolled.

"You go for the full treatment at the spa?" said Jimmy. "Manicure, pedicure, salt massage, and Brazilian wax. Yeah, I bet your husband likes you all sleek and smooth. I bet Walsh does too. Walsh couldn't call you at home, but he knew he could reach you at the spa every week. Same time, same place."

Jimmy had hoped to get a rise out of her, but Brooke just looked over her shoulder, back in the direction of her house on the hill.

"Take me to Walsh."

She started to speak, but stopped herself. He liked her for that. She had been about to lie, about to deny what they both knew was the truth, but she was smart enough to know that it wasn't going to work.

"I can't." She jerked her head toward the house again. "Michael is expecting me back in about an hour or so."

"I want to see Walsh. If you can't do it, or won't do it, I go to the cops."

Brooke Danziger looked down at him. "Men. You *love* giving ultimatums to women."

"Think of it as a promise."

"I'll bring you to see him tomorrow."

"Today."

"My husband has plans for us today. I can't get out of them."

Jimmy watched her. "*Tomorrow*, then."

The horse stirred, but she kept him in place with a gentle tug on the reins, still watching Jimmy. Her eyes were a deep brown. "Garrett was very impressed with you, Mr. Gage. None of this would have happened if he hadn't thought you could get the job done."

"Is that supposed to be a compliment?"

Brooke Danziger almost smiled. "I warned Garrett. I told him if you were intelligent and tenacious enough to be useful, you were also bright enough to be dangerous. He said it was worth the risk." She leaned forward, the saddle creaking. "You'll have to ask him when you see him if he *still* thinks it was worth it."

"I just don't know how I can help you, detective," said Sugar. "It's been a long time ago. Everything I know about the case is part of the public record."

"Don't shit me," said Katz, her voice breaking up over the phone. "One cop to another, we always save the best stuff for each other. Let's get together and kick things around."

Sugar opened his cooler with his foot, gently laid the tarpon onto the bed of cracked ice, and tossed the net aside. "From what I read in the paper, Walsh's death was ruled an accident." The fish flopped against the ice. "I thought the case was closed."

"This damn case has given me an itch. You know what that's like. I want you to help me scratch it."

Sugar looked out to the blue horizon. "I don't know. I'm kind of busy."

"You're retired, Brimley. How busy can you be?"

Sugar watched the waves. "How about lunch tomorrow?"

"Don't mind if I do."

Sugar wrote down her phone number and said he'd call her tomorrow morning and give her directions. He snapped the phone shut, tucked it back into his pocket. It seemed like all the sound in the world had been turned off. No sound, no color, no feeling. Just Sugar out there on the high seas, trying to maintain his balance on a shifting deck. He turned to the cooler and stared at the tarpon. His fist thudded against the fish without him even being aware of the desire to hit it. Ice sprayed against his bare chest as he beat the tarpon. Blood and scales drifted slowly through the air, and the only sound that Sugar could hear was his howling in his heart.

Chapter 45

"I bet you *hated* leaving your lucky sunglasses in the koi pond," said Jimmy.

"You don't forget a thing, do you?" Walsh poked at the hot dogs smoldering on the hibachi with a fork, a joint stuck in the corner of his mouth. "I was wearing those Wayfarers the night I won the two Oscars, kept them with me through thick and thin. But I tossed them in the water next to Harlen and was glad to do it. Even stuck the linoleum knife in his back pocket. Whatever it took to convince you."

"Is that what it was all about, convincing me?"

"Convince you, convince the cops. One way or the other I figured it was healthier for me to be dead than alive." Walsh's grin exposed a chipped front tooth. He slid his tongue across the rough edge, aware that Jimmy had noticed. "Busted it the night Harlen drowned. Fell right on my face and never felt a thing. The two of us were so wasted."

"Did he drown on his own, or did he have help?"

"You think I killed him?" Walsh was wreathed in smoke. "You got a mind like a corkscrew, tough guy. That's what they used to say about me, because they could never tell what I was up to. No wonder I like you."

Jimmy didn't return the sentiment. The two of them leaned against the railing of Walsh's balcony, a concrete slab overlooking the Dumpsters in the alley. The apartment itself was a by-the-week rental in Manhattan Beach, a small studio with orange shag carpeting, a toilet that never stopped running, and cast-off furniture from previous tenants. The unit was located just a couple of miles and a half-million dollars from the cottage where Heather Grimm had died. Jimmy had driven right past the Kreamy Krullers shop, thought of Sugar, and almost stopped for a dozen.

Walsh rubbed a hand across his scruffy beard. It was a lousy disguise, more vanity than anything else, thinking the world was full of fans who would recognize him. He squatted on his haunches now, wearing baggy shorts and a new red cowboy shirt with bucking broncos on the yoke. The shirt was unbuttoned in the afternoon heat, the pits stained with sweat. He balled up some newspaper and pushed it onto the coals, the flames flaring up, the hot dogs popping. "I've always been impatient," he said, stabbing the dogs with the fork. "Me and Harlen stood in the middle of the koi pond that night, pissing on the fishies. I finished first and staggered back across the rocks, in a hurry to get back to the crack pipe. I woke up at dawn, eyes swollen half shut and spitting teeth, but I still looked better than Harlen. Damn fish had already nibbled away his eyeballs when I rolled him over." He dragged again at the joint and flicked the roach off the balcony. "Put me off my Froot Loops, that's for certain."

"Don't make jokes, Garrett." Brooke sat inside on one of two mismatched kitchen chairs, wearing sandals and a short sundress the color of ground mustard. Her legs were long and tan, her toes daubed with coral. "You're going to give Jimmy the wrong idea."

"Jimmy knows I didn't kill Harlen." A truck rumbled past on the street outside, rattling the windows. "Jimmy doesn't give me that much credit."

"You'd be surprised, Walsh. I'm more impressed with you now than ever."

"The feeling is mutual." Walsh speared one of the burned hot dogs and held it up to his lips, blowing on it. "You sure you don't want one?" He shrugged. "Just for curiosity's sake, what clued you in that I was still alive? Was it this?" He reached inside his shirt and flicked the gold ring through his right nipple. "I thought about it after I left, but I didn't want to go back and try sticking it on Harlen's tit. Tell you the truth, after a couple days, I didn't want to touch him."

"No, I missed that, but it wouldn't have mattered. He didn't have any nipples left by the time they ran the autopsy."

Brooke winced at the image, but Walsh seemed unaffected, finishing the first hot dog and reaching for the other one. "What was it, then?"

"Your last two calls were to Vacaville."

"How did you know that? I used a prepaid cell phone. They're untraceable."

"Not anymore."

Walsh stopped chewing. It wasn't being caught that bothered him. It was the realization that everything had changed in the seven years he had been gone.

"I thought maybe you had been killed on some prison contract and the killer was just checking in afterward. I never considered that it wasn't you dead in the koi pond. The police had a dental match, and there was the devil tattoo. Then a friend of mine mentioned these gangbangers she had seen, and they all had the same tattoo. It made me rethink things."

"So you just got lucky?" Walsh turned to Brooke. "He just got lucky, that's all."

Brooke crossed her legs. "I don't believe in luck."

Walsh watched Brooke, dreamy-eyed. "Look at her, tough guy. She's something, isn't she? Seven years is a long time, but she was worth the wait."

"You had somebody at the prison switch your dental records with Harlen Shafer's," said Jimmy. "That's what the two phone calls were about. One to make the request, the next to confirm that it had been done."

Walsh applauded.

"Was it a guard who made the switch, or a trustee with another one of those devil tattoos?"

"A trustee, one of the boys. Vacaville is computerizing their medical records, but the state doesn't have enough money to hire out the job, so they use brainiac inmates." Walsh picked at his teeth with a fingernail. "That kind of arrangement, they're just *asking* for trouble."

"So you didn't kill Shafer. Maybe you just saw him slip and knock himself senseless on the rocks. Maybe you even started to help him, and then thought about it. Knee deep in the stink, fish going crazy— I bet you worked through the possibilities fast. You knew you weren't going to have visitors for weeks."

"You trying to make me mad?" The fork was still in Walsh's hand, held casually, as though he had forgotten it was there.

Jimmy smiled and slightly shifted position to block the strike if it came.

"Listen, tough guy, my first day inside, strung out and so scared I couldn't even talk, Harlen slipped me a quaalude, told me to hang on, said we got pie for dessert every Friday." Walsh shook his head. "Fucking Harlen couldn't read without moving his lips. He never walked past a pay phone without checking the change return. But he kept my back, and I kept his." He gripped the fork tighter. "I wouldn't have let him drown without doing something about it."

"Once he was dead though, you decided to take advantage."

"You think Harlen cared? The only good thing about dying is you don't give a shit anymore." Walsh tossed the fork aside. "You're just mad because I played you. Well, don't feel bad, I've played better men than you."

"You're going to have to get that tooth fixed. It makes you look like one of those peckerwoods from *Deliverance*."

Walsh hung on to the grin. "Make jokes. All I know is when you wanted to find me, you went to Brooke. If you figured out she's the good wife, that means you got the goods on Danziger, you know he set me up. You know he had that girl killed." He winked at Brooke. "Didn't I tell you he could do it? Jimmy here is a real bird dog."

Sugar Brimley had called Jimmy the same thing. He didn't like it any better coming from Walsh.

"You should be thanking me, Jimmy—I've given you the biggest story of your career. I'm going to make you famous." Walsh leaned closer to Jimmy and went to pat him on the back, then thought better of it. "I tried to play boy detective myself, but I didn't have the apti-tude. I made phone calls, I drove around asking questions, but nobody would talk to me, and when they did, I didn't know what to do with the information. You, though—after you and Rollo left that night, I checked you out. You're the real deal. Smack dealers, stock hustlers, assorted fuckwads and phonies—once you sink your teeth in, you don't let go. You even went after your own brother." He shook his head. "A man who sends up his own brother, that's the man I want on my side. I tried to come up with something that would get you interested." He glanced over at Brooke. "I asked her to call you, but she wouldn't hear of it. Flat out refused."

"I had no intention of letting myself be used," said Brooke. "You're the storyteller. If you couldn't convince Jimmy, then I wasn't about to try."

"Women, Jimmy. They love us, but they never love us enough."

"Getting me to dig around in Heather Grimm's murder might have brought down some trouble," said Jimmy. "You could have gotten me killed."

Walsh spread his hands. "That's a risk I had to take."

"Of course, if I had gotten killed, that would have really made your day. Killing a reporter—that's better than killing a cop if you want to attract media attention. Every newspaper in town would have assigned somebody to cover the case, just to teach the lesson that you don't fuck with somebody with a typewriter and a printing press."

"Sad but true."

"You don't look sad to me."

"I'm crying on the inside, Jimmy."

"Well, you better crank up the tears, because I can't prove that Danziger had Heather Grimm killed. I can't even prove he set you up. I *think* he did. I think he had her bump into you at the beach, and I think he had somebody call the cops, but I still don't know what really happened in the beach house that night. Not yet."

"Well, I sure as fuck didn't do it."

"You told me you didn't remember. You said you were doing dope all afternoon."

"Dope and sex," snapped Brooke.

"I told you I was sorry about that," Walsh said to her. "*You* were the one who needed time to think. Maybe if you hadn't run back to hubby—"

"I needed time to make a decision, and I made it," said Brooke. "I had an appointment with a divorce attorney scheduled for Friday. Wednesday night you were arrested. You couldn't wait for me to decide."

"I didn't plan on this little cupcake showing up on my doorstep."

"I hate to interrupt the blame game just as we're entering the lightning round, but if you didn't kill Heather, who did?" said Jimmy.

Walsh shook his head. "I wish I knew."

Jimmy turned to Brooke. "Do *you* know?"

"Don't be ridiculous," said Brooke.

"It wasn't your husband. A guy like him—he doesn't pick up a phone or flush his own toilet." Jimmy stared at Brooke. "Did Michael have anyone on the payroll who could have murdered Heather? Someone who might have done some security work, or maybe bodyguarded the two of you at some special event?"

"There—there were always a lot of people vying for Michael's attention back then. He greenlighted a lot of action films when he ran the studio, and men came up to him at social functions, trying to impress him, bragging about working for the mob. We used to laugh about it afterward."

"I'm disappointed in you, Jimmy," said Walsh. "I'm waiting around for you to get the goods on Danziger, and all you can tell me is you don't have proof."

"'Not yet.'" Brooke looked up. "He said he didn't have the proof *yet*, Garrett." She watched Jimmy, her mouth set, just like when she reined in her horse yesterday. "Jimmy's got a plan."

"That's right, Mrs. Danziger." Jimmy enjoyed the way she reacted when he called her that. "You're not going to like it, though."

"It doesn't matter what she likes." Walsh gestured at the kitchen table behind Brooke, where a ream of paper was stacked neatly beside an electric typewriter. "I finished two treatments and a shooting script since I moved in. Best stuff I ever wrote too. Clean and sober,

Jimmy, just a little weed to keep me loose. You clear my name, and every producer in Hollywood is going to be unzipping me."

"When we talked in the trailer, you said Brooke overheard her husband listening to tapes of the two of you making love," said Jimmy. "Danziger's a diligent man. Cautious. Patient. You think he suddenly *stopped* taping once he knew about the affair?"

Walsh was blank for a moment, then smiled.

"Once I listen to the tape from the night Heather Grimm was murdered, *then* I'll have proof," said Jimmy. "It may not be the kind of proof you want, though. Maybe Danziger didn't have anyone working for him. Maybe you really did kill her. You've already done the time, but if you're guilty as charged, forget lunch at the Ivy."

"I'll take my chances," said Walsh.

"What about you, Brooke? Do you just want to know the truth too?"

"I never heard anything that sounded like that girl being murdered," said Brooke.

Jimmy watched Brooke. She said she didn't believe in luck, but her timing was perfect. She had first heard her husband listening to the tapes just before Walsh was due to be released. Not during his first month of incarceration, or his first year—that would have been lucky for *Walsh*. No, she found out about the tapes seven years later, after Danziger's production deal had run out. After she and Danziger had started reneging on their charity pledges. Walsh had a devious sensibility, able to plot out the most cynical and intricate storylines, but when it came to Brooke, he was as trusting as a bridegroom.

"You can't be sure such a tape exists," said Brooke.

"It exists. I just have to find it. Where does your husband listen to the tapes?"

"The screening room."

"Then it's more than an audiotape. If it was just audio, he'd slip on a pair of headphones and listen to the two of you while he walked on the beach or drove in his car. No, if he has to get up in the middle of the night to replay your greatest hits, he's *watching* it too."

Walsh and Brooke turned to each other.

"Is there a storage locker in the screening room? A locked cabinet?"

"Yes, of course." Brooke lowered her eyes. "If Michael is watching *movies* of us, it's even worse somehow."

"The premiere of *My Girl Trouble* is tomorrow night," said Jimmy. "I assume you and your husband are attending. Will there be anyone left in the house?"

Brooke shook her head. "Raymond used to live in, but he goes home at five now." She crossed her legs. "I don't have a key to the film cabinet. Michael's very territorial."

Walsh walked over to Brooke, put his arms around her, and buried his face in her hair. He finally stood up. "You're good, Jimmy. Nice to see a man who knows what he's doing." He fumbled another joint out of his pocket and fired it up. "If none of this had happened—if Heather hadn't shown up at my house that afternoon—*everything* would be different. Brooke and I would be living in a mansion in the clouds, happily married and rolling around on satin sheets. I'd have a few more gold boys on my mantel, and you would have interviewed me about my latest movie, the one with all the buzz, and if I was in a good mood, we might have hit it off." He was lost behind the smoke again, his voice barely audible. "I don't know . . . we might have had some fun, you and me."

Chapter 46

"You can really pack it away," said Brimley.

"What's that supposed to mean?" said Katz, putting down the last of the second Whataburger Deluxe with extra bacon and triple cheese.

"No offense." Brimley wiped sauce from the corner of his mouth with his pinkie. "I like a woman who can keep up with me." He dabbed a cluster of four French fries in the pool of ketchup on his paper plate. "Most lady cops I knew were always worried about their weight. You carry yours real well."

Katz eyed him and nibbled at the soggy bun and burger, then thought what the hell and popped it in her mouth.

"That vanilla malt as good as I told you?" beamed Brimley. "Best in the city, am I right? I may not have been the smartest cop, but I could always find a good meal."

They sat at an outside table of the drive-in joint in East L.A., the umbrella drooping, speckled with bird crap, the drive-in walls thick with graffiti and posters in Spanish. Music from the parked cars provided a salsa soundtrack to their meal, a Tijuana radio station cranked and banked. Homeboys slouched in their high-polished rides, their eyes hidden behind shades as they chowed down on fish-burgers and fries, onion rings heaped high and crispy, dripping with grease, the homies watching Brimley and Katz as they ate, the only Anglos for miles.

"Thanks for meeting me halfway," said Brimley. "I usually like to come to the lady, but I'm not much for driving."

"You're the one doing me a favor, Brimley. By rights, you shouldn't have to drive."

"I told you, Helen, please call me Sugar."

"I'm not calling a grown man *Sugar.*"

"Be difficult." Brimley smiled. "It looks good on you."

The compliment confused Katz for a moment. She sucked on her vanilla malt, thinking about it, trying to figure out what he was up to. Good-looking man, brush cut at attention, a big man with a big man's quiet confidence, wearing pressed chinos and an egg-yolk-yellow button-down shirt with a little polo player on the pocket. Like they were on a date, for God's sake—but still, it was a nice thought. Brimley was right about one thing. It was the best malt she had ever had.

"I wish I could have been more help," said Brimley. "It was such a long time ago. You really think Walsh was murdered? I read in the paper he drowned in some fishpond. Didn't read nothing about the investigation being reopened."

"It's *not* reopened, not officially, and that's the way it's going to stay," warned Katz.

Brimley put his hands up. "I can keep a secret. One cop to another, you got my word of honor on that." He pushed his fries toward her. "Peace offering to seal the bargain."

Katz hesitated, then picked up a couple of drooping salt-crusted fries. She slipped one hand under the table, and undid the top button of her pants, giving herself a little breathing room. The man's brown suit was strictly thrift store, but the cut accommodated her frame better than anything from the women's department.

"What changed your mind about Walsh?" asked Brimley.

"My mind hasn't been changed. I'm just open to the idea that he was murdered."

"I keep trying to remember somebody special who might have had it in for Walsh," said Brimley, adding more ketchup to her plate. "Somebody who wanted him bad enough to wait all those years. Like

I told you, Heather Grimm didn't have a boyfriend carrying a torch or any family to speak of."

"Maybe you got a letter after Walsh was sentenced, saying Walsh got off too easy."

"I got boxes of letters like that. Heckfire, Helen, Walsh *did* get off too easy."

"Any of those letters stand out? One that you kept, even though you weren't sure why?"

"I don't know." Brimley rubbed his head, thinking. He looked like a big kid taking an algebra exam. "Heather had a fan club, did you know that?"

Katz leaned forward.

"It started up after she died. Like the world had lost this big star who died before she had a chance to shine. They had a newsletter and everything. Even made me an honorary member."

"Did you keep any of their material?"

"I—I don't think so. I got a whole storage locker full of junk though. Anything is possible. I could take a look if you want."

"I'd appreciate it. Maybe you could see if there's any of those angry letters too."

"Sure." A low-rider rumbled past, music blasting, and Brimley wobbled to the beat, still sitting down but right there with the music. "You ever been to Brazil? I'm going to get there one of these days— just listen to salsa, drink beer, and fish. You like to dance, Helen?"

"You must be out of your fucking mind."

Brimley laughed. "Now you're getting it."

Katz laughed too.

Brimley watched her finish the last of the fries. "You want to go do something?"

Katz blotted her mouth with a napkin more carefully than usual. "Like what?"

"I don't know. I guess dancing is out."

"We could go to a movie." It popped out before Katz could stop herself.

Chapter 47

Danziger's gray Mercedes rolled down the gravel road just after dusk, the headlights sending grasshoppers jumping across the high beams, beating against the grillwork. Jimmy thought again of the professor and his research project at the koi pond, imagining a scientific article that began, "Start with a recently killed fifty-pound pig." Parked well off the road, shielded by trees and brush, Jimmy watched the sedan pass. Michael Danziger was in a tuxedo, and Brooke was in a sequined dress, her hair up. He waited until the Mercedes's red taillights disappeared over a rise in the road before starting his car.

"Where are you?" said Sugar.

The phone crackled. "I'm on my way to the premiere," Danziger said, classical music in the background—that NPR station that all the moguls listened to so everyone knew they had taste.

Sugar stood in a phone booth on Malibu Drive. "Can you think of any reason our boy is parked about a mile from your house?"

"I beg your pardon?"

"Our boy is staking out your place. Are you as bothered by that as I am?"

Danziger must have turned up the CD player in his Mercedes. "Maybe—maybe it has something to do with the premiere," he said, speaking softly into the receiver. "He said he might be interested in an interview."

"He's been there for an hour. I started driving over as soon as I realized where he was."

"How did you know he was there?"

"That's not important." Sugar could see the tracking device on the front seat of his car, the pulsing red light moving now, edging across the map grid. "Darn. He just started moving. He's headed toward your house."

"You said you had taken care of things."

"I thought I did."

"You *assured* me."

"Trouble?" It was Brooke Danziger.

"Just the usual last-minute glitches," Danziger said to her.

"I'm sorry about last night," said Brooke. "I don't know what got into me."

"We're all a little tense," said Danziger. "Opening night jitters."

"What do you think our boy is looking for in *casa del Danziger?*" said Sugar.

"I really wouldn't know."

"Is that right?" said Sugar. "Well, it's been my experience that when someone tells me that they *really* don't know something, it means that they *really* do."

"Is there a problem with the theater?" said Brooke. "Or is it the caterer? I didn't like him or his fake accent, and the idea of insisting on being paid in advance."

"Your instincts are impeccable as ever," said Danziger. "Marcel only prepared *four* dozen tiger prawns instead of eight, so he's going to double up on the sashimi." A horn blared in the distance. "Just sit back, darling, I've got everything under control."

"You may be able to convince her but not me," said Sugar. "If our boy's going into your house, it's because there's something there he wants."

"I have no idea what that could be," Danziger murmured.

I bet you don't, thought Sugar. He wasn't worried. "I'm about a half-hour out of Malibu. You keep a spare key hidden outside someplace in case you get locked out?"

"I don't think that's a good idea," said Danziger.

"It's not, but it's the only idea I have," said Sugar.

Chapter 48

Jimmy punched in the access code that Brooke Danziger had given him, and the elevator doors opened. He rode it to the top level of the Malibu house, his stomach doing flip-flops as much from nerves as from the swiftness of the ascent. The doors opened, and he crossed the deck quickly. The hydraulic lap pool was covered now, bubbles visible under the slats of the decking, the smell of chlorine rising into the cool night air.

He hesitated at the front door, feeling the familiar nervous tingle in his fingertips. It was always like this when he was about to walk into someplace he wasn't supposed to be. He had been breaking and entering since he was a teenager; even grown up he still liked slipping past doormen and security guards like the invisible man. The front door lock was easy, a Schlage lever tumbler. Jimmy whipped the pick gun out of his black leather jacket, a spring-loaded contraption with various picks and tension settings. It took him less than eight seconds to open the front door. He didn't leave a scratch on the lock, but eight seconds—he was out of practice.

He had made his first pick gun in high school, using a locksmith's manual, a coat hanger, and two clothespins. It was big and awkward, but it had worked well enough for him to break into the Griffith Observatory and give his science class a late-night tour. The one he was using now was a model formerly used by the FBI—he had bought it legally over the Internet. He stepped inside, crossed to the alarm keypad on the wall, and entered the five-digit number. The house

echoed with the easy-listening music that was supposed to make potential burglars think someone was home.

Brooke had said that the screening room was on the lower level,
down the first set of stairs and to the right, but he did a quick walk-
through of the house. He had time—between the premiere of *My Girl
Trouble* and the party afterward, the Danzigers would be gone five or
six hours at least.

The kitchen featured brushed-chrome industrial appliances, polished copper pots and pans, and a two-hundred-year-old French
butcher block. Six different brands of mineral water lined the refrigerator door, and the produce bins overflowed with exotic fruits and
baby vegetables. The guest bedrooms smelled musty, but the master
suite had a king-sized canopy bed, a built-in sauna, and a pink marble Jacuzzi overlooking the ocean. Photos of Michael and Brooke
with A-list stars and Hollywood power players covered the walls.
Brooke looked bored.

Jimmy walked downstairs to the screening room, fumbled around,
and switched on the overhead lights. It was a large room with high
ceilings, a THX sound system, and thirty-six rocking-chair seats with
velvet cushions and wide armrests: four rows of offset seats, nine to a
row, each one offering a perfect sight line to the quartz-light screen.
At the rear of the room, behind an acoustic-glass partition, a smaller
room housed two 35-millimeter projectors.

He started with the film storage unit, a six-foot-high steel cabinet,
probably fire resistant and earthquake proof. He pulled out a small
flashlight and checked out the lock. Damn. Wafer tumbler, very high
quality. He made a minute adjustment in the pick gun, gently in-
serted it into the lock, and rocked it. Five minutes later he was
soaked with sweat and the lock was still cold. He stopped, listening.
The music in the house seemed louder. He opened the door of the
projection room. Nothing. He left the door wide, then went back to
the cabinet and adjusted the pick gun again. The trick was to make
just enough contact with the beaded wafers inside the lock to engage
the mechanism without sliding off. It took him almost twenty minutes
to pop it.

Danziger had a 35-millimeter print of every film he had produced or greenlighted, plus DVDs of the top hundred films of all time. Jimmy checked every DVD, opened every aluminum film can, opened every drawer and compartment; it took him almost a half-hour. Nothing. No surveillance videotapes, CDs, DVDs, or Polaroids. No microfilms, holograms, or infrared satellite images of Brooke and Walsh fucking like rabid weasels. Nothing. Jimmy closed the cabinet, locked it again, then started a search of the room, looking for something out of place.

Yesterday Brooke had told him that Danziger was up late every night now, listening to the love tapes in the screening room, while Brooke was supposedly sound asleep, overmedicated on downers. Jimmy had told her to wait until he had been in there for an hour last night, then beat on the door, hysterical, full of bad dreams and desperation. She was to cling to him and insist he take her back to bed and stay with her. A man like Danziger would have a routine, a mental checklist for putting away his stash—Brooke's interruption might make him careless.

Jimmy walked the aisles, even plucked at the carpet, searching for a hidden storage area. He paid particular attention to the seat in the middle of the first row, obviously Danziger's command center, with a CD-DVD player within easy reach. On the right armrest of his seat was a control panel, allowing him to adjust volume, start, stop, fast-forward, and reverse. On the left side was a console containing two one-liter bottles of mineral water. He lifted a bottle, checked inside, then replaced it. Too bad. He started toward the projection room, then stopped. He *definitely* heard something upstairs.

He took the steps two at a time, grabbed a large knife from the kitchen, and went through every room. There was no one there. No one on the deck either. His car was alone in the driveway. He walked back into the kitchen and replaced the knife, then heard the noise again. He had left the refrigerator door ajar—the motor kept kicking in, trying to maintain temperature. Sheepish now, he walked over and closed the door. Then he opened it again and stared at the bottles of mineral water. There were bottles with bubbles and without, waters from Poland, France, New York, and Finland. Glacial water, spring water, geyser water—every bottle was icy cold.

Jimmy walked back down to the screening room. He opened the console beside Danziger's seat and felt the bottles of mineral water. Room temperature. His heart beating faster now, he removed the bottles and lifted the metal sleeve from the console's base. There was an electrical connection in the sleeve to a refrigeration unit, but it had been disconnected. Danziger *had* been in a hurry last night. Jimmy reached down into the container, into a hidden compartment, and pulled out a small box. The box was filled with DVDs labeled by date and placed in chronological order. The last one was dated September 24, the day Heather Grimm had been murdered. His hand trembling, he slipped the DVD into the player in front of Danziger's chair.

He turned down the overhead lights from the seat. There was no prologue, no title, no credits. Just the empty living room of Walsh's bungalow, then Walsh walking back through the frame, closing the curtains in the front window. The image quality was rough, a slightly distorted wide-angle shot, but the sound was crisp—Jimmy could clearly hear the hiss of Walsh's butane lighter as he fired up a joint. He wandered back through the frame and out of sight into the kitchen. Jimmy could pick out details in the room now: a Baggie of weed and a script on the coffee table, a rumpled bed to the left, and there, gleaming on the fireplace mantel, Walsh's two Oscars.

Jimmy heard the back door of the bungalow open, heard the creaking of the hinges. The wind off the ocean whistled through the room, rippling the top pages of the script. He heard voices from the kitchen now, Walsh languid, and another voice, girlish. Heather Grimm showing up at the beginning of the disk was an indication that Danziger had either edited it or had been watching the house and knew when to start recording. For about five minutes Jimmy listened to their playful banter. Then Walsh backed into the room, followed by Heather Grimm.

Jimmy sat forward in his seat. He had seen photos of Heather before, grainy newspaper shots and her Young Miss Whittier coronation glossy, but he had never seen her . . . alive. And she *was* alive. She wore a lilac bikini, her hair curling around her shoulders. Her tan line showed at the edges of her breasts and the tops of her thighs as she sat on the bed, bouncing gently. Even with the poor image quality, she was so beautiful—coquettish and innocent at the same time, and aware enough to use both of those qualities.

Walsh bent down beside her and took her foot in his hand, examining the Band-Aid he had put on her wound. He kissed her toes while she giggled. She got up suddenly and walked over to the mantel and picked up one of the Oscars.

Jimmy fast-forwarded through the mutual seduction and saw Walsh offer her cognac and pot. Heather held the joint delicately between her thumb and forefinger. Their clothes came off sometime after that, he didn't know how long exactly, but the afternoon shadows were deeper now, and Walsh was laying out rails of cocaine on the coffee table. Later they had sex on that rumpled bed, Heather riding him like a cowgirl, calling him "Horsie" and laughing as he bucked and whinnied under her. Jimmy raced past, feeling ashamed for her, ashamed of himself for having to watch.

The DVD played on: Walsh pulled the drapes and turned on the fireplace; the flames were reflected on their sweaty skin. Walsh snorted coke off Heather's belly, then smoked brown heroin off a wrinkled square of aluminum foil. Heather asked to try the heroin, but Walsh refused, just like he had told Jimmy in the trailer.

Jimmy raced through the disk. Walsh was sluggish, dressed in a purple robe, Heather in a T-shirt and panties. Walsh smoked more heroin, shaky now; he spilled smoldering junk onto his bare thigh, and Heather laughed as he jumped up, the robe flapping around him. It made Walsh angry. He grabbed her by the hair and shook her, and she slapped him. They struggled on the bed and rolled onto the floor, and Jimmy wondered if Walsh was going to bash her brains out with the statue next. After all his investigating, all he had dug up, it wouldn't surprise him if Walsh had killed her.

Walsh staggered to his feet, his cheek bleeding where Heather had scratched him. He came after her, but he was slow and unsteady. He flopped down on the bed after a few moments, staring at the ceiling.

Heather looked down at him, drool running down his chin, then disappeared out of the frame.

Jimmy fast-forwarded until Heather reappeared, her hair in pigtails, her T-shirt torn now. She stood in front of the mirror. It took Jimmy a few moments to realize she was twisting her face up, trying to cry. A knock on the door interrupted her efforts. Jimmy jerked, and so did Heather. She checked the mirror, then left the frame again. Jimmy heard her talking with someone, sobbing. He turned the sound up louder and heard a familiar voice identifying himself as a police officer.

Heather walked into view with Sugar Brimley beside her. Sugar looked not that much different than he did today, dressed in a gray suit. "There—*there* he is," she said, lower lip quivering as she pointed at Walsh on the bed. "He's the one r-r-raped me."

Brimley laid a big hand on Heather's shoulder. She shook him off, but he put his hand back on her again.

Jimmy clenched his teeth.

"I cut my foot on a piece of broken glass under the sand. He said he would take care of it," said Heather. "He seemed so nice at first."

"Don't blame yourself. It's not your fault," said Sugar.

"My mom is going to be *so* mad," said Heather. "I'm not supposed to take the car."

"She's just going to be happy that you're safe." Sugar's hand had drifted to the back of her neck, between her pigtails. He let the loose blond strands float through his fingers.

Jimmy's chest hurt.

Sugar kicked the edge of the bed. "Wake up." He kicked it again, harder, and sent Walsh bouncing. "Hey you, you're under arrest."

Walsh slept on.

"How am I doing?" Heather was bent over the coffee table, her pinkie nail filled with cocaine, poised halfway to her nose. She looked back at him. "Was that r-r-rape thing a little over the top?"

"What?"

Heather snorted the cocaine and licked her fingernail. "Should I be crying more, or go with the brave-little-girl reading?" She dipped into the mound of coke on the table again and stood up, her eyes bright as supernovas. "I want to get it right for the cameras. You think the TV people will want to interview me here or at the hospital?"

Sugar crossed over to her and put his hands on her shoulders. "What's going on?"

Heather squirmed and waited until he let her go, one bare breast peeking out through the torn T-shirt. "Knock it off, pops. April told me about you."

"April?"

"Like you don't know." Heather glanced at the bed again. "I'm a good actress, really, *really* good, but cops make me nervous. I was freaking this morning, almost backed out, but April said not to worry, she had taken care of everything. Our little secret, that's what she called it. Like we were spies or something." She eyed the cocaine but decided against it. "Should I get dressed?"

Sugar took a long time answering. "No, not yet."

Jimmy's hands ached from gripping the arms of the chair. He could have switched off the recording, could have slipped the DVD into his pocket with utter certainty of what was about to happen, but he let it play.

Sugar walked to the mantel and took down one of the Oscars. "Is this what I think it is?"

"Isn't it *cool*?" Heather turned toward Walsh snoring on the bed. "He is just *so* famous. You wouldn't think to look at him now, but he's got like this . . . scent, and when he kisses—"

Sugar swung the Oscar down onto her head—not full force but hard enough that she crumpled to the floor. "I'm sorry. I'm so very sorry." He stared at the little gold man in his hand as though it had a mind of its own.

Walsh stirred on the crumpled sheets.

Sugar checked his suit for blood, checked his trousers and his shoes too, then went to the bed, lifted Walsh up under the arms, and carried him over to Heather.

Heather groaned and got to her feet, groggy. She rubbed the back of her head, blood dripping down her ponytail, then looked at Sugar. "What *happened?*"

Walsh mumbled something as Sugar put the Oscar into his hand, wrapped his own mitt around it, and then swung the statue against Heather's head again, swung it as hard as he could, and caught her just above the eyebrow. Blood sprayed across Walsh's face, his robe, his bare feet. The director jerked in the warm rain. Heather slid to the floor, but Sugar helped Walsh give her a few more whacks anyway. He needed to be sure.

"Hey . . . hey, let go of me." Walsh's eyes fluttered, awake now. He dropped the Oscar, the statue dripping red.

Sugar shook him so hard that Walsh's head flopped from side to side. "Gee whiz, buddy, what have you *done?*"

Jimmy put the disk on hold, Sugar and Walsh frozen onscreen. He couldn't bear it anymore. In the sudden silence he heard the sound of heavy breathing. He turned around and saw Sugar at the back of the room, tears running down his cheeks.

Chapter 49

Sugar stared at his own frozen image on the screen, Heather Grimm's lying in a corona of blood behind him.

"You surprised me, Sugar." Jimmy slipped his hand into his jacket and felt for his phone. "I didn't hear you come in."

Sugar pointed a gun at him, a snub-nosed .38. "I wouldn't do that." He moved closer, still watching the screen, unable to tear himself away. "God, what a night that was. Darn near broke my heart." He glared at Jimmy. "What happened to Heather wasn't my fault. You want to cast stones, you throw them at April. She's the one told Heather about me." He checked the screen. "Expecting a girl like that to keep a secret."

Jimmy eased his hand toward the phone again.

Sugar cuffed him with the .38, and the front sight gashed Jimmy's forehead. "I asked you to keep your hands where I can see them." His bulbous nose was peeling, and his cropped reddish blond hair spiked across his sunburned scalp—he was an overbaked doughboy turned hard and angry. "That's your trouble, Jimmy. You don't know when to quit."

Blood dripped into Jimmy's eyes. He sat down before he fell down.

"Empty out your pockets. Let me see what you're so intent on." Sugar caught Jimmy's phone, caught his car keys and pick gun too, whistled at the pick gun, then tucked them all away into his brown corduroy sports coat. He hitched up his baggy chinos. "What am I going to do with you? I keep trying to close the book, but it's like you're bound and determined to make me do something I don't want to do."

Jimmy wiped at the blood, a war-paint smear across his face as he watched Sugar.

Sugar glanced at the screen, and his ruddy complexion grew darker. "It was going to be a simple bust, statutory rape—that's all Danziger wanted. All he was paying for too. Twenty thousand dollars, enough to buy some new fishing gear, maybe a trip to the Gulf of Mexico. It should have been an easy paycheck. Heather would get a part in some movie, Danziger would get rid of Walsh, and me, I'd get a Shimano rod and reel and maybe an engine rebuild. We were all going to be happy."

"Except Walsh."

"You fool around with another man's wife, you got to expect consequences." Sugar sat behind Jimmy and nodded at the screen. "Now I understand how Danziger knew when to make the 911 call. She was only supposed to be inside for an hour, two at the most. I kept calling him, asking what was taking so long. He just said to sit tight. 'Hold your horses, Sugar, hold your horses.' I thought he had staked out the house, but he was watching her the whole time, watching everything."

Jimmy realized that Sugar had never seen the replay before, that he had had no idea the murder had been recorded. "Danziger must have gotten some real laughs these last eight years knowing he had your dick in his pocket. I bet you feel pretty stupid."

Sugar showed his large crooked teeth. "A little." He leaned toward Jimmy. "I only got here five minutes ago. Start it up again from the beginning, from where Heather first walks inside."

Jimmy restarted the DVD and saw Walsh walk off camera into the kitchen.

"You don't have to rewind it?"

"It's a DVD. Digital. You can go anywhere you want."

"Just like that." Sugar chuckled. "Anywhere you want, just like that."

Sugar kept the gun resting against the back of Jimmy's head. The moment Heather appeared, Sugar sat back in his seat and sighed, and Jimmy relaxed a little. Just a little. They sat watching Heather flounce around the bungalow, picking things up and putting them back down. Jimmy heard Sugar humming softly behind him, but he didn't turn around.

"You can stop now." Sugar laid a hand on Jimmy's shoulder. Heather was caught in midlaugh, blond and bright and beautiful. Walsh hadn't touched her yet. "That's enough. Give me that DVD, and let's take a stroll in the moonlight." Jimmy handed the disk over, then Sugar tucked it carefully into the inside pocket of his jacket, next to his heart. "Thank you for this. You don't know what it means to me."

"You want to show your appreciation, put away that punk-ass gun. You've got sixty or seventy pounds on me. What do you need that for?"

"You've seen too many movies." Sugar jerked a thumb toward the door, and they walked up the stairs, through the kitchen, and out onto the deck. Sugar was right behind him the whole way, close enough to stop Jimmy from bolting but too far out of reach for Jimmy to try any fancy moves that wouldn't have worked anyway. "Over there." Sugar directed him to the railing.

"You going to see if I can fly?" Jimmy peeked over the edge. It was a straight drop, a couple hundred yards down onto rocks. "I'm not going over as easy as April did."

"What makes you think April went easy?" Sugar growled, the .38 tiny in his big freckled hands. "*Nothing* is easy."

Jimmy leaned his back against the railing and looked up at the stars, waiting for Sugar to make his move. He thought of Jane. This close to dying, he was supposed to regret not marrying her, supposed to think about the children they had never had, the life they had never gotten to share. But the only thing Jimmy regretted was that he didn't have something he could use as a weapon—an elephant gun would be nice, but he would settle for a crowbar.

Tough luck; there was nothing on the deck but him and Sugar. A cloud edged across the moon, and he imagined Jane at home, sitting out on the balcony sipping her second drink, watching the same stars he was. *Make a wish, Jane.* The two of them bound with a single wish. Almost as good as a kiss. No matter what Sugar did to him, no matter if his body was never found, Jane was going to find out the truth. Even if Walsh and Brooke Danziger didn't come forward, nothing was going to stop her.

"What's so funny?" said Sugar.

"You'll find out."

"I'll find out? Aren't you the cocky one."

Jimmy dabbed at the blood drying on his forehead. "Secret of my success."

"All you've done is get more people killed." Sugar shifted his bulk and hitched at his pants again, and there was an ugliness to his mouth now. Jimmy wondered if he had missed it before, or if it was new. "I didn't mind taking care of Felix the Cat—worst part of it was having him blubbering on my boat while I steered toward deep water, a greasy little man huddling in the stern with a concrete block wired to each ankle." His eyes twinkled. "He tried to swim. Got to give him credit, he tried." He tapped the .38 against his leg, watching Jimmy, his eyes bloodshot. "Stephanie was different. That bothered me."

Jimmy's legs went soft.

"She was a good woman, Jimmy. What you made me do to her—I think you owe me an apology. I'm going to have nightmares about that for years."

Jimmy took a step toward him and stopped, the .38 centered on his chest now. If he looked at the gun much longer, he was going to fall into the barrel. Jimmy smiled instead. The smile confused Sugar for a moment, and in that moment Jimmy rushed him.

Sugar had time to fire, but he tucked the gun into his pocket instead, casual, as though he had made a decision. Jimmy punched him twice, three times, hit him hard, full force. Sugar took the hits, grunting with the impact, but too heavily padded to be knocked off his feet. They grappled on the deck, and Sugar seemed to welcome the contact, butting heads, driving their knees and elbows into each other, around and around on the deck, the two of them gasping for breath.

Winded now, Sugar wrapped his arms around Jimmy, shared his sweat and his cologne with him. "It stings, doesn't it," he panted, holding on as Jimmy kicked and struggled. "You killed Stephanie as much as I did, and she didn't deserve it. We both got to deal with that." He flung Jimmy back against the metal railing, and Jimmy almost went over, his back arched in space. "That was good," said Sugar, one eye starting to swell. "I needed that."

Jimmy stood up. His forehead had opened up again. He thought of Stephanie in her house in the desert, the house with the handmade curtains and the doorbell that played the theme from *Zorba the Greek,* and wished she had never answered his ringing, wished she had been long gone with no forwarding address.

"What am I going to do with you?" Sugar said, pacing, the deck creaking with the weight of him. "Yesterday I met up with Detective Katz. She had all kinds of questions, thanks to you."

"What did you do to her?"

"I took her out to a movie. Bought her some buttered popcorn and a large Coke. Oh, I came close—I came *this* close—but that's all I did. She's a brother officer. Gives me a stomachache to think what might have happened. You see what you started?"

Jimmy didn't respond. He was waiting now.

"Just when you think everything is settled and forgotten, somebody like you start it all up again." Sugar kept pacing. "Answer me one question. *Why* did you do it? I mean, what was in it for you? Nobody cared. It was over and done with."

"Maybe I just don't like seeing the bad guys walk off into the sunset, whistling a happy tune. It just plain pisses me off."

"I used to feel that way too, but I got over it." There was a beeping from Sugar's pocket. "You mind if I get that?"

"Fuck you."

Sugar pulled his phone out. "Yeah?" He winked at Jimmy. "He's right here. . . . I don't think he's too happy about it either. I'm not too happy myself. . . . We got some things to talk about, you and me." He grimaced. "Where you calling from? . . . How many times I told you to use a phone booth when you call my cell? When are you going to learn?" He rolled his eyes at Jimmy. "I've heard that one before. Take your time getting back here after the premiere. I'm going to have to ditch our boy's car. . . . I won't. . . . I *said* I won't leave a mess at your house." He hung up, shrugged. "This is the part I hate."

"Be kind to yourself then. Get in the elevator and leave."

"Can't do it, Jimmy. Turn around."

"No, thanks."

"Don't be like that. We've already settled who's going to win the argument. Go on, just do what I ask." Sugar took off his belt, looped it through the buckle, and made a noose. "Turn around and check out the view—that's what the rich folks pay for. It's a clear night. Maybe you'll see a whale or something." He moved closer, the belt loop held loosely in one hand. "You got a girlfriend. I'll make it easy on her— I'll stash your body where no one will ever find it. She'll think you just took off for greener pastures. She'll get past that quicker than a homicide. I'll do that for you, Jimmy. Just turn around."

Jimmy held up the DVD that he had slipped out of Sugar's pocket when they grappled. "What should I do with this?" He made as though to fling it off the deck. "It would make a great Frisbee."

Sugar patted his jacket for confirmation, then held out his hand. "I'd like that back." He stepped closer. "I've been good to you, Jimmy. I gave you time out here under the stars, time to prepare your-self. I could have treated you lots worse."

"I guess I'm an ingrate."

"There's no way I can let you go, you got to know that. I been in-quiring into that fishing trip to Brazil we talked about. Bluest water in the world, just like you said, and fish that fight you all the way to the boat. Sounds good, but I'd be looking over my shoulder the whole time if I let you live. Give me my property. I promise you won't feel a thing."

"I like feeling things. Pain, pleasure, love . . . regret. All of them. Otherwise, what's the point of being alive?"

"Brave talk." Sugar sidled closer. Jimmy was within arm's reach now, holding the disk over the edge, ready to fling it into the darkness. "Hand it back, Jimmy, or you won't want to feel what I got in store for you. That's a promise."

Jimmy gripped the disk tighter as he watched Sugar's eyes. As Sugar lunged for him, Jimmy snapped the disk in half on the railing and slashed Sugar's throat with the jagged edge, ripped him wide open.

Sugar staggered back, eyes wide, not sure what had happened. He clamped a hand over his neck, blood leaking through the fingers. There was a rhythm to the leak, an ebb and flow, and Jimmy knew he had nicked Sugar's carotid artery, knew there was nothing more to be done.

Jimmy and Sugar looked at each other. Sugar's free hand drifted toward the .38 in his pocket, but he stopped himself and let his hand fall. Jimmy didn't know if it was another decision or if Sugar couldn't concentrate on two things at once right now.

Sugar pressed harder against his neck, the blood running across his knuckles. "Do you . . . do you believe in love at first sight?"

"Uh . . . yeah. Sure."

Sugar's hand shook, blood seeping down the collar of his brown corduroy jacket. "Was that the way it was with you and that girlfriend of yours? What was her name . . . Jane, right?"

"It took a while for Jane and I to get together. I don't think we liked each other very much at the beginning."

"Well, maybe that's best." Still standing, Sugar gazed at something past Jimmy. "I didn't get a good look at Heather until that day on the beach. She had a towel spread on the sand, reading a magazine. I was just checking . . . making sure she was alone. I watched her from the street through a pair of binoculars. Made me feel like I was right there beside her, close enough to smell her suntan oil." He exhaled slowly, as though he were deflating. One hand still on his neck, he sat down heavily on the deck. "I'm tired."

Jimmy sat down facing Sugar. It was long past time for feeling sorry for Sugar, but that didn't mean Jimmy wasn't about to keep him company.

"Heather was wearing these . . . silly red sunglasses shaped like hearts. Kind of thing a kid would wear thinking it made them look grown-up. Strange the things that touch us. . . ." His head drooped, but he fought it. "You asked me before . . . you said I could have called things off with Heather. Heck, Jimmy, I almost *did*. Back on the beach, I wanted to run out there and tell her not to go ahead with it. I wanted to tell her that she didn't need to dirty herself. Tell her to go home and grow up." His grip had loosened, blood streaming through his fingers now.

Jimmy leaned toward him, their knees brushing.

"It was too late though," croaked Sugar. "She was already on her way, heading right for him. Her big break. *Hooray for Hollywood,* that's what I said to myself. I didn't hold that against her. We both had a job to do. So I went back to my car, drove around doing police business, and waited for Danziger to call. Waited for him to say she had given the signal. But it took so long. . . . Then I finally get inside, and Heather tells me she knows everything—"

"You didn't have to kill her. You could have told her the setup was off. You could have called the station, told them it was a false alarm."

"Young girl like that . . . she would have just *had* to tell someone." Sugar's eyes closed, then flew open, and he struggled to lift his head. "She was only supposed to be with Walsh for an hour or so. That should have been plenty of time. Plenty. He didn't call 911 for six hours. I was off duty by then. I had to hustle to step into the case." He shivered, his face paler than the moon. "Six hours. What could she have been doing in there with him for *six* hours? I could never have trusted her after that. She was ruined."

Jimmy listened to Sugar's teeth chattering.

Sugar suddenly squinted at Jimmy. "First time I saw you . . . some bruiser was beating you half to death with a basketball. A *basketball*. Darnest thing I ever saw." He tried to laugh but it came out as a wet cough, a bubble of blood popping on his lips. "Wonder where I'd be now if I hadn't stopped him. Some folks would just have kept walking."

"Once a cop, always a cop."

"That's right. Once a cop . . ." Sugar's hand dropped from his neck and flopped into his lap beside the other one, the blood gushing down his jacket. His eyes were fading, but he hung on. "We should go fishing together, you and me. I'll take you out where they're really biting. I know . . . I know all the best spots. . . ." He looked at Jimmy and the warm night closed in around them. "I think you killed me, Jimmy."

Jimmy took his cold hand and squeezed it. "I think I did, Sugar."

Epilogue

Jimmy peered through the smoked glass of his limousine at the other limos stacked up outside the Hollywood theater, camera crews jostling for position as stars got out, their smiles in place for the fans packed ten deep behind the velvet ropes. Spotlights danced in the sky. *HAMMERLOCK,* proclaimed the theater marquee. "I can't do this."

Holt stroked his cheek. "You're the guest of honor."

"Don't say that."

"Shall I get in line, sir?" The limo driver watched Jimmy and Holt in his rearview mirror, nervous after Jimmy had told him to park across the street. "The studio wanted you delivered curbside five minutes ago."

"Stay where you are," said Jimmy.

The crowd screamed and started chanting "Walsh! Walsh! Walsh!" as a gold limousine pulled up. Garrett Walsh stood up inside, his torso emerging from the sun roof, waving to the fans like he was the pope or something. A pair of Wayfarers were perched on his forehead, the return of nighttime cool.

"Gold?" Holt shook her head. She was more beautiful than usual tonight, dressed in a seafoam-green designer original and her grandmother's pearls, her hair up high, showing off her long neck.

The crowd cheered louder as Walsh exited the limo, remembering to help Brooke Danziger out almost as an afterthought. Strobe lights flashed from the photographers lining the rope, and Walsh assumed various poses for the paparazzi, giving them what they wanted. Every magazine and newspaper in the world would have a different shot to choose from. He looked around, reveling in the moment. Walsh's recut *Hammerlock* was having its world premiere tonight, opening wide next week. Critics were already talking about a third Academy Award for his mantel. Walsh urged the crowd on, waving his hands. Oh yeah, the golden boy was back.

It was a good story, Jimmy had to admit—the innocent man triumphant, the artist redeemed. In the four months since Jimmy had killed Sugar Brimley, Michael Danziger had been indicted for conspiracy to commit murder, partially based on a series of phone calls to Sugar from his cell phone. Danziger was currently ensconced in the L.A. County Jail, held on two-million-dollar bail. Based on images pulled from the shattered DVD, it was now known that Sugar had killed Heather Grimm and was a suspect in the "suicides" of April McCoy and Stephanie Keys and the disappearance of Felix the Cat. The issue of *SLAP* with Jimmy's Walsh cover piece had sold out three print runs. Even Detective Katz had something to celebrate— she was praised for reopening the "Walsh" drowning investigation, albeit too late to have determined the true circumstances; and she was characterized as "one tough cop," by the *Orange County Register*. Yeah, everyone was a winner.

"Look, there's Rollo," said Jane. "And Nino."

Rollo and Napitano broke off their interview with *Entertainment Tonight* and greeted Walsh with hugs. Rollo's short documentary on the supposed death of Garrett Walsh was slated to precede *Hammerlock* tonight. The Monelli twins flanked Rollo, air-kissing Walsh. Brooke Danziger was a step behind, looking uncomfortable.

"Mrs. Danziger doesn't look happy," said Holt.

"She's smart," said Jimmy. "She knows what's coming."

"Rollo called me this morning," said Holt. "He told me—"

"Rollo called *you?*"

"He said his documentary had been accepted at Cannes, and he had more meetings set than he knew what to do with. I'm quoting here: 'I'm not going to have to buy lunch for fucking *months* at this rate, Jane.'" Holt laughed. "He's really rather charming."

"Rather."

Holt punched him in the arm. "You sure you don't want to go to the premiere? You look so nice in your tuxedo."

Jimmy watched the strobe lights popping across the street. "Just before he was about to kill me, Sugar asked why I did it. He was really bothered. He had a pretty good life, living on his own boat. Nothing flashy, but it was the life he wanted. Then I showed up. He wanted to know why I had made such a big deal about something that was already settled. You know what I told him? I said I just couldn't stand to see the bad guys heading off into the sunset whistling a happy tune. Look across the street, Jane. Look who *is* heading off into the sunset. Traveling first class too."

"You brought a killer to justice. You cleared the name of a man who served seven years for a crime he didn't commit. Don't complain."

"Sometimes I think I should have let well enough alone. I didn't bring back Heather Grimm. I just got Stephanie killed. And Felix the Cat—although that was no loss. Jesus H., listen to me—that's just what Sugar said. I should have let him go on fishing."

"You didn't murder those people. Sugar did."

Jimmy didn't answer.

"You did the right thing, and it didn't turn out the way you wanted," said Holt, her eyes flashing in the limo's dim interior. "There's not a cop in the world who hasn't felt the same way. We arrest a woman for killing her husband, a husband who was abusing their daughter or their son, and *she* goes away for twenty years. A man burns down his house to collect the insurance money, and we arrest him. Then we find out at trial that he needed the money to pay for his kid's transplant, an operation his insurance company wouldn't pay for. The law doesn't care. The man goes to jail, the insurance company doesn't pay off, and the kid doesn't get the transplant. Next case. If you don't like it, Jimmy, get off your white horse and go back to writing film reviews."

"Gee, thanks for the pep talk."

"Are we going in or not?"

Jimmy could see Walsh under the marquee, smiling at the cameras, signing autographs. He kept glancing around though, trying not to let his annoyance show. "Excuse me, driver? How long do we have the use of this thing?"

"The studio hired the vehicle for the whole evening, sir."

"Good. Let's get out of here." Jimmy kissed Jane and hit the privacy button. An opaque screen blocked off the driver's view of the rear compartment.

"Where to, sir?"

"We'll let you know," said Jimmy, as the limo slid away from the curb. "Right, Jane?"

A B O U T   T H E   A U T H O R

Robert Ferrigno is the author of six previous novels, including *Heartbreaker, The Horse Latitudes,* and *Flinch.* He lives with his family in the Pacific Northwest. His website can be viewed at *www.robertferrigno.com.*